Guy N. Smi[illegible], runs a mail-order b[illegible]rror and crime and [illegible]e Welsh border. In [illegible]ied with four children.

GUY N. SMITH

Phobia

THE SHERIDAN
BOOK COMPANY

This edition published in 1994 by
The Sheridan Book Company

First published by Grafton Books
8 Grafton Street, London W1X 3LA
A Grafton Paperback Original 1990

Printed and bound in Great Britain by
Cox & Wyman Ltd, Reading, Berkshire

ISBN 1–85501–496–3

This one is for Frank Norulak, a friend and fan

PART ONE
Summer

1

The house was frightening – all the more terrifying because it had not seemed so during the viewing; nor in the frequent visits prior to today. Not even five minutes ago. Just now. Suddenly.

Leah Strike shivered in the warm summer sunshine and felt her skin prickle beneath the cotton dress she was wearing. Goosepimples triggered off a shudder, and for one awful fleeting moment she experienced an urge to turn and flee. Anywhere. Then, with an effort, she got herself under control.

The feeling had not gone away. It was still lurking in the dark recesses of her mind, but it was uneasiness now rather than terror. A kind of inexplicable revulsion.

She thought she was going to be sick, then that she would faint. She sat down on the low brick wall, leaning forward until the sensation passed. But when it did, she was still left with a nagging sense of foreboding, almost afraid to look again at the house across the street.

Tall and fair-haired, she could have been attractive but for her stubborn resistance to the use of cosmetics. At thirty-five, there were lines on her face that could have been camouflaged, and a visit to the hairdresser's would have put some life into the long strands that straggled about her neckline. Even a smile would have helped, but she rarely smiled because life had become drudgery, a boring routine of cooking, cleaning and washing for a husband and three children. The dutiful but meaningless role in a humdrum existence had left its mark upon her.

She squinted in the bright afternoon sunlight and

forced herself to look across at the house again. It was partly hidden behind the tall removal van parked outside. Number Thirteen, it had to be unlucky – she had not thought of it until now. She shivered once more. It was a typical south London terraced house, no different from the fifty or so others which lined both sides of the road; the same as those in the next street and the one adjoining that. Soundly but unimaginatively built prior to the war to meet the demand of a population explosion, they had cost £750 in 1935, £125,000 in 1989. Identical boxes, they had no room for extensions except the addition of bow windows, stone cladding and anything else which might put their owners one up over their neighbours in their own estimation. Outside, they each had a pocket handkerchief of a garden, a shrub outside the front door. Claustrophobic, drab; it depended upon your expectations of life, she thought. It was basically somewhere to live. Property values were escalating so she kept telling herself that it was a good investment and in a year or two they would be moving on. John had assured her of that. In the meantime, she had to convince herself that it was trendy.

The house in Chiswick had been much the same only more modern; cramped, but light and airy. At least she had looked out on a playground with its untidy grass and strewn litter. Unsightly but not *creepy*.

Leah would have been happy to have stayed there for another year or two but that had not been possible. They had had no choice but to move once the bank promoted John; the promotion was costly when they weighed the mortgage repayments here against the increase in salary. John had said they must look to the future, and maybe he even believed it himself. Being an accountant at a larger branch was a status symbol. Or, at least, he pretended it was because nobody else would even notice;

London banks were big and impersonal, not like provincial ones where you could establish a reputation on the golf course or in the country club. And the bank had not even given him the day off to move house; that responsibility had been left to Leah. So she passed the buck to the removers and let them get on with it. If anything was in the wrong place then John would have to move it later, and serve him damned well right, she thought.

She felt better now, eased herself off the wall and stood up. The house didn't look anything more than just dull; nothing wrong that a coat of paint wouldn't put right. It had all been in her mind, she decided, with the stress, the upheaval and a kind of wanting to reject this new home. She ought to go inside and see what the children were up to.

Sarah was moving things around in her new bedroom, a determined expression on her freckled face. She was mature for her thirteen years, had bought her first bra a fortnight ago and was proud of it. Leah noticed that her daughter had put on some mascara, and some lipstick that was a shade too dark and made her look precocious. But she wasn't going to start that row all over again, not now, anyway. John had said she could wear make-up because most of the girls at school did and it was wrong to try and make your own child different. Leah considered girls grew up too fast these days and looked older than they really were. Which was why a lot of them got into trouble. She experienced a feeling of guilt, one which she had not been able to rid herself of and never would. Because she had got pregnant out of wedlock, and one day she would have to tell her own daughter. And it was no good blaming John; it took two to make a baby.

'You okay, Sarah?' Leah sounded tired, strained, as if she was saying something for the sake of it.

'I'm fine, Mother.'

'Where are the boys?'

'Probably in the garden.'

God, the garden was a like a tip. Leah stood looking at it through the open french window. Twenty metres by ten, at a guess; one would have thought that the previous owners could have taken the trouble to keep it tidy. Sam was playing football amidst the debris and weeds, kicking that new plastic ball which he had bought out of his pocket-money. It bounced back off the rickety fence and the nine-year-old drove it back hard, rattling a panel of so-called peep-proof. Little Ben gurgled his delight and ran after the ball, but Sam beat him to it and whacked it against the dilapidated shed. Ben screeched his frustration.

'Sam!' Leah's shout sounded shrill, almost hysterical.

'What, Mum?' Sam picked up the ball and held it clear of his younger brother's outstretched hands.

'Let Ben play as well, Sam.'

'I am.'

'No you're not. You're making sure he doesn't get the ball.'

Ben screamed his rage, jumped and fell over, then began to cry.

'You'd better come inside, both of you.' Oh, Christ, they were going to start squabbling again. Maybe it would have been better to have left them out here after all. 'The men have nearly finished. I'll start getting some tea.'

'I'm not hungry, Mum.'

Leah sighed. Any excuse not to stop playing. 'There's a fish and chip shop in the next street. Maybe we'll have chips for tea.'

'Oooh, yes!' Sam's mood changed. 'I'll have fishcakes, please, Mum.'

'All right, in about twenty minutes.' Even Ben had stopped crying after she'd taken the easy way out. 'Now go and get cleaned up, Sam, you're filthy. And I'm going to give Ben a wash, too. Then we'll see about chips.'

And if John wanted any when he came home he could fetch his own.

Ben's enthusiasm for chips ended after the first half-dozen or so when he threw one across the table at Sam.

'Stop it, Ben!' Leah tried not to shout and resisted the urge to slap the three-year-old when he deliberately dropped the next two on to the floor. He was overtired but probably wouldn't sleep in his new surroundings, and would end up in bed between John and herself. And would probably wet the bed into the bargain. 'Ben, why don't you play with your Lego?'

'Don't want to.' Which was just as well because Leah could not remember in which carton she had packed it.

'All right, you can get down. And no fighting. Do you hear that, Sam?'

The boys were getting on her nerves. Since school finished a week ago they had done nothing but quarrel and fight. Sam should have known better, he was becoming a bully.

'Okay, Mum.'

'Any fighting and it's straight up to bed, both of you. D'you hear?'

They nodded, but she knew it wouldn't make any difference. Sending them up to bed was not the solution because they would continue their quarrelling upstairs.

Sarah was still in her bedroom, probably sticking posters of pop groups all over the walls with Blu-Tack. And anything would be an improvement on the existing interior decorations, Leah decided. The Graftons must have lived like pigs; they had obviously been quite happy to let the place fall into a state of disrepair all around them. Which was why John had been able to knock the estate agents down a thousand. She was glad she had never met the previous occupants of Number Thirteen.

The boys were back outside playing football, and for once Sam seemed quite happy to allow Ben to kick the ball. Apart from their ages the two might have been mistaken for identical twins. Both had John's olive skin and dark curly hair, even the makings of his strong lithe physique. Handsome like their father, and doubtless they would pull the girls just like he did, she reflected wryly.

She heard a vehicle in the street outside and went to the window. A bright red Suzuki four-wheel drive, gleaming with its latest coat of turtle wax, scintillated in the late evening sun as the driver expertly reversed into a small space, edged it to within an inch of the green Golf parked behind, and switched off the engine. John was home.

'Hi.' John Strike stood surveying the row of unpacked tea chests and cartons in the hall. 'Everything go all right?'

'I suppose so.' She sensed a criticism because the containers had not been emptied and their contents put away. 'I wouldn't know, because you supervised our last move.'

'It's bound to be chaotic for a day or two.' He looked around for somewhere to deposit the waxed Barbour jacket which hung limply on his arm, and draped it over one of the boxes. 'God, the traffic! That's the first and last time I go to work in the jeep. I wouldn't have done today except that I'd've had to go all the way over to Chiswick this evening to fetch it. What's to eat?'

'Fish and chips,' she answered, 'and they're ready and waiting for you at the shop in the next street.'

Outside in the garden, Sam and Ben were just beginning another quarrel.

* * *

Thankfully the children were all asleep. Leah had checked on them one last time before she and John turned in. Sarah's room resembled a record shop, posters of Police and Michael Jackson hiding the frayed and grubby wallpaper. Sam had begun putting up his soccer stars, mostly centre spreads torn from football magazines. Tomorrow Leah would have to find something to paste up for Ben so that he did not feel deprived. She gently closed the door of the small end bedroom and tiptoed away.

John was already in bed, sitting up reading a copy of *Today*, immersed in his favourite feature article about some man who had made a million from nothing, a fellow who kept a jeep parked outside his house, polished it every weekend and went to the office in a thornproof jacket, rain or shine. And wore green wellies in winter. And if you hadn't made your first million and just worked in a bank you did exactly the same. He was like a bloody child with his fantasies.

She pretended not to notice his erection as she pulled back the duvet, slid in beside him and turned to face the other way. Surely this was one night on which she might be spared!

She tensed as his slender fingertips began to stroke her buttocks, easing up her nylon nightdress. She experienced the same feeling of guilt that she had had earlier, because Sarah was growing up and soon she would have to warn her not to do what she had done – and that made her a hypocrite.

In a way it was worse with the light off. She was lying on the back seat of John's old Cortina thirteen years ago. She had not lost her virginity until after her twenty-first birthday, and even then it had scared her to hell. All right, she was old-fashioned, everybody slept around these days. Except her. She had only let John because all the girls were after him, and if she wouldn't there were plenty who would. Strangely, she had enjoyed that first time and had been almost willing the second.

She'd insisted he used a condom every time but, all the same, periods were a relief, a nightmare if they were a couple of days late. It had taken her two months to become really passionate and make it to an orgasm. She'd got an engagement ring off him and provisionally fixed a wedding date six months hence. And then disaster had struck.

It was just like tonight, in the dark with John desperate to push into her. God, she had been a damn fool letting him have it without a Durex. His glib tongue had worked on her soft warm lower regions until she would have agreed to anything, and then he had convinced her that as her period had only finished a couple of days ago it would be safe without a condom.

She had moaned as his naked hardness slid right into her and started to thrust. No, John, *please*! Oh, *yes*. I want you to. She hadn't had any choice. She'd been writhing and pushing at him as he started to orgasm. Just like tonight.

And she had known right away that she was going to be pregnant, lying there in the darkness with his sperm warm inside her, convincing herself that she could feel a baby moving in her womb. At least that couldn't happen tonight, she thought thankfully.

That was when she heard Ben start to scream. In one panic-stricken moment she uncoupled and groped for the light-pull. Smoothing her nightdress down, she ran for the door, with the warm wet patch seeming to scald her fingers. And then her guilt was replaced by fear, that same gut-wrenching terror that had almost made her faint out in the street a few hours ago. The scream started to rise in her throat.

Ben was out on the landing, standing there in his sweat-creased red and white Arsenal pyjamas, his eyes closed as if he was still asleep, his features a ghastly greyish colour that might herald a sudden bilious attack. But his black curly hair should have been lying flat, damp with fevered sweat. *Instead it stood upright, stiff and straight, like a blighted cornfield.*

She was already reaching out for him when John caught her arm and pulled her back. 'Don't touch him!' His voice was tinged with fear, the fingers that clutched her shook uncontrollably.

She just stood there helplessly, seeing the child's expression of rigid terror, the lips moving, mumbling; dribbling saliva. And then Ben's eyes flickered open, and roved around but appeared not to see his parents. He screamed a second time, and that was when Leah grabbed him and pulled him to her.

'He's had a nightmare,' John muttered.

'What is it, my darling?' Leah picked the boy up and cradled him to her as he began to cry. 'Tell Mummy what the matter is.'

Ben's expression was vacant, puzzled. He was afraid but unable to explain the reason for his fear. Babbling incoherently, he pointed back towards the open door of his bedroom, struggling in case they tried to return him to his bed.

'He'd better sleep with us.' Leah began to carry her son into their own bedroom. She heard her husband check the child's room, then come back.

'Well, there's nothing in *there*.' There was no mistaking the relief in his voice.

'Why, did you expect there to be?' Leah snapped as she laid Ben in the middle of the bed and began to smooth his hair back into place. There was a vestige of colour returning to his cheeks and he had stopped crying.

'No, of course not.' John's tone lacked conviction. 'I just thought that . . . well, something very ordinary can frighten a child in the dark. It's the strange surroundings that are responsible; they've given him a nightmare and made him sleepwalk. Maybe we ought to get some sleeping mixture from the doctor tomorrow. Nothing to worry about, it happens to kids.'

Leah put the light out and held Ben close against her until she heard his breathing steady and become rhythmic. They should have had him in their bed in the first place, she thought. It would have spared the child and her an unnecessary trauma.

She was aware that she was lying on a damp patch, but to have moved might have awoken Ben again.

2

It was a long time before Leah drifted into an uneasy sleep, in a cramped position on the edge of the bed with Ben's tiny fingers clutching her nightdress into a ball. And then she was awake again.

Her immediate realization was one of acute bodily discomfort. Not just the stiffness brought on by her posture; a burning desire to go to the toilet. A glance at the bedside radio alarm clock showed her that it was just after three o'clock. There was no way she would be able to hold out until it was time to get up.

Gently she loosened Ben's grip and eased herself out of bed. There was no need to switch on the light; she groped her way out on to the landing, then had to pause to remember where the bathroom was situated. The floorboards creaked beneath her bare feet. On her way back to the bedroom, she noticed a light shining beneath the door of Sarah's room.

Her surprise turned to apprehension; perhaps Sarah was poorly. Or else Ben's screams had alarmed her. Leah glanced at Sam's door and was relieved to see that his room was in darkness. She moved towards the lighted door and stood listening. Silence, except for a roaring in her own ears. She grasped the handle, depressed it slowly and pushed the door open a few centimetres.

Sarah was lying in bed amidst a rumple of sheets and blankets, the result of a fevered tossing and turning, perhaps. Eyes closed, her features pallid, she certainly did not look well. Leah stepped inside and moved towards the bed, hand outstretched as her maternal instinct prompted her to feel at her daughter's forehead, anticipating an unnatural warmth that indicated a high temperature. A bout of summer 'flu, possibly, or a bilious attack.

Sarah's eyes opened wide in an expression of fear, and she cringed back into the pillow. Then she gasped her relief aloud as she recognized her mother.

'Sarah . . . are you all right?'

'Yes, Mother.' The eyes roved round the room. 'I'm fine, thanks.'

'You don't look it.'

'I'm okay!' She was irritated, churlish, now.

'Then why have you got your light on?'

'I . . . I couldn't sleep. I've been reading. Fell asleep.' A lie, Leah realized; Sarah had never been a good liar.

Leah looked around, there was no sign of a book or a magazine. 'All right, go back to sleep. I'll put the light out for you.'

'*No!*' the girl shrieked, coming up into a sitting position, and there was no mistaking the sheer terror in those wide blue eyes.

'Whatever's the matter?' Leah seated herself on the edge of the bed, guiltily crossing her hands over that small patch of dampness on her negligée. 'You're frightened and upset, love. Come on, you can tell me.'

'I'm all right.' She hesitated, and then, 'What's the matter with Ben?'

'He had a nightmare. Sleepwalked. I suppose he's disturbed by his new surroundings . . . like you are!'

'I'm not!'

Oh, God, teenage pride and stubbornness didn't help. 'Then you won't mind if I put the light off?'

'No . . . *please*!'

Leah took a deep breath, then let it out slowly. Strewth, there wasn't room for any more in the parental bed! Maybe she could sleep with Sarah; it would be a bit of a squash, but no worse than having Ben in between John and herself. But the suggestion would be rejected, there was no doubt about that. 'All right, leave your light on, then. Call me if you want me.'

Leah let herself out, leaving the door ajar behind her. And as she crossed the landing that fleeting terror which she had experienced earlier threatened to return; an inexplicable childish fear of things that lurked in the darkness and might leap out at her at any second. But it had passed by the time she squeezed herself back into bed alongside Ben's sleeping form.

And she understood why Sarah had been afraid.

John Strike caught the tube at Balham underground. The carriages were packed with early-morning workers. He carried his Barbour over his arm, realizing he should have left it at home because the weathermen were forecasting the heatwave would continue until the weekend at least. It was a kind of uniform, a hallmark, of those trying to create an image of rural life in the metropolis – and it spread like some contagious disease. A man standing in the aisle was even wearing his coat, his face shiny with sweat, a folded copy of the *Financial Times* clutched in the same hand that gripped the safety rail. It was a game that everybody was playing.

John alighted at Tottenham Court Road and walked the rest of the way to the bank. The traffic was at a standstill. There was an ambulance caught up in the jam, its blue lights flashing. Coming or going? he wondered. A traffic accident or a heart attack? Life or death was a common occurrence in the city, you just minded your own business like everybody else because it was none of your concern.

He still felt heady over his promotion to accountant in

the large branch. It was an admin job – a staff of forty-two did all the running about, he just took the responsibility for their balls-ups – with a rostrum to work at, an elevated lookout post, in fact. His authorized signature verified everything that everybody placed in his in-tray. If everything went okay, that was fine; if it didn't, he got his arse kicked. He was a paid whipping boy, the manager's stooge.

Mostly the staff were girls in their mid to late twenties, working for pin money to buy things for themselves whilst their husbands paid the mortgage. It was a cushy job until they either got tired of the daily routine or else became pregnant. The men had more at stake: promotion if they played their cards right and their faces fitted. The late entrants, the ex-university ones, were the worst, John decided. Too bloody clever by half for their own good, brilliant when it came to theories and systems, but give them a mundane routine task to do and they took the rest of the day to cock it up.

Periodically his glance strayed towards the door of the manager's office. He was relieved to find it still closed. Kenton was a nasty bastard and the staff were scared of him. A small, thickset, balding man, he had a permanent supercilious leer on his face as if to say, I'm the manager, I'm God, and don't you forget it. He was sarcastic, and if anyone crossed him he got them moved and demoted. Power, that was his thing in life. He created a sense of unease even when he was shut in his room granting overdrafts to customers.

John found his gaze straying to the number three cashier on the counter. She had short dark hair, a shapely figure and a split skirt that rode up and revealed an area of bare thigh every time she bent over to take money out of her reserve till drawer. Her nameplate stated that she was Ruth Ford and she wore a wedding ring. Which didn't mean a lot these days. He found himself watching her idly, and it was some time before he realized that she had given him an erection.

And going home on the tube that evening his thoughts strayed to her again.

Leah had a headache, one of those that began with a nagging ache behind the eyes and became progressively worse as the day wore on. She prayed it wouldn't turn into a migraine. She had not had one for over a year now. Tiredness, that was the cause, without a doubt, after a sleepless night and all that fuss with the children. Well, you had to get the first night in a new house over; it was over now, and that was that.

She had spent the morning unpacking the boxes in the hallway, finding a place to put everything. Doubtless it would all have to be moved again, but at least she had got it out of the way. The empty cartons were in the skip outside, along with a lot of other rubbish. She thought a skip was a bit unnecessary, a special refuse collection could have been arranged easily enough. But John had insisted on ordering a skip; he had almost made an issue of it. Well, if he wanted one that badly she wasn't going to involve herself in a heated row over it.

She came to the conclusion, somewhat reluctantly, that the house could be made really nice. At some stage, definitely not during the Graftons' time, extensive alterations had been made to the interior. Two front rooms had been knocked into one, and the kitchen had been extended to incorporate a dining area. There were patio doors that once probably looked out on a neatly planted rear garden with a lawn and rose bushes. The framework was all there; it could be restored with a few coats of paint, and a weekend in the garden, which John would put down to grass, naturally. Somewhere for Sam and

Ben to play football and scuff the turf bare. A place to fight and quarrel.

Sam had already made friends with the boy two houses away and had gone round there to play. With any luck he would stay to tea. Ben was upstairs sleeping off his disturbed night, and Sarah was up in her room finishing a painting which she had begun weeks ago: a watercolour of their former house in Chiswick. Was it nostalgia, Leah wondered, or maybe even homesickness? Anyway, for Leah it was a period of unprecedented peace and quiet during the summer holidays, and it might not occur again.

She was tempted to go up to the bedroom and lie down for an hour. Maybe she would, but first she ought to wash up the breakfast things and prepare a meal for this evening. John certainly would not appreciate a second successive visit to the chippie. A salad, a pizza out of the freezer, she decided. Something nice and refreshing, and easy. But first the dishes.

As she ran the taps and squirted washing-up liquid into the water, she wondered why whoever had altered the kitchen had not moved the sink beneath the window. It seemed the obvious and easiest course, certainly more pleasant for the housewife lumbered with the irksome daily task of washing crockery. Admittedly, one only looked out on to the fence, but that was preferable to staring at a blank emulsioned wall. She could put a bird table out there and watch the sparse population of city birds feeding during the winter months; anything to break the monotony.

She tried not to think about last night but it was inevitable. Not Ben. Nor Sarah. Just nightmares brought on by childish fears. John dominated her thoughts. God, he disgusted her at times. She wondered if all men were like that; she didn't know because she had never been with anybody else. Not seriously, anyway. All he wanted was sex and more sex. She only let him have his way because if she didn't he would get it somewhere else, she had no doubt about that. Sometimes she wondered if he did anyway. It wouldn't be the first time. She screwed with him for the children's sake, convincing herself she was some kind of martyr. Marital sex to promote family harmony. But there were limits, Jesus Christ, there were!

She would never forget that occasion when he bought a Polaroid camera. He said it was to take snaps of the kids with, and, fair enough, he had done just that. In the beginning.

Sarah was eight at the time, so that was five years ago. They were on holiday in North Wales, staying in a rented cottage, and the relaxed atmosphere even made Leah feel like sex. The kids were asleep in bed and she and John were engaged in a lengthy session. Strewth, she had even taken the initiative and kissed him where he liked being kissed most of all, so she had really been turned on. But that rare moment of passion came to an abrupt end when her husband reached under the bed and produced his Polaroid already loaded for action.

She was aghast. He wanted her to lie there with her legs lewdly spread and let him take a close-up picture inside her thighs. Not only that, he asked her to hold her lower lips open for him! And, to make matters worse, he *presumed* that the idea would excite her: I'll snap yours and you snap mine – like dirty little schoolkids playing with one another behind the coal bunker during break-time. Leah flatly refused and pulled the sheets right up to hide her body, and that ruined the rest of the holiday.

So now he just took her when the urge was upon him, which was most nights. And when he didn't, she would worry in case he was getting a bit on the side. She sighed. When the children were grown up she would probably leave him. Right now it was a reassuring thought. She began washing plates and stacking them in the rack on the draining-board.

Suddenly she stiffened and felt her breathing quicken, her pulses speed up. The instant hot flush turned icy cold and goosepimpled her skin. Her vision swam so that the scratched and faded paintwork of the wall above the sink misted.

She clutched the edge of the working surface. She had to hold on to it or she would have fallen. Her dry mouth wanted to scream but her vocal chords refused to function. Inexplicable escalating terror froze her.

Somebody was watching her.

She knew the feeling but it had never been as strong, as frightening, as this. It was like when she used to sunbathe on the lawn at home in her mid-teens, clad in only a bikini, and she knew darned well that Mr Moore next door was lustfully spying on her, peeping through the privet hedge. Only this was a thousand times worse.

Somebody was out there in the garden watching her. Moving her head barely an inch, she strained her eyes until they hurt. Her vision was distorted because sweat was running into them and stinging her. The mass of debris and weeds was not enough to hide anybody; unless they were skulking in the shed. No, they couldn't be there because it was locked. The lock was rusted; John said he would have to force it and fit a new one.

Where, then?

Don't move, don't let them know that you know, she told herself. She was shaking and her legs felt as if they would buckle under her and throw her to the floor. A plate slid in the rack, clinked against another, tilted at a precarious angle, and threatened to domino the rest.

Her body was taut, so tight it might split open. She felt an urge to flee straight back through the hall and out into the street, slam the door behind her and leave the children at the mercy of . . .

I can't remain like this forever, she thought. But I don't want to *see*.

If whoever it was wasn't out in the garden, then they had to be . . . *in here*. Because there wasn't anywhere else.

She heard a movement, a kind of shuffling noise like somebody sliding a bare foot along the tiled floor of the kitchen. She was incapable of movement. Holding on to the unit top for dear life, taking a deep breath, she knew that the hidden watcher was directly behind her. Less than a metre away. Any second a hand might stretch out, *touch her*.

She could hear the intruder breathing, snuffling breaths through nostrils clogged with mucus. Another slithering step. He must be right behind her now. Bracing herself, she tried to force a scream through constricted lungs. And then the plates fell, clattering and crashing, tumbling out of the rack and sliding, avalanching on to the floor. Shattering and smashing, they broke the spell that had held her rigid and helpless.

Leah got her scream out at last, a piercing shriek as she turned and crunched a shard of crockery beneath a sandalled foot. Slipping, almost falling, she threw up a hand to protect herself.

And that started Ben screaming, too. Standing there, wearing just the bottom half of his Arsenal pyjamas which he had wet during his daytime sleep, he began yelling hysterically, eyes wide with shock and fear.

Amidst the debris of a smashed dinner-service, mother and son clung to each other, sobbing uncontrollably as stark terror subsided into blessed relief. Shaking as they embraced, they murmured incoherent reassurances until finally Leah carried her son back upstairs and lay down on the bed alongside him.

But she still trembled because she knew it had been something more than just Ben standing there behind her in the kitchen. Somebody else had been watching her. Just as they had yesterday afternoon when she stood across the road watching the house. They had been out there on the darkened landing last night, too. And in Sarah's room.

Somebody or *something* sinister.

3

John Strike was tense behind the wheel of the Morris Minor. He slowed to 25 mph and changed down to second. Nervousness that bordered on fear made him sweat profusely. Watching the narrow one-track road ahead of him, he kept to the near side so that the overhanging foliage of the high straggling hedge brushed the side of the car. Hawthorn branches whipped the windscreen as though trying to urge him on, angry with his slow speed.

He had always had a lurking terror of side roads; no vision, miles of narrow bends, no warning of approaching vehicles. Already he had had to back up for a tractor and trailer, reversing a couple of hundred metres until he came to a gateway, wheels spinning in the soft grass. But tractors were only a nuisance, they travelled slowly. With a car coming at speed in the opposite direction, he would have no chance. There was loose gravel everywhere, the remnants of frost grit spread by locals from the intermittent piles dumped by the council in winter. If he braked hard he would skid. With luck it would be no more than a crunched wing, a time-wasting nuisance, with each driver paying for his own damage because neither wanted to lose his no-claims bonus.

This was one facet of rural life which lost its appeal, he'd found. Living out in the sticks sounded idyllic until you experienced the drawbacks. Clumps of nettles and cow parsley grew densely on the high banks, narrowing the highway still further.

He was going somewhere; he could not remember

where, only that he wanted to emerge from these dangerous side roads on to the main road; to join speeding cars and heavy goods vehicles, nose to bumper. At least the dangers were there to be seen. Danger lurked everywhere, but you lived with it, with everyday hazards. Oh, God Almighty, how much further?

The surface was breaking up. There were deep potholes filled with water from that heavy shower this morning. The old bullnosed Morris bumped its way over them, the chassis creaking its protests. Down to 15 mph now, the car was trying to straddle a miniature ravine in the tarmac, the off side wheels sliding down into it and sending up a spray of muddy rainwater.

John's mouth was dry and he felt a headache coming on. His shirt clung damply to his body and he felt slightly sick. Jesus, this stretch of so-called road had to come out somewhere before long . . . unless he came to a dead end and had to travel all the way back again. To where? Just concentrate on your driving, he told himself.

And then he saw the car coming towards him. In a split second that became an eternity, every detail clearly burned on his tortured brain as though with a smouldering branding iron: a light blue Ford Escort, ravaged by rust, with only half a front numberplate remaining and hanging at an angle; a silly green sticker on the windscreen revealing the driver's name – Mick; a doll swinging crazily in the rear window like a hanged murderer kicking his last; a face staring at him through the glass, with brown hair and boyish features that were contorting into an expression of horror and disbelief. The driver mouthed his terror in mute exhortations and curses. *Fucking hell!*

John was braking, slewing. Gravel pinged on the bodywork like a hail of enemy machine-gun bullets. Ploughing into the bank sideways on, the seatbelt contracted on his chest like a sledgehammer blow; pinioned, trapped, he waited for the impact. And waited.

Metal buckling, glass showering, all was opaqueness. Then he was able to see. Staring, he waited for his numbed brain to comprehend. Waited until he was able to scream.

The other driver had not been wearing a safety belt, or he would not have been thrown forward. The front of the Escort had disintegrated. The rusty metalwork was compressed against the buckled near side of the Morris, its windscreen entangled with the framework of John's car so that the youth's head protruded through a jagged hole and hung there inside the Morris.

John stared into the terrified blood-washed features only a metre away; the other driver was not even struggling, suspended by a jagged piece of glass embedded firmly in his neck. His throat was gashed, pumping blood with force; drowning the screams. He was dying.

Blood sprayed, a crimson fountain that bathed John Strike and saturated his sweaty shirt. He screamed, struggled to free himself of his belt, and tried to depress the release catch with slippery fingers. The ragged glass was cutting into the youth's neck, guillotining him with the weight of the hanging body, slicing through flesh, grating on bone.

And then John Strike was free, panicking as he struggled to force the door open. It was embedded in the soft earth; there was just a gap which he might be able to squeeze through. He tore his clothes, but didn't care. His trousers caught on the window winder and ripped. Blood was washing over him all the time.

Falling clear, he crawled away, aware for the first time that both engines were still running, with a steady tick-over. The fuel might ignite, explode. Run, he thought, you can't do anything to help *him*.

Kneeling there in the road, he saw the youth's eyes fixed on him, as if pleading, Don't leave me, you bastard!

John wrenched his gaze away and almost vomited. He knew the youth was done for, beyond help. All the same, he had to get help, an ambulance to remove the corpse . . . Suddenly he stopped and began examining his own body. *Oh, God, I must be hurt!*

There was blood all over him; his shirt and torn trousers were soaked and it was drying on his skin in the warm sunshine. He looked for wounds but it was impossible to find any in this mess, trying to tell himself that the blood had all come from that poor sod in the Escort, and half believing it. He had bruises everywhere; they would come out later. Stumbling away, he was still conscious of the steady *drip-drip* of blood in the crushed cars.

Dazed, not knowing where to go, he just followed the narrow lane, bend after bend. The high hedges made it impossible to see any landmarks. Surely there were farms around, he thought. There weren't, just gateways and empty fields. Breathless, he had to stop and rest. There was no hurry, he told himself. That fellow would be dead by now. Scared, he listened in case a vehicle came hurtling round one of the bends; there was nowhere to get out of its path.

His watch was gone and there was no way of telling the time. The sun was high in the sky. It had been like that for hours, just as if time had stopped. Stumbling along, he fought against the urge to lie down and sleep. Exhausted, he fell once and had difficulty in getting back on to his feet. He had lost all sense of direction, but if he kept going he would reach *somewhere*.

Some time later, hours, it seemed like days, weeks, he rounded yet another bend and recoiled in horror at the scene which greeted him. Shying away from it, he covered his eyes with his hands in an attempt to shut it out, but even then he saw it in his twisted and tortured mind.

The heap of mangled metal was barely recognizable as

the remnants of a Morris Minor and a Ford Escort. Scrap. The engines had cut out, perhaps because they had used up all the fuel. Everything was just as he had left it. No, not quite.

The broken windscreen had cut right through the youth's neck and his head had fallen inside the Morris, rolled like a ball, and somehow found its way out through the partly open door, then come to rest on the road. Upright, it was like a roadman standing up in a deep hole he had dug and looking out. Eyes wide and staring, it accused him: You abandoned me, you bastard, and left me to die!

The blood had dried and it was difficult at a glance to tell it from the rust. There was a smell which he did not recognize but knew was the stench of death. John stood there, aware of the total silence, a kind of finality about it. *He's dead, and you're not going anywhere.*

There was no escape. Whichever way he walked, however far, this road would bring him back here. It was just him and that decapitated bloody corpse. He moved back and sat down on the bank.

Later, much later, he heard the drone of an approaching vehicle. Comprehension was difficult. He thought at first it might be the buzzing in his ears, or a bee hunting pollen amidst the dense cow parsley. No, it was a car all right, coming this way. Louder by the second, full revs and not slowing on the bends, it was gathering speed all the time.

Hope turned to stark terror and had him trying to climb the high bank. The grass was wet and his feet slipped. Sliding back, he twisted his ankle. Lying on the frost-ravaged tarmac, he dragged himself along, a wounded crab stranded on a beach and trying to reach the receding tide. Cursing because the wrecked cars blocked his progress and there was no way past them, he beat at them with his blood-encrusted fists so that they reverberated. Sobbing his frustration, he was forced to look at that severed head again. It had turned round and was watching him with its wide dead eyes, mocking him. *There's no escape. Like before!*

The oncoming car was deafening now, just one bend away. Bracing himself, he screamed.

And he was still screaming when Leah shook him awake.

'Wake up!' There was alarm in her tone. 'Are you all right, John?'

'Uh?' He was aware of the darkened room, his wife's voice.

'You've had a nightmare.' She was whispering, afraid that perhaps it was too late and the children had already been woken up.

No, he knew it was too real for a dream. Smoothing his hands over his naked body, he found it slippery with sweat. Or blood. His mouth was dry. There was a sour taste on his palate and a smell that lingered in his notrils. The stench of death; he thought he could even detect the odour of scorched tyres. He was trying to get everything together but it would not come, because there was no escape whichever way you went. You always arrived back at the accident.

Leah tugged the light-pull and the blinding glare made him cover his eyes. *No, I don't want to look!*

She nearly said, You're as bad as the kids, but checked herself just in time. He'd had a bad one, there was no doubt about that, and he wasn't out of it yet.

'What happened?' she asked.

'I . . .' He stopped. God, he didn't want to think about it, couldn't go through it all again. 'Nothing really,' he said lamely.

'Shall I go and make a cup of tea?'

'No.' He shook his head. 'Just put the light out.'

Back in darkness, neither of them talked. He could feel Leah trembling with him. Hell, it was as bad now as it had been in the dream. It was a dream, it had to be, or he would not be here in his own bed now. He felt his body, just to be sure. It was aching; maybe there were bruises. His head was the worst, with his temples pounding. There were some aspirins downstairs, he remembered.

He waited for Leah's breathing to become heavy and regular; he did not want any more questions. Sliding out of bed, he was aware how his legs shook.

Just a bad dream, he told himself, like the ones he used to get as a kid when he was sickening for something. Only much worse. He wondered what had brought it on. He'd never had a Morris Minor, and the only time he had driven around narrow lanes was when they had holidayed in Devon and Cornwall, and spent half the time sitting in a traffic jam because a coach was blocking the route. *But it didn't have to happen in a country lane: you could have a head-on anywhere!*

Oh, God!

You're getting paranoid, he thought. No, just logical. A main road, speeding traffic, a lorry coming towards you overtaking and misjudging. Or a wet road, that same lorry jack-knifing.

Stop it!

Five thousand a year killed on the roads – the luck of the draw. You didn't have to go far; he had read somewhere that statistics proved the majority of fatal accidents occurred on short journeys.

Out on the landing, he closed the bedroom door behind him and leaned up against the wall. He felt faint. Maybe he would give up driving and sell the jeep, he thought. They didn't really need it except to stand outside in the road as a status symbol. They could go on holiday by coach.

The luck of the draw again. That news feature on the television last week came back to him with frightening clarity in the darkness of the landing. A coach carrying fifty-four passengers . . . a tanker careering across the central reservation of the M6 . . . a head-on . . . seventeen killed, twenty-four injured.

He almost screamed again.

The feeling of faintness receded. He walked unsteadily towards the top of the stairs, then stopped again.

There was a light showing beneath Sarah's bedroom door. She was either reading late or ill. He'd better check.

The girl's eyes opened the moment he looked into the room, fixing him with a curious, half-frightened stare. She said in a low voice, 'You don't look well, Dad.'

'A headache.' He leaned up against the doorpost. 'What are you doing with your light on at this hour?'

'Mother said I could sleep with it on. Ask her if you don't believe me.' Stubborn defiance; she wasn't going to put the light off.

'All right.' I'm not going to ask if you've had nightmares, he thought. I don't want to know. He stepped back outside and closed the door.

The aspirins tasted as sour as his palate and his head throbbed viciously in the glare of the fluorescent light in the kitchen. He went back upstairs. Leah was asleep, thank God.

He could not shake off the dream. The details didn't matter, a fellow he'd never seen before and didn't give a shit about. People were killed on the roads every day, and as long as it wasn't somebody you knew, it didn't matter. Just statistics. But it could be *you*.

Lying there, still trembling, he was back behind the

wheel; the jeep this time. He had a kind of compulsion to drive. He'd keep out of the narrow lanes and off the motorways. London, then; traffic lights on red, a triple line of cars easing forward on amber, surging on green. Somebody was jumping the lights. A police car, an ambulance, maybe a drunk or an armed raiders' getaway car. No chance!

John jumped, the way people do when they fall down a flight of stairs in a dream. Except that he wasn't dreaming, he was fully awake.

He licked his lips and felt how his breathing had become shallow; each breath was a conscious effort. Sleep was out of the question.

He tried to think of other things. That cashier at the bank, Ruth Ford. He couldn't even make an erection now.

Maybe it was a premonition, a glimpse into the future. *This is how you're going to die, John Strike*. Death was a certainty; you accepted the inevitable but hoped it wouldn't be tomorrow, next week, next year, but in old age, senility, when you didn't know anything about it, or if you did you wouldn't care because there was nothing left for you in life.

Perhaps he was ill, mentally, and stress was bringing on a nervous breakdown. He did not really believe that because he had never let it get to him. Moving house, then. Whatever the reason, it put him back on the road. Now it was a suburban street, with cars parked on either side. He was driving slowly, down to 15 mph in case one of them suddenly pulled out in front of him, checking each to see if there was a driver behind the wheel. Too late!

There was a darting figure. He had not seen the ball bounce into the road in front of the boy. Standing on the brakes, the tyres squealing, he felt just a faint bump, and then a wheel went over something. Jumping out, he rushed to the lifeless bleeding form, treading on the red football cap that matched the blood in the road. Sobbing, he turned the boy's body over. Seeing the face, recognizing it in spite of the disfiguration, he screamed hysterically.

Because it was Ben.

Afraid to sleep, John Strike was still awake when the first grey fingers of dawn slid into the bedroom.

And whatever it was that was the matter with him, he knew it was bad.

4

The Cellar Wine Bar was crowded by five-thirty. Office workers were seeking a brief relaxation before returning home, managing directors were finishing a long luncheon meeting with customers, or a farewell drink with a colleague who would be moving on to another firm on Monday morning. Friday evenings were always busy, and there was an atmosphere of exuberance, almost sheer relief at having completed yet another week of routine stress.

John Strike was in no hurry to leave the bank. Most of the female staff had left half an hour before. Kenton was in his room with the door closed, a squat silhouette through the opaque glass, busily writing at his desk; it might have been notes on overdrafts to be typed up and filed away on Monday, or even personal letters. Nobody knew the workings of that inner sanctum except the manager himself, and nobody was really interested.

There was an atmosphere of tranquillity in the main office after the bustle of a busy day, with waste-paper bins overflowing, ledgers untidily stacked on the shelves – the hallmark of a workforce eager to be gone from this humdrum place. They worked five days in order to enjoy two; there was nothing to be gained by lingering here. Unless they had a reason. Which John Strike had.

He busied himself sorting out his pending file of letters awaiting replies and some diary cards for next week. Killing time, he was trying to seem busy in case Kenton emerged from his office. The manager liked the staff to be away by five, not for their benefit but because they might book overtime if they worked later and that reduced the branch's annual profits. An accountant was not eligible for overtime; it was considered beneath his status, and his salary was supposed to compensate for unsocial hours, anyway. Nevertheless, John needed a reason to be here after five if the boss queried it.

Five-fifteen. John shuffled the last of a pile of letters and placed them neatly in the wire basket, then capped his pen. It was less than ten minutes' walk to the Cellar. He had timed it just right. One quick phone call; he watched the outline of the bank manager as he waited for the phone to ring at the other end. The bald head was bowed, the podgy hand still scribbled. There were a few moments of tension for John, a sense of guilt. But he was back under control when Leah answered.

'Hi, love.' He tried to sound a trifle piqued, the hard-done-by chief clerk who had had an inconvenience imposed upon him by the boss at the last moment. 'Afraid I'll be a bit late back tonight. Dinner with a customer.' Lowering his voice, he prayed that Kenton would not decide to come out just at this moment. 'Got it dropped on me, you know how it is.'

'What time shall I expect you home?' There was neither disappointment nor suspicion in her voice; it was just a routine question.

'Can't really say. Might be latish, midnight even. You can never gauge a business meeting. Don't wait up for me.'

'That's fine.'

'Everybody okay?'

'Yes. Sam's with those kids down the road. Sarah's painting. Ben's a bit restless, might be sickening for something. Nothing serious, I don't expect.'

'See you later, then.' He dropped the phone back and had to check the urge to grab his Barbour and rush from the office. Everything had worked out; he had an alibi and a date. He was slightly nervous, but that was all part of it.

All kinds of fears plagued him on the short walk to the wine bar. Ruth might not be there; she might have had second thoughts and decided not to turn up. Or somebody from the office might be in there and see them together. Forget it, play it as it comes, he told himself. She'll be there, and, anyway, hundreds of office workers have a drink together on a Friday before going home.

She was there, all right, sitting at a corner table, looking strikingly lovely in the dim light. He collected two glasses of house red from the bar and joined her.

The initial awkwardness was only to be expected on such a meeting between accountant and cashier. John wondered if his invitation to join him at the Cellar had been understood or naïvely misinterpreted. He'd had to play it cautiously, he was in a position of trust and authority. One brief chat when she brought some documents for him to sign, had been time enough in which to learn that Ruth's husband was away on a company course for three weeks, weekends included. She had agreed readily enough to meet John after work, but he was still testing the water. He left it until they were on their second glass.

'Fancy something to eat? There's a good Indian not far from here.'

'Suits me,' she smiled, but even then he did not know for sure. 'What time do you have to be home?'

'When it suits me,' he replied, and she laughed.

They were halfway through their meal, before she volunteered any information about her husband.

'Keith's a workaholic.' There was bitterness, resentment in her tone now. 'Married to his job and his company car. Away all week, then spends the weekends trying to catch up on a mountain of paperwork. The only time he breaks off is either to eat or to watch the football on telly. But I've got used to it over the years. Sometimes I go out with my friend Jenny, but really it's a bore and a waste of time being married. I've thought of leaving him but I suppose I'm just too lazy. One day, perhaps.'

The signs were good. And he was not altogether surprised when she declined coffee at the table and suggested that they went back to her place and had some there.

Ruth's house was similar to the Strikes', only smaller – one room at the front, the dining room and kitchen combined at the back. But there was something more homely about it, John decided. Cosy, that was it. It wasn't . . . *eerie*. A stark contrast to Number Thirteen. It was the first time he had been able to relax since moving house. And that awful nightmare and its subsequent phobia were almost forgotten. Almost but not quite.

Her lips were upturned to meet his when he leaned across the sofa to kiss her. He felt her body tremble slightly against his own and their tongues touched. She had not misunderstood him, after all.

'Your wife will be worried about where you've got to.' He wondered if she was calling time: a kiss and a cuddle, that's all you're getting, John Strike. Thanks for the evening, I've enjoyed it.

'She's not expecting me until I arrive,' he laughed. He was not ready to discuss Leah yet. It was early days.

Ruth kissed him again and he knew then that everything was going to work out.

His heart beat wildly as he stroked a breast through her dress and she pressed herself up against him, crushed her lips on his and moaned softly as he began to unfasten her buttons. Then, suddenly, she freed herself and whispered, 'We'd be more comfortable upstairs.'

The marital bedroom – a double bed with a duvet, a bow window, a chest of drawers that might have come from a secondhand furniture dealer's. Again it was cosy; he wished that he could stay the night.

Ruth was in the bathroom. She was certainly taking her time, he thought. He undressed, folded his clothes on the bedside chair and slid under the duvet. This delay was disquieting; he had lost his arousal. Then he heard her bare feet padding swiftly across the landing.

She was wearing a long nightdress and seemed nervous now, checking that the curtains were closed. A moment of indecision, and then she slid into bed to join him, kissing him. He thought that she would have reached for the light-pull had he not been pinioning her on the pillows.

She let him pull her nightdress up over her head and he feasted his gaze on beautiful small breasts, the pink nipples firmly erect. Throwing back the cover, he saw her lithe body with its flat stomach, her thighs pressed closely together deliberately obstructing his view of her lower regions.

'I'm afraid I'm terribly inhibited,' she whispered, her eyes closed. 'It's the way I was brought up.'

Her words had his erection back to full stretch. This was so much more erotic than some floosie flaunting herself at him, lewdly spreading her legs and inviting him to look. She was sexy in her own way and . . . loving. This realization came as a shock, one that both thrilled and worried him. Then he noticed the scar.

At first he thought it was the mark of an adolescent appendix operation, but it was too high, too long. He stared in curiosity until he heard her say, 'I got that in a road accident when I was nineteen.'

His brain whirled, his vision misted. He felt himself tautening and became slightly faint. Oh, God, *no*!

'I'm afraid it's rather unsightly.' Ruth was blushing, self-conscious. 'Keith says it's off-putting.'

'No, it isn't.' He had to force the words, fighting to dispel that inexplicable phobia which was starting to stir like some frightening revolting serpent in the dark caverns of his mind. 'I . . . I think it's . . . rather erotic.'

Then he was kissing her neck, flicking at her nipples with his tongue, tracing a path downwards, leaving a trail of saliva glistening on the soft skin of her pulsing body. Circling her navel, he was going on downwards. And her thighs began to open in readiness for him.

Her dark pubic hair was closely trimmed so that the pink warm flesh amidst it stood out starkly, inviting him to kiss its softness. She shuddered and started to writhe, and he tasted her sweetness, smelled the fragrance of her body and knew that he could wait no longer.

The bed groaned beneath their coupled bodies and Ruth's inhibitions were gone. Pushing at him, claiming him, encircling him with her long legs in case he might try to withdraw from her, she cried her pleasure aloud as her orgasm mounted, urging him on and on. And as they exploded into ecstasy he heard her whisper, 'Oh, I love you, John.'

They lay embraced for some time afterwards, two people in a world where husbands and wives did not exist, kissing tenderly now that the fires of passion had died down to glowing embers.

'I must get home.' He was reaching for his clothes.

She was close to tears. 'Do you have to go?'

'Afraid so.' He pulled his shirt over his head. 'But I'll be back.'

'When?'

'As soon as possible. One night next week, probably. See you at the office on Monday.' He kissed her, went downstairs and let himself out into the street with cars parked on either side, the orange streetlights glinting on their metalwork. It might have been his street, the house he had left, Number Thirteen. Much of a muchness. But it wasn't the same. People were different. And houses, too. He shivered, wishing for more reasons than one that he did not have to go home.

John Strike paused at the end of Schooner Street and hung back, a guilty child who had played truant all day and was afraid to return home and face the interrogation that was bound to ensue. *Where have you been? What have you been doing all this time?*

Infidelity was nothing new to him – one-night stands he had forgotten by the following morning. No strings attached, no involvements. He had thought tonight would be like that; it could be if he didn't make another move. But he would, because a physical relationship had suddenly become much more. Oh, God, you're tired, you don't have to make a decision tonight, he told himself. Put it off, procrastinate. But it won't go away.

Suddenly the warm summer night had chilled and he shrugged himself into his Barbour. It was as if the warmth and tranquillity ended here at the top of his own street, that Number Thirteen breathed cold hostility at him.

He walked down the opposite pavement with slow, dragging steps, counting the houses because it was too dark to read the numbers on the front doors. 7 . . . 9 . . . 11 . . . *13*. Stopping, he cringed before it.

Windows that were dark eyeless sockets picked him out of the gloom, glowered malevolently at him. The doorway was a wide toothless mouth emitting fetid odours. He smelled them, recoiled from them. It was a house of brooding evil that spawned terrible nightmares.

Which, he knew, was too bloody silly for words. He gave a low laugh that came out like a whimper and began to cross the road. His legs felt weak; a thought crossed his mind that he might not make it. But he did. Standing in the porch, he fumbled for his keys. The Chubb for the lower security lock, the Yale to open the door. It creaked a kind of warning growl.

The feeling of guilt was strong now, like in his teenage days when he had stayed out late with a girl and his parents were lying listening for him. A flood of lights heralded their anger, the questions, the accusations. *Where have you been till now? The pubs close at eleven.* Once he had hidden his briefs deep in the dustbin in case his mother checked them for stains. The fear now was as it had been then. Only worse.

Maybe Leah was asleep. He did not need an excuse, he had made it hours ago. If you wanted promotion, a better standard of living, then you had to be prepared to work unsocial hours. He didn't have to explain in detail, banking was veiled in secrecy. He almost kicked off his shoes and left them down in the hallway. But he didn't because that was only pandering to his guilt.

Walking on the balls of his feet, he tested each stair in case it creaked. For the sake of the sleeping children. Realizing that he was still wearing his waxed jacket when he reached the landing, he stood there, listening to the beating of his own heart. He was so cold, his teeth were chattering like castanets.

It was as though time had stopped and he was suspended in a dark void. *As if this house was waiting for something to happen.*

The scream shattered the awful stillness. It came from nowhere and was everywhere, a piercing infantile shrieking that had him reeling back, clutching at his ears in a vain attempt to shut it out, a sound that embodied pain and terror. And somewhere in the darkness he heard a rush of bare feet.

Blinding light dazzled him, people seemed to be rushing in every direction. Leah pushed past him, ignoring him. Sarah, eyes wide with terror, was standing in the lighted doorway of her bedroom. Sam peeped round his door, frightened to come out and ready to slam it shut if necessary.

John was a helpless spectator, wanting to help but powerless to do so, terrified of what might have happened.

Leah was back on the landing, Ben in her arms. The child's hair was wet, as though it had just been washed, his pyjamas a clinging wet suit where he had urinated in his terror. He was clutching his mother, crying.

'So you're back, creeping about in the middle of the night!' There was both scorn and suspicion in Leah's expression, then she dismissed her husband with obvious contempt. 'Come on, my darling.' She kissed Ben and carried him into the parental bedroom. 'Tell Mummy what happened.'

John followed, pulling off his Barbour, dragging it along with him. Standing just inside the bedroom door, he watched his wife peel off Ben's soaking trousers and pull him into bed with her. Maternal reassurance stemmed the tears, and Ben buried his face in her bosom. She was saying words that John did not catch; they would not have registered in his confused mind anyway.

He undressed, left his clothes where they fell and slunk into bed. Leah had her son, she did not need him. But he wished she would put the light out.

Ben was asleep in her arms. He watched her laying him gently in the bed between them, covering him.

'He's had another nightmare,' she said. 'Sleepwalked again. Or rather, sleep*ran*. If I hadn't dashed out the moment I heard him start to scream he would have gone headlong down the stairs. Right past *you*!'

John swallowed. 'I wonder what's bothering him.'

'Whatever it is, he's having some very nasty nightmares. I got this one out of him.'

'Oh?' *I don't want to hear, don't tell me.*

'He dreamed that he got knocked down in the road. *That you ran over him in the jeep!*'

5

Leah was relieved when it was Monday morning again. The weekend had been dreadful, claustrophobic and overpowering. Nothing specific, just the atmosphere that was partly due to the children's obvious disturbance by the move to this depressing house. And John.

She tried to convince herself that he had been drinking heavily on Friday night. Certainly she had smelled alcohol on his breath, but she sensed a deeper reason. Another woman. It had happened before. She had closed her eyes to it and pretended that it had not happened. But this time it had affected him badly, from the way he tried to keep out of her way. His guilt created tension.

He had busied himself clearing the garden for most of Saturday, wheeling barrowloads of rubbish out to the skip at the front. He had certainly tidied up the small patch of land that backed on to the house and even started to make a border along the fence. Then he had gone down to the shops and returned with bunches of dried herbs which he had hung in the kitchen. She wasn't impressed; the leaves would drop off and litter the working surfaces. The dead foliage would gather dust and provide a refuge for spiders and other loathsome insects. She wouldn't use the herbs for culinary purposes, they were too much trouble. She already had a rack of powdered ones . . . But it was all part of this stupid image he was attempting to create, along with the Suzuki, that ridiculous waxed jacket and the green wellies under the stairs: a country squire living in south London. That was only one step up from the little boy who dressed up to play cowboys.

On Sunday they had slept late, and he had taken them to a restaurant for lunch, his one redeeming action of the weekend. She could not remember how they had passed the rest of the day; she thought John had been out polishing his jeep whilst she had gone upstairs for a lie-down.

At least Ben had not had a recurrence of that ghastly nightmare. But she knew that it was preying on the child's mind. He didn't like going out of the front door and was scared of the road.

Now it was Monday again, thank God! John had got up early and was out of the house before eight, as if he was running away, eager to be gone before she could ply him with questions. Maybe later there would be a phone call to say that he had another evening engagement. *Sorry, love, don't wait up for me*. I won't, she thought, don't worry. At least while you're screwing her you're not pestering me. That was one consolation.

She wondered about leaving him. She had considered it before, a couple of years ago. She could go to her parents, take the children with her. But ultimately she would be the loser, she would give up her home to some unknown woman.

'What are we going to do today, Mum?' Sam had finished his wheatflakes. Ben was busy spreading his over the drop-leaf formica top of the breakfast bar.

'Shopping,' she replied.

'Aw, Mum!' – a groan of dismay that Ben imitated – 'I want to go and play with Jeremy.'

'Well, you can't.'

'Why not, Mum?'

'Because I shall be away for a couple of hours and I'm not leaving you. Anyway, Jeremy's mother must be getting sick and tired of you being round there all the time. He'll have to come and play here one of these days.' *One more child to add to my overflowing cup of joy!*

'I've invited him but he won't come.'

'Why not?' *I'm not really interested, but tell me.*

'He doesn't like this house.'

'Oh!' She felt the base of her spine begin to prickle. 'That's silly, I don't expect he's ever been inside it.'

'He has. When Timothy Grafton lived here, they used to play together. Jeremy says that this house is spooky. He used to have bad dreams after he'd been here. Ask him if you don't believe me.'

Leah steadied herself against the sink. Bad dreams. Nightmares. Like Ben. And John. And maybe that was Sarah's problem, too, but she was keeping it to herself and sleeping with her light on.

'Jeremy's just being silly.' She tried to sound indignant. 'I suppose we're not good enough for him. Did he say whether Timothy Grafton had nightmares, too?' *Oh, Christ, I shouldn't have asked that.*

'Dunno. He didn't say. Mum, do I *have* to go shopping?'

'Yes, you do, Sam. And Ben and Sarah are coming as well. Now go and change out of those filthy jeans. There are some clean ones in your drawer.'

It was a relief to get out of the house, like waking up the day after a migraine and realizing that the pain was gone. Leah held Ben's hand; he did not protest for once but insisted on walking on the side furthest from the kerb. Sam trailed behind sulkily. He was in one of his moods, determined to be as difficult as possible. Sarah was a yard or two in front. Leah noticed that she had put some lipstick on. In all probability she would spend her pocket money on make-up. But John had okayed it so there was nothing to be gained by making a scene.

It was hot again and it wasn't eleven o'clock yet. Ben's hand was sticky in hers. He was gripping her, pinching her skin. Poor kid! She went cold just thinking about his nightmare. But it would not become reality, she would see to that. She would not allow him to play in the street, as a lot of the children did.

They needed to cross the road to the big supermarket on the opposite side. The traffic was continuous and delivery vans were parked on both sides. Leah spied a pelican crossing ahead. A queue of shoppers was waiting for the lights to turn red to halt the speeding vehicles. They went red, then almost immediately back to green. Some of the people retreated as the vehicles eased forward threateningly. But she was not in any hurry. She glanced round and called to Sam to catch up with her. Sarah was already at the crossing.

Some youths were fooling about, using obscene language; she tried to close her ears to it and hoped that if Ben heard he would not understand. Sam was immediately behind her now, thank goodness, among the women with shopping trolleys. An old man, obviously a vagrant, rummaged in a litter bin and found a half-smoked cigarette, muttering to himself all the while. He should have been put in a home and looked after, Leah thought. He was filthy and smelled.

A bleeping. The traffic had stopped. The youths were running across the road, probably on a shoplifting expedition, she guessed. An elderly woman was hindering everybody's progress. Leah held Ben's hand tightly and checked on Sam again. Damn these lights, you didn't stand an earthly of getting right across in time unless you ran.

Sarah was on the opposite pavement. Leah dragged

Ben to safety with her and would have grabbed Sam if he had lingered. Engines were revving; tyres screeched as a driver let his clutch out too quickly.

Then came a sickening thud and squealing tyres. All around, people were screaming.

Then there was silence as they realized and backed off, staring in disbelief at a huddled bundle of bloodied rags that lay beneath the twisted bumper of a blue transit van. The driver was gripping the steering wheel, deathly white, trying to tell himself that it hadn't happened. Or if it had, the vehicle in front was responsible.

Human ghouls clustered on the pavements on either side, huddling for safety, craning their necks in an attempt to obtain a better view. Dead; whoever it was could not possibly still be alive – a crushed skull, a mass of bone splinters and grey ooze streaked with crimson, flattened out of all recognition where the heavy wheel had gone over it.

The watchers glanced at one another, thinking, Somebody go and help him. Or her. But they shied away. An ambulance will come soon, they rationalized, it's bound to. But they stayed and watched. The crowd was swelling. The youths were back, pushing roughly for a better viewpoint.

Leah's vision blurred. Only the fact that she was hemmed in by others prevented her from falling. Her sticky hand slipped from Ben's. She felt faint and almost threw up. A split second of oblivion and then she was conscious again, her sagging knees straightening as a terrible thought gave her the strength to move. A voice, her own, echoed words she had spoken a few nights ago, regurgitating them with awful clarity. *He dreamed that you ran over him in the jeep.*

Oh, my God, my baby!

Pushing, shoving people out of her way, she screamed

as she ran forward into the road. All eyes were on her but she saw nothing except that mangled bloody heap and threw herself down beside it. Touching it, trying to piece the pulped human jigsaw together. Sobbing, oblivious of the unwashed odour that wafted up from the ribboned clothing, the strewn brains that adhered to her probing fingers like slimy frog-spawn. *My baby, give me back my baby!*

She heard Ben's screams ringing in her ears and thanked God that the child still lived. It was impossible but true. Then a harsh resonant sound obliterated all else. Even she recognized it as an ambulance, and shouted incoherently for it to hurry. *Save my baby whilst there's still time!*

Somebody had hold of her and was trying to pull her back. She kicked and fought, tore herself free. Seeing uniformed ambulancemen, she pointed, but could not get the words out.

'Madam . . . perhaps somebody could look after the lady?' *Restrain her, hold her down if you have to, but keep her out of our bloody way.*

'*My baby!*' Leah shrieked. She freed a hand and pointed at the crimson morass on the ground. '*Are you mad? My baby's dying. Save him!*'

The two men exchanged glances. One muttered, 'Maybe it's her father. Or grandfather.'

The spectators were closer, a ring of curious faces all round. A death was exciting but this one had an added flavour. One of the youths said something, the others roared with laughter.

'The police will be here in a second.' The ambulance driver doubted whether they could hold this berserk woman for much longer. In any case, they had a job to do; shovels and a black plastic bag. It was that tramp, the one who hung around the High Street most days and slept in the underground. It had to be, it couldn't be anybody else with garments as filthy as that. If only the crowd would fuck off, but they wouldn't; they flocked around any road accident. Vultures in human form.

A crimson-streaked fog closed in on Leah. She fought against it, sure that if she passed out then Ben would die. These people were blind to the fact that he was miraculously still alive. She could hear him screaming her name. Oh, my poor darling! She made one final effort to escape from the hands that held her, kicking out, twisting her head round in an attempt to bite her captors.

'*Mummy!*' The cry was coherent now, just behind her.

And then Ben was there, his tear-stained features deathly pale, standing in front of her with outstretched arms.

Again she nearly blacked out. Her vision was cut off for a moment, then came back distorted, as if she were in a house of funny mirrors at the fairground. Ben, his head elongated, was widening, his legs long, then short, one grubby sock around his ankle. Running to her, he clutched at her, gripping one of her arms until the skin pinched tight and she gasped with pain. Burying his face against her body, he rubbed his black curly locks on her bosom so that she *felt* him, knew that it was no mirage sent to taunt her in her moment of grief and madness. Not understanding, she was just relieved. She did not even feel foolish when those holding her released her and she heard those yobs guffawing their sick mirth in the background.

'There seems to have been some terrible mistake,' she heard herself say as she knelt to examine her son and left streaks of old man's brains on his clothing like snail tracks on a patio.

'Mum, are you all right?' It was Sam, confused and frightened. Sarah was holding his hand.

She nodded. 'I'm all right. I thought . . .' But she

dared not put her thoughts into words. It had been a trick of the mind, a macabre hallucination, all because of Ben's dream. But now she was back to reality, thankfully, and he was safe.

'I think you should come to the hospital for a check-up, Madam.' The taller of the two ambulancemen saw with relief that a police car had arrived. The traffic was building up. The jam of cars would stretch back to Streatham before this mess was finally shovelled into a sack.

'No, I'm fine, thank you.' She was not, but they made no attempt to bar her way back to the pavement, her three children holding on to her, fearful in case she might be taken from them.

And it had not even been *her* dream.

They were all back home, safe inside 13 Schooner Street. Leah could not recall the walk back, just that they were here in the kitchen and Sarah had made a pot of tea and given Ben a drink of orange juice. Sam was looking at the latest copy of *Match* but she could tell he wasn't taking in its contents.

She refrained from asking Ben yet again if he was all right. He wasn't, he was clearly shocked, but she had to stop reminding him of this morning's happenings. The accident itself was bad enough, but for her to react that way in front of him must have been frighteningly disturbing. She realized it could leave its mark on him for the rest of his life.

Sarah had changed him, and those blood- and brain-smeared clothes were in the washing machine. He was wearing the football kit that matched his pyjamas. She glanced at the clock on the electric cooker: three-thirty-five. They must have been home four hours at least. They couldn't just sit here for the rest of the day.

'I'll make something to eat.' She had to bring about an atmosphere of normality. 'Or do you – ' No, we're not going down to the chippie, she decided. We're not going outside again. Ever. *Now you are being bloody stupid.*

'Or do we what?' Sam looked up.

'Nothing. Who's for beans on toast?'

'I'm not hungry.' A chorus, a familiar one when children were busy. But today they were just sitting around, reliving that accident on the pelican crossing.

'All right,' she sighed, straightening up in her chair. 'You're not hungry. And neither am I. But look at it this way, that man was a tramp, old and sick, no home, no family, probably eighty. He might have died in his sleep tonight. It's not like . . . like somebody *young* getting killed, is it?' Her words brought a tightening of her stomach muscles. She reached out to clasp Ben, to hold him close. He was still all right. *Oh, please, God, don't let this be a dream and I'll wake up to find it really happened.*

'Why did you run to the old man, Mum?' It was Sam who asked the question which had doubtless been bothering them all.

'I just wanted to help.' She winced inwardly at the lie, knowing she would not have gone near under normal circumstances. 'Everybody else was standing back.'

'That was very brave of you, Mum.'

Oh, Christ, that made her feel worse. 'We have to try to forget it.' She stood up, swaying slightly. 'What we need is a good rest. Let's take the lounger out into the back garden. Sarah, go and get a big towel out of the airing cupboard for you lot to lie on. Let's do like we do at the seaside, sunbathe.'

'I want to dig sandcastles.' Ben spoke for the first time since they had arrived home.

'All right.' She smiled weakly. 'Go and get your seaside

spade. You can dig in that border that Daddy made at the weekend.'

And sod John if he didn't like it!

The children were quiet but that was only to be expected. She hoped that their rest in the sunshine had helped. Sarah was back up in her room, Sam was pasting football stickers into his Panini book and Ben was sitting on a chair watching her prepare the evening meal. She could not expect John to fast even if everybody else seemed intent upon doing just that.

The potatoes were peeled and boiling. The steaks which she had taken out of the freezer earlier were thawed. She regarded them with a feeling of nausea. Bloody meat, just like that on the crossing. *Shut up!* Too much fat. John loathed fat. She had better cut some of it off before she grilled them. She could understand why so many people were turning vegetarian.

The sight of blood was sickening, *any* blood. She had always been squeamish over blood and could not bear to watch any of those Jonathan Miller programmes a few years back. She knew that if it had not been for that awful fear that it was her son lying there in front of the van she would surely have fainted. Subconsciously she had called upon her reserves and they had seen her through. The human mind was too complex even to try to understand.

A wooden block stood on the working surface, a polished triangular holder for six knives of varying sizes. She selected the largest, tested the blade with her thumb and grunted her annoyance. It was blunt. She scrabbled in a drawer until she found the old-fashioned wheel sharpener that had been her mother's and began putting an edge on the blade. The grating sound made her grind her teeth; it was almost like running a thumbnail down the side of a bus. The blade was razor-sharp now.

She saw that mutilated corpse in her mind once more, and shuddered. Not Ben; that thought wasn't worrying her because it had not been him and could not possibly have been because she had been holding his hand the whole time. The body itself did not disturb her unduly any more – a dropout she had never seen in her life before, a dirty old man; it would lessen the taxpayers' burden, to be realistic.

The *blood*! She saw it as clearly now as she had then, thick and bright; a pool of it on the tarmac, splattered all over the front of the transit; oozing out of the crushed form, soaking through the filthy lice-ridden clothing. Leah smelled it, tasted it, like those sour iron tablets she'd had to take after Sarah was born. She tried to spit the taste out of her mouth.

'Mummy, stop spitting!'

Shut up, you little bastard. 'All right, Ben. I'm sorry.'

'You said *I'm* not to spit, Mummy.'

'That's right.' She took a deep breath and closed her eyes. But she could not get the sight of blood out of her closed eyes, the smell of it out of her nostrils, the taste of it out of her mouth.

'What's the matter, Mummy?' He was becoming alarmed again.

'Nothing, darling, I'm just tired.' Forcing herself to open her eyes, she picked up a steak. 'Now, you just watch how Mummy cuts the nasty greasy fat off.'

'That's *blood*!' He leaned forward and pointed. 'Just like – '

'Yes, we know all about that.' She wanted to slap him but that wouldn't solve anything. 'Now . . .'

'Mummy?'

'*What?*'

'Do cows bleed when they're killed?'

What stupid bloody questions children ask! 'I expect so.' *You know damned well they do.*

The knife was sharp, the blade passed effortlessly through the layer of fat. So easy. Her eyes flicked back to Ben. *And then she was screaming hysterically for the second time that day.*

Blood.

It jetted upwards, spraying a near-perfect figure-of-eight pattern on the ceiling. Horizontally across the wall, four separate rivulets travelled sluggishly downwards, tributaries which would merge on the formica surface. Turning one way, then the other, she tried to plug the gash in her wrist with her thumb but only served to spray the blood in three directions at the same time; a human lawn-sprinkler that left a fine crimson film on everything it touched.

To her horror, Ben's shocked face was suddenly mottled red as if with an instant outbreak of measles. The freckled blood gave him a vampirish expression as it dripped from his open mouth when he shrieked his shock aloud.

Leah was screaming. Ben was screaming. Panicking, standing there, they were screaming at each other.

Sarah ran downstairs and stood in the kitchen doorway. She dropped the paintbrush she was holding. It bounced, rolled, and left a bright red trail across the tiled floor. Her mouth opened to join in the screaming but somehow she controlled herself. She had already witnessed death today; an everyday household accident did not warrant panic.

Suddenly mature for her thirteen years, she crossed to the sink unit and grabbed two tea towels to make a bandage and a tourniquet. She worked fast with fingers that shook, then pushed her mother down into the chair.

'Here.' She beckoned Sam, who had stood in the doorway throughout. 'Come and help Mum to hold these in place. Tightly! That's it. Now, keep them there whilst I go and phone for help.'

Leah groaned as she heard her daughter talking to somebody on the phone. *Which service, please? Police, ambulance or fire?*

Fire! Leah found herself sniffing the air but all she could smell was blood. Or she thought she could. But suddenly it did not matter; it was as if her blood phobia had been building up in a crescendo and now that she was bleeding it was out of her system. She almost laughed at her own unfunny joke. But right now it was the thought of fire that was bothering her most. Sarah was still talking but Leah was not listening.

She must insist that John fitted a smoke alarm, she decided. There had been one at the head of the stairs in their Chiswick house. She had taken it for granted, and had not even started when it was accidentally set off. A slice of toast burning in the toaster was enough to trigger off the sensitive mechanism.

She remembered that chimney fire they had had at home when she was small. She was about eight at the time, and had almost forgotten it until now. The fire had suddenly started to roar in the open range, and the chimney had sounded like an angry dragon. Her mother had pushed her out into the garden and phoned for the fire brigade. The ladders and hoses had been intriguing to a child. The men had climbed up on the roof, squirted foaming water down the chimney and filled the kitchen with hissing steam and sooty water. It had taken Mother the rest of the day to clean it up. An adventure at the time, she had written an essay about firemen in English at school the next week. *But the episode had taken twenty-seven years to make its full impact upon her!*

Smoke can kill! But smoke meant *fire*. Almost every day you heard of a fatal fire somewhere – children burned to death, trapped in an upstairs bedroom; a spark from a cigarette smouldering on a foam-filled sofa, then suddenly *whoosh!*

She would check that settee in the front room, just to be sure. Instinctively she made an effort to rise but Sam pushed her back, still clasping the tea-towel bandage.

'Are you all right, Mum?'

'I'm fine.' The cut wasn't hurting, she just felt slightly faint. 'Sam, I want you to do something for me.'

'What, Mum?'

'Just check upstairs to . . . to see that everything's all right.'

A moment of puzzled silence, then, 'Like what, Mum?'

'I . . . I'm not sure. But just go and check, there's a good boy.'

'I can't, I have to hold this.'

'Then Ben can go.'

'I don't want to, Mummy.' His small hand found hers and squeezed it tightly, pleading, I don't want to leave you, Mummy.

Just then Sarah came back into the room. 'They're sending an ambulance, Mum. As soon as possible.'

'But I can't leave you three.'

'We'll be all right.'

Leah sensed her panic returning. There was a definite stench – not of blood now, that was gone – of scorching, like a garment that had been hung to dry in front of an electric fire. 'Sarah, is something burning?'

'I can't smell anything.'

'Go and look. *Please!*'

Leah listened to her daughter's footsteps, through into the front room, back down the hall, clattering upstairs.

Doors were opened and closed. Across the landing, down the stairs.

'No, Mum, there's nothing burning.'

'Good.' Leah failed to hide her relief, aware that she was damp with sweat.

And then she heard the ambulance drawing up outside.

6

Ruth Ford was fast losing her inhibitions. And, John told himself with no small amount of smugness, it was due entirely to him.

She was eager for sex now, even though it was only their third date. Tonight they had gone to another wine bar – there was always the risk of bank staff turning up in the Cellar – three tube stops and a five-minute walk away. She pulled him to a stop within fifty metres of their destination and her lips were already moving in on his in a passionate kiss that had heads turning. He tried to disengage tactfully.

'I needed that,' she whispered. 'I couldn't wait till later.'

Later was back at her flat. As he undressed, John wondered what was going to happen when Keith returned to the roost. He decided to meet that problem when it arose. He also told himself that he ought not to be too late home tonight. Because of what had happened to the family yesterday, they were still pretty shaken. Leah had had four stitches in her wrist, he had spent the evening cleaning up the kitchen, and Ben had slept in their bed again. He had bought Sarah a small battery-powered night-light, a step towards encouraging her to go back to sleeping in the dark. At least Sam wasn't bothered by all these phobias that they were developing. And he himself had not thought about road accidents for the last couple of days.

He lay on the bed, naked and aroused, waiting for Ruth to return from the bathroom. In spite of her eagerness she would be wearing her nightdress and she would not remove it until they were in bed. He heard her footsteps hurrying across the landing.

'Sorry to have kept you.' She made sure that the curtains were closed and made for the bed.

'Hey,' he laughed. 'I want to see you naked.'

'You already have.' She blushed as his outstretched arm prevented her from throwing back the duvet and sliding beneath it.

'Yes, in the glow of the streetlamps,' he answered. 'I want to see you *properly*!'

She pursed her lips. 'Next time.'

'No, now!'

'You won't like my body.'

'I think it's gorgeous.'

'Oh, all right, then.' With some reluctance she peeled off her nightdress, dropped it on to the floor and stood there coyly, embarrassed. 'I feel like a stripper,' she giggled.

'You are.' He noted how her hands were crossed over her pubes in a kind of human fig leaf, the way she tried to hide her bottom from him. Then he let her slide into bed.

Her lips were warm. Their tongues touched, then she was more than willing for him to kiss his way down her slender figure.

'I want you to kiss me now.' He knelt up, half expecting a promise of 'next time', but instead she pulled him towards her and now it was his turn to moan his delight aloud. If she had never done it before then she was making a damned good job of her first attempt!

It was just nine-thirty by the radio alarm clock on the bedside table when they uncoupled. She held him tightly, not wanting him to go even though they were both spent.

'I told you I wanted to be home early tonight.' He tried

to keep the irritation out of his voice. 'As I said, we've had problems at home.'

'I know.' She sounded genuinely sympathetic. 'But there's something I have to tell you, John.'

He was relieved that the semi-darkness of the bedroom hid his surprised expression. She couldn't be pregnant because he had had a vasectomy. What then?

'I love you, John.'

Strangely, he wasn't shocked. He nearly replied, 'And I love you, too, Ruth', but that would keep. They had moved fast in three dates. All the same, it was disconcerting. He had not yet thought seriously in terms of a steady relationship.

'I'm going to have to tell Keith when he comes home,' she whispered, and his heart missed a beat.

'We'd better do some talking.' He dressed more hurriedly than usual. 'Wednesday night, we'll go for a meal at Joe Allen's.'

'All right.' She slid off the bed, stood up and embraced him. As their lips crushed together her fingers explored him, found him. Clearly, she could have made it again even if he couldn't, and suddenly an office affair had taken on a different complexion. Complications were looming on the horizon.

It was as he emerged from Balham underground station that he felt a sharp twinge in his chest. Not painful but uncomfortable. It lasted for maybe three seconds and then it was gone. He slowed his pace, experiencing a sense of unease. He'd read about chest pains and thought they would never happen to him. Of course, it could be a strain, muscular. He had done a fair amount of physical work tidying up the garden. It must be that, he had convinced himself before he turned into Schooner Street and dismissed the matter from his mind.

Again he was apprehensive as he let himself into the

house. He half expected Ben to come rushing across the landing, screaming. But the boy was safe in the marital bed, nestled up to his mother. Sam's room was in darkness but a light shone from beneath Sarah's door. John thought it seemed too bright for that glowing night-light but he wasn't going to check now.

Leah was asleep, or else she was feigning slumber. He did not mind which. It excused him from having to account for his movements tonight. Lying wasn't easy when you were tired, you risked a slip-up. He was grateful that his wife had turned in early.

He undressed as quietly as possible and left his clothes on a chair. He felt guilt at his nakedness because he had been unfaithful to his wife; she would lie against his tainted body. But Ben was a barrier in between them, and John was grateful to the child for that much.

He still was not sure whether Leah was asleep. It didn't really matter. He stretched out, feeling mentally and physically tired, but suddenly it was impossible to relax. His thoughts hopped from Ruth to Leah, back to Ruth. He thought he might get an erection and then his chest twinged again.

The feeling was sharper this time, a pain, vicious. It lasted for maybe three or four seconds. It was frightening in the darkness of night when he was struggling with his conscience.

A warning, the forerunner of a heart attack? Sweat beaded on his body and he thought about going downstairs and making a drink of tea – or even something stronger. But that was not the solution.

He had read an article on heart problems fairly recently. The author claimed that they were hereditary. John's sweat chilled. His own father had died of one, collapsed in the street. But he had been seventy-two. Age was not a determining factor, though – what about that fellow at training college? John could not recall his name but the young man, no more than twenty-three, had gone home seemingly fit on the Friday afternoon and was dead by Saturday morning, cremated on the Thursday. John's sweat was icy now and he shivered.

But his pain was, in all probability, muscular. The pectoral muscle could be pulled without him knowing it, lifting a heavy file at the office, as he was doing daily. Just a slightly different stance, maybe a sudden jerk, when he was concentrating too hard to feel it go. Yes, chest pains could be caused by any one of fifty or so reasons. Like . . .

Lung cancer!

His mouth was dry and there was a sour taste on his palate, as there used to be in the days when he smoked – heavily, fifty a day. He had cut it down to twenty after that first bout of bronchitis, then ten after the second, and given up altogether last Easter. He'd sweated it out through Lent and never touched a cigarette again. It was supposed to take three years to get nicotine out of your system, he remembered. How long did it take cancer to develop? *Oh, Jesus Christ!*

Henley, the chief cashier at John's first branch, had died of lung cancer less than a year after he retired. John could see him now, stocky, bald, chain-smoking on the counter against all regulations, but Henley had been an institution, a law unto himself, and even the manager had dodged the issue. The old feller had stopped at the newsagent's every morning on his way to the office; a standing order – the *Guardian*, twenty cigarettes and an ounce of strong pipe tobacco. He had smoked all day long, alternating between pipe and cigarette, creating a fug of thick smoke in the bank. Passive smoking they called it today. That *could* have sown the seeds of John's own cancer.

He remembered going to visit Henley in a hospice three days before he passed away; wasted to a skeleton, a ghastly parchment colour, coughing continually, spitting pink-streaked phlegm into a bowl which he scarcely had the strength to hold. Please, God, I don't want to linger like that, he thought. Rather a thrombosis, here one minute, gone the next.

Or a head-on car crash.

He writhed inwardly. It wasn't just dying that scared him, it was the manner in which he died. He imagined himself behind the wheel of the Suzuki, travelling a road of tortuous bends, double white lines all the way. He kept well over to the left. There was traffic behind him, nothing in front. Until that oncoming car overtook a van which had been holding it up for the last half-mile.

Wrenching the steering wheel hard over to the left, he attempted to get out of the way, but there was nowhere to go. Only a high bank like that one in . . . Christ, this wasn't even a bloody nightmare! Bracing himself for the impact, he sat up, mouthing curses, half anticipating another stabbing pain in his chest.

Then it was all over, leaving him shaking and frightened. He had to go downstairs, not for tea or Scotch, simply because if he stayed here it would happen again. And again.

Sarah definitely had her light on. It was far too bright for the night-light, but who could blame the poor kid? The kitchen fluorescent flickered and took its time coming on. He must remember to pick up a new starter switch tomorrow. Mundane things like that helped to make life bearable.

He sat in a chair at the table, still naked, staring at the wall and seeing a spot of Leah's dried blood which he had missed. That had not been a dream but stark, awful reality.

Tensing and wondering if his chest might explode with the next spasm of pain, he waited for it to happen. Like Chinese water torture.

Leah had not been asleep when she heard her husband arrive home. He was earlier than the last time; perhaps he had had a row with his new girlfriend, whoever she was. Wishful thinking, she told herself. There would always be another woman. She pretended to be asleep, partly for Ben's sake. She did not want to wake the child, fearing what it might trigger off. Neither did she want to go through a rigmarole of lies, asking John where he had been and who with, pretending to believe his contrived answers. Because it was all totally pointless.

John was restless, threshing about. Serve him bloody well right! She did not move even when he sat bolt upright. Her only worry was that Ben might wake up. The boy stirred, moaned in his sleep, and slept on. Now John was out of bed. She followed his footsteps with her ears, thinking that he might be going to the bathroom, but was surprised when he went downstairs. She sighed her relief when he did not return immediately. Their marriage had nose-dived and she almost wished they could end it here and now. Not just because of his infidelity, though that was bad enough. It was the little things that got on her nerves, like those dried herbs hanging up in the kitchen, the way he tried to create an image to keep up with neighbours he didn't even know.

She was listening to Ben's rhythmic breathing when she first heard a scuffling noise directly above her. It sounded like something running over the ceiling, a huge spider with a bloated body and repulsive legs. Ugh! If it had not been for Ben she would have put the light on. Listening, she heard her own heartbeat becoming faster and faster. Then the noise came again, and she knew instantly what it was. Mice in the attic!

Of course, there would be mice up there; there might even be *rats*! On the day after they moved in she had fetched the stepladder and peeped through the trapdoor out of curiosity, wondering if there might be a useful storage space up there. She had dropped the hatch cover back into place almost immediately. Her torchbeam had revealed an area of sheer filth, dust and cobwebs, and there were wires running all over the place. Cowboy wiring, a cheap job carried out by the Graftons or maybe even the owners before them. Dangerous. And small rodents had a fixation with electric wires, chewing through the casing . . . She began sniffing to see if she could smell smoke. Not yet.

Don't worry, she told herself, it has probably been like that for a decade or more. Like the slagheap at Aberfan, threatening to avalanche for years; but one day it did. Living with danger, you hoped it wouldn't happen. But one day, or night, it might.

The scurrying had stopped, to be replaced by another sound which she could not work out at first, a kind of rustling and crunching like cornflakes being crushed. *Gnawing!*

Leah felt her stomach contracting into a ball and experienced an acute desire to urinate. Nature's way of lightening the body in preparation for flight, she thought. Her arm encircled Ben, ready to sweep him up and run with him. She'd tell the other two to follow, hammer on their bedroom doors on her way and check to make sure that they followed downstairs, fleeing before a serpent of thick black pungent smoke that squirmed after them. Then through the hall, out into the street and across to the opposite pavement, to stand there, sweating and trembling, watching the flames licking at the windows, the glass cracking in the heat.

She realized that she had not given a thought to John.

The rodent gnawing continued. They must be pretty well through the covering on the wires by now, and she wondered if there was any way to stop them, such as standing up on the bed and banging on the ceiling. It was too high to reach. Use something, a coat-hanger, she told herself. No, it wouldn't do any good. The mice would only stop temporarily, then continue their ravenous feast after the human occupants were asleep. The only way was to kill the verminous creatures, put some poison or traps up through the square hole over the landing. But it might already be too late; exposed wires could start a blaze any time.

She knew she was not going to be able to sleep. She dared not. She would lie awake trying to scent the first wisp of smoke that infiltrated the bedroom. She had forgotten to speak to John about fitting a smoke alarm; that accident, spurting her own blood all over the kitchen, had taken it right out of her mind. She thought about going downstairs and telling him right now. Except that she had no wish to converse with him. What the devil had he gone down for? Was something wrong?

She had to go to the loo, the pain in her bladder was excruciating.

Carefully she extricated her arm from beneath Ben and slid across to the other side of the bed. Was it safe to leave him? She still could not smell anything burning, and she would only be a minute.

On her way back to the bedroom she decided to check on the other two. She could hear Sam snoring; he was all right. She eased Sarah's door open, blinking at the unexpected brightness of the electric light. The girl was awake, sitting up in bed; not reading, just staring straight ahead of her.

'Sarah, what's the matter?'

'Nothing, Mother.'

'Why aren't you using your night-light?'

'I don't like it. It isn't bright enough.'

'You'll never get to sleep in this bright light!'

'*Don't!*' Sarah's shriek halted Leah's hand within an inch of the light switch. '*Please!*'

'You're frightened, aren't you, darling?' Leah moved into the room and seated herself on the edge of the bed.

Sarah nodded, close to tears. Gone was the rebelliousness, the stubbornness, leaving just a very frightened little girl. 'I can't bear being in the dark, Mother.'

'You've slept in the dark all your life.'

'Yes, but not *here*!'

'I know how you feel.' Leah's hand found her daughter's and squeezed it with a reassurance which she did not feel; body language, a lie. 'It's a cold, unfriendly house, but perhaps we can alter that once we've redecorated and – '

'Nothing will change this place!' Sarah's words came in a frightened rush. 'It's as if . . . *as if there's somebody watching you all the time!*'

Leah's spine started to tingle. She felt eyes on her at this very moment, hostile invisible orbs that watched her every movement.

'Can't we leave, Mother?' The plea incorporated the desperation of a child on the brink of sheer terror. 'I'll never be able to sleep in this house, I know.'

'I'll speak to Daddy about it.'

'When?'

'Tomorrow. I promise.'

'You won't be able to because he's gone to work before we're up and he doesn't come home until we're in bed.'

Children were perceptive, Leah reflected, hoping that Sarah would not pursue John's absences from home any further. She would lie through her teeth to protect the children from that.

'Daddy went downstairs,' Sarah went on after a pause. 'Almost an hour ago, and he hasn't come back up. Can't you go and speak to him now about moving. Please.'

'All right.' Leah stood up. 'In the meantime, do me a favour . . .'

'What, Mother?'

'Oh, it doesn't matter. Forget it.' Keep sniffing the air in case you smell smoke, she wanted to say. They had thought she was mad when she had sent her upstairs for that very reason that afternoon. The children were scared enough as it was without alarming them further. 'I'll go and talk to Daddy now.'

John was sitting at the kitchen table just staring in front of him, naked. It would have seemed hilarious at any other time, in any *other* kitchen. But here, in Number Thirteen, Schooner Street, it was starkly terrifying.

'John?'

He looked round but did not even register surprise at seeing her. He did not speak.

'John, what the hell's going on?'

She read guilt in his eyes but she had not come down here to discuss his infidelities.

'I couldn't sleep,' he replied weakly and dropped his gaze.

'Like the rest of us in this household.' Her tone was sharp, accusing. After all, he had insisted on buying this property. But, to be fair, there had not seemed to be anything wrong with it then. Not until they moved in. 'John, I think there's something wrong with this house.'

'Like what?' He sounded tired, uninterested.

'As if it's . . . *haunted!*'

‘You’re crazy.’ His attempt to sound incredulous failed. His eyes flicked round the kitchen as if he expected to see something lurking in a corner. But fluorescent lighting threw no shadows to hide anything.

‘No, and I think you’re as scared as we all are.’ She sat down opposite him at the table. ‘Crazy, awful nightmares – I’ve had ’em, Ben’s had ’em, Sarah has, too, but she’s trying to hide them. And I know damned well *you* have, and don’t try to deny it. You’re as white as a sheet and scared to hell. Want to tell me about it?’

‘I’ve had pains in my chest.’

He might be seeking sympathy now that the chips are down, she thought.

‘Then go and see the doctor.’ She wasn’t going to pander to him or let him off lightly. ‘I’ve just come down to say that we’ve all had enough, we can’t take any more.’

‘So?’

‘We want to leave. Sell up. Find another house. Is that an unreasonable request in view of all that’s happened?’

‘It’s impossible!’

‘Why?’

‘Because we’re mortgaged up to the hilt with the bank and we’d never get our price.’ Despair was evident in his expression. She knew that he was telling the truth and her hopes plummeted.

‘The bank wouldn’t have granted a rip-off mortgage. They check everything out.’

‘I know, but we’d never get a buyer. We’re stuck with this place.’

‘Not in London.’

‘Anywhere. We got it because . . . *nobody else would buy it!*’

‘Oh, God!’ She buried her face in her hands. ‘But at least we could *try*!’

‘Kenton will have a fit.’

'Sod Kenton, he doesn't have to live here. At least put it on the market, John, and see what happens.'

'All right.' He nodded. 'If you insist. But I didn't realize, not until it was too late . . . no estate agent in London drops the asking price because you crib about a bit of shabbiness. He couldn't believe his luck when I said we'd buy if he dropped a grand. I ought to have twigged. But what *is* wrong except a feeling that we didn't get until it was too late? It seems that others sensed it right away, or it wouldn't have stayed unsold. On the face of it we got a bargain, an investment. But it's a bloody liability if we can't get rid of it.'

'But you promise you'll try?'

'Yes.' He scraped his chair back and stood up. 'I'll give it a go.'

'Because we've all suffered,' she reminded him.

A sudden disturbing thought crossed her mind. They had all had some kind of terrifying experience, except Sam. So far.

And that was very worrying.

7

'I think you should see the doctor.' Leah had risen before her husband, been downstairs and made some tea. She set a steaming mug down on the bedside table alongside a beaker of fresh orange juice for Ben when he awoke.

'I'll be all right,' John groaned, closing his eyes. Jesus, his head was going to burst open at any second. He wished Leah would close the curtains and shut out that shaft of early morning sunlight. The events of last night came back to him, making him clutch at his chest in an attempt to locate the source of that pain which had frightened him. Pressing down on the pectoral muscle, he was trying to make it hurt. He took a deep breath, then let it out slowly; testing his lungs, and trying not to think of oncoming vehicles on narrow roads. His forehead was damp with sweat; he had a migraine, and no wonder.

'You won't be all right.' She sensed an advantage over him, a rare occurrence. 'You look like death!'

Death.

'I have to go into the office.' Because of Ruth. 'Damn it, I've only just started there, I can't earn myself a reputation for going sick every five minutes.' He recalled his early days when he had been junior clerk under another tyrannical manager. During his second week he had gone down with an attack of flu, the kind that put you to bed for a week. That bastard Dillon kept ringing, not to enquire after his health but to urge him to get back to his desk. As a result, he had gone back too soon and had a relapse on the third day. No sympathy; instead, a warning that if he persistently took time off it would jeopardize his future. And Kenton was the same breed. John groaned aloud. Give me ten minutes and I'll be okay, he thought.

'You are not going to the bank today!' Leah was aware of a kind of sadistic satisfaction that he was too ill to argue; a sense of dismay, too, because the house was mortgaged to the bank and John would not be able to tell them today that he was putting it up for sale. 'I shall ring the office at nine and tell them you're ill. And that's final.'

He did not reply because he knew that his resistance would be feeble. All he wanted to do was to sleep. *And pray God I don't get any more bad dreams.*

He had no idea how long he had slept. The curtains were drawn and the sunlight did not hurt him quite so badly when he squinted through slitted eyelids. The sheet beneath him was damp where he had sweated, so he edged on to a dry patch. Ben had gone and there was no sign of Leah. She had probably taken the children out somewhere in case their shouting and squabbling disturbed him, he decided. Like the driver in a car crash getting back behind the wheel the next day; *no, don't think of road accidents!* But they all had to go out again some time. In fact, they had recovered remarkably well from their trauma.

John found himself thinking of Ruth but not in a physical way; he wasn't in the mood to become aroused. Hell, he had let their affair get out of control. When a bit on the side fell in love with you, you were in big trouble! Ending their relationship too abruptly might blow it all up in his face. She might phone Leah, or come round to the house. And if she told her husband, Keith, he might do just that. Christ, it was difficult. There were other ways – a gentle cooling-off process, making her get tired of *him*. But there wasn't time; she might already have phoned her Keith to confess all. It was easy for her. She didn't have much to lose.

The bank would take a dim view of an affair between an accountant and a cashier, and transfer both parties to separate branches. That certainly would damage John's career; they would probably demote him, post him to the relief staff. And the jungle telegraph would tap out its warning – watch this fellow, he's likely to screw your female staff! It didn't really matter about girl cashiers. Turnover was rapid, and they were expendable, anyway.

His head still ached but not the way it had, more of a dull throbbing behind the eyes than the expanding and contracting of cranium bone that threatened to crack open.

He had a lot of thinking to do. He would have to put the house on the market, as Leah insisted, but he had the gut feeling nobody would buy it. All right, it *was* spooky, but only if you let it get to you, as they had. There had been a string of unfortunate coincidences, that was all. And his chest wasn't hurting any more. Take a middle course, he told himself, put Number Thirteen up for sale, and when there were no takers the Strikes would carry on living here.

Downstairs, somebody was starting to scream.

Leah breathed a sigh of relief, if only a temporary one. John wasn't going anywhere, neither to the bank nor to his mistress. *If* he had a woman on the side. He was overworking, that was his trouble. The A-type personality, as the media termed it; an ageing whizz kid trying to burn the candle at both ends – what they called a yuppie.

The children were eating their breakfast in the kitchen. So far everything seemed more normal than it had since they moved in here. Ben was spooning his wheatflakes into his mouth with rare relish, probably because he had not eaten yesterday. Sarah was munching muesli, trying to convince Sam that he should eat more healthily. That was the current trend, wholefood purveyors concentrating on the kids to sell their products, TV ads designed to convert the gullible. Sam wasn't impressed. But for God's sake, Leah thought, don't start an argument over it!

'Children.' Leah exaggerated her whisper. 'I want you to play quietly today because Daddy's poorly and he needs his sleep.'

'What's the matter with him?' The inevitable question from Sam.

'He's . . . been working too hard, been at the office very late recently.'

'Oh!' At least the boys believed her; she wasn't sure about Sarah.

'Would you like to go out somewhere?' Leah asked half-heartedly. *I hope not because I wouldn't. Not after yesterday*.

'No, thanks.' Sarah's reply was positive, curt. 'I've got things to do.'

'No.' Ben sprayed half-chewed flakes across the table. He might have been emulating his sister's reply. Or else remembering yesterday.

'Nor me,' Sam added, and did not give a reason.

'Very well, but you mustn't make a noise. Sam, you can go and play with Jeremy and take Ben with you.'

'You said I was spending too much time there, Mum. And, anyway, Jeremy doesn't like Ben – says he's too babyish.'

You can't bloody win! 'If you two get quarrelling and fighting I'll wring your . . . I'll give you a good hiding.' It sounded trite, a feeble threat. 'Sarah, I shall have to pop down to the shops later. I'm leaving you in charge, and you're to see that these two don't play up and wake your father.'

'All right.' Sarah nodded without looking up. She would go up to her room, draw and paint, turn a deaf ear to her brothers' behaviour. She always did.

Leah began collecting up the empty cereal bowls, put them in the sink and ran the tap. Sarah made for the stairs. Sam went out through the open patio doors. He would doubtless kick that semi-inflated football around the untidy garden for hours. She watched Ben out of the corner of her eye but he made no move to go outside. He was clearly in one of his clinging moods and would stick with her all morning. Maybe she could persuade him to come down to the corner shop with her. She had to buy a few things, enough to tide them over until they could face going down to the supermarket again.

Shortly after nine o'clock Leah telephoned the bank. A female voice answered; Leah left a message to the effect that John Strike was ill and would not be into work today. That would suffice; she had no wish to go into details.

She busied herself consciously, killing time. The soft ball thudded against the fence with annoying regularity but she could think of worse irritations. She gave Ben a colouring book and some soft crayons; he seemed to have an obsession with red. He did not talk and was subdued. Poor kid, today was going to be difficult for all of them.

She wondered about phoning the estate agents and decided against it. They would probably come up straightaway and insist on measuring up every room. It wasn't fair on John. Was he ever fair to her? All the same, one more day wouldn't make any difference. Would it?

Sam's goal was a fence panel with cracked boards, the one leaning towards him a crouching goalkeeper. He had to put the ball wide of the keeper but in between the stanchions on either side. The football wasn't bouncing back properly today. It needed blowing up. The foot-pump was in the jeep outside, locked up, and Dad had the keys in his pocket. But he could not ask him for them just yet. Finally the ball was too soft to play with and Sam kicked it away in disgust, then wandered idly across to the far side of the small garden, the area that was still high with straggling, sun-browned weeds, like a miniature jungle.

And it was there that he saw the reptile.

Everything inside him froze instantly; a sudden constriction of his stomach threatened to throw up his wheatflakes. A swallow stuck, creating a blockage in his windpipe. Sweat was oozing out of his pores. Immobile, his eyes protruding in terror. He remembered in his fear a terrible, dimly lit place that glowed green with subtle luminosity where slimy, malevolent creatures stared through the plate-glass walls of their prison cells and hated the human audience that goaded them in safety. A small boy tapped on the thick pane with his forefinger so that an evil snake spat at him, its venomous tongue flicking in and out. Others might have been specimens provided by a taxidermist, except that their eyes moved balefully. Repulsive toad-like things dragged their bellies across the floor of the artificial tropical setting. But worst of all were the alligators, especially the hatchlings, only twenty centimetres in length, that screeched and flung themselves at the steep concrete bank in an attempt to sink their sharp teeth into human flesh. But always they slipped back into the water, threshed their tails and tried again. And again.

Maddened, an obsession for revenge and a hunger for human meat fuelled their frenzy. Their mother, lying half-submerged in the far corner of the pool, seemed oblivious to it all, almost as though she had abandoned her hatch. People were laughing, leaning over the safety rail, teasing, taunting the reptiles. A dirt-smeared slice of limp bread was thrown. The occupants of the alligator house ignored it as it tossed in their waves and began to break up. Whistling, somebody reached across and tapped the concrete with a stick. And then one of the baby alligators, against all odds, made it to the top and clung precariously to the edge, its jaws gaping as it shrieked its anger at the watchers.

Sam Strike had been in the crowd that day, hanging back, tugging at Leah's dress. 'No, Mummy, I want to *go*!'

His terror and loathing were reaching a peak, his cries were hysterical. His fear was not just of the reptilian inhabitants of that stagnant water, but of all cold-blooded creatures. His phobia had begun when he entered the reptile house, eyes tightly shut so that he would not see, clutching Leah's hand. Ben was asleep in a sling around her shoulders, Sarah was unmoved, even bored, yawning in the stifling atmosphere of a pseudo-Amazon. Frantic now, Sam was trying to free himself from maternal protection and run for the doorway behind with its neon exit sign.

'Don't be silly, Sam.' Leah was tired but determined that the children should have their money's worth; it had cost an extra two pounds to come in here. 'They can't hurt you, they can't get at you.'

That one can!

Sam watched almost hypnotized as the tiny alligator maintained its hold on the concrete lip surrounding the pool, a toy monkey swinging on a stick. Except that it wasn't a monkey, neither was it a toy. It was a fierce man-eater.

And then its tiny eyes met his own, as if it had singled him out, in a malevolent glare. The mouth opened, slavering slimy water as it squeaked, *I'm coming to get you, boy!*

Sam was screaming but his cries went unheard amidst the noise from the spectators. If that wriggling fiend managed to clamber up on to the ledge, then it would come for him. The mesh surround would not stop it, it would wriggle beneath. Lusting for Sam, blaming him for the baiting.

It almost made it, and had its belly half over the top when the youth with the stick stretched over and poked at it, pushing it back. Sam gave one last look into those tiny eyes. It had not removed its gaze from him. *I'll get you one day, boy!*

Then it was gone, dropping back into the maelstrom created by its threshing brothers and sisters. Sam did not forget it and was terrified to sit on the toilet for weeks in case it came up the waste pipe and dug its sharp teeth into his buttocks. He was scared of the bath, of puddles in the street and drain grids where he could hear the rushing water below. Two years later, he still shied away from ponds and streams, just in case. *I'll get you one day, boy!*

And now that same baby alligator had finally tracked him down and was here in their own garden!

It had not grown in size. If anything, it was smaller. A freak, perhaps, its growth stunted by the confines of a zoo pool, but none the less deadly, crazed by two years of burning hatred, surviving in the concrete jungle into which it had escaped. Living in drains and sewers, eating garbage, hunting, scenting; and now its unerring powers had brought it to the home of the boy it sought.

It moved forward a couple of centimetres, perched on a tussock of browned grass and lay watching him with eyes that scintillated in the bright sunlight, flashing red and green alternately. Stop. Go. Stop again. Despite its jerky progress there was no mistaking its intention to close in on him.

Sam glanced behind him. The fence was rickety but unscalable, in the far corner of the garden, and there was nowhere to run. He managed to swallow. The garden narrowed here. The reptile was in front of him and had placed itself in a strategic position, with a gap of barely a metre on either side. He might make it with a dash, Sam thought, but he dared not. His legs were weak and shaking and he might slip. He remembered how swiftly it could move, darting like a rat. No, he would not make it.

The creature moved forward another few centimetres and flopped down again. Its eyes never left his own and its mouth was open in an awesome grin. *I told you I'd come for you, boy!*

Sam looked around for a weapon of some kind. There was none, just that burst football, and in the awful stillness he could hear the air hissing out of it. His lips moved but no sound came from them. You've got it all wrong, he tried to say. It's not me you want. I didn't intend to hurt you in the zoo, I wasn't the one poking at you, throwing at you. Please believe me.

Liar!

He saw it start to move again, more purposefully now, a cat that had tired of playing with its prey and was closing in for the kill. Sam forced the scream out of his constricted throat. It was a croak to begin with, then sheer desperation gave it volume, and the yell of terror shattered the suburban silence and hung in the air.

The reptile paused less than forty centimetres from him. It was in no hurry now; the boy wasn't going anywhere. Sizing him up, selecting an area of exposed flesh in which to sink its vicious teeth, it was savouring the kill, bracing itself for the attack.

'*Sam!*'

Sam saw his father through a haze. John Strike, dressed in only yellow pyjama trousers and bare-footed, was threading his way through the scattered rubble. Panic was stamped on the pallid features, then relief to find his son still alive and unharmed.

Sam was trying to warn him, his words incoherent whispers, a shaking finger pointing at the reptile. Leah was now behind her husband, and Sarah was on the patio restraining Ben. Spittle dripped from Sam's mouth, and he was wide-eyed with fear as he saw his father approaching, now only a metre from the vicious baby alligator.

'*Alligator!*' Sam got the word out, a half-scream as he pushed himself back against the fence. He felt it wobbling and threatening to collapse.

He saw his father stoop, then straighten up with the reptile struggling between forefinger and thumb. Holding it aloft, he was laughing, almost hysterical. Sam thought he was going to faint. That mist was back, streaked with crimson. Any second, the creature would squirm in his father's grasp, sink its teeth into his flesh and spring for his throat.

'It's only a bloody *newt*!'

Sam was already starting to faint as the words penetrated his spinning brain. With one final glimpse before he blacked out, he saw his father's arm go back, the fingers unclench and hurtle a wriggling long-tailed creature high into the air. Spinning, it reached its apex, then it was falling. Sam followed it with his darkening gaze until it was lost from his view on the other side of the boundary fence. He thought he heard it thud on to the neatly mown turf next door and then he fell forward, slumping into his father's outstretched arms.

8

Amazingly, Sam had recovered from his ordeal within the hour. It was barely midday and the whole family was sitting in the kitchen sipping soft drinks. The patio door was open; it would have been foolish to pander to the boy's fear and even suggest that there was something menacing out in the garden.

'A newt!' John forced a laugh. 'I think it was a crested one, but I'm not sure. They're quite rare, especially in London. I expect someone close by has a pond and they've caught it on a trip to the countryside. Anyway, it's all over and done with now.'

Sam nodded. He was old enough to feel slightly foolish. But he wasn't going to play in the garden again, not until Dad had tidied it up so that there weren't any patches of tall weeds where . . . *things* could hide.

John realized that his headache was gone. Perhaps it was the shock of this morning's events. Whatever, he was just left feeling slightly lethargic, and guilty at having taken a day's sick leave.

'I think we all ought to go out.' Leah was wondering whether to suggest that they ate, but if her own appetite was anything to go by, nobody would fancy food. She was still trembling slightly. Sarah had gone back upstairs to her painting, and Ben had tipped his Lego out on the floor. But she still needed to go to the shops.

'I reckon I ought to go into the office,' John said.

'No way,' she snapped. 'You're not well enough. You're better, though, thank goodness.' But this is one night when your fancy woman will have to miss out, she decided. 'Maybe we could go into town. Or to the Tower. Or somewhere.' *But not the zoo.*

'Would anybody like to go to the swimming baths?' John spoke loudly so that maybe even Sarah might hear him upstairs. The baths, nice and easy, close by; he wouldn't even have to use the Suzuki.

'Yes!' Sudden enthusiasm from Ben.

'Suits me.' Sam looked up. 'We haven't been to the baths for weeks. What sort of baths have they got here?'

'We'll have to find out.' Leah smiled as she heard Sarah's footsteps coming down the stairs. Obviously going swimming was a popular idea. Not for herself, but she could leave them all in the baths and go to the shops. 'All right, swimming it is.'

John was glad that Leah was not coming to the baths with them. He had not expected her to; she could swim a few strokes but she did not care for the water. She would only have sat on one of the benches lining the pool and reminded him at intervals that they ought to be 'making a move soon'.

Shopping would take her a good hour, and they did not have to be ready when she called for them. Of course, his own activities in the water would be limited. Most of the time would be spent in the shallow end with Ben, but he could trust Sam to look after his younger brother for a few minutes and enjoy a decent swim. In any case, it was a break from routine, from the office. And I hope to Christ word doesn't filter back to the bank, he thought.

John was surprised how crowded the baths were; mostly young people, probably the unemployed trying to forget the realities of life. It was noisy, too. Voices echoed in the spacious building; shrieks as somebody was pushed into the water, and laughing and shouting. He would have to keep a strict eye on Ben in there.

Sam appeared to have forgotten his trauma. He dived in and swam amidst the seething bodies. Some youths were indulging in horseplay with a teenage girl; a mother was supporting herself on the rail, holding a small boy. Fun for all the family. Ben was tugging at John's hand, eager to get in the water.

'All right, feller, give me a chance,' John laughed, nearly slipping in a puddle. 'We've got ages to . . .'

And then he saw the body in the water.

The din was a background noise now. It was as though he had suddenly been isolated from the other swimmers. Ben was still pulling at him, and he was aware of the strong smell of chlorine, feeling it harsh at the back of his throat. Tensing, he tried to back away, but he was anchored by the boy. Staring down into the bluish-green depths, he was sure that he had made a mistake. It was a distortion underwater, or somebody fooling about.

But there was a corpse down there, all right.

John saw it clearly now, a fully dressed man in a shabby dark overcoat, navy blue creased trousers clinging to thin, almost skeletal legs; still wearing shoes.

He didn't want to look at the face, but some irresistible morbid curiosity made it impossible to drag his eyes away. *Oh, God!*

It was an old man, maybe eighty or even older, with thinning grey hair that floated like marine growth on the seabed. He had aquiline, pinched features, hollowed cheeks and eyes that bulged and might have belonged to a dead cod. Dead but *seeing*.

That was impossible! John's mouth was dry and his legs threatened to buckle beneath him. He saw those thin lips open, a bubble forming in the mouth cavity, and then shooting up to the surface. Another. Now the lips were moving, forming words, *speaking*. No, it was impossible, just air leaving the body.

Those eyes held him. They seemed to move as though a cataract had peeled off them and the mouth was stretching in a malevolent leer. And talking again.

Then an arm floated up, and from the clenched fist a finger straightened out, hooked, flexed and *beckoned to him*. There was no mistaking the gesticulation, an invitation from the dead man to join him beneath the water.

For one terrible second John Strike's body threatened to obey the summons. His bare feet moving half a pace forward before he stopped himself and drew back. *No, I'm not going in there!*

'Daddy . . . let's swim in water.'

Thank God that Ben had not seen, John thought. Possibly he was too small to see over the edge from here.

'Wait, Ben.'

'Why, Daddy?'

His confused brain had to present a reason to pacify the child. It wasn't easy – the water's too cold? I don't feel like swimming today? The chlorine's too strong?

'I don't feel well.' Which was true right now.

'*Again*, Daddy!'

'Yes, again.' He was watching the corpse down below. It was mocking him, an old man who looked as if he had died from malnutrition except that he had drowned instead. Repulsive. *Evil.*

He heard laughter, splashing. That girl was getting her own back on her tormentors, trying to pull their trunks down. And they had not even noticed the dead body in the pool. Nor, the realization came as a shock, *had anybody else*.

'Wanna go in water, Daddy.'

Shut up! But it was not Ben's fault, he knew. There would be a lifeguard around somewhere; it was his duty to fetch the body out of the water, administer resuscitation. John almost threw up at the thought.

Looking for a lifeguard, he saw one on the opposite side of the baths, a tall figure dressed in a light blue tracksuit. Some girls were chatting him up. John was angry, cursing under his breath. The bugger wasn't doing the job he was being paid to do! A man had drowned in the pool and he hadn't even noticed.

'Hey!' It was meant to be a shout; it would have been, but the noise all around was deafening.

Ben was jerking his arm impatiently. 'Daddy, when can we go in water?'

'Later.' It was doubtful whether the boy had heard him. 'First I've got to talk to that man over there.'

Ben was being stubborn, digging his heels in like a tug-o'-war competitor and starting to cry. But at least he had not seen what was down there in the water. John stooped, lifted up his struggling son and turned away. One last glimpse at that corpse down on the bottom showed the features all screwed up, the lips moving, cursing. The extended fist was clenched, shaking; enraged because John Strike had disobeyed, spurned that call to join the dead.

With an effort John dragged himself away from the edge of the baths and began pushing his way through a crowd of bathers. Ignorant bastards, he thought, they wouldn't move to let him through. As if they were in league with that thing down there!

Almost slipping again, he resisted the urge to run. *Don't look back, whatever you do! Keep going.*

Now where the hell had that lifeguard gone? He was probably in one of the cubicles screwing with those birds, John decided. He was angry, looking all around but making an effort not to glance down into the water again.

The baths were even more crowded now. That mother with her child had been forced into a corner for safety. They were all yelling, shrieking, splashing one another.

God, they were all bloody blind, surely somebody must notice. But they didn't.

Then he saw the lifeguard. The fellow was kneeling by the side of the pool, shouting to somebody in the water. This time John looked, steeling himself. *Oh, my Jesus, they've found him, they're bringing him up!*

A swimmer in red trunks, a slightly built fellow gasping for air and struggling beneath the weight of his burden, was trying to hold a figure in a black overcoat out of the water whilst he floundered towards the rail, grabbed for it and held on. He was supporting the other man, keeping the head above the surface. Don't waste your time, John thought, he's bloody dead!

Somehow the rescuer dragged the corpse up on to the wet concrete and clambered after it. The lifeguard was standing back, laughing, making no attempt to help.

'Daddy, what's the matter with that man?'

How the hell did you explain to a three-year-old that a man had fallen in the water and drowned. That business at the crossing with the vagrant would be preying on Ben's mind; he couldn't thrust another violent death on the child.

'Can we go swimming yet, Daddy?'

'No.' He was still shouting. Then an awful thought struck him. '*Where's Sam? Where's Sarah?*'

He blamed himself, tortured himself because he had let them out of his sight, out of his mind. They were in that pool when –

'Dad!'

Sheer relief made him feel weak and sick again as he saw Sam and Sarah coming towards him, dripping water, shaking themselves.

'Sam! Sarah! Are you all right?'

'We're fine.' Sarah was eyeing her father, noting that

he and Ben were still dry. 'Haven't you been in yet, Dad?'

He shook his head, not trusting himself to speak, and tried to spread himself so that they would not see beyond him.

'I think we ought to be going.' He was still holding Ben tightly.

'But we've only been in here a few minutes!' Sarah was incredulous. 'We've been watching the life-saving.'

'Life . . . *saving!*'

'Yes. Behind you.' They were leaning over, trying to see.

'Don't look!' He was trying to spare them the awful sight; this morning had been bad enough. And Sarah was sleeping with the light on, anyway; the last thing she needed was to see a dead old man who blew bubbles and spoke with wasted lips.

Too late, they were past him, joining the ring of onlookers. John turned. The swimmer was leaning over the corpse, head bent, lips on those dead ones. *The kiss of life, only it was too late.*

Clutching Ben to him, he shouted to Sam and Sarah to come away.

'What's got into you now, Dad?' Sarah was grinning.

'He's . . . dead. That fellow's too late. I – '

'Relax, Dad.' Sarah came towards him and rested her fingers on his bare arm, sensing now that her father was genuinely disturbed. 'It isn't a *man*, you know.'

'Not . . . a . . . man?' Hearing her words, John was trying to understand. But it was a man; he had seen him down on the bottom of the pool. A revolting old man, possibly a vagrant. Just like the one who had been run over on the crossing, according to Leah's description. Nobody would miss him, but that was no consolation for those who happened to be around at the time.

'Of course it isn't a man.' Sam came away from the spectators. 'I've seen it before, they keep it specially for life-saving exercises. Dress it up in old clothes to make it lifelike. It's a *dummy*!'

John Strike still felt weak and sick. Not like this morning; that had been a physical ailment and he could accept it. This was different, a fear that knotted his stomach and threatened to squeeze anything that was in it either up or down. Or both.

The children were talking normally, chattering. Sarah had taken Ben into the pool and splashed with him in the shallow end until Leah arrived. John had dressed surreptitiously, hoping the others would not remember that he had not been in the water. There was no way he could have gone in.

It wasn't just that lifelike dummy. That had been bad enough and it had shaken him. A mistake on his part, and he was still trying to convince himself that it was one that anybody could have made – anybody who had experienced the effect that a house like 13 Schooner Street could have on you. Phobias. Hallucinations. You could convince yourself of almost anything.

But it was only afterwards that the root of his terror became apparent, the undoubted reason why he had seen a repulsive senile corpse in the pool. *Because suddenly John Strike was terrified of water!*

It was illogical, he knew. He had learned to swim at eight years old; had managed a length by the time he was nine. He had won his life-saving badge before he left school, and he always took advantage of any opportunity to visit the baths. Now, suddenly, this inexplicable fear had manifested itself.

He followed the others and turned right into Schooner Street. And saw Number Thirteen.

Identical in structure to the other terraced houses, but it was instantly recognizable and had him cowering for a second. Because it *saw* him with its dull eyes, just as that figure in the water had seen him. It scowled with its mean and twisted mouth, breathed icy fetid odours at him in the heat of the afternoon sun and seemed to beckon him.

Because evil festered within its four walls. A malignant invisible cancer was eating it up, its occupants too. A brooding hatred by day, an inescapable terror by night. Warping their minds. Destroying them.

And John knew that they had to get away. Before it was too late.

9

The Johnsons' kitchen was, for Leah, an insight into how John's plans for their own would look. Frightening, in a way, except that it would never come about because Number Thirteen would be on the market as from today. All the same, it was a revelation.

The hanging herbs, of course. She had had to stoop to avoid the bunch of apple mint suspended from the beam above the doorway. The beams served no purpose other than ornamentation but were cunningly implanted so that they gave the appearance of supporting the upper storey. They were made of varnished pine with irregular planing to give the impression of antiquity.

Ornaments hung from them: a recently restored duelling pistol clamped next to a black-leaded gin trap, horseshoes, an array of brasses.

Nothing matched; it wasn't intended to. Pine panelling and a Welsh dresser; an oak plate rack; an array of jars with cork lids, probably filled with powdered herbs to avoid spoiling those hanging up. She wrinkled her nose as she detected a faint whiff of garlic. The open-plan downstairs was as much a part of the scene as the BMW parked outside. *Real* yuppies; John was still playing at it.

Janet Johnson was overweight and even her Ralph Lauren two-piece could not hide the spreading waistline and capacious bottom. A fleshy chin and thick lips gave her a sullen appearance which was deceptive. Friendly, but smiling rarely, she was too engrossed in her life-style to notice others. Attractive, though; she made sure of that with skilled use of cosmetics and an expensive hairdresser, but Leah doubted whether she was a natural blonde. But it was really of no consequence.

Janet placed two earthenware mugs of steaming coffee on the scrubbed pine table, seated herself opposite Leah and said, 'I'm *so* glad Sam comes round to play with Jeremy, and I'd like Ben to feel free to come as well. Jeremy really does miss his friends at boarding school during the holidays.'

'It's very kind of you.' Leah fought to dispel a creeping sense of inferiority. Our two only go to a state school, she wanted to apologize. And so will Ben when he's old enough. 'I was afraid they might be getting a bit of a nuisance.'

'Not at all.' Janet Johnson lit a cigarette. 'As a matter of fact, I'd like to take Jeremy to Hampton Court one day this week and I was wondering if you would like to come along with your three. Educational for the kids, an outing for the mothers.' She allowed herself one of those infrequent smiles.

Leah's roving gaze noted the squash kit on a chair in the corner. She wondered if it was ever used.

'I just never see anything of Brian these days,' Janet went on. 'That's the penalty of being married to a stockbroker. But you can't have it all ways, can you?'

'No,' Leah sympathized, 'it's the same for me, being married to a banker.' Even if John is only a branch accountant, she thought, we'll leave it at 'banker' for the time being.

'Your house could be made *so* nice with a little planning. You need the right architect, that's the secret. Of course, Brian has a lot of contacts in that field.'

'Actually,' Leah's words came out in an embarrassed rush, 'we're putting the house up for sale.'

'Oh, *no*! What a shame, you've only just moved in. Oh, dear, I'm so sorry, and Jeremy will be, too, when I tell him. But you have to accept these things in banking and the like – rapid promotion, moving on, whether you like it or not.'

'The truth is . . . we don't like the house.'

'But, my dear, a house is what you make of it. The thing is to buy cheap and make it how *you* want it. And I'll let you into a little secret.' She lowered her voice, a habit of confidentiality which she had perfected. 'This place didn't cost what you might think. Contacts, that's the way to do it. You talk to your husband (I'd love to meet him, one of these days) and tell him to chat up a builder customer, one with a large overdraft who relies on the bank. No problem.' She winked. 'Don't throw the towel in, take my advice. I know the place is a bit of a mess but it has *potential*.' She was whispering now. 'You should have seen this place when we moved in. A pigsty wasn't in it. I'll show you round properly before you go.'

'Why did the Graftons leave?' Leah hoped that Janet would not detect the tremor in her voice. This was her real reason for calling on a near neighbour, apart from apologizing for Sam's lengthy daily visits.

'Oh, I don't really know.' Janet waved a hand. 'I didn't see much of them. The boy used to come round in the holidays. He was *all right*, company for Jeremy, but I think they were really out of their depth here. Financially, I mean. Grafton, I forget his first name, was only a glorified clerk, a wage-earner. I suppose they had to sell when the debts caught up with them.'

'Didn't the boy ever say why they were leaving?' Leah felt her skin starting to prickle. *Come on, tell me the truth*.

'Oh, he was a bit of a romancer, had a vivid imagination.' Janet Johnson stifled a yawn. 'You know what some kids are, bogeymen under the stairs and all that sort of rubbish. Thank God we sent Jeremy to a prep school and made a man of him. That Grafton boy tried to make out that his parents were scared, too, but that was only to justify his own nervousness. Then they just upped and left, and we haven't heard a word from them since. Not that we really want to,' she added. 'But it's such a pity that you're going when you don't have to. Now, you come and look at the rest of our house, and I guarantee I'll change your mind.'

It was after five when Leah and the children finally arrived home. As she opened the front door the telephone was ringing. She knew before she answered it that it would be John calling to let her know he had been 'lumbered' with a late appointment. She sighed; back to normal. But if he had arranged with the agents to put the house up for sale then that was some consolation.

In a way, Ruth Ford was a means of escapism, John Strike reflected as he lingered over some trivial routine jobs in the office. For once Kenton had left early, and that was a relief after today. One of *those* days, to employ a popular phrase that incorporated a mixture of stress, frustration and general harassment.

The day had not got off to a good start. The manager was scathingly sarcastic over John's absence on the previous day. 'We'll have to prune some of these small unsecured overdrafts tomorrow, Mr Strike, and send out a few letters. That is, *if* you're going to be in tomorrow!' And other unsubtle insinuations. 'Well, if *your wife* really wants to sell the house, go ahead. Maybe a house nearer the branch would assist you to be at work daily. I suppose tube travel *is* rather exhausting and conducive to migraines, or whatever you call them!'

John had telephoned Lester & Co., Estate Agents & Valuers, during his lunch hour. Kenton did not appreciate staff, even the accountant, making personal calls both at the bank's expense and in the bank's time.

'Yes, I want 13 Schooner Street put back on the market.' It was as though the agent doubted his own hearing. 'That's right.' John sighed beneath his breath. 'I want to *sell* it! My wife is there today, if you want to go and measure up and take particulars.'

'I don't think that will be necessary.' There was a definite lack of enthusiasm in the voice at the other end. 'We still have copies of the brochure from last time. Any particular reason for selling, Mr Strike?'

'It wasn't really what we wanted.' It's a fucking awful place and it's only by the grace of God that any of us are still sane, he added silently. 'And I think we can put that grand back on. To cover expenses.'

'We can try, but property isn't selling as fast as it was a couple of months ago.'

Which is a fucking downright lie, John thought. You know it'll stick as well as I do, that you'll lose out on the paperwork involved. Only yesterday, the *Financial Times* had reported a twenty-five per cent increase in London property prices.

But at least the bloody house was up for sale. A positive step; he couldn't do any more.

All of which culminated in a need for Ruth Ford tonight.

John's arousal began in the wine bar, an exciting relief from everything which had happened today, a welcome distraction which blended with the house red. Tomorrow was another day; live for today, or tonight, he thought, in a kind of pleasurable oblivion.

'I've told Keith,' Ruth breathed, as she found his hand beneath the table and squeezed it.

'Christ!' The shockwave sat him upright in his chair.

'Surprised?' Her eyes narrowed. 'Or worried?'

'Both,' he replied. 'We'll both be in trouble if he turns up and . . .'

'Don't worry,' she laughed. 'I've written to tell him. He won't get it until tomorrow at the earliest.'

'Oh!' A reprieve! Live for tonight – I'm in the shit, but why worry? he told himself.

Tonight was different. It was as if Ruth had shed a great weight from her mind. Her husband had been told because the letter was written and posted. The fact that he had not received it was of no consequence. The die was cast.

This time there was no delay in the bathroom. John was lying on the bed, fully erect, and as she came into the room she began pulling off her nightdress. She was still embarrassed but the guilt was gone. The letter was a decree nisi as far as she was concerned. Only the details had to be finalized.

She knelt on the bed alongside him, moaning her pleasure as he reached up and stroked her, pushing his fingers into the soft, warm flesh and rubbing until she was shuddering. Only then did she straddle him, lowering herself on to him.

Her previous inhibitions had disappeared. She rested her hands on his shoulders, a jockey testing a new mount, walking it, cantering – then breaking into a full gallop, holding on for dear life as its bucking and twisting threatened to unseat her.

John knew there was no way that he could hold back. For once he was not in command. His passion escalated and rushed towards a climax. Writhing, convulsing, rider and mount were falling, a trembling heap of pulsating flesh as their combined ecstasy hit its peak and began to subside slowly.

They lay there for a long time in the darkened room,

with their own thoughts, not talking, as if afraid to ask or answer questions.

'John?' Ruth's voice trembled as she broke the long silence.

'Yes?'

'You do love me, don't you?'

'Yes.' It was true; he had given it a lot of thought lately. It was a complicated kind of love where a family and a job were at stake. A situation had arisen that could not go on indefinitely, although that would have been the ideal solution if only it had been possible. 'Yes, I do.' He had to sound sure of himself, there could be no half measures from now on. This was a relationship he could not live without.

'Good.' There was relief in her voice. 'I'm glad I wrote that letter, then. We'll have to sell this place and I'll put my half-share towards *our* place.'

Oh, Christ Almighty!

'What's the problem?' Anxiety crept into her tone.

'Just small ones.' He licked his lips. 'Like a wife, three kids, a mortgage and a position at the bank which I'm likely to lose. Demotion to relief staff, disgraced and lost in the faceless milling crowd of bank workers. Or hadn't you thought of that?'

'Aren't I worth it?'

You selfish little bitch! Instinctively he eased himself away from her, but her hand closed over his wrist and tightened. He resisted the urge to extricate himself.

'If you're going to ditch me, you've wrecked my marriage!' She sounded angry, disillusioned.

'I never said that, but it will take time. I have to work things out.'

'You're stalling me. All you have to do is tell your wife and move out. It's straightforward, as I see it. I've done just that.'

Yes, without asking me, he thought. He found himself craving for a cigarette, although he had not smoked for three years now.

'I'll fix it,' he replied, and began groping for his clothes. 'Look, I love you and – '

'If you love me then you'll do what I've asked!' She was close to tears of anger and frustration.

'I told you I'd fix it.'

'I want you, John.' She was pleading now, starting to cry.

'If you really want to know' – a sudden inspiration, a means of defusing the situation – 'I put our house on the market today!'

He heard her catch her breath. *Don't ask me why I did it because I didn't do it for you. Not consciously, anyway.* But he had unwittingly taken the first step on an unknown path.

He heard the click of the light switch and was dazzled by the blinding glare. In that instant he saw her as a beautiful, tear-stained pathetic figure of a girl. Gone was her sensuousness, her seductiveness; in their place beautiful innocence. It hurt, wrenched at his stomach, and then he was leaning across the bed to kiss her as he had often kissed Sarah after a tearful tiff. A make-up-and-forgive kiss. Except that this time the proverbial ball was well and truly in his court.

'Don't worry, just leave it to me,' he murmured. 'See you in the morning.'

The same boring return trip, only this time he never noticed it. In the sparsely filled tube carriage, a youth had been sick on the floor. A well-dressed businessman had changed his seat because of it. A young couple kissing at the other end were oblivious of everybody. Up the escalator, then he flashed his travel pass at a ticket collector who wasn't looking. And outside, the night had turned unexpectedly chilly.

John shrugged on his Barbour as he hurried across the pedestrian crossing. Badly lit side streets led to Schooner Street if you knew where to turn right and left. He slowed his pace, then stopped.

He felt an urge to retrace his steps, without having any alternative destination in mind. Not because of Leah. Nor Ruth. They were but pawns in this terrible inexplicable business. *Triskaidekaphobia*: the fear of the number thirteen. The fear of 13 Schooner Street.

It almost turned him. It was a warning: *flee now, while you still can*. If it had not been for the children, he knew he would have obeyed his instincts, and probably gone back to Ruth. More than her love, her body, she offered *safety*.

He was walking again, dragging his feet past a trickle of late-night passers-by, faceless silhouettes, all going somewhere. He envied them.

Schooner Street. He stood on the edge of the opposite pavement, reluctant to cross, trying not to look at the house because he could feel it looking at him. He was shuddering inside his waxproofed jacket because the brickwork and windows were a face again, with demented senile features, hollowed cheeks and bulging dead eyes that still saw. The mouth formed bubbles then released them, uttering a mute command which he could not disobey.

The corpse in the pool had returned and was summoning him.

He heard Ben crying even as he struggled with the Chubb lock and clicked the Yale. The kitchen light was on at the other end of the hallway; the clock on the wall told him that it was one-ten.

Scared of what he might find, he hurried down the dark passageway and stopped in the doorway.

Leah was seated in the big rocking chair, Ben on her lap, his white tear-streaked features turned towards his father. Leah did not speak, but her expression was angry and frightened. Accusing. *You've been with another woman, John, deserted us. Left us to the mercy of this dreadful house.*

He almost shouted, 'I've put the house up for sale'. Instead, he asked, 'What's the matter?'

'Ben refuses to go upstairs,' she answered.

'Is that all? We had this trouble not so long ago, this not wanting to go to bed and then wetting himself to get his own back on us when – '

'It isn't like that at all!' Her voice was curt, tinged with fear. 'It started earlier, after tea. He absolutely refused to go up the stairs to fetch his Lego. I tried to make him and he screamed the place down. So, in the end, I gave in. Which is why I'm here now.'

'There's nothing up there, Ben.' *God, what a bloody liar I am but I have to say that.*

'It isn't that,' Leah sighed. 'Nothing like that at all. He adamantly refuses even to sleep in our bed. It's nothing at all to do with what's happened to all of us – not directly, anyway. He's suddenly terrified of *heights*!'

'I put the house up for sale today,' John said, and hoped that perhaps Ben would understand. But even if he did it could not make any difference tonight.

'I'll pull the divan bed down in the front room.' Leah handed the trembling child to John. 'I'll sleep downstairs with him. You sleep where you like – you always do!'

John felt the vibes that came at him out of the walls, the cold hostility. Warning after warning – the house was becoming impatient now. It was driving them out, as it had the Graftons and maybe others before them. An evil place that wanted to be left alone to brood.

And if they did not leave soon, then something terrible would happen.

10

'Mummy, we won't get lost in the maid, will we?'

'The *maze*, darling.' Leah noted Ben's nervousness, his pallid complexion after a near-sleepless night on the sofa in the front room. 'No, of course we won't. It's just hedges, like a big garden. And we'll all be there, Sam and Sarah and Mrs Johnson and Jeremy.' And there won't be any heights, she thought. Or newts. It'll be daylight, so nobody will be scared of the dark. Nothing to set on fire and no blood, either. Oh, Christ, what a relief to get away from this place! 'Now, go and fetch your clean shorts from off your bed . . . No, I'll go.'

For once he did not follow her as she ran up the stairs, grabbed the denim garment and ran back down. He was standing in the hall, watching her with dismay on his face because she had been upstairs. *God, we can't go on like this for ever!*

'Sarah, Sam, hurry up and get ready, we have to be round at the Johnsons' for ten-thirty and it's twenty past now.' Leah heard the other children moving about. Sarah didn't want to go and had come up with all kinds of excuses. She was an industrious child who wanted to spend the day painting and drawing. Talented children could be as much a problem as average ones, probably more so, Leah decided. But today *everybody* was going out. No exceptions.

The three children were waiting in the hall. Leah had gone back into the kitchen for her handbag. One of the sink taps was dripping, so she turned it off tightly. A sweet wrapper lay on the floor, so she put it in the pedal bin. One of the drawers in the dresser was not closed properly, so she shut it. Checking the room over, she looked to see if anything else needed doing.

'Hurry up, Mummy.'

'I'm coming . . .' She stopped, felt faint for a moment and had to hold on to the flap of the breakfast bar. The kitchen tilted, then steadied. She felt beads of sweat on her forehead, a goosepimpling of her skin. *And then the fear hit her, a terrifying, inexplicable sensation that almost had her screaming.*

Somebody's watching me! The presence was so close that it might have been right behind her, but when she turned round there was nobody there. Just an empty kitchen. You're being stupid again, imagining things, she told herself.

She thought she heard somebody breathing, faint rasping breaths that rattled phlegm in ageing lungs. She waited for a spasm of coughing but it did not come. There was silence, except for the children moving about in the hall.

'Come on, Mummy!'

She opened her mouth to reply, and in that awful instant she knew that she was not going anywhere – *a frightening realization that there was no way she was going to be able to leave this house with its lurking terrors.*

Agoraphobia.

She recognized the symptoms even in her initial panic, and succumbed to them because she knew it was futile to fight them. She was safe in the house. Rubbish! But she could not face the world that lay beyond the front door, either.

'Mother!' That was Sarah getting impatient, annoyed because she had been made to accompany the others and now it was her mother who was procrastinating.

'Sarah . . . come here a moment, please.' I mustn't

alarm the others, she thought, particularly Ben. The kitchen walls seemed to have moved in, and the room was reduced in size, a prison cell from which there was no escape.

Leah heard footsteps coming down the hallway, fast, irritated ones. She did not turn round, did not want Sarah to see her expression.

'How much longer are you going to be, Mother?'

'I . . . I can't go, Sarah!'

Silence. Leah heard her daughter's sharp intake of breath, then, 'Why ever not, Mother?'

'I'm not well.'

'Oh! I'd better stay and look after you.'

'*No.*' I don't want any of you to stay, she realized. I want you out of here, somewhere where it's safe. 'I just want to be left alone, and no arguments, please. Now, I want you to take Sam and Ben down to the Johnsons', explain to Mrs Johnson that I'm not well and ask her if she would mind taking you lot along with her. And those boys have got to behave themselves, d'you hear? No quarrelling or fighting, and I want you to be in charge of them. Don't let them out of your sight for a moment. My handbag's on the table, take a ten-pound note out of my purse to pay for everything.'

'All right.' It was a sullen acceptance of the situation. Leah heard the clasp on her fake crocodile bag click.

'*Mummy!*' A shriek from Ben. She heard him running into the room, coming towards her. 'Mummy, I'm not going without you. I want to stay with you.'

Oh, Christ, that's all I need right now! 'Ben, listen to me.' She pulled him to her and stooped to kiss his forehead. The room began to gyrate again. 'Mummy's not well, I'm going to bed for the day. So please go along with Sarah and Sam. And Jeremy. You'll enjoy it, and before you know where you are it'll be time to come home and Mummy will be better and Daddy will be home from work.' A faint outside chance that one or the other might come true, she reflected grimly, but she had to be optimistic. 'Now, run along. Please.'

'Don't want to.' Ben was starting to cry. Sarah had him by the hand and was pulling him out of the kitchen. *Oh, God, don't have a tantrum, I can't stand it!*

The front door shut and Leah breathed a temporary sigh of relief. It would be just my luck to have them all trooping back in five minutes because Janet can't manage three kids on top of her own, she thought. She can't handle children, that's why Jeremy was sent to boarding school.

Leah lowered herself into a chair and closed her eyes. She still had that feeling of a presence, of invisible eyes that never left her, and watched her every move, as if . . . it was waiting for something!

The cooker clock was ticking loudly, like a time bomb nearing its detonation. She was sweating, the perspiration chilling on her skin and causing her to shiver. She raised her head and looked at the clock. Ten-thirty-five. Janet Johnson had obviously agreed to take the children with her to Hampton Court. Leah felt momentary relief before her terror surged back. Now she was alone with whatever was in this dreadful house!

This was too stupid for words! She rose unsteadily and moved towards the hall. All this time she had been longing to get away from Number Thirteen and now, without warning, she was afraid to go outside. Well, there was only one thing for it . . . Her feet moved in a shaky, uncertain rush, making her stumble along the hall. The door was there before her; all she needed to do was grasp that Yale latch, turn it, rush outside and slam the door behind her – and to hell with the fact that she didn't have her key. It was in her handbag back in the kitchen and she was not returning there. Just get outside, she told herself, and play it from there.

She was within a yard of the door when it was as if she had run into an invisible barrier. Her legs stopped moving. She recoiled and cried out, then turned away because the door was a terrifying prospect. *There's something awful out there. I don't know what, but I can't face it.*

And there was undoubtedly something equally awful inside this house.

I'll go out through the patio doors, then, and run into the garden, she resolved. At least I'll be in the open air, the sunshine. Dreading the kitchen again, she hesitated in the doorway, realizing that the rear entrance was no different from the front; an impassable barrier that confined her to this abominable hell.

She did not even attempt to approach the french windows, just stood there looking at them. She saw a reflection of herself, a pathetic, scarcely recognizable, cringing figure. Listening for everyday mundane sounds, she heard only a dreadful stillness. Even the clock on the Belling seemed to have stopped ticking. With a start she saw that the hands still showed ten-thirty-five. They had not moved since . . . since when? Since just after the children left. How long ago was that? Twenty minutes? Or an hour, several hours? She wanted to scream because time itself had stopped, marooning her in a ghastly void.

Her frightened eyes roamed the room. It *did* appear to have contracted. Her breathing was shallow; she was having to draw breath consciously and expel it forcibly. *Don't panic*. I *have* panicked, she knew.

She'd try upstairs. Even if she couldn't escape, at least she could look out, see cars going by, people walking down the road – a normal world. She would be an onlooker, a convict serving a life sentence gazing wistfully out of a barred cell window.

She had to hold on to the stair rail and pull herself up a step at a time. This same staircase had terrified Ben last night. But Leah was not afraid of heights, just of what might lie up there. Or down below her.

Reaching the landing, she paused. The main bedroom overlooked the street; she would try that. This time the door did not present an obstacle and swung inwards at her touch. She left it open.

Standing in the bow window, she looked down. Cars were parked on both sides of the road. The Suzuki was glinting in the morning sunshine – if it *was* morning. A world of stillness in which nothing moved; no passing vehicles, no pedestrians on their way to the shops, a silent, empty street. She willed a car to drive by, somebody to emerge from their house. But neither happened and gradually the terror of gazing down on a dead place seeped into her. She backed away, knowing that it would be no different from the rear bedrooms. She was abandoned, trapped.

She experienced an urge to beat on the walls, to scream her fear. Her pulses were racing, her temples pounding and bringing on a slight headache. Try to think rationally, she told herself. I can't, this whole business is irrational.

She had a sudden idea. It wouldn't work, but at least it gave her something positive to do. The telephone was in the hall, her sole contact with the outside world. Except that there was nobody out there, and even if the phone was working it would not be answered.

The journey back downstairs seemed to take an eternity. It was more arduous than climbing up. But eventually she was standing in the hallway again and the telephone was within reach. Her shaking hand reached out for it. The instrument would be dead, naturally. It wasn't!

She could not remember the number of John's bank and had to consult the directory. A near-impossible task; the pages flipped out of her fumbling fingers, the print was so small that she could barely read it. Finding the entry she sought, she pushed the buttons like an infant struggling to master the intricacies of numbered wooden play blocks. At least there was a dialling tone. She had not expected even that. Ringing out, too. But nobody would answer because . . .

They did. A girl's voice – she sounded distant as if she was concentrating on something else and not listening properly. But it was the right number. The bank!

'I want to speak to Mr Strike, please.'

A long pause, then, 'I'm afraid he's engaged. Can anybody else help you?'

'No, I'm afraid they can't. Will you ask him to call me back, please. It's his wife speaking.'

'I'll give him your message. Does he know your number?'

Stupid bitch! Leah replaced the receiver and let out her pent-up breath. She was euphoric because she had actually spoken to somebody. There *were* other people out there. John would ring back. When? She did not know, but she would wait right here by the phone and snatch it up the moment it rang.

The feeling of being watched was much stronger now. She glanced around but there was nobody there. She sensed the hatred in those unseen eyes, a malevolence that burned into her, an anger because she had defied whatever it was, and called for help.

'Damn you!' She could not remain silent any longer. She shrieked at the walls, which were closer than ever now, as if they meant to crush her like an apple in a cider press. 'Look what you're doing to us. We've done nothing to you. We just want to leave. D'you understand? We want to leave as much as you want us to!'

The sensation seemed less strong after her outburst but she knew that the presence was still there.

And then the telephone shrilled, an agonized scream as though even an inanimate object felt the terror of this house.

Leah snatched up the handset. 'Hallo. John?'

'This is Lester & Co., Estate Agents.'

'Oh!' Her hopes were dashed but at least it was somebody to talk to.

'We have somebody interested in your property. Is a viewing possible?'

'Yes. Oh, yes, *please*.'

'Good. The gentleman has just rung in and insists on coming round right away.'

'That will be absolutely marvellous.' Leah felt a surge of hope and found herself wishing that she had not phoned John. 'I shall be in for the rest of the day.'

'That's fine.' The estate agent sounded in a hurry. 'If he wants to proceed then ask him to come to the office.'

She leaned up against the wall and found herself looking at the front door again. It was still an illogical barrier, but if necessary she would go upstairs and throw the key down to her expected caller when he arrived.

She did not want to return to the kitchen. She would stay right here within view of her prison door, waiting, listening for footfalls, the catch on the front gate clanging, the ring of the doorbell. Bracing herself, she willed it to happen *now*.

A harsh ringing made her jump. It was the phone. She did not need it now, but she answered it. It was John.

'No problems?' He sounded tense. Damn him, she wouldn't have rung if there had not been problems. He was as stupid as that girl who had answered her call a short time ago. Or was it a long time ago?

'No.' She tried to sound normal, slightly excited. 'Just to say that there's a man coming to look at the house.'

'Oh, I see.' *Is that all you rang to tell me?*

'I thought you would like to know,' she replied haughtily.

'People are always viewing property.' His voice was flat, expressionless. Perhaps he was disappointed because somebody might actually buy the house, she thought. 'Let him see round. I'll talk to you tonight. Must go, I'm terribly busy.'

You bastard! She slammed the receiver back. If I'd needed you, as I did a short while ago, it would be just the same, she thought. *See you tonight – late. Because I'm going to screw my fancy woman first.*

She was waiting again, for the doorbell, this time. And still being watched. She jerked round once because she thought she heard that rasping breathing. Or was it mice up in the attic gnawing at the wires? The house might go up in flames. If it did, she knew she would not even try to get out because there was no escape. *Oh, hurry up, please, I need you.*

She was aware of the timelessness again. The cooker clock had stopped but there was always the radio alarm upstairs by the bed. No, she wasn't going up there again. She could have phoned the speaking clock but she didn't. Because time itself was of no consequence.

Exhausted, slumped on the straight-backed chair by the phone, she waited.

When the doorbell finally rang she did not even jump. As she struggled to her feet she felt a sense of relief, not because the expected caller had arrived but . . . *suddenly she realized that she was no longer shackled by those inexplicable bonds, that she could have walked right out into the street had she wished. It was a feeling akin to a sick person awakening to discover that the fever had left him whilst he slept, that only the weakness remained.*

She turned the catch, pulled the door open and stared in disbelief.

'I liked the maze, Mummy.' Ben pushed his way inside and grasped her arm.

'It was okay.' Sam walked on through and mounted the stairs.

'Are you feeling better, Mother?' Sarah asked. 'You don't look too good.'

'I'm all right now.' Dazed, she wondered if the children were real or if it was some mirage sent to torture her battered, bemused brain. 'Just tired. Go on in, cut some sandwiches, will you, please. Dad will be home soon. And I'm expecting somebody to call to look at the house.'

'The boys were very good, they didn't quarrel,' Sarah said as she went through to the kitchen. 'Goodness, it's hot in here, you haven't had the patio doors shut all day, have you?'

Six o'clock; the cooker clock was working again, had somehow caught up on itself. Leah shivered. Everything was back to normal, as normal as anything could be in 13 Schooner Street.

It was after nine, and Ben was already asleep on the sofa in the front room when John arrived home. Late, as she had expected; he was not even bothering to come up with excuses now.

'How did you get on, was he interested?'

'He never came,' she replied, and almost added, 'I didn't expect him to.'

It would not have made any difference because the atmosphere, the vibes, here were too strong. The Strikes, the agents, were wasting their time. Nobody would buy.

11

For Leah there was one terror that transcended all the other horrors in this dreadful house. Not the mice in the attic, which still gnawed the electric wirings nightly and would surely cause a fire before long. Not the omnipresent invisible watcher who followed her every move and whose breathing she could hear in moments of rare silence. Nor the fact that she might cut herself on any one of the sharp kitchen knives and spray arterial blood all over the walls and ceiling again. Not even the inexplicable terror of going outside, which she seemed to have overcome now. Something much, much simpler than any of those and a thousand times more terrifying.

The telephone.

The squat inanimate monster crouched on the hall table ready to scream without warning when she least expected it. Lately it had been quiet; it had not rung for two days now. Waiting, like everything else in 13 Schooner Street.

August was gone and the pictorial calendar on the kitchen wall showed a tranquil September setting with a faint hint of brown amidst the thick foliage of leafy chestnut trees. Sam and Sarah had started at their new school and seemed to have settled in without any undue problems. Ben followed her about the house, bored because he had nobody to quarrel with. A week ago she managed to coax him upstairs, had even persuaded him to sleep in the bed with her. John was out late at least three nights a week but she had resigned herself to that, had even contemplated leaving him and going back to her parents' house in Wales, taking the children with her. But the priority was to get rid of Number Thirteen; when that happened she would think positively. At present they were in the midst of a kind of lull; she didn't try to con herself that everything was all right, because it wasn't. A breathing space, nothing more.

She busied herself preparing the evening meal: sliced meat from the supermarket – that way she did not have to use a knife; pre-packed potatoes ready for boiling; frozen peas. Nothing canned because cans had sharp, ragged edges. She was pandering to her phobias, but it was only until she got away from here. Then it would be different.

Ben had fallen asleep in the chair, his picture book lying on the floor at his feet. The radio was playing softly. Without it, she would have had to endure the awful silence, would have heard that breathing again. She kept glancing round, checking on Ben, making sure that there was nobody standing behind her.

On impulse she tiptoed to the door and peered into the hall – at the phone. She knew it was going to ring, that was a certainty. It might be in five minutes or an hour. But it would ring, she knew that much. Listening, bracing herself for the first shrill shriek, she willed it to ring; then she was praying that it would stay silent, as it had done recently.

Telephones were a curse and a blessing, she thought. You had to have the good and the bad. You could not escape them. Even if you did not have one, if anybody wanted you in an emergency they would get bad tidings to you somehow. Via a telephone, of course. Whether it was a neighbour hammering on your door or a stoic policeman breaking bad news, the phone found you. There was no hiding place.

One phone call from the estate agents in three weeks!

It was unbelievable. That first prospective viewer had never materialized. Leah had not expected him to. But the Craigs were real enough. A middle-aged conventional couple, they had gone through the proper channels, booked a viewing appointment via Lesters for three-thirty on Wednesday afternoon. They were punctual almost to the minute. That was a fortnight ago yesterday.

He wore a dark suit beneath a light fawn macintosh, and had polished shoes and an office umbrella. She had her grey hair tied up in a bun on the back of her head, dark red lipstick and an empty shopping bag. Early retirement, Leah thought, on their way to the shops, probably a weekly routine to break the monotony. She didn't understand why they wanted to retire in south London. She didn't care, as long as they bought the house.

'I'll just have a look at the downstairs and the garden, dear.' He obviously took all the decisions. 'You go up and look at the bedrooms with Mrs Strike.'

For some reason Leah got an uneasy feeling as she led the way up the stairs in front of Mrs Craig. She had sent the children out of the way, round to the Johnsons', had tidied up all their strewn toys. Nevertheless, she had a foreboding, just as she had had that afternoon when she sat on the wall over the road watching the removal men carry the furniture in. Her momentary feeling of faintness passed almost immediately. She glanced back at Mrs Craig, but she was engrossed in the new wallpaper, maybe already planning to strip it off and replace it with something to her own taste. Just buy it and do what the hell you like to it, Leah thought.

'This is the main bedroom . . .' Leah was suddenly aware that her companion had not followed her across the landing. Instead, she had gone into Sam's room. *Oh, well, please yourself.*

Silence. Leah could even hear the ticking of the clock in the hall; Mrs Craig had paused to study something in the small bedroom, and her husband was probably outside in the garden. A coincidental synchronization of stillness had created a frightening silence. Leah whirled round, hearing that rasping breathing again. It was faint; it might have been on the stairs or even in Sarah's room, it was impossible to place it. *But the watcher was back, because somebody else had infiltrated his domain.*

Mrs Craig came out of the room in a rush, caught her foot and almost fell. Breathless, she was trying to conceal something, the lipstick on those moving lips starkly crimson against the whiteness of her ageing features.

'I . . . I think I've seen all that I need to see, Mrs Strike.' She was holding on to the top of the stair rail and it was clear that she was about to descend. 'I'll . . . I'll just give my husband a call, if you don't mind.' Shakily going downstairs, she clung to the pine rail. 'George . . . George, are you there?'

Leah heard George Craig coming in through the patio doors. *Damn it, what was the matter now?*

'George, I think I've seen all I need to see. Shall we go?'

Craig looked surprised, embarrassed. 'You haven't been long, dear. The kitchen's very nice and roomy, and the garden's just about the right size for me to manage. You go and have a look and I'll see upstairs.'

'No, dear!' Her insistence almost bordered on panic. 'I really don't think this is the place we're looking for.' She was edging towards the front door. 'Thank you so much, Mrs Strike, I'm sorry to have taken up your time.'

All of two minutes, Leah thought bitterly. 'Is there . . . something you don't . . . like, Mrs Craig?' *Go on, tell me, for God's sake!*

'Oh, no!' Formally polite again, she already had the

front door open. 'Nothing at all, it's a *lovely* house, Mrs Strike. It's just that I can see that it's not what we're looking for and it would be unfair of me to take up any more of your time. Thank you so much for letting us see, and I'm sure you'll have no trouble selling such a nice house. Good afternoon.'

Mrs Craig had seen or felt something, Leah reflected, and that was not altogether surprising. But when she and John first viewed the house there had been nothing amiss; it was tatty, certainly, but nothing that couldn't be rectified with a grand knocked off the purchase price.

But nobody had been to look at the house since the Craigs. Which was crazy in London. It wasn't like a small village where rumours circulated and became embroidered by local gossips. In the metropolis, houses were houses – and they were at a premium.

And then the telephone rang, as she had been expecting it to do all afternoon.

Standing with her fingers sweaty on the handset, she was afraid to lift it up. She wished that phones had some way of signifying the nature of the call before you answered them – good news, indifferent news, bad news – a neon light to signify the nature of the call so that you could prepare yourself for whatever tidings awaited you. Which was silly. All the same, it was some seconds before she found the courage to lift the receiver.

'Leah, is that you?'

Identifying the voice, she was perturbed by the tone. Her mother phoned only infrequently, and then after six on the cheap rate.

'Mother, what's the matter?' Something certainly was.

'Your father's not well.'

'Oh!' She clutched at the table and felt a sinking sensation in her stomach. 'What . . . what's the matter?'

'When he got up this morning I thought he didn't look

right, and he was an awful long time in the bathroom. When he came out, oh my goodness, you should have seen the *blood*!'

The wall in front of Leah started to spin. She saw again the spurting crimson from her own wrist, the way it sprayed everywhere; and she started to feel faint.

'Oh, it wasn't *that* bad,' her mother went on, 'although it gave me a turn at the time. Your dad had been trying to shave and made a bit of a mess of himself. So I called the doctor – you remember Dr James? Well, the doctor says your father's had a slight stroke, nothing to worry about but he has to rest. And I was wondering if you could come up for a few days?'

Nothing to worry about . . . just nicked himself . . . a slight stroke . . . Letting out a long breath, she tried not to visualize the blood. A slight stroke; lots of people had them when they were over sixty, she told herself. Some recovered, lasted another ten or twenty years. Others had a massive one soon after; the first had been a warning.

'I . . . don't know.' Leah had difficulty thinking. The children were the problem, Sam and Sarah. She could take Ben with her. 'Do you *really* need me, Mother?' Much as I'd love to get away from here for a few days, she thought.

'I do, really.' It was a kind of self-pitying whine. 'There's an awful lot to do when your father can't help me. And I'd like somebody to stop with him whilst I pop out to the shops. It would only be for a few days. The doctor says he'll be up and about by next week.'

'All right.' Leah was still shaking. 'I'll fix something. I'll ring you back about nine to let you know my plans.'

'Who was that, Mummy?' Ben was standing in the kitchen doorway rubbing his bleary eyes.

'How would you like to go and stay at Gran's by the

sea for a few days?' Maybe it was the answer to her current problems.

'Ooh, yes, Mummy. When are we going? Are Sam and Sarah coming?'

'Sam and Sarah can't come because of school.' That was definite. 'I'm going to see if Mrs Johnson can help out. Your daddy will have to come home early each night to get their tea.' And he'll have to babysit, too. Which gave her a surge of satisfaction. For once, she was going to disrupt other people's plans.

Janet Johnson was glad that she had insisted on Brian having a vasectomy after Jeremy was born; otherwise every mealtime would be like this one – two extra helpings, double the washing-up. Thank goodness Leah had taken the youngster with her.

Of course, everybody helped out in a crisis, she told herself. So long as that crisis wasn't prolonged. Leah hoped to be back on Monday. Probably she would take advantage and pinch an extra day. Tuesday, then. John Strike would look after the children over the weekend, so there was really only today, Friday, to cope with, and only until about eight o'clock; John had said he would be home by then. Not too bad, in that case, and maybe in return she could persuade Leah to have Jeremy for a couple of days. Children could be a bind at times.

'I'm just popping round to make sure everything's all right and to take the washing in,' she announced once Sam, Sarah and Jeremy were seated at the table. 'I'll only be five minutes.'

The Strikes weren't making much progress with Number Thirteen, Janet thought as she inserted the security key in the front door. A bit of tidying in the garden, some interior decoration, and that was all. They should have had the builders in by now to gut the place.

God only knew, it *needed* gutting. Knock the bloody place down and rebuild it! It was so old-fashioned. Maybe they didn't have as much money as they pretended to have. Well, now was her chance to have a good nose round and see what they really had. She could soon tell.

The moment Janet stepped inside she had a feeling that something was wrong, so she left the front door open behind her, an escape route if she needed it.

It was just a feeling; she could be wrong, prayed that she was. But she knew that she wasn't the moment she saw right through to the kitchen. The patio doors were wide open, the glass smashed. *Oh, Jesus Christ, burglars!*

Standing there, she felt a sensation of helplessness. She saw the phone and knew that she would have to dial 999. In a minute. She wanted to scream but knew it wouldn't do any good. Then she wondered if she ought to run home and phone from there, seeing the devastation in the kitchen, cupboards tipped out, broken glass on the floor; even the hanging herbs had been ripped down.

She was aware that the trail of destruction led into the hall, right to where she was standing beneath the stairway. Fragments and shards of broken pine – the bastards had even wrecked the stair rail and smashed that wooden bannister with its upright struts. She looked up – and saw the dangling feet, rumpled blue socks, a frayed black trainer on one foot; the other shoe was missing. The feet swung gently to and fro . . .

She whimpered her fear aloud as her eyes followed on up, to the blood-streaked shredded jeans, the ripped T-shirt. And then the head, a broken strut of railing impaling the throat and somehow suspending the body just below the level of the landing where it had fallen through. Arms hung limply by the corpse's side, and the twisted, dead features were agonized beneath the mask of dried, caked blood. Creaking beneath its own weight, the body was waiting for the executioner to come and take down his victim.

There was blood everywhere. She had not noticed it until now. The jugular had sprayed it all over, on walls and ceiling, and it had dripped down to the floor below. And dried.

The woodwork above creaked, cracked; the corpse lurched, dropped another few inches but still hung there as if it was being gently lowered to the floor below. It started to creak again . . .

That was when Janet Johnson ran screaming hysterically into the street outside.

PART TWO
Autumn

12

It had been a traumatic evening for John Strike, beginning with a phone call at the bank just as he was about to leave. Brian Johnson, obviously shaken, explained what his wife had found when she went to check Number Thirteen over. Of course, the Johnsons would help as much as they could; they were even prepared to bed Sam and Sarah down in sleeping bags in the spare room for tonight. Just for tonight.

The police were in the house when John arrived. Scenes of crime men, a slightly officious inspector who interrogated John for over an hour, even implying that the bank accountant was not entirely above suspicion. Could he find alternative accommodation for tonight? There were extensive forensic investigations to be carried out which would take up most of tomorrow. And, after all, nobody would want to sleep in the house after *this*, would they?

The dead man, the policeman reluctantly revealed, had three convictions for burglary, two with violence, and was currently on bail over another break-in. So nobody was really sorry, but the correct procedures had to be adhered to.

John would stay with Ruth, but first he had to call Leah – and that wasn't going to be easy.

'How's your father?' He'd eased into it gently. He didn't give a damn how his father-in-law was, a grumpy old bugger who thought that no man was good enough for his daughter.

'He's much better.' Which meant that he had not been all that ill to begin with. 'Just a slight loss of the use of one arm, but the doctor says it should come back in a few weeks and so long as he takes it steady he might go another twenty years. How's – '

John told her, sparing her the gory details. A second spraying of arterial blood on the walls was enough to make anybody want to move house. Even John himself.

'Oh, my God!' He pictured her features blanching with the impact of the shock. 'John, I *can't* go back *there*!'

'No, I'm not asking you to.'

'And I don't want the children through the door of Number Thirteen again. Ever. It's jinxed. Haunted. There's something terribly evil lurking there.'

'Yes, I'm inclined to agree with you. Now, what I propose is this . . .' He had thought it all out carefully once the initial shock wore off. Leah and Ben could stay in Wales with her parents. He would put Sam and Sarah on the train tomorrow and they could stay with her for the time being. The school in London would understand. Or, at least, they probably wouldn't give a shit. He had to stay in town, of course, because of the bank. And Ruth. The situation was turning to his own advantage. That old adage was true, it was an ill wind . . .

'It seems the only possible solution.' Her agreement was reluctant. 'Can't you put some pressure on the agents to get the house sold?'

'I'll do that first thing in the morning,' he promised. Jesus, the sooner he had 13 Schooner Street out of his hair, the better.

'Poetic justice.' Ruth took the news philosophically, her obvious delight at the sight of John's suitcases in the hall over-ruling everything else. 'A fellow with convictions for burglary with violence falls downstairs and breaks his neck, so society is rid of one more leech. But I can understand what a shock it must be if it happens to be *your* house he chooses to have his fatal accident in.' But it meant that they would be together, for a time at least.

Her husband had reluctantly accepted that their marriage was over. She had expected a fuss, arguments, pleading. But he had taken her letter calmly. She wondered if he, too, had somebody else. No, it wasn't likely; he just welcomed the prospect of his freedom. The house would be sold, there would be a divorce in due course.

'When are you going to tell your wife about us?' she asked, as they made their way upstairs.

'The moment we've sold the house,' he replied. 'Obviously, I can't spring it on her in the midst of all this. I'm going to get tough with the agents tomorrow. Christ, if they can't sell a house in London, they can't sell anything!' Except when it happened to be 13 Schooner Street.

John experienced an unexpected feeling of euphoria. Possibly it was due to the relief of getting away from Number Thirteen, coupled with the knowledge that tonight he did not have to invent excuses or alibis to account for a late homecoming. In fact, he was not going home at all. This was to be his first full night with Ruth. And the result was a full erection before he had even finished undressing.

He stood there and let her fondle it as he began unbuttoning her blouse and unclasping her skirt. Kissing her, kneading her naked buttocks, he pushed her slowly back on to the bed. Once more his tongue traced that familiar downward path, flicked her erect nipples tantalizingly, explored her navel. The trimmed black pubic hair was erotic to touch. Her thighs opened readily, stretched wide for him.

'Kiss me *there*, John, *please*,' she groaned.

The soft wet warmth, the scent of talc was making him heady with an urge for much more than loveplay in a semi-darkened room. Suddenly he straightened up and said, 'Hang on a minute.'

She watched wide-eyed as he went to the suitcase in the corner of the bedroom. She heard the locks snap open, then a rustling of clothes as he searched frantically for something, a grunted 'ah!' when he found it.

'What's that?' she asked in trepidation; it looked like a camera he was holding.

'A Polaroid.' He was watching her carefully for a reaction. 'People buy them for taking naughty pics. Instant developing, no risk of a voyeur lusting over them in the lab.'

'Oh!' She felt a mixture of nervousness and excitement but she made no move to close her thighs. 'Oh, I see.'

'You don't mind . . . do you?'

She closed her eyes. No, she didn't mind, the very thought was almost enough to make her orgasm there and then. 'I don't mind.' She stopped herself from adding, 'If you really want to' because she wanted him to. Very much.

He lay on the bed between her outstretched legs, the camera positioned close to that throbbing, tingling part of her body. She wanted him to look at it, stroke it, to photograph it. And afterwards to . . .

A brilliant flash blinded her for a few seconds and when her vision returned he was kneeling up, holding the camera by a flex; counting. He tugged the white tab that protruded from the side and peeled off a square of paper, then studied it. 'Perfect,' he breathed, 'absolutely perfect!'

She looked at the photograph, saw every detail in the picture and knew that she could not contain herself much longer.

'Will you do me a favour?' he asked, and his voice trembled slightly.

'Yes.' Her reply was instant, her hand reaching out for the Polaroid camera. Because right now, more than anything else in the world, she wanted to photograph that erection, to keep the picture in some secret place where she could sneak off and lust over it; and maybe do those things to herself which she had been doing during the last couple of years of her ailing marriage.

John Strike was back in Number Thirteen, because there were things he had to do, things which had been preying on his mind all day. He felt a furtive stranger in his own house, like that burglar. He tried not to look at the broken stair rail and the blood-spattered walls. But in an hour or so he would be leaving, going back to Ruth.

Sam and Sarah had gone to Wales that morning. John had taken the day off work and driven them to Euston to put them on the train. A long journey lay ahead of them, the inter-city to Wolverhampton then a slow train to Aberystwyth, changing for Barmouth at Machynlleth. Leah would meet them off the train. She had done that, he had phoned to make sure that they had arrived an hour ago.

'Where are you staying, John?' The inevitable question.

'At home.' *For a little while*. 'There's a lot of cleaning-up to do if we're ever going to sell the place.'

'Which we won't.' She didn't believe him and sounded despondent.

'We will, I promise you.' But not in the way she meant. Because he had planned it all today, here in this awful depressing house with its cold dampness with the heating turned off. Autumn had announced its coming. Outside it was already dark and it was drizzling. He shivered.

Leah was right, of course. There was no way anybody was going to buy 13 Schooner Street. The estate agent wasn't saying so outright, but John could tell by his tone. Maybe he, too, had sensed what lurked here, that feeling of foreboding and hostility. Maybe the atmosphere stretched beyond the house, even, and in some way manifested itself in the agent's brochure, a sense of eeriness that came over in the description of the property. 'Suited to renovation.' In other words, it needed work doing on it. Like thousands of other pre-war houses on the market.

Two enquiries in six weeks; a fellow who had not turned up for his viewing appointment and a couple who had virtually fled the place in terror. Nobody else would come, John had resigned himself to that. Which was why he had to do what he planned to do tonight.

The feeling was strong tonight, stronger than before. There was definitely somebody else here. He couldn't see them; he thought he heard somebody breathing, but when he stopped to listen there was only silence. *A silence that lived and moved around him.*

John moved with a purposefulness now. He gathered up the pieces of broken stair rail that littered the hall, an armful of tinder-dry pinewood, and glanced round instinctively. I know you're watching me, he thought, you might even guess what I'm going to do. But you won't stop me!

I stopped that burglar in his act of desecrating my house.

Sweating in spite of the cold, he went through to the front room. The existing fireplace was still there, a yawning cavern beneath the ugly tiled mantelshelf, still caked with a covering of soot from yesteryear. Unused but unblocked, its concealment had been one of his priorities. He was glad that he had never got round to it. Because tonight he needed it.

He was crumpling up a newspaper, stuffing it into the old cast-iron grate, laying the sticks criss-cross fashion – the way he had done when he was a boy and they had an open range in the kitchen. The pile of wood would surely be sufficient. More newspapers, he was filling the hearth with them and making a trail that led across to the cheap sofa. In all probability it was foam-filled, and that was an added bonus.

He straightened up and stood back to survey his handiwork, aware how he trembled. Not just the house, his whole crazy plan terrified him. Number Thirteen would not sell, so he had a choice: either continue to live here with this escalating catalogue of phobias that were becoming terrifying reality or . . . get rid of it. Fire was the obvious answer. An accident. Nobody could possibly prove otherwise. Could they?

Even in London, people had open fires. Smokeless-fuel ones, of course. He should have purchased a small bag of Phurnacite. Wood was a forbidden fuel because it gave off smoke and smelled sweet. But you had to use kindling to light a fire. Actually, it was so bloody cold in there, and I couldn't get the central heating to work, so I just burned some bits and pieces of rubbish, he rehearsed. It sounded plausible. To him.

Damn it, if I don't light it now I never will, he told himself. Light it and get the hell out of here. Tomorrow morning there will be a message at the bank. *We've some bad news for you, Mr Strike. Last night your house burned down. Gutted. You shouldn't have lit an open fire and left it*. But that wasn't a crime, just crass carelessness. The insurance company would fork out, albeit grudgingly.

Just one match, that was all that was needed. It reminded him of an old TV commercial, he couldn't remember the brand name. The matches were in the kitchen on the shelf above the gas cooker.

Turning quickly, he stumbled because for one moment he had the impression that he was about to bump into somebody. A stifled curse died on his lips. He was sweating; trembling, too.

Almost running through into the kitchen, he half expected the box of cook's matches to be missing or the box to be empty. Neither; he grabbed them, shook them, heard them rattle. Fuck you, you're beaten now, you bastard, he thought. You're going to roast in your own hell!

Back in the front room, the matchbox in one hand, the drawer open an inch or so, he was fumbling to get a grip on an elusive sliver of wood. *And then the doorbell rang.*

Blind terror almost had him fleeing through the rear patio doors and scaling the rickety fence. Instead, he just stood there clasping that partly open box in guilt and fear. *All right, you've caught me, I was going to set fire to the house.* With an effort he pulled himself together.

Who the hell could it be? He felt apprehensive about a direct confrontation with an unknown caller.

The police?

A possibility.

A viewer called on spec?

Another possibility, but an unlikely one.

The Johnsons?

No, they wouldn't come round, they would telephone, as they always did; a trend of the nouveaux riches.

The doorbell rang a second time, more insistently; three peals.

All right, I'm coming. He closed the matchbox and put it on the mantelshelf. He stooped to gather up the balls of newspaper that spilled out of the hearth and across the carpet, stuffing them back in the fireplace. *I was thinking of lighting a fire, just enough to keep me warm until I'd finished.*

He thought he heard an intake of breath, almost a snigger, out in the hall. He darted to the door but there was nobody in sight. Just somebody outside in the porch, reaching out to press the bell push again. He beat them to it, wrenched the front door open and stared in shocked surprise at the girl who stood on the threshold, her green mac and dark hair dampened by the drizzle.

'*Ruth!*'

'John, are you all right?' Her smile changed to an expression of concern, her hand reaching out for his. She squeezed past him, pushing the door closed behind her.

'I'm okay.'

'You don't look it.' She regarded him closely. 'In fact, you look ill.' Her features softened into a sympathetic smile. 'Still, I suppose it's no wonder after what has happened. All the same, you could have found a minute to phone me today. When you hadn't turned up at my place by eight I thought I'd better come and look for you, and this seemed the obvious place to start.'

'You could have phoned.'

'I've been trying to call you since six!'

Those icicles were sliding down his back again. 'Oh, the phone must be out of order. I haven't tried it.' *And I'm not going to now*.

'Making a fire?' She had followed him back into the room, glancing at the heap of rumpled papers which had already begun to unfurl and were falling out into the hearth.

'Yes!' He was abrupt even though he had not meant to be, his tension erupting into that monosyllabic reply. *Mind your own bloody business!* 'I'm sorry, this place has got on my nerves. I was just going to burn some rubbish for a little warmth. The central heating has gone wrong.'

Damn it, I could still light it! When he left here, Ruth would go with him. He searched for an excuse to be left alone, just long enough to strike one match. *Look, you go on ahead, get the tube. I'll finish off, follow on the next*. No, that wouldn't work; she'd ask why and be suspicious. Or: *Look, I'm going to burn the house down, claim the insurance. I know you won't shop me*. She wouldn't. Yet. Unless things turned sour between them, and it did not necessarily have to be because of Leah. That was too dangerous.

I'll have to come back and light the fire tomorrow evening.

He stiffened because he thought he heard those lungs rattling again – in the kitchen? Or on the stairs? He turned round quickly.

'You're jumpy, John. Your nerves are all on edge.'

'Yeah, it's this place. It'll never be the same again.'

'I think it's . . . *eerie*!' She pressed up close against him. 'I don't think I could spend a night here. It's as if . . . *as if there's somebody around who you can't see!*'

His flesh went cold. 'Let's go.' He steered her out into the hall, averting his gaze so that he did not have to look at those blood-streaked walls again. 'I don't need to do any more here tonight. I might pop back tomorrow after work. If I do, then you'll know where I've gone. Don't come traipsing after me, I'll come back to your place when I've finished.'

He was beaten. No, just thwarted, he told himself. A postponement of arson. He would see it through tomorrow.

The door banged behind them, echoing down the hallway like the slamming of a tomb entrance on its latest occupant. And as they moved out on to the pavement he heard the laughter.

Just one peal, mocking him because it had defeated him. The sound jarred his brain and brought back reminders of death that would have had him screaming his terror aloud had it not been for Ruth clinging to his arm. His thoughts kaleidoscoped: a road accident, the decapitated head in the Morris Minor; drowning, a corpse mouthing its curses on the bottom of the swimming bath; writhing in pain as a thrombosis took him. And then seeing the crushed infant body beneath the wheels of the Suzuki and knowing that it was Ben.

Somehow he fought them all off, dispelled them. But this time it was more than a phobia; it was a premonition of death.

But whose?

13

'All this business isn't doing your father much good in his state of health!' Leah's mother came into the spare bedroom shortly before eight o'clock, drew the curtains back with obvious displeasure and stood with folded arms at the foot of the bed.

Leah stirred and propped herself up on an elbow. Ben was still fast asleep.

Marjorie Bourne was sixty-five, five years younger than her husband, slight of build and walked with an arthritic limp. Sharp-featured, she wore an expression of perpetual dissatisfaction and was usually at her most bad-tempered during the first two hours after rising, until her limbs became fully mobile. Looking after George was bad enough, she thought; he needed constant nagging to do as he was instructed. She didn't mind Leah and Ben for a few days, but the other two children filled the small seafront house up, shattered the peace and quiet she craved and generally made life intolerable. The next thing, John would be turning up without so much as a by-your-leave, and that would be the limit. She had not liked her son-in-law from the first moment she saw him, and she liked him a whole lot less after he got Leah into trouble. She would never forgive him for that.

'Would you like us to go back home then?' Leah snapped irritably. She realized that if she left John she could not stand living with her parents. Already, Mother was trying to make her feel guilty for coming here, even though she had asked her to come. Whatever you did, it had to be on Mother's terms even if you were doing her a favour.

'No.' Marjorie Bourne looked startled. 'No, you can't go back to that dreadful house. But I should have thought your husband would have taken steps to find you alternative accommodation.' She avoided referring to John by his name; it was usually 'your husband' or, if she was particularly annoyed, 'that man'.

'*You* asked me to come and stay for a few days, which I did, even though it wasn't convenient.' Trying to make *her* feel guilty, Leah knew, was a ploy that never worked. 'But it wasn't my fault that a burglar broke into our house and killed himself, was it? Sam and Sarah couldn't stay behind with nobody to look after them, so John did the obvious thing and sent them on here.'

'How long are you going to stay?'

'I don't know. A week, perhaps a fortnight. We'll have to play it by ear. The children are too frightened to go back to Schooner Street, so we'll have to find another house, rent one if necessary.' She wondered again where John was staying. If he was still at Number Thirteen then he wasn't answering the phone. Presumably because he was shacked up with some floosie and taking advantage of the situation. But her mother must never even guess. Much as her mother disliked John, in her book marriage was for life, for better or for worse. She would never accept a divorce.

'It's your father I'm worried about.'

'The children have been exceptionally good. Apart from one argument, which I stopped. You can't blame them, Mother.'

'It creates an air of disquiet having children in the house. It mithers your father.'

'It didn't appear to yesterday. In fact, he seemed to be enjoying having them here.'

'Your father puts up with a lot.'

That was true. He had tolerated her mother for forty-one years! Leah sighed. She knew only too well what her mother was hinting at: You'll have to keep the children out of *his* way because they're getting on *my* nerves.

'I'll take them out for the day.' Leah heard the wind buffeting the window, but at least it did not appear to be raining. A typical autumn seaside day, cold and blustery.

'I don't want to drive you out of the house . . .'

You do and we'll go. 'I'll take them somewhere for the day.' *Christ knows where*. 'It might have been better to have let them sleep in for an hour, they need all the rest they can get.' *And so do I*.

'I would have done, except that I have to get the house cleaned.' Marjorie had been unable to extricate herself from the routine she followed when the place was a seaside guest-house. Breakfast at nine, everybody out of their rooms by ten and not allowed back until four-thirty. Now her daughter and grandchildren were her boarding-house guests and the old rules were in force again.

'I'll get the others up and give them some breakfast.' Leah swung her legs to the floor and watched her mother leave the room. Her mother was next in line for a stroke if she did not ease up. Leah sighed, and went across the landing to the bathroom.

She thought about phoning John at the bank but decided against it. If he had any news he would call her, and right now he was the last person she wanted to talk to.

The children seemed to sense the atmosphere in the big kitchen, and ate their cornflakes and toast and marmalade in relative silence. They were in obvious awe of Grandma and kept glancing nervously in the direction of the sink, where she was washing their crockery the moment they had finished with them.

‘Hallo, Grandpa.’ Ben broke the silence. Heads turned towards George Bourne, who appeared in the doorway wearing a tartan dressing gown over his striped pyjamas.

He was thickset and bald-headed. His usually ruddy complexion had paled with his illness, but his thick lips smiled and he beamed at his grandchildren through heavy-rimmed glasses. ‘Good morning, children. And how are you all this morning?’

‘Okay,’ Sam replied, and Ben shrilled, ‘We’re going out for the day today.’

‘George!’ Marjorie’s exclamation of surprise at seeing her husband downstairs so early bordered on the hysterical. ‘George, you should be resting in bed!’

‘I’m fed up with damned bed.’ His reponse was jovial. ‘If I’m going to die then I’ll die downstairs, not like some damned invalid.’

‘Mind your language in front of the children!’ Marjorie snapped.

‘They’re not going out on a day like this!’ He was incredulous. ‘They’ll catch pneumonia! Make the fire up in the lounge for them, Mother.’ He had called his wife ‘Mother’ ever since Leah could remember. Nowadays it seemed to reflect a nonsexual marriage. Which had probably been the case for the last thirty years, she reflected.

‘It’s bracing.’ Leah attempted to defuse the situation. ‘A good walk along Marine Parade will do the children good, and then I’ll find somewhere under cover to take them.’

Where? It was out of season; even the amusement arcades were closed. Definitely not the swimming baths. Nor a zoo, if there was one nearby. Maybe a coach trip if she could find a coach that was running. She would think of something, take a bus to Harlech or Portmadoc. The priority was to get out of the house.

Twenty minutes later, clad in their Barbours with rainproof hoods, except for Ben, who insisted on wearing his red and white Arsenal peaked hat, they left the house. The wind was strong, coming off the sea and driving spray and fine sand across the road. Foam-tipped breakers crashed against the sea wall, and part of the promenade was under water. Leah had to turn her head to get her breath.

The seafront was deserted, except for half a dozen parked cars and a man in the distance walking his dog. Ben was carrying his new football, the one John had bought to replace the old punctured one. He had insisted on bringing it along and Leah had not forbidden him, because the last thing she wanted was a scene in front of her mother. Just something extra for me to carry in ten minutes, she sighed to herself; there was no chance of the boys being able to kick a ball about anywhere today.

She decided to head for the harbour. It would be more sheltered that end and it was only a couple of minutes' walk from the town. The place had an air of desolation about it – the funfair all boarded up, seafood and ice-cream stalls shuttered and abandoned until next season. Even the harbour café was closed.

Leah made for a shelter alongside the harbour, a three-sided concrete structure with its back to the prevailing winds and a bench, a refuge for the elderly on inclement summer days. It was a breather, somewhere to plan the next move. Across the road was the lifeboat station. That, too, was locked up.

'Mum, what are we going to do?' Sam asked.

'We'll go into town in a minute and have a drink somewhere.' The first of endless rounds of coke and coffee to pass the time.

'Don't want a drink.' Ben was bored. She couldn't blame him; it was going to be a difficult day.

'Perhaps the wind will drop and the sun will come out in a bit,' Leah said. She knew it wouldn't; the forecast was bad for the next couple of days. Soon it would start to rain.

'I want to play football.' He bounced his ball in a puddle, splashing the inside of the shelter.

'Well, you can't, Ben, and don't bounce that ball, you'll soak everybody.'

He looked at her defiantly. The ball floated in the pool of water and came to rest against his foot. Ben's foot went back, hesitated, and then drove forward with all the force that the three-year-old could muster. There was a spray of water as the football cannoned against the side of the shelter. It bounced back, spun, and rolled across the road towards the lifeboat station.

And before Leah could grab him, Ben had darted in pursuit.

It was the moment that every mother dreads and is alert to; but when it happens she is unprepared. Her reactions froze for one terrible second during which Ben was lost to her view behind the shelter. Neither Sam nor Sarah had moved. Leah leaped; ran.

She saw Ben. He was already on the opposite side of the road. The ball had hit the shed doors and was rolling back on the gradient. He reached for it in a clumsy infantile way, but somehow it eluded his outstretched hands and gathered momentum.

'*Ben! Stay . . . where . . . you . . . are!*'

In that moment of panic Leah found herself absolutely helpless. She might have screamed, but for some reason she didn't. Ben was shambling after his football, totally oblivious of the oncoming vehicle.

Even in her terror Leah thought that for some unaccountable reason John had arrived. She saw the approaching jeep, a red Suzuki which might for one moment have been the Strikes', except that it was mud-spattered and being driven at speed. The driver's face was in shadow but she knew now that it was not her husband.

She managed to scream at last. It made no difference. She wanted to throw herself into the road; *run over me, then, but spare my boy*. She only made it to the kerbside, but by then the Suzuki was level with her; past her; braking; a screech of tyres; skidding; slewing.

She heard the impact, the crunch, even though she tried to close her ears to it, then the terrible sound of the locked wheels going over something in the road and that something being broken up, splintering. She told herself it was that stupid football – it had burst and was shredding – and Ben was still on the opposite side of the road. She almost believed it.

Until she saw the muddied football cap and the blood that matched its Arsenal colours.

The crowd was huddling, gawping. She had to fight her way through. Somebody caught her sleeve but she tugged herself free. *For God's sake, let me go to my baby!*

Heedless of the blood, she was cradling the crushed, bleeding form to her, smearing herself with the grey substance that oozed out of the splintered cranium. It was unrecognizable, except to her.

Vague hope infiltrated her crazed mind. The stink of an unwashed body, the filthy ragged clothing. Her screams took on a note of hysterical relief. She turned to the crowd, but it had mysteriously vanished except for three faces: Sam and Sarah, and the driver, puking.

'It's all right!' She was yelling at them. 'I tell you, it's all right. It's only a vagrant.' *Like before*.

Except that it wasn't.

This time it was Ben.

14

'Time to get up.' Ruth Ford shook John Strike gently as she placed a mug of tea on the bedside table. 'It's nearly seven and we have to get a tube around eight.'

'Uh?' He stirred, opening his eyes, blinking, waiting for everything to come back to him. It did, and he groaned inwardly. It was Ruth who had prevented him from setting fire to Number Thirteen last night. 'It's Wednesday and we have to go to work.' She was wearing her pink housecoat and he could tell from the way her damp hair straggled that she had already bathed.

'I . . . I'm not going in today.' He closed his eyes and let them stay closed.

'John, aren't you feeling well?' There was genuine concern in her voice as she leaned over him.

'No.' He paused, giving himself time to think. 'I . . . I have migraines from time to time. Do you think you could close the curtains?'

She moved swiftly to oblige him, and the room was plunged into the kind of dismal gloom that seeps through the curtains on a rainy autumn morning. 'I'm sorry, I'd better tell them at the bank . . .'

'No, don't do that!'

'Oh, I forgot. Of course not. Will you ring in later?'

'I suppose so. But don't you worry about me, love. I'll still be here when you get back.'

'All right.' She walked towards the door. 'Maybe I'll phone later to see how you are.'

'No, please.' Migraines were useful alibis, he thought, because the sufferer did not like being disturbed. 'I'd rather just be left in peace. It'll probably start to go about lunchtime. Mine rarely last more than twelve hours.'

'All right.' She was on her way back to the bathroom to get dressed. 'Don't worry about a thing. I'll be home around six.'

Eight-ten and he had the house to himself. More than that, he had his freedom – and an alibi, if necessary. But there was no hurry. He lay there but sleep was out of the question, relaxation nigh impossible. He knew what he had to do and he did not want to slip up by rushing things. He had eight hours in which to finish what he had started last night.

About nine o'clock he rose, bathed and dressed. He made a mug of coffee in the kitchen and took his time. Nobody was going to stop him today. And shortly before ten he let himself out of the house into the rain-lashed morning. With luck, he would be back here by midday.

It was like a rerun of an old film, standing there on the pavement looking across at 13 Schooner Street, the house with features that were twisted into a malevolent scowl and eyes that saw and recognized him. *So you've come back, but it won't do you any good, John Strike.*

Fuck you! He was angry and defiant, and told himself that he was not afraid, because it was broad daylight and nothing could harm him.

That burglar had been killed, and that was afternoon.

This will take me about two minutes, he reasoned. And I can even leave the front door ajar, in case I have to make a run for it.

Standing out in the street was unwise, people might see him, recognize him. *Yes, officer, I saw Mr Strike in the vicinity around . . .*

Ten-forty.

The collar of his waterproof turned up, he headed

across the road. There was nobody in sight, just parked vehicles on both sides. The Suzuki looked forlorn, almost as if it would never start again. He would come and fetch it tomorrow. It might arouse suspicions if he drove away in it now.

He glanced at the Johnsons' house; there was no sign of life. Brian would have been in the city three hours ago, Jeremy was back at boarding school. And in all probability Janet was still in bed. The lazy cow, John thought, she's probably got a vibrator. She was the sort, definitely; fucked herself every morning with a plastic cock and kidded herself that she had a string of lovers. Another fantasy to add to the yuppy image she was trying to create.

He sensed the presence that lurked in the house even as he pushed open the front door. It seemed to come at him down the hallway in a cold fetid rush of air, clammy fingers stroking his face, his hands. But this time he would beat it. Whatever it was, it would be destroyed, incinerated in its own foul lair before this day was out.

The crumpled newspapers had unfurled and spilled out of the fireplace in the front room, arranging themselves virtually how he had strewn them originally, before he had panicked and stuffed them back in the hearth when the doorbell rang. Now they were back across the carpet and up against that foam-filled sofa.

Like the tobacco advert of yesteryear, all he needed was one match.

The matches were back on the mantelshelf. He picked them up, shook the box and heard it rattle. It will only take a second and then I'll be gone from here, he thought. And when I return I'll be standing in that same place across the road, only everything will be different because Number Thirteen will just be a blackened heap of rubble, the ashes of a funeral pyre. And whatever lives here will be dead!

He heard a sound that seemed to come from the kitchen, a sharp intake of breath. *Fear!* Jesus, it was scared now. He wondered if spooks could shit themselves.

A sense of elation, gloating, overcame his own fear. 'Can you hear me, you bastard?'

No reply. Just total silence. It was bloody frightened, and so it should be – because nothing could stop him now.

He opened the drawer of the matchbox, extracted a match with his forefinger and thumb, and held it against the emery paper. It was like holding a pistol, he thought, fingering the trigger but not applying pressure, savouring the situation. *You're going to die and I don't want it to be too quick because I want you to suffer.*

He imagined the fire – the papers catching, the kindling crackling as the flames licked at them, showering sparks. A tongue of fire shooting up the old chimney, smoke billowing back because it was blocked by an old sootfall that had never been cleared. More flames running down into the hearth, hungry for the balls of paper, jumping from one to the next, scorching the settee, blackening it. Then *whoosh*, going up in a ball of fire right to the ceiling, like in those public information films on telly warning of the dangers of inflammable furniture, engulfing the entire room, a raging inferno that spread in all directions. By the time the windows were cracking and smoke pouring out into the street it would be too late. *Oh, sweet Jesus, it would!*

Then fire engines blocking the street, those yuppy BMWs obstructing the crews as they raced to spray foam on a lost cause. *We can't save Number Thirteen but we have to stop the blaze spreading to the adjoining houses.*

Firefighters wearing breathing apparatus trying to determine if anybody was trapped inside but being forced back by the heat, sure there was somebody inside – or, rather, *something*. Listening above the hiss of foam and the crackling of the inferno, and hearing its wheezing screams, the sound of phlegm sizzling in wasted lungs . . .

John was aware of its presence, its cloying foulness. He smelled it, *felt* it closer than ever before, the sheer evil that surrounded him, clutched at him and tried to stop him. Fighting it, he forced his fingers to move, rasping the matchhead on the emery, scraping for a flame. Just one match . . .

And then the doorbell chimed.

Fucking hell, I don't believe it. Déjà vu. It was that same old film, you couldn't change it. Outside Ruth Ford would be standing, a bedraggled figure in the morning rain, relief on her face because she had found him. *Oh, John, I was so worried when I came back home and you weren't there. But I knew you would be here.*

As before, he gathered up the papers and stuffed them back into the fireplace so that they would fall out again and be ready for the next time. And the time after that.

Hearing that wheezing laughter follow him down the hallway, he paused to pull himself together and then opened the door.

'Ruth, I . . .'

It wasn't Ruth, it was a uniformed police officer removing his flat hat and preparing to step inside. His companion was at the wheel of a car in the road, trying to back into a space opposite. Clearly they were likely to be here some time.

John stepped back. He almost dropped the matchbox as he missed the pocket of his waterproof with it. *Oh, God alive, they know!*

'Mr Strike? Mr John Strike?'

He nodded, gulping his guilt . . . attempted arson, attempting to defraud the insurance company.

'I'm afraid I have some bad news for you, sir. May we go into the room' – *the one where you were trying to start the fire to burn down this house* – 'and sit down?'

John sat in the armchair, the policeman on the foam sofa. The papers were rustling their way out of their crumples, starting to lay the trail again as if they had been specially trained in the job.

'Your son, sir.' The officer was white-faced, his lower lip trembled. A rookie, the sergeant had done the dirty on him and sent him inside whilst he parked the car. 'He was run over in Barmouth earlier this morning. I'm afraid he's . . .' The word that everybody chickened out of.

'*Dead!*' For John Strike it didn't register. Not at first. He barely listened to the words because those damned newspapers were set on proving his guilt, constructing the crime before it was committed, louder and louder, trying to attract the policeman's attention. *Look, officer. See, this is how it was going to be*. But the policeman wasn't looking anywhere except at John Strike's deathly white features.

'He was killed instantly. Your wife is under sedation with her parents. Would you like me to get you a doctor, sir?'

The room began to tilt, in stages. The floor heaved one way, then the other, then started to spin. The blur went faster and faster until the uniformed man's features were unrecognizable. They might have been those of an old man in a navy blue overcoat mouthing mute words.

Then, for John Strike, everything went black.

The rain had eased to a fast drizzle with the coming of darkness. Schooner Street was shiny wet. Cars threw up spray as they rushed by, suburban evening traffic that found its peak around ten-thirty then died down to an intermittent trickle of closing-time homecomers. The quiet backwater was near silent by midnight, with just the occasional hurrying footsteps.

Mike Gilson's sweater was damp from the drizzle during the half-mile walk from the Indian restaurant, his jeans clung wetly to his legs, and his erection was causing him considerable discomfort. Tall and well-built, his strong arm held the girl at his side close to him, impeding their walk. He bent his head and kissed the top of her wet fair hair.

Tracey was pretty, but that wasn't the only reason he had dated her every night for a week – except for Sunday, when her parents had insisted that she accompanied them on a visit to relatives. Her folk had money, and she herself had an eighty-pound-a-week job at the coffee bar where he had first chatted her up. That was a lot of money, when he was out of work. Tracey had paid for the meal tonight, as she had done for the past five nights. But tonight he wanted more than that; his arousal was demanding it.

She was eighteen and a virgin, and always told the truth. She was innocent in present-day terms. He was looking for a darkened porchway, a shelter where they could smooch and he could try his luck again. Two nights ago she had let him slide a hand up her blouse, had not really objected to having her tits felt. Last night he had progressed another step. She had not put up too much resistance when that same hand found its way up her skirt, but she had not been too eager to ease her legs apart so that he could stroke in between them. The tip of his finger penetrated enough to tell him that she was sopping wet but he couldn't go any further. *Keep working at it, feller*. Jeez, just thinking about it was enough to make him come in his pants!

There was a house with unlit windows, the gate half open as if it had been expecting them. *Come on in, try your luck here.*

'I mustn't be late home tonight,' she said, as he steered her into the porch and the shadows cast a protective mantle over their pressed bodies.

'You won't be.' He kissed her, grasped her tight buttocks and pulled her close to him so that his hardness dug into her closed thighs.

He went over the ground he had gained so far, flipping her coat buttons and going up her blouse. Her nipples were like sharp spikes inside the cups of her bra. Then under her denim skirt, rubbing in an attempt to make her lubricate. She still kept his finger partly at bay but her pants were dampening, and that was a hopeful sign. He prodded at her with his erection; if he had not been holding her tightly to him she would have backed off.

'I'd like to go home.' She was tense suddenly, and it made her all the more desirable, had his hardness stretching still further, throbbing and pulsing.

'Soon.' He had made up his mind to have her tonight. He had been thinking about it all day; now it was a driving obsession. This very place spurred him on, gave power to his lust. It was like a void apart from the rest of the world, where nobody would hear if she screamed.

His left hand went down, found his zip and ran it. Fumbling his thick length of turgid flesh out of the vent, he forced her unwilling fingers against it. She was resisting, trying to snatch away, but he rubbed her fingertips on his own slippery warmth.

'Don't!' A frightened plea, but he had her in a corner. 'Please, I don't want to.'

'*I* do!' The laugh did not sound like his own. 'Look, let me just touch you with it, put it against you. No further than my finger went.'

She began to struggle as he found the elastic of her pants and pulled hard. A ripping sound, then he was up against her, feeling her silky pubes, but her pressed thighs still denied him. He was breathing heavily, aware of the mounting tension in his lower regions. He could not hold off much longer. The beginnings of an orgasm fuelled his desperation.

Take her!

The whisper might have been inside his lusting brain, or borne on the damp autumn night. Insistent, goading, it was urging him on, like a voyeur in the deep shadows impatient and eager to witness the full act.

His strong fingers prised her thighs apart. He thrust forward, found her entrance, and her softness closed over him. Now she was fighting him, trying to pull apart, but there was nowhere to escape in the corner. She clawed at his face with her fingernails but he was impervious to any sensations other than the one which obsessed him. He powered into her with his sheer strength, his orgasm beginning, escalating.

He heard a soft laugh somewhere in the darkness but he ignored it, pinioning her against the rough brickwork as he shuddered and groaned his delight aloud.

His ecstasy was short-lived, giving way to fear as she began to scream, hysterical now that he had had his way and his lust had subsided. He was aware of what he had done, and of the consequences. He apologized, pleading with her, but she did not hear him. She was shrieking, yelling for somebody to help her because her virginity was no more. Her cries echoed in that dark porch and gathered volume. But amidst them, at the height of his fear and panic, he heard that rasping whisper again.

Silence her!

Once again he had no control over his body. Hands

moved uncontrollably, fingers encircled the slender neck and tightened.

'Shut up, you bitch!'

Her screams were now choking gurgles, her arms flailed and struck him feebly. She was afraid but hated him. There could be no forgiveness. No compromise.

His hands tightened still further, squeezing until even the croaking whispers were silenced. Her eyes bulged like air bubbles about to burst but did not see. Not struggling, she hung limply in his grasp like an outsize rag doll. And when he loosened his hold she crumpled into a heap at his feet.

He stared down at the huddled form and poked at it with his foot. It rolled back, the head striking the wall with a sickening thud of finality, twisting round as if to look at him. Obscene in her posture, her thighs were now wide as if inviting him to take her this time. In death.

He glanced about him, peering into the darkness, seeking the owner of the voice that had urged him on; perhaps now he could offer help. But there was nobody there, just the cold dampness of the autumn night reaching out to touch him.

Then he was fleeing blindly from the porchway of that dreadful house where death lurked and where the number on the door was thirteen.

15

Number Thirteen Schooner Street had become a source of acute embarrassment for Don Lester. His sense of relief when the Strikes bought it had been short-lived. Now they wanted to sell it again, fast! Why?

He stayed on in the office after the rest of the staff had gone, poring over the photocopied brochure of the house. There *had* to be a reason why nobody wanted it, and when at last it was bought the new owners put it up for sale again within a matter of months.

He could, of course, have refused to handle it; sent the Strikes down to those new cowboy agents, passed the buck. But the easy way out was not his way, because he thrived on challenges. Never mind that very ordinary property in Hampstead was currently on offer at a cool million and gave him a generous cut; that was routine bread and butter, that type of residence sold itself. He would not rest until contracts had been exchanged again for Number Thirteen, and then that would be it! He certainly would not take it on again.

In the meantime, he decided, he needed to conduct a very thorough investigation into this problem house.

Don Lester was thirty-two and slight of build. Every movement he made was decisive, positive, even if it was only to pick up his pen and sign a cheque with a flourish. Fresh-faced, he wore glasses for astigmatism, had expensive suits specially tailored in Savile Row and drove a Jaguar XJS. He lived in Balham, worked seven days a week, and his only relaxation was a game of squash on Sunday mornings and a fortnight's skiing in January. A millionaire within weeks of his thirtieth birthday, he had set himself a target of his second million before he was thirty-five. So, logically, he should have ignored such incidentals as a jinxed property. Except that it rankled; he felt it reflected on his professionalism, was bad publicity for his firm. Sod it, he'd take it on personally and get it sold by the end of the week, drop everything else if necessary.

He checked the details methodically, ticked each one. The price was cheap if you took the latest increase in London property prices into consideration. There was no need to reduce it at this stage; in any other case he would have persuaded the vendor to add another three grand.

The surveyor's report was not brilliant but there were no major structural faults, just an overall shabbiness – which was usually the case before moneyed customers took over. Damn it, they had sold Number Fifty-two only a month ago for £125,000, and there had been scope for gazumping.

It was ideally situated for commuting to the city and set in the 'Gateway to the South', a catch phrase that had become tired and worn out. Selling houses was merely a matter of bringing seller and buyer together and taking a profit. Except in this case, he thought.

So the problem must rest with the house itself. Don had not been inside it, only seen it from the street on his way home. Therefore the next step was a personal inspection. He looked at his watch. Nine-thirty. He wondered if the Strikes would be at home; fuck it if it was inconvenient to look round, they'd have to put up with it if they wanted a quick sale. If they weren't, then he had a duplicate key; it was unethical, snooping round somebody's house when they were still living there, but fuck it again!

It wouldn't take long and it wasn't out of his way. He

thought about calling Melanie to tell her he would be late but decided against it. Once you began reporting your movements you were pandering to accountability like some bloody nine-to-five clerk. And you didn't make your second million that way.

There were no lights showing in Number Thirteen. Neither was there a parking space big enough for the Jag. He found one further up the road and reversed expertly into it. The heavy rain had slowed to a fine drizzle so he shrugged into his waterproof jacket and strode confidently down the street, the key in his hand. One ring of the doorbell; he could sense that there was nobody at home, so he went inside.

Jesus on a bike, what a bloody mess! He stepped back a pace and surveyed the broken stair rail and the blood-splashed walls in the dim hallway light. He thought that Strike would have cleaned that up by now, repaired the damage. No client would buy when he saw *that*! Don almost switched off the light and left, but he realized that this was not the problem. This had only happened a day or two ago; the problem went back much further than that. In all probability the police had asked Strike not to clear up yet. He'd better take a look over the rest of the place.

What was the silly bugger up to in here? Don Lester stared in amazement at the heap of crumpled newspapers that cascaded from the grate across the carpet. Surely he wasn't thinking of lighting a fire!

John Strike's talents, if he had any, certainly did not stretch to home decorating or any other form of DIY, for that matter. Don glanced over the kitchen: a right bodge-up. A would-be yuppie and no mistake!

It was not until he was upstairs that Don became aware of a sense of unease. Standing there in the main bedroom, he felt as though he was not alone in the house. He glanced behind him, resisting the temptation to glance into the wardrobe in case there was somebody hiding in there, and told himself that he had seen all that was necessary. He'd advise Strike to get the place cleaned up and repaired, that was all that was the matter with it. *But it wasn't.*

Don Lester swayed, feeling dizzy. Overwork, tiredness, probably. He knew he had an A-type personality, heart attack material. It was a suddenly frightening thought. Oh God! Anticipating chest pains, he stood there waiting for them to strike. There had been a lot in the papers recently about people who worked seven days a week, kept themselves fit, ate the right foods; and just went out like a light! Like himself.

Out on the landing, he had to clutch at the broken stair rail. This was where the burglar fell through, he remembered, speared his neck on a broken strut and hung there until they found him, jetting his blood all over the walls and ceiling. *Because he felt like I feel now!*

Don had to cling on to that flimsy support otherwise he would have fallen. He recognized the symptoms, one of them, anyway. Vertigo! The last time he had experienced it was on a skiing holiday in Switzerland, on a trip up the Jungfrau, when he'd gone out on to the balcony of the Ice Palace. Heights had never bothered him before but they had then. A sheer drop – the thought made him giddy, his breathing went shallow, and he wanted to sit down on the ground, to hold on to something. *Like now.*

He sank down to the floor, gripped the base of one of those uprights which was still intact and hung on grimly. Once again he had the feeling that somebody was watching him, sniggering. *Shut up, you bastard!* It was terrifying.

I'm not well, he thought. It was the logical explanation. The carpeted landing floor seemed to heave up; then settled again. He worked out how he was going to get downstairs – easy, the way he used to when he was two, before he could walk. He'd slide down on his arse, holding on to the rail all the way. Feet first, take it slowly and don't look down whatever you do, he told himself.

It was a slow process and he was aware that he was shaking, afraid. *Because there was definitely somebody watching him.*

It seemed like hours before he was finally sitting on the bottom stair. I won't get up for a minute. I'll just rest, he thought. I'll feel all right soon.

The vertigo passed and he stood up shakily. Maybe he would tell Strike to try those cowboy agents, after all, and just get the hell out of here!

Two, perhaps three, steps towards the front door, then he stopped abruptly. *Because the thought of going outside into the night was as frightening as those sensations upstairs. It was as if there was some invisible barrier between himself and the front door. He couldn't go outside. He was trapped in here!*

He was in a shabby prison with bloodstained walls, where the inmates were executed and the executioner hid and watched him. The sentence of death had been passed.

'This is bloody stupid!' Don Lester spoke aloud in an attempt to bolster his waning courage, but there was no mistaking the fear in his voice.

The telephone! One phone call and he was safe. Somebody would come and rescue him.

He stepped towards it, then checked himself. No, he couldn't do that. He could not even phone Melanie because that would be the end of his male domination. Anybody else would be ridiculed; and even his reputation was at stake. *Just let me out of that fucking door!*

With an effort, fighting all the way, he made it to the door and leaned up against the scratched paintwork. But there was no way he was going to open it and face the world which lay outside.

Sweating, he panicked within himself. He couldn't go outside, yet the thought of going back upstairs was too terrifying to contemplate. And remaining in this house would surely send him mad before morning.

Then he heard footsteps, outside, turning in from the street, clinking the small iron gate, and low, muffled voices. He knew that they were in the porch.

The Strikes, it must be them! They had returned from an evening out. Thank God! In sheer relief, Don Lester was already preparing the mental script of his story: I'm awfully sorry to have intruded but we had a call from a prospective purchaser, and in view of the problems with this property I thought I ought to have a look at it. I dared not leave it till morning, so I used the duplicate key. You'll have to get this mess cleared up. Get a carpenter to mend the stair rail, wash those walls down and make the place look respectable. You won't sell it if you don't. He thought that sounded feasible. And if he looked white and dishevelled, it was because he'd worked a sixteen-hour day.

He waited. Christ, what were they fucking about at in the porch? Probably they couldn't find their key. But he couldn't open up to let them in. Christ, the hall light was off; he hadn't noticed. He felt another stab of fear, then he realized he must have leaned up against the switch. *Hurry up, don't leave me a second longer!*

A rustling of clothing; probably turning their pockets out for that bloody key. The voices were too low for him to hear what they were saying.

He was still waiting. Something was wrong but he didn't know what. Movements that sounded like a struggle, then came a shrill, piercing scream that had Don

Lester backing away from the door. He heard a man's voice, rough and angry. 'Shut up, you bitch!'

The scream became a choking gurgle, then died away. There was a thud, as if one of them had fallen to the ground, and footsteps again, hurried ones that went back out into the street. Then just an awful silence, except for somebody breathing somewhere; it sounded as if they were inside the house, but that was impossible because the front door was still shut.

Don Lester crouched there in the darkness of the hallway, huddled against the cold, damp wall, afraid to flee; afraid to remain. It was a process of gradual insanity; he gave up willing the door to open, because there was something even more terrible beyond it. He grabbed the phone but was unable to make a call because his fingers would not respond to his fear-crazed brain. The handset swung on its coiled flex, bumped against the wall and purred its anger.

Some time later he heard movements outside again, people in the porch, raised voices. They went away and then came back again; this time they were more authoritative. Somebody was trying to break in, using a sharp, scratching instrument on the lock, bumping the door. The woodwork cracked, then it yielded.

The figures framed against the street lighting outside were uniformed men in flat caps. A glare of light, and then they saw the man huddled behind the hall table, watching them through splayed fingers.

'The bugger's here!' a policeman grunted, and came towards the cowering estate agent. 'What's the game, mate?'

'I . . . want . . . to . . . go . . . outside.' Don spoke falteringly, and fell against the policemen as they dragged him to his feet.

'Another bloody burglar and a sex-killer to boot.' A

constable handled him roughly. 'We'd better take him down to the station and charge him with illegal entry for now. Then we'll see what the forensic experts come up with.'

Don Lester made no attempt to resist as the two policemen dragged him out to the waiting car with its flashing blue light. He was bundled into the back seat and a policeman slid in beside him. Something hard and cold encircled his wrist and snapped shut; he was handcuffed to the officer.

His stark terror had subsided. The sheer relief of getting out of that house was overwhelming, bringing with it nausea and trembling. Take me away, please, he thought. Do what you want with me, only don't take me back inside that place!

An unmarked police van had pulled up behind them, ready to remove Tracey's body once the forensic experts had completed their initial investigations.

16

John Strike drove directly to Barmouth with only one stop to fill up the Suzuki with petrol. He went at a steady pace up the M1, then on to the M6 and the M54, in driving spray the whole journey. His eyes ached with tiredness and grief. His sorrow had temporarily overridden his terror; later it would give way to anger. God, how he hated that bloody house and what it had done to him and his family. He would have his revenge on it, he promised himself that. So far it had thwarted him. Luck, pure luck, but its luck would run out eventually. But first he had an awful lot to face, and as he neared Dolgellau he steeled himself for the ordeal ahead.

Kenton had been only as sympathetic as his dictatorship over the branch allowed. 'You had better take a fortnight of your annual leave and sort out all your problems,' the manager had offered with bad grace. Later John would broach the subject of the compassionate leave to which he was entitled. But at the moment there were many things that would go unchallenged.

Leah was under heavy sedation but that did not mask her accusing expression as she opened the door of her parents' seafront house to him: You wanted that house, and now it has cost us our son's life, because it drove us here, drove Ben under that . . . vehicle. She was trying not to look at the jeep parked on the partially flooded Marine Parade.

Sam and Sarah were asleep upstairs. George Bourne had aged a decade since John had last seen him at Christmas. Marjorie's glare was hostile, too: It's your fault, John Strike, because you got my daughter into trouble. Without you, it would have been another child somewhere else, still alive.

'You'd better come in.' She spoke hoarsely from dry grief, the sort that hurt most after the tears had all been shed.

John did not dare to think about the funeral; he wondered if he could endure it. Ben was gone, he wouldn't be coming back, but accepting that would be nigh impossible for a long time.

Sitting there in the front room with rain and sea gales lashing the windows, nobody talked because everything had been said. He had been blamed in his absence; they were mutely blaming him now. And then the front doorbell rang.

'It's the police.' Marjorie Bourne came back into the room. 'For you.' *What have you been doing now?*

The CID sergeant had called to inform John of the rape and murder committed in the porch of Number Thirteen the previous night. And of how they had found Don Lester gibbering in the hall. The estate agent had been released, he had had nothing to do with the crime. Perhaps, after treatment, he would regain his sanity. 'We understand your problems, Mr Strike' – his first real sympathy so far – 'but when you return to London our chaps would like a word with you. Nothing desperate, only that there *have* been two deaths on your property recently.'

'I want Ben buried in London.' Leah's dazed expression was momentarily determined, a flash of stubbornness: Just in case you thought I wanted him buried in Wales. We can't leave London because of the bank, can we?

John nodded, surprised. 'All right. I'll arrange it. I have to go back the day after tomorrow.' Because he had a job to do. This time, Number Thirteen and whatever lived in the house would pay dearly for what it had done to them, he vowed. He tried not to think of Ruth; that was something else he had to face up to. Later.

It was a relief to be on his way back to London, mainly because of Marjorie Bourne. The cow could not even bury the hatchet at a time like this. It wasn't anything she said, more what she didn't say; at times it was as if he did not exist. Maybe she sought refuge from her sorrow in hostility.

The rain had cleared. It was a bright sunny day after the first frost of autumn. At least the roads were dry; he would not have to contend with incessant spray thrown up by other vehicles this time.

The Suzuki gave him a sense of invincibility, with its pseudo-ruggedness, its macho design. Which was stupid really, because it only had an 800 cc engine and would crunch up like an ordinary car in a pile-up. But he could give rein to his fantasies, or just keep it to park outside his house in a south London suburb.

The traffic was sparse, but it would build up later on the M1, it always did. Funny, this last couple of days his phobias had not troubled him, almost as if the entity in Number Thirteen was satisfied now. There had been warnings, and John had not heeded them. He had ignored that last premonition of death, and Ben had paid the price.

God, he was going to have his revenge! The house had survived two arson attempts, it could not survive a third. If necessary, he would pile all the furniture up and set fire to it, and to hell with it if they found out it was deliberate. When your son is in his coffin you don't give a damn about much else. Except revenge.

John was angry now, but knew that wasn't a good thing

to be when he was at the wheel on a motorway. Apart from impairing his judgement, it pumped the adrenalin round his body and he didn't have a chance to burn it up. So he could have a heart attack, slump over the steering wheel, career across the central reservation . . . He eased his foot off the throttle and a Sherpa van blared its horn at him as it swung out sharply into the fast lane. Jesus, it might have clipped him!

Ahead of him the traffic was bunching, braking. Everybody was slowing, stopping. He had read somewhere recently that the majority of motorway accidents happened in daylight, in dry weather, when visibility was good. Like today on the M54, where the volume of traffic was light. Because some silly fucker was daydreaming and lost his concentration for one second, enough to get clipped by the vehicle behind. Or else had a thrombosis and –

There *had* been an accident.

John rolled to a standstill, the jeep's engine ticking over smoothly. A high-sided van immediately in front obstructed his vision and he had no idea how long the queue ahead was. Glancing in his rear mirror, he saw cars and lorries pulling up behind him. It only needed some stupid bastard in an artic to come hammering up and see them too late . . . He braced himself at the thought and felt the sweat breaking out on his forehead.

Everybody was switching off their engines; it looked like being a long wait. There wasn't any hurry, he didn't have to rush back for anything.

The driver in front had climbed out and was walking forward to see what the delay was. Sirens like wailing banshees made John wince. He caught a glimpse of a police patrol car followed by an ambulance speeding down the hard shoulder. He heard them slowing, stopping. Not too far ahead. Now everybody was getting out of their vehicles.

John fought with himself to stay in his seat. He only unclipped his seat belt for comfort; he unlatched the door because it was becoming unbearably hot in the Suzuki with the direct rays of an autumn morning sun beating in through the windows. He stepped out on to the tarmac because his legs were stiff and cramped and needed stretching. He did not need to walk on down towards the scene of the crash. But he did.

He came upon the accident almost before he realized it, a mountain of mangled metal. It was impossible to be sure how many vehicles were involved. An articulated lorry had ploughed into whatever cars were immediately in front of it, gathering them up as if in a breaker's yard, crushing them, steamrollering them, then finally slewing to a halt. There was broken glass everywhere, debris strewn across the three lanes; blood seeped out of the twisted car bodies, dripping steadily.

People were screaming. A hand that spouted blood was thrust out of a shattered window. A body lay in the road, a girl seemingly unmarked by the impact, a shapely teenager, legs spread wide, as if to say: Come on, somebody, screw me!

John recoiled. He wanted to look away but it was impossible. He was a victim of some macabre hypnotism. Bile scorched his throat as he began to vomit. Oh, Jesus God, I don't believe it!

He hated himself as much as he despised that crowd of ghoulish spectators, not helping, just watching, revelling in the carnage. Police were shouting for everybody to get back, but they were too busy to enforce their orders and roughly pushed their way through the crowd. More ambulances were arriving; two fire crews with cutting equipment; stretchers; ambulancemen and police with black plastic bags. Shovels scraped on the hard surface.

A rookie policeman was throwing up. There was screaming everywhere, from the trapped and dying.

The dead girl was on a stretcher, a blanket screening her in a final touch of dignity. Steel cutters were beginning to saw their way through the mashed metalwork. A doctor was in attendance, syringe in hand.

John Strike's legs were weak and threatened to buckle under him. He glanced down, wondering if his shoes had become adhered to the tarmac. The bitumen had partially melted in the warm autumn sunshine. *I want to get away but I can't!*

'Move to one side, sir!' There was contempt in the policeman's voice. A hand pushed John. He staggered and almost fell. He supported himself on a Ford Escort, an undamaged one, the driver having managed to stop within a few centimetres of the rampaging lorry in front. He was a lucky man, but that had not stopped him from going to gloat over the misfortune of others.

When John saw them bringing out the child he almost screamed. The boy could not have been more than three, a slight figure in torn bloodied football kit. Red. Arsenal colours to match the blood. And when John saw that the head was missing the vomit began to spout from his mouth. He tried to rush forward to claim the infant corpse because it was Ben. It had to be. He stumbled, fell forward and lay in the road.

It wasn't Ben – logic came to John's rescue – because Ben had been dead for two days. But, Jesus, it might have been because it had been just like that. He had chickened out of viewing his son in the mortuary, but he had seen him now.

The crowd was growing, streams of latecomers threading their way along the queues of parked vehicles as if this was a major attraction and they might miss it, hustling one another. Those at the back were standing on the balls of their feet and craning their necks in an attempt to see.

John was on his hands and knees trying to crawl away. *Move, you bastards, and let me through!*

And then he saw the old man. The rescue crew had cut through to him and dragged him out on to the road. He had broken limbs, clearly, and there might have been some internal injuries, too, but he did not seem to be in pain. Slumped in the arms of an ambulanceman, he was like a scarecrow in tattered clothes, a ribboned navy blue overcoat and scuffed shoes below his skeletal white ankles. The pinched face had deep-sunken eyes that roamed the spectators, found John and settled on him. Seeing him, he was mouthing obscenities with those wasted lips.

It was him again, there was no doubt in John Strike's mind, that evil ragbag blowing bubbles at the bottom of the pool, the harbinger of death, the spectre that haunted his nightmares and lurked in the dark shadows of his mind during the daytime hours.

John was cringing, cowering, whimpering his terror as he scuttled away like a wounded crab. He heard the old man's laughter ringing in his ears, the muted revelry in death. And he smelled him, the rancid odours of his unwashed body clothed in stinking rags. The malevolence was a living force that emanated from the shrunken form, directed at John, the one who had murdered Ben as surely as if he had been at the wheel of that ill-fated jeep.

Then John was dragging himself through a forest of legs, feet that trod on him and did not notice, bunching because there was safety in numbers. Drawn by the irresistible scent of death and blood, the pack of human scavengers feasted with their eyes, hungered for the sight of a motorway battlefield.

At last he was clear of them and able to stagger to his

feet. Lurching away, he tried to run. He saw the Suzuki, its bodywork glinting in the bright sunlight, but shied away from it. No! Not the scarlet monster that preyed on children.

He turned for one fearful glance back. The crowd had swelled, but nobody was interested in him, except that living dead thing that had emerged from the wreckage and would pursue him even though its body was crushed and broken. He sensed its power and fought to repel it from infiltrating his crazed mind yet again. He was giving way to panic because he could feel the evil even more strongly than before. A beast of the chase fleeing before his pursuers, he was running now, and he would run until he dropped.

A grassy bank sloped steeply down to the ploughed field below. John's feet slipped on the wet grass and he slid most of the way to the bottom. Picking himself up, he was confronted with a barbed wire fence. He snagged his trousers as he straddled it. A ripping noise, then he was free, his shoes sinking in the newly turned earth. He had to step over deep furrows and tread in the ridges. Mud clogged his feet; each step became heavier; and he had to pause frequently to dislodge the cloying soil. His socks were saturated and his footwear was ruined, but what was that, compared with the fiend on his trail?

It was as if a steel band encircled his chest and was being tightened slowly but surely. He gasped for breath, the taste of vomit still sour on his palate. And he was barely halfway across this massive field. He shaded his eyes and saw a small spinney beyond the far hedge, a mixture of dark green spruce and silver birch with delicate autumnal colourings. A place of refuge, somewhere to hide! He knew only too well that that copse was his destination, the limit of his endurance.

It might have been easier and quicker to have skirted

the field and followed the fence and hedge, treading on grass instead of earth. Too late now, he was beyond the point of return.

So far, he had resisted the awful temptation to look behind him. Weary, pausing for a brief rest, logic prevailed. This was nonsense, succumbing to childish fears. After Ben's death, the multiple accident had been the breaking point, leading to the fear of a mythical bogeyman. It was impossible for the man in the swimming baths – it had only been a dummy – to be here now. And impossible for this awful caricature of malevolent senility, albeit with broken limbs, to be hounding him across heavy terrain. Shock and terror had driven John Strike to flight; all he had to do was to retrace his footsteps, wait until the motorway was cleared and head back south. He breathed more easily, and felt foolish in case others had witnessed his panic. No, they were too busy gawping at the mass mutilation.

The impossible had become reality! Two hundred metres to his rear, lumbering over the furrows, came that relentless nemesis. His shattered limbs miraculously knitted, the figure in navy blue was bent almost double as he strode doggedly in the wake of the one he hunted with such tenacity. Most terrible of all was the sheer persistence of the pursuer, his obvious determination to be in at the kill.

Because John had tried to burn down his house.

John was stumbling forward again. His body protested but he ignored the tightening pain in his chest, the aching of his calves. There was no time now to knock the mud from his shoes. He felt like a screen cartoon character with oversized feet, his strides now barely stepping over the high ridges, losing speed, losing ground. The pursuer was no more than a hundred and fifty metres away now and gaining all the time, head bowed so that his features were hidden, because they were too terrible to look upon.

John cried his relief aloud as he saw the small wood was no more than twenty metres ahead. He would make it. And what then? A terrifying game of hide and seek, that old man parting the undergrowth in search of him, sniffing for a scent with his mucus-caked nose. John listened for the phlegm rattling those rotting lungs, fearful lest the pounding of his own heart would give his hiding place away.

Thankfully there was no barbed wire this end, just a straggling hawthorn hedge that formed the fringe of the spinney. John squeezed through a gap, impervious to the wicked thorns which tore his clothing and gouged his skin. Still on all fours, he went through an avenue of rhododendrons, the overhead foliage shutting out the sunlight and creating an atmosphere of eventide. The shadows were frightening, and it was cold and damp in here, with an earthy smell that was reminiscent of gravesoil.

He came upon a clearing amidst the trees, an area of browning bracken and seeding wild willow herb. He lowered his aching body to the ground, lay flat in the undergrowth and listened.

He could hear his pursuer coming and followed his progress by the sounds he made. Rhododendron boughs brushed a stooped body, then sprang back as it passed. Feet squelched in the soft ground. Emerging from that leafy tunnel, the old man straightened up and John could hear his bones cracking. Now he would be looking around, seeing the flattened grass that led on into the clearing.

John had given up, surrendered. Physically he was spent, mentally he had almost cracked. Flight had been his last resort. He had failed in his attempt to destroy the cancer that pulsed and grew in the confines of a suburban house. Now it had turned on him and was methodically hunting him down in this remote wood.

There was silence except for the heavy breathing. The old man must surely discover John's hiding place soon. Given the strength, the banker would have run on, found a better place of refuge and stood at bay like a wounded stag. But now he knew what the stag felt like when its heart had burst and it lay down awaiting the end. *Please let it be quick.*

He heard movements again, slow and deliberate; the swish of tall grass and the rustling of dry leaves as bushes were parted. The pursuer was searching, coming closer all the time.

Yet the spark of hatred still glowed within John Strike, a desire for revenge upon this monstrosity from the bowels of hell. His enemy was frail in stature, perhaps even in his own exhausted state he could overcome him, pull him to the ground. John's fingers flexed at the thought of encircling that scrawny neck; squeezing until those sunken eyes bulged from their dark sockets, straining until they burst like party balloons; the protruding tongue, swelling and purpling; the diseased lungs drowning in their own phlegm; matchstick arms and legs flailing, quivering until they hung limply and the woodland atmosphere became sickly with the stench of death.

John lay with his face pressed against the damp ground, eyes tightly shut. He sensed the proximity of the old man now and knew that he had been found. Lie still and maybe it will go away, he thought, like a child cowering beneath the bedclothes when it heard the creak of a floorboard in the dead of night. He would be an ostrich; if he did not see then he was not seen.

He almost screamed as a hand touched him, extended fingers stroking the back of his neck so that the hairs stiffened. He jerked and clawed into the soil beneath him as if trying to burrow his way to safety. Turning his head and looking up, he saw that awful funereal navy blue which was suddenly not so tattered, only mud-streaked, and followed it upwards with frightened eyes.

'I think you'd better come along with me, sir.' There was a trace of sympathy in the policeman's firm touch. 'It's bad back there, the worst I've ever seen, enough to push strong men over the brink. But I think you'd better see a doctor before you continue your journey. Just to be on the safe side, if you see what I mean.'

17

John had not continued his journey back to London. He tried not to think of it as an excuse not to return, but the doctor who checked him over at the hospital strongly advised against lengthy travel, particularly driving, for the next forty-eight hours. He gave him some tranquillizers; John dropped them into a waste bin and then drove the Suzuki back to Barmouth.

Thankfully neither Leah nor her parents asked for a lengthy explanation. 'I got caught up in that multiple pile-up,' he told them. And that was that. 'I'm quite happy to sleep on the sofa tonight.'

The local undertakers were already making arrangements with a firm in London for Ben's funeral. The body would travel back tomorrow. Then John and the family would follow the day after. George Bourne insisted on attending the funeral, so that meant that Marjorie would be coming as well. God forbid! And everybody would be staying at Number Thirteen because there wasn't anywhere else, except an hotel, and nobody even suggested that.

Oh, Jesus Christ, whatever festered in Number Thirteen was damnably clever, one move ahead of him the whole time. John was angry in that darkened front room after everybody else had retired. Twice it had thwarted his arson attempts before, and now it had done it again. Carnage on the motorway, seven killed, four seriously injured, just to prevent him returning and setting fire to that hellish house! And it knew that it had a respite until after the funeral.

For a whole day nobody wanted to eat or talk. They just sat about the house, drenched in their grief. In the end, John took Sam and Sarah for a walk down to the harbour. Tense, he watched their every move. *Don't go near the water. Keep away from the road.* A depressing sea mist saturated his trousers beneath his Barbour, the endless grey gloom coming in from the sea like an opaque shroud.

Funerals were supposed to be therapeutic, he had heard it said, an escalation of sorrow that came to a peak and afterwards you were left with just the dull ache. But it wouldn't be quite like that, not for him anyway. All that was left now was revenge. The thought kept him going and he wondered what it would be like afterwards.

The Bournes had elected to travel by train and take the children with them, as if to say, Because we don't like you, John Strike, and the idea of being cooped up in that jeep with you for hours is unthinkable. That was fine by John, and when at the last minute Leah also decided on rail travel, he did not try to change her mind. He was starting all over again, right from square one – M54, M6, M1 – and maybe this time he'd get there.

He arrived in London in plenty of time to collect the others from the station. Another depressing day, but this time there were things to do – preparations for the funeral and after. The Johnsons would be coming back to the house after the burial, so that meant tea and cakes. Stupid, meaningless things, but at least it gave him something to do.

A carpenter had been to repair the smashed stair rail, and for an extra tenner he had washed the bloodstains off the hall wall. Leah and her mother cleaned the house whilst George sat in the lounge smoking his pipe. Sam and Sarah were round at the Johnsons' house, they would probably stop the night.

Number Thirteen seemed strangely serene; John found himself listening, testing for vibes, but even his distraught senses could not pick up any. Maybe the entity was satisfied now and had moved on elsewhere. No, it would be back all right, he was convinced of that. He tried not to think about what he was going to do afterwards in case it picked up his thought waves. There would be plenty of time later.

It was a small family service, eleven people huddled together in the front pews, staring at the small pitiful coffin. Only he and the Johnsons were not sedated in any way. John held Leah's arm but she seemed oblivious of his presence, withdrawn into her own drugged thoughts. For the undertakers and the curate it was just another job; grief had its price, too. The spoken words did not register, nor the two hymns and the twenty-third psalm, which nobody sang. It was all finished in under half an hour, then they were being ushered back to the cars so that they would not hear the clink of shovels on gravesoil, earth thudding on to polished oak. So final.

The thing was back in the house. John sensed it the moment he stepped into the hall – a coldness which the central heating failed to warm, a lurking presence that followed him to the toilet, an overriding atmosphere of escalating tension again, as if something was about to happen.

Suddenly he was aware that it was dark outside. British summer time had ended last week but it took some time to adjust to the prospect of winter evenings. The Johnsons were gone; they would keep Sam and Sarah tonight. It was just himself and Leah and her parents. It was going to be a long night.

Everybody was in the lounge seemingly impervious to the thick fog of tobacco smoke created by George's pipe and the aftermath of Brian Johnson's cigarettes. Leah was crying, and that had started Marjorie off; George was attempting to comfort them when John opened the door.

He almost retreated except that it was too late. His own emotions were an unhealthy mixture of grief, fear and his dislike for his mother-in-law. Even now she was regarding him with that reproachful stare of hers: I'll never forgive you for getting my daughter pregnant out of wedlock. I would not have wanted her to marry you if she had not had to for the sake of respectability.

Everybody was looking at him, an unwelcome intruder.

'We have to face up to things.' George Bourne was standing up. He seemed slightly unsteady on his feet and spoke with his heavy pipe threatening to dislodge his dentures. A trickle of saliva and nicotine appeared on his square chin. 'I mean . . .' He was speaking for the sake of it, uttering clumsy words amidst a spray of spittle. 'Leah's young enough to have another child . . .'

'George!' Marjorie spat his name out with venom and horror. 'George, how dare you say such a thing!' Her meaning was clear: she didn't want *that man* ever touching her daughter again.

George recoiled visibly. The pipe slid but held, showering ash down his waistcoat. He was embarrassed, his wife's words hammering him like a physical blow.

'It's all right, Mother.' Leah attempted to defuse the unfortunate situation. 'Dad meant well. I know what he's saying . . .'

'And so do I!' Marjorie Bourne whirled on her husband and for one moment it seemed as if she was about to strike him. 'George, how insensitive can you get?' She glanced at her son-in-law. Licence for you to give vent to your filthy lust, she seemed to say.

For one awful moment everything seemed to stop. The cessation of time caught everybody in the room and held them immobile with their expressions of sorrow and bitterness, a movie still displayed in the foyer of a cinema.

And that was when John sensed something push past him into the room. He did not see it, only felt its coldness as it brushed him. *But he knew what it was, all right; and if he could have yelled a warning to the others he would have done so, however futile it might have been. Death had just touched him, and was even now in this very room.*

Marjorie's anger restarted like a sluggish engine suddenly firing on a winter's morning. This time the screech of anger was directed at her husband, her son-in-law, maybe even her daughter. The volatile assault turned George Bourne's pallid complexion deathly white.

'*You* survived, George, but how I wish it had been you that had died instead of Ben!' She seemed to regret her spoken thoughts instantly, trying to recall them with lips that moved mutely. But it was too late, they were uttered.

George swayed on his feet. The heavy briar slipped from his mouth even as his thick lips began to twitch then slacken uselessly. His eyes protruded, glazed. He half raised a hand as if to clutch at some part of his anatomy that was in sudden excruciating pain, but it fell back down to his side. Tottering, he was striving to maintain his balance, but the use was gone from his legs and they were giving way. Crumpling, he fell sideways, striking his head on the hearth with a resounding crack and setting off an avalanche of crumpled newspapers from the grate.

'*George! Oh, my God!*'

Papers hid the upturned features in a shroud of newsprint. The bulky human form was strewn lifelessly on the floor, not even a twitch from the outstretched fingers.

Marjorie had backed off and Leah seemed trapped in her chair. Only John Strike was released from the atmosphere of frozen petrification which had gripped the gathering. He moved forward, knelt down by the still form and knocked the papers away, and even then wished that he could set fire to them this very moment.

A rush of stale, fetid air nauseated him. It might have been a gust of wind down the chimney that had gathered foul fumes in passage, but he knew it was not. He felt that stroking touch again as the unseen entity headed for the open door and out into the hall. *Death had come and gone*.

There was a babble of female panic and fear at his shoulder. He heard himself saying, 'I'm afraid he's gone. Somebody phone for a doctor.' He was kneeling there because it was easier than standing up and trying to explain, to console.

He heard the phone being used in the hallway. Leah was speaking. Marjorie went with her because she was frightened.

Then the long wait in the kitchen, the door shut to keep death at bay. The two women were shocked, numbed. Dry-eyed, they would cry later, sitting there holding hands, companions in bereavement.

It was half an hour before a doctor arrived, superciliously fresh from medical school. He only rushed for the living, the dead could wait. After a cursory examination of the corpse, he telephoned for an undertaker's death wagon. It might be some time, he said.

An hour later, George Bourne was gone. He would be in the mortuary for viewing tomorrow if anyone was interested.

'I want him cremated at home.' Marjorie Bourne spoke with remarkable calmness as she poured herself a second cup of strong tea. 'George would have wanted that. He hated London, he shouldn't have come.' She looked up at John. It's your fault again, her eyes said. If George had stayed at home he would have been alive now. 'I don't like this house.'

Marjorie disliked most things, but her most recent dislike sent shivers up and down John's back. Of course she didn't like the house, because her husband had just died in it. No other reason.

'I'm going home with Mother tomorrow,' Leah said. 'Sam and Sarah had better come with us. If you're too busy then we'll go by train again.'

'I have to go to work soon, I can't stay off indefinitely.' He had not confessed to having a fortnight's leave. He was relieved that they were going, because he had a job to do here. *Don't think about it.* He looked furtively behind him in case his thoughts had been eavesdropped.

'I might stay up there for some time.' Leah spoke almost vindictively. 'I'll see if I can get the children fixed up with schooling in Wales.'

'All right.' He hoped his relief did not show. 'I'll be okay. In fact, I'll put pressure on Lest . . . on the agents to get the house sold.' Nobody was safe, not even the estate agents. This place was like a dangerous monster that savaged everybody who came within its reach.

Morning. Leah, her mother and the two children had gone on the nine-forty from Euston. They would be in Barmouth around half past two. John came back to Schooner Street and managed to park the Suzuki in a vacant space directly outside the house, ready for a quick getaway.

The skies had cleared and the sun was shining brightly. It was going to be a beautiful autumnal day. His thoughts returned to that pile of kindling and papers in the hearth. Only five weeks until the fifth of November. Well, this year bonfire night would come early! Night was best, though; by day the smoke might be spotted and the alarm raised before the flames got a hold. Which meant that he had to pass the day somewhere else because there was no way that he could stop here. And then he remembered Ruth Ford.

She would be at the bank, of course, but he had a key to her house. It was the obvious place to go.

He travelled by tube, arrived outside Ruth's house shortly before ten o'clock. He inserted his key in the lock with instinctive stealth. He knew he should not be here. His son had died; so, too, had his father-in-law. He should have been with his family in their hour of grief. Instead, he had sneaked off to his mistress. He had a diversion whereas the others did not. It gave him a feeling of guilt. And also an erection, but that was silly because Ruth would not be there.

He had that feeling again that the house was not empty. It was an annoying habit that was growing on him. He tried to ignore it, but all the same he crept furtively up the stairs. And when he reached the landing he realized that his senses had not let him down, because there *was* somebody in the house. He could hear them breathing, groaning. Oh, Jesus, no! He almost turned and fled.

From where he stood he had a partial view of the bedroom through the half-open door. He saw Ruth, it could not be anybody else, her head jerking from side to side, eyes closed, moaning loudly, convulsing as if she was in the midst of shooting abdominal pains as her naked body threshed and writhed, her legs kicking out, tossing the duvet to the floor. She was clutching at herself, a hand pressed to her groin, the other flung wildly in time with her flailing legs.

An appendicitis, perhaps, he thought. Whatever her illness, she was undoubtedly in terrible pain. Fate had sent him when he was most needed. He must go to her, then phone for an ambulance . . .

Even as he stepped through the doorway, he knew. The realization made him want to shout his relief aloud, combined with a surge of eroticism that had his arousal struggling to escape from the constriction of his trousers.

Her eyes flickered open and her body was temporarily rigid with the shock of seeing an intruder in her bedroom. Her slender fingers ceased in their frantic manipulation of the soft pink centre of her pleasure in embarrassment. But she was too close to her orgasm to draw back, it was already starting to shudder her like the beginnings of a miniature earthquake.

Long before Ruth's climax had reached its peak John had joined her, his clothes strewn untidily on the floor, pushing deep into her as her fingernails gouged his bare back.

It was a respite from grief and terror. Number Thirteen Schooner Street would have to wait until he was ready. It had a few hours left.

18

Ruth lay on the bed watching John dress. There was something definitely strange about him; more than just uneasiness – furtiveness, the way he avoided her gaze. She sensed that he was going out somewhere. Somewhere which did not involve her.

Okay, he had lost a son and his father-in-law in the space of a few days. How would that affect his marriage? Would it be the final wrench? Or would it pull him and his wife back together in their combined grief? It was as if he was weighed down by a sense of guilt, too; as if he ought not to have come here at this time.

They had barely spoken this last hour, each engrossed in their own thoughts. She had not gone to work today on an impulse. Her troubled mind could not have coped with routine bank work. She had phoned in, given a trifling excuse and gone back to bed, then lain there thinking of John Strike. In due course she had become aroused, and had been unable to resist the urge to masturbate. And then, just when she was hitting a climax, he had walked into the bedroom. It was now four o'clock; they had passed the day in each other's arms, but suddenly he had extricated himself and reached for his clothes.

'I'll be back soon.' Still he did not meet her searching eyes, just looked down at the floor.

'Where are you going?'

'Back home. I want to collect one or two things. I'll bring the jeep back here when I've finished.'

'I'll come with you.' She swung herself off the bed.

'No!' It was more than a refusal, an angry command: You won't because I don't want you to.

'Why not?' Damn it, this was an issue she was determined to force.

'Because . . .' He hesitated. 'That house is evil. People have died because of it. I . . . don't want to take any more chances.'

'I want to go with you.' It sounded petulant.

'No!' His lips tightened; he was becoming angry. 'I won't let you. Look, I'll be back in a couple of hours.'

She sighed, then nodded reluctantly. 'If there is danger in that house then I don't want you to go alone.' That wasn't the reason; she was suspicious. Maybe he wanted to phone his wife in Wales, a make-up-and-forgive call. Or even another woman. He wanted to do something devious, she was sure, and that was the reason he did not want her to go with him. 'Don't be any longer than you can help, John, please.'

She heard the front door slam behind him, and began to dress hurriedly, her fingers trembling in her haste.

Dusk had turned to darkness as John Strike emerged from the underground station. It was raining again, a fast drizzle. Autumn had truly arrived with its wet pavements and raw atmosphere. He zipped up his Barbour. Hurrying because he knew what he had to do and wanted to get it over and done with, he felt that foreboding again. Something would happen, some unforeseen event would prevent him from putting match to paper. No, sod it, he wouldn't let it, not even if it meant going to prison for arson. This time there would be no stay of execution for the entity which lived in Number Thirteen.

He went past a piece of waste ground on his left, and then there was another road to cross. A stream of traffic kept him waiting, and in the end he had to dart across between oncoming vehicles. Horns blared. He was trembling and felt sick.

The house looked sullen from across the road; sulking rather than brooding, as if even it could not keep him at bay indefinitely. Unlocking the front door, he tried not to think of that burglar speared by a broken stair rail and spraying blood all over the place; or that girl who had been raped and strangled in the porch; or Lester going crazy – he was still undergoing electric shock treatment. And Ben . . .

He left the door partly open, then jumped as the telephone began to ring. No, I'm not going to answer you, he thought. It was as though it had waited all day for him and was screaming its hatred at him.

It was impossible to ignore its harsh, incessant noise. It vibrated his head, increasing the feeling of nausea. He forced himself to think. No, there was nothing he needed to take away from here, it was all in those suitcases at Ruth's house. There was nothing remaining here which could not be replaced by an insurance pay-out. There was no reason to delay.

Shut up, you bastard! The phone seemed as if it was becoming hysterical, louder and louder. All in the mind, he told himself. Go on, light that fire.

The matches were still on the mantelshelf, spilling out when he opened the box the wrong way up, but it didn't matter because he only needed one. Just one. And then the telephone stopped.

It took him several seconds to realize that it was no longer ringing, that what he heard was merely a resonant echo in his own mind. It, too, had given up. *Because you know you're bloody well beaten this time*.

He scraped the match along the emery paper; they never ignited first time, did they? The head snapped off. Fuck it! He fumbled another out of the box. A ball of paper rustled and started to unfurl, as if there was something hiding in there, a mouse maybe. As if everything knew. But if they did, it was too late now.

No, I don't bloody well believe it!

John almost dropped the match as he felt that icy presence again, even as he heard the front door being pushed open, creaking on its hinges. *Somebody had stepped inside the hall!*

Tensing, he was afraid to go and look, afraid of what he might see. That emaciated old man in the frayed and moth-eaten navy blue overcoat mouthing mute obscenities. Or the police.

He hesitated, the match poised to strike again. And then a voice called out, 'John?'

Recognizing the woman's voice, he felt relief then anger. Oh, Jesus wept, what the hell was Ruth doing here?

'Oh, there you are!' She was white-faced, standing in the doorway staring at him, seeing the matches, and the newspapers that spilled out of the hearth as far as the sofa with its inflammable stuffing.

'You!' he hissed, feeling an urge to hit her, to shake her. 'What the hell are you doing here?'

'I . . .' She faltered, and almost said, 'I don't trust you, that's why I'm here.'

'Look.' He rattled the matchbox in his anger at being disturbed. 'I told you I didn't want you to come here with me. Didn't you understand?' He thrust his face close to hers.

She was frightened by what she read in those eyes: the obsession, the mania. She recoiled, shocked because she had never imagined him this way. It wasn't John Strike, it was some fiend inside his body.

'Go and wait in the jeep for me!' he hissed. 'Go on,

you stupid cow! I'll maybe explain later.' When I've thought up a suitable story, he thought. Don't trust her.

Ruth backed into the hall, turned and ran for the open door. And as he heard her go it crossed John's mind that the Suzuki was locked. But that didn't matter, he wouldn't be a minute. Just long enough to strike one match . . .

The brimstone head flared with a bright orange flame that hurt his eyes as it wafted in the draught from the open door. He felt the coldness again, that presence coming for him, clawing at him with its icy fingers in a last desperate attempt to stop him. Fighting it, cursing it, forcing his hand down to that nearest rumple of paper, he struggled to hold the flame against it even though that unseen entity was exerting every power to drag him away.

He saw the newsprint starting to brown, to blacken. Oh, Christ, it's damp, it fucking well won't burn! Then the flame took hold, ran along the edge, spread. Its warmth dispelled the enshrouding coldness, dispersed it; creating flickering shadows and then destroying them.

He stood there watching the flames in the fireplace, how they made the kindling crackle. Burning balls were already starting to fall out into the hearth, igniting the paper trail. Smoke was billowing back; the chimney was surely blocked. He moved away, stared through smarting eyes and gave way to a spasm of coughing as the fumes penetrated his nose and mouth. *Don't go, stay and watch! Stay here and be cremated, as George Bourne will be the day after tomorrow!*

He was fighting to escape now before it was too late. Hearing maniacal laughter that just might have been in his own mind, he struggled down the hall towards the partly open door, dragging himself free of those cold clutching hands. The bastard knew it was done for, that it was going to burn in its own hell, but it wanted to take him with it to some dreaded place of everlasting torment.

One last desperate wrench, and he had made it out into the porch. Stumbling, he cried his terror aloud because he thought that he had stepped on a human body, a partly clothed girl lying huddled in the corner. But there was nothing there.

Laughter followed him, insane babblings, Don Lester screaming after him because he couldn't escape. Or perhaps it was that burglar kicking his last as he hung from the stair rail. Not looking back, not daring to, he somehow found the keys to the jeep and managed to unlock the door. And only when he was behind the steering wheel did he remember Ruth.

He looked for her but she was not there. The street was empty, not so much as a commuter walking wearily home after a hard day in the city. Nobody.

John started the engine and revved it. Ruth had probably gone on home. Which was just as well, because it gave him time to think up a feasible explanation. He pulled out into the road, feeling weak with relief.

I beat you in the end, you fucking pig, he thought. Now go roast. This is for Ben.

Mike Gilson had given way to blind panic after he raped and strangled Tracey. Scarcely able to believe what he had done, finally accepting the awful reality of his crime, he fled. Walking fast, afraid to run in case late-night passers-by glimpsed him beneath the streetlights and recognized him, he sought refuge in filthy subways, mingling with dropouts under the influence of drugs and meths. They scarcely glanced at him, accepting him as one of themselves.

He spent a night and a day of sheer terror, feigning

sleep and hiding his face in a crooked arm. Until the urge came upon him again.

He fell into an exhausted slumber, oblivious of passing footsteps, not even disturbed by the twanging of a busker's guitar and a deep voice that sang tunelessly, the same song over and over again. His deep sleep was finally broken by an erotic dream.

It wasn't Tracey, he knew even in his subconscious that she was no more and now his conscience did not trouble him. Another girl; he could not see her face in the shadows but he was not interested in her features, however beautiful they might have been. Just her slim body, the way she moaned and gyrated her thighs against his hardness, running his zip, beating him to it, laughing as he unbuttoned her. Willing, she wanted him to go all the way. And for some reason that angered him, because he wanted her to struggle, to fight him. He had to have her against her will, stroking her soft neck and then closing his hands around it, squeezing and cutting off her scream before it left her throat, feeling her quivering feebly as he thrust into her. And then he woke up seconds before the ultimate pleasure, hungering for a woman he had never seen and knowing that he had to go and look for her.

A beast of prey back on familiar territory, he felt the urge to mate and to kill predominating. Alert to every sound, every smell, crouching amidst the debris on a stretch of waste ground, he heard voices; laughter and shouting.

He listened to approaching footsteps; heavy ones made him draw back into the shadows, seeing silhouettes and knowing that they were not right. He knew what he wanted, and curbed his impatience. Everybody used this short cut to the tube, it was only a question of time.

Then his straining ears picked up the light tip-tapping

of hurrying feet, and Gilson knew that his wait was over. He straightened up and checked that there was nobody else in sight except the slim, hurrying girl in the zipper jacket with the hood pulled up so that her face was in shadow. But her face did not matter.

He waited until she was less than a metre away before he stepped out to bar her path.

Ruth Ford was both angry and frightened. In a matter of a few hours John Strike had changed; she had barely recognized him as the man back there in that awful house.

Shaking, she had run out into the rainy autumn night and looked back at the gate in case he was pursuing her. He wasn't, thank God! His eyes, she would see them in her dreams for months, perhaps years, to come; orbs that smouldered with fury yet at the same time reflected an inner terror, stark fear. A man possessed, she thought, a madman who might have killed her, such was the rage boiling inside him. And she remembered that poor girl's body that had been found raped and strangled in the porch of 13 Schooner Street . . .

No way was she going to wait by the jeep. Her priority was to put as much distance between herself and John Strike as possible. It was incredible to think that he was accountant at the bank where she worked, a civilized boss whom the staff respected. Or the man she slept with. The thought hurt her. And yet every day there were stories in the papers about mild-mannered family men who for no accountable reason murdered their wives and slaughtered their children in cold blood. A brain, a personality, had become unhinged, turning them into homicidal maniacs.

She stopped again at the end of the road and checked that he was not following her. There was nobody in sight. Her bosom was heaving and she slowed to a fast walk. It was his son's death that was responsible, had done this to him, she decided. She felt pity but it did not make her any less scared, because, whatever the reason, her life was at stake and the initial cause was irrelevant.

She debated whether or not to return home. Doubtless John would turn up at her house, and it might be dangerous. She wondered about staying elsewhere overnight; her friend Margaret was always trying to persuade her to go and stay with her. Margaret's husband had walked out, gone to live with another woman. Oh, God, men were all the bloody same!

Ruth decided that she would phone her; there was bound to be a telephone at the underground station. Another thought, what the hell had John Strike been doing with those matches? He had looked as if he was going to light that pile of screwed-up papers in the hearth. Which seemed rather silly when he was about to lock a house up and leave it. But, there again, his reasoning had flipped.

She could see the road on the other side of the tract of waste ground. A pavement bordered by a high wall led down to the tube station. A hundred metres, possibly less, she calculated.

It was an oasis of darkness amidst a maze of streetlighting. But as long as you could see the light ahead of you it didn't matter. She began to hurry. And then, without warning, a man stepped out in front of her.

For one terrible moment Ruth thought that it was John Strike, that he had guessed her destination, taken a short cut and got ahead of her. But this man was too big, too tall. And before she could cry out a hand had found her neck, suffocated her cry for help before it began, and was dragging her struggling body back into the deep shadows.

She was borne to the ground, broken bricks and sharp stones gouging her back, and held powerless as her attacker shredded her clothing and pawed at her body. A blackness that was blacker than the shadows mercifully spared her the final pain and ignominy as the crazed stranger began to vent his uncontrollable lust on her nakedness.

Ruth had obviously gone home, John decided. Now that he was away from Schooner Street and the fire had actually been lit, he felt more relaxed than he had for a long time. There was just the ache caused by Ben's death; he knew that that would be with him always. Time was a great healer, but it would never really heal this one. It was something he would have to learn to live with.

First, he thought, he would go back to Ruth's house and wait for her there if she had not already arrived. This whole situation had to be defused. He gave up trying to invent stories that sounded feasible; once she read in the papers that Number Thirteen had been razed to the ground she would put two and two together and she wouldn't make five! If he cut her in on the deal she wouldn't shop him. Which, he supposed, meant marriage, or, at the very least, cohabitation.

He wasn't really a criminal. Of course, he would claim on the insurance and look for a full pay-out, but it was only so that he could purchase another house as nobody would buy this one. He would not be any better off financially and it wouldn't harm the insurers; they made vast profits, anyway. It wasn't like picking up an old lady's purse in the gutter, stealing the cash and leaving her on the poverty line. He was trying to put his conscience right and had almost succeeded by the time he parked outside Ruth's house.

He knew instantly that she was not at home, not just because there were no lights showing but from the sense of emptiness that came at him. It was similar to the feeling that emanated from Number Thirteen, a foreboding, a sense of . . . *death!*

No, not here, he decided. It was the lingering sensations from his own house which were doing this to him. He laughed aloud in the darkness because by now there would not be much left of 13 Schooner Street. Even if there was, there was nothing anybody could do to save it.

Standing there in the orange-tinted artificial lighting of an October night, he visualized the scene in Schooner Street. Oh, sweet Jesus, he could almost feel the heat from the inferno. In fact, it was making him sweat . . .

Fire engines hampered by the line of parked cars; residents being knocked up out of their beds and told to shift their BMWs or whatever; the face on the house like a halloween lantern, flames showing in all its orifices, eyes burning their hatred out of blackened sockets, distended nostrils breathing out thick smoke from the smouldering mucus; the twisted mouth with its orange tongue of fire screaming pain and fury in the cremation of the living dead.

Crowds thronging the pavements, being pushed back by police; ladders up to the windows; firemen with breathing apparatus trying to determine if there was anybody inside – there was, but it would die there – then being driven back by the heat and retreating into the road and playing their hoses on the pyre; wanting to let the house go but to stop the blaze spreading to the others; to sacrifice Number Thirteen, because they had no choice . . .

God, it was tempting to go back to mingle with the crowds, a spectator incognito. *It* would know he was there, and that in itself would almost have been worth it, to mock and taunt it. And watch it die.

John decided not to go inside Ruth's house. He was impatient now and regretted his earlier edginess, the way he had reacted. He hoped she would understand. He wanted to see her, to apologize and explain.

Pacing the shiny wet glinting pavement, he watched closely every figure that approached. They were all too tall, too short, had the wrong walk, or were male instead of female. He hated each and every one of those who passed by because they were not Ruth.

Downstairs lights came on, went off and were replaced by upstairs ones. Then there was total darkness in every window, a sleeping street. He glanced at his watch. One-thirty A.M. And that was when he knew that something was very wrong. He also knew that Ruth would not be coming home.

At two o'clock he had made up his mind to return to Schooner Street because she might still be there. He trembled at the awful possibilities: she had been lured back inside, trapped there to die in the blaze; or driven beneath the wheels of an oncoming vehicle, like Ben; or under a tube train.

Driving was not easy, he had lost his concentration. He edged the Suzuki cautiously down side streets with cars parked on both sides because he was not sure of its width. Once he lost his way; a wrong turn, and it took him ten minutes to find the right road again. Until finally he recognized the end of Schooner Street.

He would have to park in the adjacent street and walk back, he realized, because it would be impossible to drive any closer. There would be a road block, fire engines, double or even treble the original crowd.

He parked, climbed out and stood listening, expecting the rush of chemical foam, the liquid hissing on the blaze, maybe a loud-hailer to keep the watchers back, and flashing blue lights that would reflect on wet roofs, creating a psychedelic scene. Instead there was nothing.

Except a brooding silence.

It was all over. Number Thirteen was finished, burned to the ground, just ashes and rubble. He sniffed the night air, hoping to scent the stench of burning, the sour smell of hot ashes. There was only the odour of suburban London, the petrol fumes.

He had to force himself to walk to where Fanthorpe Road adjoined Schooner Street. For a few moments he dared not look. He had that feeling of being observed again, of hidden eyes focused on him.

Glancing fearfully out of the corners of his eyes, he started to count the houses. 7 . . . 9 . . . 11 . . .

And 13!

It did not look any different. It was still dark and forbidding. But this time there was an unmistakable leer on the shadowy face.

No, it's impossible!

Looking up and down the street, he tried to will the vulturous crowd, the fire engines. He concentrated all his forces on that house in an attempt to ignite it, but it did not work, had no more effect than that one match.

Number Thirteen Schooner Street was unburned, and the evil within it still festered.

19

'I notice *he* hasn't phoned!' There was scathing criticism of her daughter's husband in Marjorie Bourne's tone. Brooding rather than grieving, she needed a scapegoat for having the children here, for George's death. For everything, in fact.

'He's busy trying to sell the house.' Leah wished that she had had time to think up a better reason.

'Huh, he could leave that to the estate agents. You don't have to do anything except put the property in their hands. And, anyway, I saw a programme on telly the other week about London houses. They sell themselves; often the board isn't up for more than a day.'

'Number Thirteen happens to be different,' Leah snapped. 'Or hadn't you noticed?'

Marjorie pursed her lips. 'Isn't it time for Sam and Sarah to go to bed? It's past nine and we have . . . a lot to do tomorrow.' She avoided mentioning the cremation. She skirted round the subject, made vague references to it, just as she did about her son-in-law.

'They'll go to bed before long.' Leah was tired. She was still listening for the phone in the hall, willing it to ring and for the caller to be John. 'Sam's going to have a bath. I've ordered him to. I've put the immersion heater on, Mother.'

'I think he's . . . up to something.'

'Who . . . Sam?' Leah looked up in surprise from the cookery magazine she was pretending to read.

'No.' Marjorie's expression was disapproving. 'That man of yours.'

'His name is John, Mother.' Oh, Christ, don't start a bloody argument now!

'Well, I find it all very suspicious. He isn't even coming to . . . tomorrow, which I find rude of him, a downright insult to my George. And he can't even be bothered to phone. *I* think he's got another woman on the quiet, Leah!'

Leah tensed. The magazine fell from her knee and fluttered to the floor. Her mother was telepathic, she thought. No, just being nasty, stating what nasty people always thought. What *I'm* thinking!

'I wouldn't put it past him, my dear.'

'I'm sure John wouldn't.' But she knew he would, and in fact he probably was having an affair right now. But I'll never degrade myself by admitting it, she realized. A divorce because of incompatibility would let us both off the hook.

'I think he would.' The older woman was distraught, and the argument had come readily to hand. 'After all, he got *you* into trouble, Leah, and a man who will do . . . *that* before marriage is quite capable of doing it with some other woman behind his wife's back.'

'Mother . . . I did it with him as well. He didn't do it on his own, you know. Now, shall we not continue this ridiculous conversation? I'm too tired to argue with you.'

'It's ridiculous!' Marjorie said.

'Yes, it is . . .'

'Not having a crematorium in Barmouth is ridiculous. The nearest one is somewhere up Colwyn Bay or Bangor way, but for some reason they can't fit us in there. So we have to travel all the way to Shrewsbury. I ask you! If it didn't mean going against George's wishes I'd have him buried here in town. In fact, I'd much prefer it but – '

'We'll do what Dad wanted.' Leah felt the tears welling up in her eyes again. 'It'll be a long journey, about a hundred and fifty miles the round trip, but we'll do it. I'm most grateful to your neighbour for agreeing to look after the children.'

'I feel I'm putting on Mrs Jones,' Marjorie sniffed. 'If your husband had been here he could have stayed and looked after them if he didn't want to go to . . . to Shrewsbury.'

'Well, he isn't here and I'm sure Mrs Jones doesn't mind.' Play it all down, she told herself.

'It really is time those children were in bed. Sam is only nine and – '

'I'm fully aware of his age, Mother. I'll go and remind him . . .'

Sarah's voice came from somewhere upstairs, angry and complaining. 'Sam, will you *please* have your bath because I want one too, and I'm not going to wait up all night for you.'

'Sam, it's bathtime and bedtime . . .' Leah was halfway up the stairs before she realized that something was wrong. Sam was standing on the landing wearing just his pyjama bottoms. The bathroom door was open, steam was billowing out and she could hear the taps running. 'Sam, what's going on? Get in that bath at once!'

'No!' There was more than defiance on his face, an expression that bordered on terror. 'I . . . I don't want a bath, Mum.'

'You've got to have one, whether you like it or not. You haven't had a bath since – '

'No, *please*!' It was almost a scream, and he was backing away towards his bedroom. Sarah stood in the open doorway of her room, her features flushed with anger.

'Sam.' Leah caught his arm and felt how he trembled. 'Sam, what's the matter? Come on, you can tell me.'

'I . . .' He was still trying to pull away from her but she

held him, firmly but gently. *'I'm scared, Mum. Of the water. Like Dad was at the swimming baths that day!'*

Oh, God, so that was why John hadn't joined the children in the pool that time, because he was frightened! Now it was all coming out. 'There's nothing to be frightened of in the bath, Sam. Come with me and we'll both take a look.'

'*No!*' This time it was a scream, a shriek that bordered on hysteria as childish fears scaled their topmost peak.

'All right, *I'll* go and take a look, then.' As Leah walked into the steam-filled bathroom, she heard her mother's whining voice from down in the hall enquiring what all the fuss was about. For God's sake, don't you come up here, Mother, she thought. I've got enough troubles as it is!

There wasn't anything untoward in the bathroom; Leah had not expected there to be. She turned off the taps, stood there in the swirling steam and felt it dampening her. It was like a thick fog; she could imagine all kinds of weird shapes, if she let herself.

'There's nothing there.' When she emerged on to the landing Sam was back in his bedroom and had pulled on his pyjama top as if to ensure that he did not bath. 'But if you're too tired to have a bath, then get straight into bed. I want you asleep in five minutes. D'you hear?'

'Yes, Mum.' With sheer relief, he hurried into bed and pulled the sheets up. 'And, Mum?'

'What?' *What now?*

'Can I sleep with the light on?'

'There's no reason . . .'

'Sarah does. She has for months.'

'Sam.' Leah saw how pale he was, how his eyes roamed the room as if he suspected that somebody might be hiding in there. 'Are you . . . frightened of something?

We're not at home now, you know. There's nothing to be scared of here.'

'I know.' He screwed his face up; his bottom lip was trembling. 'But . . . it's as if we sort of . . . brought it all with us, if you know what I mean.'

Out of the mouths of babes! She knew what Sam meant, felt it herself. But it was crazy, and she wasn't going to pander to it. 'Go on, get to sleep. And leave the light on if you want to.'

'What's the trouble?' Marjorie was standing at the foot of the stairs.

'Nothing, Mother, nothing at all. Just childish prattle.' *Which you would not understand.* 'I think we all ought to have an early night.'

It was just eleven o'clock when Leah went up to bed. Her mother appeared to want to sleep downstairs again, and she could not deny a widow that right on the eve of her husband's funeral. Leah went into the bathroom and cleaned her teeth. She was surprised when she opened her bedroom door to discover that the light was on. She was even more surprised to find Sarah in the bed.

'May I sleep with you, Mother?' the girl asked nervously, and there was a note of pleading in her voice.

'I suppose so,' Leah whispered, in case Marjorie heard downstairs. 'Now, what's *your* problem?'

'I'd sooner sleep with you, Mother.'

Leah wasn't going to ask further, knowing the reply would be much the same as Sam's. Leaving 13 Schooner Street wasn't the answer to the problem because, it seemed, you took your phobias, your terrors, with you, carried them around. *Oh, Christ, how the hell did you get rid of them?*

'Why can't Grandpa be buried, Mother, like Grandad Strike was?'

'Because he wanted to be cremated.'

'*I* don't want to be cremated, Mother. I couldn't bear to be *burned*, even when I'm dead.'

Leah felt herself tensing, the muscles in her stomach contracting as she remembered how the mice gnawed the wiring in the attic back in London and might have started a fire at any time, cremating them. *Alive*.

'You're not going to be cremated, darling. And neither am I. Now, shall we both go to sleep?'

Leah made no move to switch off the light and knew that her daughter would not, either. Even here, three hundred miles away from London, the dark was still a terrifying prospect.

Leah was awake before six. She crept downstairs to make a cup of tea. Sarah was fast asleep, and so was Sam when she looked in on him. Her mother was obviously still in the lounge.

Leah switched on the kettle and, on impulse, went into the hall and picked up the phone. She did not expect John to be at Number Thirteen but she had to try, because of what her mother had said last night.

It was ringing out at the other end. Nobody would answer, of course. She counted the rings . . . 11 . . . 12 . . .

It was a strange sensation; she wanted to slam the receiver back on the hook but was powerless to do so, like that day when for some unexplained reason she found herself trapped in the house. *It was as if the telephone wires had rejoined her to the evil and it was holding her prisoner*.

Manacled to the phone, unable to tear herself away, she was forced to listen to that sinister *brrr-brrr*. The mechanical whisper of evil mocked her, its monotony threatening to snap her reason. She knew nobody would speak at the other end; they did not need to. *You cannot escape, wherever you go.*

'Leah, who are you phoning?'

The complaining reprimanding tones did the trick. Something seemed to snap inside Leah, like the breaking of a frayed rope, and threw her forward. The handset slipped from her fingers, banged against the wall and swung crazily to and fro. Her mind was temporarily blank; her mother was speaking again but her words did not register.

'You *are* worried about that man, aren't you?' Marjorie Bourne sneered.

Leah turned slowly and saw her mother's haggard face with its black-ringed eyes, the thin lips curled into a what-did-I-tell-you leer; and her funereal clothes, even a black hat covering the grey hair.

'I don't want to argue with you now, Mother.'

'He's not at home. What did I tell you? Well, put the phone back!'

No, I don't want to touch it. In case it traps me again.

'Helpless as always.' The frail woman pushed past her, grabbed the swinging telephone, clicked it back on to its cradle and stopped that awful purring sound.

'I've got the kettle boiling, Mother.' The kitchen was full of steam, as if the kettle had been boiling for several minutes. But it could not have been more than twenty seconds, Leah tried to convince herself. 'We've got plenty of time. The taxi won't be here until nine.'

It was twenty past nine before the taxi drew up outside, an ex-London cab with a T registration. The young driver was wearing an anorak and jeans. A sea mist had reduced visibility to less than a hundred metres; it was a damp, depressing day.

There was little traffic once they were through Dolgellau. The mist thinned, then thickened again as they began the steep ascent of Dinas-Mawddwy. The driver changed down from third to second. The engine missed, but picked up.

A sudden fear that they might break down made Leah glance nervously out of the window at the swirling opaqueness. It was like that steam in the bathroom; she could imagine all kinds of shapes, things that floated, formed, disintegrated to make way for other nameless horrors. She glanced at her mother, but Marjorie Bourne sat with bowed head, eyes closed. She might have been asleep, or grieving silently. There was no point in disturbing her.

The driver was cutting it fine, Leah thought, when they reached Welshpool at ten-thirty. The cremation service was scheduled for eleven and the undertakers would not wait, because they had a full day of funerals. Death was a cold, calculating business.

The chapel was so impersonal, so lonely, with just Leah and Marjorie and three undertakers. The chaplain rushed his words because he, too, had a full workload. The coffin was terrifying in its simplicity, only a box with a corpse in it. Marjorie's husband, Leah's father.

Leah watched her mother carefully. She was bearing up well; she would not break down. Not until later, anyway.

'*Ashes to ashes, dust to dust.*'

Hurried words again, but they hit Leah with the force of a physical blow. She heard a scratching sound somewhere; it could have come from anywhere. Her father, not dead after all, trying to attract attention in his coffin: *Let me out!* She felt slightly dizzy.

Or maybe mice, chewing through electric cables to start a fire. *To burn the body*.

She felt a surge of panic and had to grip the pew in

front tightly, to hold on; not in case she fell but to stop herself fleeing this place, running screaming out into the mist. *Because there was a faint smell of burning in her nostrils*.

Marjorie stood with bowed head. The curtains were starting to close around the coffin. Leah had to fight against the desire to run for the exit.

That permeating odour was stronger, a rancid stench . . . *the smell of burning flesh*. No, it's all in the mind, she told herself. It is all in the mind, as everything else has been.

But the blood had been real that time she cut her wrist. And so was Ben's blood, a scarlet mulch on the tarmac.

Suffocating now, she was fighting for her breath. She looked for the undertakers; they were on their feet, edging towards the door. Follow them, she thought. But Marjorie had sunk down on to her knees, buried her face in her hands and started to sob.

Mother, we have to leave before it's too late, she wanted to say.

Grey wisps that might have been the fog or smoke were infiltrating through the open door and beginning to fill the chapel. Did they burn the corpse now or later? she wondered.

'*Mother!*'

It came out as a hoarse whisper, a strangled cry of terror. Marjorie Bourne lifted up her head; her face was red, her tears were wet and her eyes were trying to focus out of black-ringed sockets. She said, 'They're going to burn my George.'

Oh, God, there's bodies burning now! Can't you smell them? Leah thought.

Her hand came off the pew, found her mother's and gripped it firmly. Tugging the frail, bemused woman up on to her feet, she started to drag her towards the doorway.

And that was when the greyness darkened for Leah and the smoke thickened so that she could no longer breathe. Legs that suddenly refused to support her sent her tumbling down into the yawning black abyss before her, pulling her mother after her.

20

John Strike sat on the singed sofa, staring at the mass of charred papers in the fireplace. He did not believe it. Yes, he did, because he should have realized that no way was 13 Schooner Street going to burn down. He could douse it in petrol and ignite it, but somehow it would survive. Its unknown, unseen evil occupant would protect it against anything he could throw at it. It was an invincible fortress of evil, an indestructible bastion of the forces of darkness.

It was afternoon now and it seemed light years ago that he had returned to Ruth Ford's house to await her return. She had not come back, but some time after dawn the police had arrived. God, that malevolent force had punished him for his attempt to destroy it. Ruth had been found raped and strangled on a piece of waste ground only a few hundred metres from Schooner Street. A man was 'helping the police with their enquiries' according to the lunchtime edition of the *Standard*. The killing was linked to that of the teenager found in his own porch. But that did not spare John a lengthy interrogation.

How long have you known Miss Ford, Mr Strike? What was your relationship? Why had she been to your house? *Because I've been screwing her for weeks and she wouldn't let up pestering me. I didn't ask her to come to the house. In fact, I sent her packing. Sent her to her death.*

Everything would be out in the open now, he realized. Leah would know what she had undoubtedly already guessed. Kenton would refuse to have him back at the bank, would have him transferred, demoted, to avoid bad publicity for the bank; he'd lose the offender in a faceless army of behind-the-scenes clerks. Female cashiers were dispensable, but soiling the good name of the banking profession was inexcusable.

The police had let John go around lunchtime and he had returned to Number Thirteen. He had sat here surveying his failed handiwork ever since, in a kind of trance. The newspapers had burned, all right; they were charred and flaked, but the sofa had not ignited the way public information adverts warned you it would. Singed, that was all. The carpet was scorched, but a shampoo might bring it back to its original state, or it could be turned round so that furniture would hide the burned area. The ceiling was smoke-blackened but would probably wipe clean. *If* anybody was interested in clearing up the devastation.

Ruth was gone, Leah would not be coming back now, and job prospects were nil. He thought about relighting the fire, and standing here until the blaze caught. But it wouldn't work, some obstacle would be thrust in his way.

He realized that he was not scared any more, because he did not care. He considered suicide in an abstract sort of way. There were paracetamol tablets upstairs in the bathroom; eight were supposed to be fatal. He wasn't afraid of death but it was too much trouble. If it was going to happen he would not flinch; neither car accidents nor drowning bothered him now.

But revenge was still uppermost in his mind.

'You bastard!' He spoke aloud and listened for a reaction, but there was none, no laboured breathing from the hall or the kitchen. Perhaps the thing was satisfied now. It had killed his son, his mistress and his father-in-law.

But he knew it was still here, even if he could not hear it. It was too much to hope that it had left.

There had to be a *reason* for everything that had happened. He wondered why he had not thought of it before. He sat up. The terrors, the killings, surely there had to be a purpose behind them, behind the phobias that had driven the Strikes away. But *why*? If it was a ghost, then *whose*?

He had regarded it simply as an evil entity. How far back did the terror go? Further than the Graftons, because they had left. John had to know, and the obvious starting place was the deeds to the property, which his own bank held as security against his mortgage.

'I'll be back,' he shouted up the stairs on his way to the front door, 'and when I return I'll know just *who* you are.'

Then he was outside in the greyness of an autumn afternoon, hurrying towards the tube station because the bank closed at three-thirty and there was no time to lose.

The bank was crowded with a last-minute rush of customers and the uniformed messenger was standing by the door, ready to lock it promptly at half-past three. John went to the side counter and rang the bell. He noticed with some relief that the light was out in Kenton's room; probably the manager was out on a late luncheon date with a customer. He would face Kenton later, but right now there were more important things to attend to.

'Hallo, Mr Strike.' Jack Armstrong, the chief securities clerk, was within a year of retirement. Conscientious, fussy to the last detail, he had never been managerial material and had occupied his current job for the last twenty years at the branch. Formal as always, he showed no surprise at seeing the accountant unshaven and dressed in casual, creased clothing. In all probability, John thought, he would pass no comment afterwards, either. 'What can I do for you?'

'I need to look at my deeds. Sorry to come at the last

minute. I'm afraid I don't have the receipt with me, but I don't want to take them away.'

'Just a minute.' Armstrong turned away. Five minutes later he returned with a bulky, frayed envelope. 'Ring the bell when you've finished, Mr Strike.'

John seated himself at a customer desk and began browsing through the documents with a practised eye. He skipped over sheafs of legal jargon, then began tracing the title back from his own name. The Graftons. The Smiths. 1952, the Jorgensens had lived there for barely a year. So many names; nobody had stayed long at 13 Schooner Street. The Wilkinsons, 1948–49. *Joseph Nason, 1928–47*. That had to be the one he was looking for! John stuffed the documents back into the envelope and rang the bell again.

'Finished, Mr Strike?' Armstrong was obliging, unruffled, in no hurry to go home amidst a staff who were working feverishly to finish the day's work.

'Jack.' John always called him by his first name even though it was not reciprocated. 'Do you by any chance know anything about a certain Joseph Nason who lived in my house up until 1947?' Did anybody know anything about anybody else in London? But there had to be a starting point.

'I'm afraid I don't, Mr Strike.' He seemed genuinely sorry that he was unable to help. 'But, let me see, Schooner Street . . . Now, Mr Denby lived in Schooner Street. Number Fifteen, unless my memory fails me. He lived there from the war years up until about 1968, when he retired.

John's pulses raced. 'And who is Mr Denby, Jack?'

'George Denby was manager of this branch. He retired just as I started here.'

'But he doesn't live in Schooner Street now.' It was twenty years since Denby had retired. That meant the fellow was around eighty now. *If* he was still alive. John felt his initial surge of euphoria starting to plummet.

'Oh, no. He left London soon after he retired and went to live down in Hastings. Why do you ask?'

'He might be able to help me. If he's still alive.'

'Oh, he's alive, all right.' Armstrong smiled wanly. 'At least he was last Christmas. Every year he sends a Christmas card to the branch, even though nobody except myself knows who he was. I can find his address for you if you'll hang on a minute.'

John Strike arrived back at Number Thirteen with George Denby's address. He attempted to find the telephone number from directory enquiries. No, there was no Denby listed in the Hastings area and he wasn't ex-directory.

'I know who you are, Joseph Nason.' John was frightened by his own voice, that note of near-manic exultation echoing back at him in the empty house. 'And I'm going to find out why you're doing this to everybody who lives here.'

Which meant a trip down to Hastings. Tomorrow. And now he didn't give a damn about staying in the house overnight.

The telephone rang seconds after he had moved away from it.

'Mr Strike, this is Lester and Co.' It certainly wasn't Don Lester; he might well spend the remainder of his life in a mental hospital. The young clerk was just doing a routine job and seemed in a hurry. 'We have a prospective buyer for your house, a Mr Matheson. Is it all right for him to call and view tomorrow afternoon?'

Oh, Christ, Nason is putting the spoke in again. It's a trick to stop me from going to Hastings! John felt his neck beginning to goosepimple. He glanced around but he knew he would see nobody, just feel a presence. Nason was back. *If* he had ever been away.

'I have to go away tomorrow but if he makes it late afternoon then I could well be back. Or else you could send somebody round with him.' And earn your bloody percentage, he thought.

'We don't have anybody to send, sir, but I'll ask Mr Matheson to call on the off chance.'

Five minutes later the phone rang again. This time it was Leah.

'We're coming home tomorrow, John.' She sounded tired, fed up. Her mother was probably getting on her nerves, nagging about having the kids.

'Oh . . . fine.' It wasn't fine, but she was coming and that was that.

'We're coming by train, should be home about two.'

'I won't be home till later, but there's a bloke coming to look at the house, so you can let him in.'

'All right.' He heard a sudden note of relief. 'But whether or not he buys it, the children and I are going to find alternative accommodation. You understand? I really can't keep them off school any longer; Sarah has her mock GCSEs next year.'

That was it, then. Leah and the kids were on their way home; and, apart from Ben's tragic death, life looked like resuming a normal boring routine. He no longer had Ruth as a diversion. And if it had not been for a burning desire for revenge upon this mysterious Joseph Nason, John would not have bothered to go down to Hastings. In all probability he was wasting his time, anyway.

21

George Denby was eighty-three, he told John Strike three times within the space of ten minutes. He and his wife had moved to this small seafront house in 1969 and dear Elizabeth had passed away in 1970. Not because of the move; she had had cancer three years previously. Today, with modern medicine, they might have kept the growth in remission a few years longer.

John had arrived in Hastings just after midday and found Denby's house within twenty minutes. A typical retirement dwelling, it was the kind of place where you could die of boredom if you didn't have a hobby. John was sure the retired bank manager would explain his own interests in detail before long.

Denby was short and stocky, with thinning grey hair and a limp. He had been advised by his doctor to have a hip replacement, he told John as he escorted him through to the small front room, but what was the point when you were already thirteen years over your allotted span? If Elizabeth had still been alive it might have been different, Denby smiled, but he believed in living from day to day.

Somehow the old man's dentures managed to grip the huge blackened briar pipe which he smoked continuously throughout the daytime hours. The distinctive odour of the aromatic honeydew tobacco had permeated the whole house.

'Do have a sherry.' Denby opened a cocktail cabinet in the corner and lifted out a bottle of Bristol Cream and two glasses. 'The staff presented me with this cabinet as a retirement present. And that, too.' He indicated a china leopard crouched on top of it. 'Good days, they were, wouldn't mind reliving them. I'd have Elizabeth again then, wouldn't I? Did you say that you're in the bank, too?' He was suddenly enthusiastic, a man dedicated to a profession discovering someone with whom to discuss his memories of bygone days. Pouring out the sherry, he spilled some but seemed not to notice. 'I don't think I'd like to be in the bank today, all computerized, too impersonal. The customer's just a name. Or rather,' he laughed, coughing at the same time, 'a number. But I wouldn't mind going back to the old days. You did say you were in the bank, didn't you, Mr . . . ?'

'Strike. John Strike. Yes, I'm in the bank, accountant at your old branch . . .'

'Well, goodness me, how simply amazing!' Denby removed his pipe to sip his sherry. 'Now, that really is a coincidence, isn't it? We really do have a lot to talk about.'

'I also live in Schooner Street,' John put in quickly before Denby could launch into the virtues of the banking profession again. 'Number Thirteen.'

'Well, I never!' George Denby's pipe had gone out; it gurgled ominously as he attempted to relight it. 'This really is quite unbelievable. I used to live in Number Fifteen. Do you know it? The one with the laburnum tree by the gate. I expect it's grown big now. Or else somebody's cut it down. There's a lot of guppies living there now, according to what I've read in the papers.'

'Yuppies,' John corrected him. 'Yes, your tree is still there. I was a bit concerned because the pods fall on our side and they're poisonous to children. Tell me, Mr Denby, did you know a fellow by the name of Nason who must have lived next door to you then?'

'Joseph Nason?' Denby removed his pipe from his mouth and nodded. 'Oh, yes, I remember Joseph. He was a customer of the bank from well before the war. A wealthy man, worth a fortune and too miserly to spend it. And then he left it all to charity – can't remember which one. You wouldn't know him, though, he would be dead before you were born.'

'Tell me about him.' John leaned forward.

'A queer chap.' Denby knocked his pipe out into the ashtray and began to refill it. 'Got queerer as time went on. I think it was the war that did it, the blitz and then those doodlebugs – enough to send you off your rocker, particularly if you lived alone as Nason did. I know that my Elizabeth was scared to death of him, which was silly because we never saw him from one day to the next and he was harmless enough. It was towards the end of the war that he became a recluse. We didn't notice it for a time, and then one day, it was just after Christmas, I remarked to Elizabeth that we hadn't seen him for about three weeks and we hadn't noticed any smoke coming out of the chimney. So I said I'd better go round and check that he was all right.'

John experienced that all too familiar tingling in his spine.

'It took me ages to knock him up.' The banker finally got his pipe going to his satisfaction and puffed out thick clouds of sweet-smelling smoke. 'Eventually, though, he opened the door about six inches and peered out, and I can tell you I got the shock of my life. I scarcely recognized him. He had wasted away – he looked like a bloomin' skeleton – and was wearing his hat and coat because he hadn't got any heating. Not because he didn't have any fuel,' Denby added, 'but because the blighter was scared stiff that he might set the house alight, that the chimney might catch fire or else a hot coal tumble out of the hearth. I ask you, near freezing and he wouldn't risk a fire! And he was starving himself, too . . . because he was frightened to go out of the house to buy food. Hypothermia, agoraphobia, and that was only the start!'

'My God!'

'Oh, yes. I went inside that house, just the once, about a week before they found Nason dead, and I can see every detail to this day. I never told Elizabeth, it would have scared her out of her wits. I went and fetched some food for the old boy. In fact, I never got paid for it, but that's by the way. I suppose in doing so I prolonged his miserable life a week or two. When I got back with it he asked me in, and sometimes in the middle of the night when my hip's troubling me and I lie awake, I think about that afternoon.

'Nason was frightened of just about everything. He had rat- and mousetraps set all over the house; he was terrified of any small living creature, even harmless insects. And he stank to high heaven because he hadn't had a bath for years. *He was petrified of water*. Would you believe it? Afraid of drowning in the bath. And when I handed him a loaf I'd brought, he began tearing off chunks, stuffing the bread in his mouth. I asked him if he didn't have a breadknife and he said no, because he'd thrown it in the dustbin . . . and every other knife in the house with it. *And not just knives, anything that was sharp enough to cut you! Because he was terrified of the sight of blood, and phobic about bleeding to death!*

'Then I discovered that he wouldn't go upstairs, at any price. *He hadn't set foot on the stairs for years in case he fell down and broke his neck. He reckoned that even the first stair made him feel giddy. Vertigo, I think they call it.*'

'And he lived in dread of cars?' John Strike's voice was a shaky whisper. He had to know.

'Yes, that, too. All part of the agoraphobia, I suppose. He was scared to go out in case he got knocked down by a car. He told me he'd been in an accident once. The fellow who was driving him was killed, and the driver of the other car was thrown forward and *cut his throat on the broken windscreen!* Mr Strike, you've gone as white as a sheet! Are you all right? Would you like a glass of whisky?'

'I'm all right.' John forced an insipid smile on his trembling lips. 'But please go on, Mr Denby.'

'Of course, Nason died.' Denby sucked on his pipe. 'And I felt guilty about it for ages afterwards. I should have done more for him, fetched him food, persuaded him to light a fire to keep warm. If I could have got him out of that house I would have taken him home, stinking dirty as he was, but nobody could have got him outside the door. One day I went round but couldn't make him hear, so I called the police. The policeman broke a window and asked me to go in with him. There was Joseph Nason, dead on the kitchen floor. He'd been dead several days . . . God, it was an awful sight, it really shook me up! *And those traps he'd set all over the house to catch the rats and mice in the attic . . . well, it was as if the creatures had had their revenge on him. They'd been at him, eating him so that he was scarcely recognizable!*'

'What . . . what did Nason look like?' John was afraid to ask but he had to have confirmation. He already knew.

'Cadaverous, to put it bluntly. Eyes sunk deep into their sockets, gaunt, almost skeletal. And you never saw him without his greasy trilby hat and a navy blue overcoat that reached almost to his ankles. I say, are you sure you're all right, Mr Strike? I think you really ought to have a glass of whisky.'

It was after three o'clock when John Strike left Denby's house. John had guessed most of it, maybe hoping he was wrong, yet he had been shocked because he wasn't. Suddenly the confirmation of his fears made it all a thousand times worse because it was no string of dreadful coincidences. Nason had skulked for years in Number Thirteen, a hermit, a victim of his own fears; his phobias had seeped into the stale atmosphere of a closed house and been born again, so strong that they *lived*, manifested themselves. And they had to be destroyed before there were more deaths.

He considered an exorcism. Was it possible? How did one go about it? Was there time?

Or should he just get out and leave it to somebody else?

No, because he had a personal score to settle with Joseph Nason.

The wind tore at John and almost threw him into the road. He struggled to keep his balance, turning his head to one side in order to draw breath. Salt spray stung his face. On the opposite side of the road a woman was clutching at an umbrella which had been blown inside out. Overhead, clouds raced, caught up with others and merged into larger formations. Christ, there was one hell of a gale blowing in off the sea, hurricane force!

The London train was running half an hour late due to a fallen tree across the line, according to the Tannoy. It didn't matter, John thought, what time he arrived home. Leah would be there, and it was going to be difficult anyway. He needed time to think about Nason.

The delay turned out to be nearly two hours and it was after eight before he arrived back in London. A news placard caught his eye: BATTEN DOWN WARNING; HURRICANE HARRY ON THE WAY. He paused and bought a late edition, half-ashamed of himself for being susceptible to Fleet Street salesmanship. The headlines were a sure seller; the debris from that October 1987 hurricane had not been completely cleared up yet. The cowboys had jumped on the bandwagon and there could be another one very soon.

The hurricane which has ravaged the east coast of America, causing millions of dollars' worth of damage and claiming twenty-two lives, is now heading for Britain, weathermen warned today. 75 mph gales are already lashing the south coast and these could increase to 100 mph in the next twenty-four hours. The core of the hurricane is expected to centre over the south-east of England where structural damage could be severe. Motoring organizations are warning people not to travel unless their journey is unavoidable. The Severn Bridge has already been closed to high-sided vehicles . . .

John started as he noticed a subheading at the bottom of the front page: SEX ATTACKER CHARGED. It could have been any one of a dozen perverts arrested daily but he knew it wasn't, from a gut-wrenching sensation. The pending hurricane was forgotten. 'A man has today been charged with the murders of Tracey Wilson and Ruth Ford. He will appear before magistrates tomorrow morning.'

A mention, no more, because girls were raped and killed nearly every day but a hurricane was still a novelty, he thought. It could affect *you*. Your garden fence might be blown down or you could lose tiles off your roof. Sod some poor wretch lying naked and mutilated on a piece of waste ground; it wasn't any of your business, so why worry?

It was eerie seeing the windows of Number Thirteen lit up. A kind of truce, almost. In some ways he found the darkness and the shadows preferable because he knew what he was up against.

As he crossed the road John experienced a sensation of escalating terror that urged him to turn and run. Now, whilst there was still time. A feeling of portending doom came at him on the shrieking wind, more pronounced than ever before. Not phobias this time, because he understood them, knew now why they happened and could come to terms with them. They were figments of the mind, but what was happening to him now was something real and frightening.

For he knew without any doubt that a man who had been dead for over forty years was inside that house now.

Waiting for him.

With faltering steps, fighting against the wind, for even the elements were bent on preventing him from entering his own home, John gained the shelter of the porch and cowered in the very place where a teenage girl had been brutally murdered. He thought he heard her death cries but it was only the wind. Dead leaves rustled in a heap and blew around his feet.

Voices came from inside, muffled and unrecognizable, perhaps shouting to warn him. But his key was in the lock and turning.

22

'Mum, do we really *have* to go home?' Sarah asked.

'Yes, I'm afraid we do.' Leah avoided her daughter's searching gaze, afraid to reveal her own feelings.

'But it isn't *just* because of school, is it?'

Leah sighed. 'No, it isn't. Mind you, that's partly the reason. You can't afford to miss much more school with your GCSE mocks next year. But I'm afraid Grandma doesn't want us to stay any longer.' That was only a half-truth. Marjorie Bourne wanted Leah to send the two children back to John, and to stay on here on her own. Apart from its being an unreasonable request, Leah was not having her son and daughter back in 13 Schooner Street without her. She and her mother had come close to a row over it. The older woman was distraught, clinging. But she did not want the children here any longer because they 'got on her nerves'.

'I don't like Grandma any more,' Sam muttered.

'Ssh! You mustn't say things like that, Sam. She might overhear you.' Which was unlikely because Marjorie Bourne was still spending the nights downstairs in the front room. George's death was really hitting her now and Leah felt guilty about leaving. But if her mother wasn't prepared to tolerate Sam and Sarah, then they were all going home.

'She didn't make all this fuss over Ben getting killed,' Sam answered sulkily. 'I don't mind going away from here but I don't want to go back to our house.'

'We won't be staying more than one night, two at the most, I promise you that,' Leah said with determination.

'Just long enough for me to find us somewhere else. I'll probably rent a flat.' *If* I can find one, she thought. But it would be safer sleeping in the subways than in that house of death.

The overnight gale had strengthened. The breakers were crashing against the sea wall, partly flooding Marine Parade. Leah heard them when she awoke just after six, and groaned. It was funny how the weather controlled your moods. A sunny day and you could face anything, grey skies and you were depressed. She heard something bouncing and sliding on the roof above, then crashing into the patio garden at the front. A tile. This really was some gale!

The train was running on schedule; they were in Shrewsbury by eleven and the eleven-four intercity to Euston was already waiting. The last lap, into London around two, home by about three. She remembered John's mention of a prospective buyer coming to view. That was a joke; he wasn't likely to be any different from the others. Whoever he was, he would either take a quick look round and flee like a scared rabbit or not turn up at all. She was philosophical about it; if he arrived she would show him round, but she didn't give a damn whether he bought the house or not because she wasn't staying there to wait for surveys and solicitors and contract dates. It might take months to sell. No, whatever the outcome, she would find alternative accommodation in the meantime.

Just one night was bad enough. They would all sleep in the same room for safety. Or rather, spend the night together, because nobody could possibly sleep from now on in Number Thirteen.

She found herself blaming her mother, almost hating her, for without Marjorie Bourne she would not be condemned to taking the kids back to that awful house. Her mother was embittered, blaming Leah because she had got pregnant out of wedlock. It was her way of punishing her daughter. Leah sensed an animosity towards Sarah that had not been there before, because Sarah was the direct product of pre-marital sex. She told herself that her mother would not outlast her father by long, and she was surprised that the thought did not disturb her.

The news placards carried warnings of 'Hurricane Harry'. Already the winds were gusting down the streets. Sheets of cardboard, refuse sacks that had not been collected and almost every imaginable form of litter were piling up in any sheltered place. It had stopped raining and there was a grittiness in the atmosphere that stung her eyes.

Half an hour later Leah and the children alighted at Balham and began to fight their way against the gale. A chimneypot had smashed in the road, broken tiles were everywhere. And the weathermen were still claiming that the full force of the hurricane had not arrived in Britain yet.

'What the devil's been happening here?' Leah stared in astonishment at the singed carpet, the smoke-blackened ceiling, the hearth full of charred newspapers.

'I think Daddy's been trying to get a fire going,' Sarah replied.

'The damned fool! He could have set the house on fire. Well, he'll have to pay for a new carpet. But I don't give a sod whether he does or not, because we won't be here after tomorrow.'

The doorbell chimed, making them jump.

'That will be the man come to look at the house.' Leah regarded the fire damage and pulled a wry face. There was no time to clean the mess up. 'Well, I suppose I'd better let him in.'

Mr Matheson gave Leah the impression of a retired clerk, a bachelor without a doubt, set in his own ways and unwilling to change. He was respectably dressed but his dark overcoat had seen plenty of wear and the shine on his shoes failed to hide the thin leather. Grey-haired, and sharp-featured, he had to force a smile; he was ill at ease, unused to company, with eyes that darted and noticed detail. Rubbing his thin hands together, he was a kind of living caricature of a miserly, poverty-stricken office worker from the last century, perhaps a misogynist, from the way he kept his distance from her.

'I'll show you round,' she smiled, wishing that Sam and Sarah would stop crowding her the way they used to do when they were very small. 'I'm afraid my husband has rather foolishly tried to light a fire. We shall, of course, either replace the carpet or deduct the cost from the price, whichever you prefer. Now, shall we look at the kitchen, and then I'll take you upstairs.'

Matheson seemed uncommunicative almost to the point of rudeness. Staring intently, once trying to peer round Leah at Sam and Sarah so that they shrank back like shy infants, he watched her every move; his very presence was disconcerting. Yet he asked no questions. A cough rumbled in his lungs; she thought that either he was a heavy smoker or else he had bronchitis. Or both. He was so painfully thin, he looked ill.

'Really, it is a very comfortable and conveniently situated house.' She was talking to break the awful silence. I sound just like an estate agent, she realized. Like Lester, and he's at a head farm now. 'Twenty minutes by tube to the city . . .'

'Mum, I'm cold,' Sarah complained in a whisper. She was shivering.

'Yes, Daddy must have forgotten to switch the central heating on.' Because he's been away sleeping with some whore, she suspected. Or else it's broken down, and that's why he tried to light a fire and risked burning the house down. 'I'm going downstairs in a minute and I'll turn the heating up.'

But their visitor appeared to be in no hurry. He leaned forward to examine items which interested him, as though he was totally oblivious of their presence. And, outside, the wind was shrieking to an even greater velocity, rattling the windows.

'When you've finished, we'll go back downstairs, Mr Matheson.' Leah spoke almost in awe, despising herself for it. Look, we're getting bloody frozen up here, she wanted to say. And what's our wedding photograph got to do with you?

The cheek of the man, he even picked it up and examined it minutely, and when he put it back on the dresser it fell over. He did not bother to set it upright again. His long bony fingers stroked an ivory hairbrush and turned it over.

'I shall have to go downstairs and turn the radiators up, Mr Matheson. The children are getting cold. I've only just returned from . . . holiday.'

'Oh . . . yes.' He turned and seemed to have difficulty focusing; his eyes were glazed as if cataracts covered them. 'Please carry on, Mrs Strike, don't mind me.'

Will you bloody well come on downstairs! She tensed, feeling suddenly afraid. 'All right, come down when you've finished.'

She almost fled the bedroom, Sam clutching at her dress, Sarah gripping her hand. The children were hurrying, dragging her with them.

And then she heard a key being turned in the front door lock.

'Hi! Whatever's up with you three?' John Strike stood in the hall. He saw the fear on the faces of his wife and children, their obvious relief at seeing him. *Oh, Christ, whatever's wrong now?*

'Mr Matheson's here,' Leah blurted out, then lowered her voice. 'He's upstairs, looking at *everything*, poking his nose into – '

'So long as he buys the house . . .' John's voice tailed off. He felt the tension, as powerful as that rising hurricane outside, the atmosphere charged with evil, the damp coldness, the odour of staleness. And it had nothing whatsoever to do with a house that had been unoccupied for a few days.

'How long has he been here?'

'About . . .' Leah was going to say 'a quarter of an hour' but that could not be right. Because they had been home just after three-thirty and it was now fully dark. 'What time is it?'

John consulted his watch. 'Six-thirty.'

Matheson had been here three hours!

'John, I'm frightened!' She gave a whimper and rushed to her husband. Sam and Sarah clung to their father. And in that moment of terror everything was forgiven.

'He's coming now,' John muttered, as the dragging, shuffling footsteps sounded on the landing above. Bracing himself, he tried to pull Leah and the children behind him, offering his body as a shield against whatever would appear at the head of the stairs in a couple of seconds. He heard its approach, felt its malevolence; the rasping cough that was a death rattle of a mirthless laugh. *And John almost cried his fear aloud when he saw the man who called himself Matheson.*

George Denby's description was terrifyingly accurate: cadaverous, emaciated, eyes sunk deep into their sockets. The greasy trilby was jammed firmly on his head and the frayed navy blue overcoat fell almost to his ankles. His aquiline features were partly hidden in the shadow cast by the brim of the hat. Standing there at the top of the stairs, thin lips drawn back in a leer as he perceived the fear of those below him, he was rubbing his gaunt hands together in sadistic satisfaction. But there was no mistaking the sheer hatred in those features.

'*Joseph Nason!*' John shouted.

'So you know me.' The voice was a croak, reminding John of a record with scratched grooves. Staccato. Venomous.

'I know you!' Suddenly anger transcended terror for John Strike. Above him stood the man who was responsible for death and madness – the death of his own son, his father-in-law. 'And, by God, you've got a lot to answer for!'

'I have merely returned to claim back what is rightfully mine.' Nason's head was thrust forward and his eyes appeared to smoulder in the shadows. 'This is my house and you have stolen it from me. Not only that, you have attempted to burn it down. Leave now, or you will surely regret it!'

Sam and Sarah were sobbing with fear, Leah was trying to hold back a scream. And in that moment John Strike's anger exploded within him and threw him into an uncontrollable rage. In his mind he saw Ben, a tiny, limp, crushed and bloodied form, the red football cap lying pathetically in the road. With a choking cry of fury he pushed the others from him and ran for the stairs.

'I bloody well want *you*!' he yelled. 'By Christ, you're going to pay for what you've done to my family!'

Sarah screamed. John felt her clutching at him, yelling, 'Come back, Daddy! Don't go!'

Leah was grasping his arm, white with fear, trembling. Sam, too. All three of them were attempting to hold their father back. Whilst up above them the man called Joseph Nason laughed harshly. John shook them off, pushed them away and ran for the stairs.

'I'll bloody kill you!' he hissed, as he began to mount the stairs.

Two steps at a time, he was halfway up when a strange sensation flooded over him. It was as though his feet were leaden weights; it was an effort to move them, but still he managed to do so. Everything about him was slowing down, not just himself, in a kind of action replay, a feeling of timelessess. And the stench which came at him was overpowering; an odour of mustiness, of stale air combined with the smell of unwashed bodies and stinking clothing. It was so cold, too, that he heard his teeth chattering like distant machine-gun fire.

And up there in front of him Joseph Nason stood triumphant, his face no longer in shadow, gaunt and almost skeletal, the wide lips displaying blackened and uneven teeth, old man's saliva trickling down his wasted chin; not moving, because he knew he was invincible, beyond the vengeance of ordinary mortals.

John swayed, and would have toppled backwards had he not grabbed the stair rail. *Like that burglar. Any second it would snap, a broken strut would pierce his throat; he would hang there, speared, jetting his blood all over the walls and ceiling. He felt the wooden balustrade start to give under his weight.*

Somewhere, it sounded far away, he heard Leah still screaming, the children hysterical. His vision blurred. He could not see Nason properly now, just an outline that might have been a farmer's ragged scarecrow. But he felt his presence, his awful power, the sheer malevolence, the evil that had lived on in this house for forty years.

A cracking sound; the stair rail was starting to snap. He let go, and the vertigo robbed him of his balance. It was like one of those awful falling dreams; he would wake up with a start any second and find himself safely in bed. But he knew he wouldn't because this was no dream.

As he went backwards, his feet felt light now. He seemed to hang suspended as if he had suddenly found a way to defy Newton's law. Maybe he would float up to the ceiling, the way he sometimes did in dreams, a sort of freeing of his astral body.

No, he was falling, clawing the air, gathering speed. One last glimpse of Nason, arm upraised in a kind of Nazi salute, a phlegm-rattling laugh of triumph, and then John Strike's world was gyrating, spinning faster and faster.

He felt himself hit the hall floor, slide, then knock over a chair. The pain was not as bad as he had expected. Lying there winded, he saw the shimmering faces of his wife and children, their hands exploring him, searching for broken bones.

'I'm . . . okay,' he grunted, waiting for the walls to steady and everything to slow down. He closed his eyes for a second and saw again that terrible apparition on the stairs. He mentally cringed from it.

But when he opened his eyes everything was apparently as normal as he could have hoped. He was shaken, but he knew there was no permanent damage. Looking to the stairs, he found nobody up there, just Leah and Sarah and Sam bending over him, concerned for his safety in the midst of their terror.

He struggled up; the feeling of dizziness had passed. He lurched for the stairway again.

'John, come back!'

'I have to . . . to be sure.' He began to climb, and this time there was no invisible barrier to halt his progress.

There would not be anybody up there but he had to satisfy himself, checking every room, switching on the lights and leaving them on. Once they flickered momentarily but it was probably the storm outside. There could well be a power failure. He shuddered at the thought, the prospect of spending the night here with no electricity, no light except for flickering candles which created weird and terrible shadows. Then he was going back downstairs, holding on to the rail, testing its firmness.

'He's gone.' He did not expect them to believe him. He was not sure he even believed it himself, except that George Denby's story had been confirmed. The recluse who had once been Joseph Nason had created phobias that lived on here. *So strong that now the man himself had been called up from his hermit's grave.*

'John, we can't stay here a second longer!' Leah was holding the children to her. 'We must go now before some other terrible tragedy strikes us.'

'I have to stay.' He sounded tired but determined. 'I can't run from it now I know.'

'But you can't fight it, whatever it is!' Hysteria was creeping back into her voice. 'Do what you want, but I'm taking the children to safety.'

The lights went off; came back on. Sarah screamed.

'All right, you go.' He picked up the fallen chair and leaned on it. There was no point in relating the retired bank manager's story, not now, anyway. 'Book in to an hotel or somewhere. Call me and let me know where you are and I'll join you later. But first I have a job to do.'

An impossible task; it was madness, for nobody could destroy something that was already dead. He had tried and failed. But there had to be a way. Even if there wasn't, he was not running. Because of Ben. And Ruth. The desire for vengeance was too strong.

It wasn't going to drive him out as it had driven out the Graftons and those before them. Defeat for John Strike was the ultimate in degradation. He would never be able to live with himself if he ran now. He had to stay here because there was nothing left for him anywhere else.

He heard the front door slam behind Leah and the children. And then the lights went out.

23

The door flew inwards the moment Leah turned the catch. It took all her strength to prevent it from slamming into the hall wall. A howling, shrieking wind whipped the words off her lips as she called to Sam and Sarah to get outside. Holding the door, disentangling her children's frightened grip on her, she pushed them out into the porch. Dragging the door closed as it almost leaped from her grasp, she struggled with it until she felt the Yale click shut.

The three of them huddled together. Leah had no idea where they were going; the first cheap bed and breakfast accommodation they found would suffice. There were crashes everywhere. Chimneys and tiles were cascading into the road, buckling the roofs of parked cars, smashing windscreens. In the orange-tinted holocaust, trees were bent almost to the ground.

'*Look!*' Sam screamed, and pointed.

That laburnum tree in the front garden of Number Fifteen had been uprooted, bringing the dividing wattle fence down with it. A heap of debris blocked their exit to the pavement. The branches were straining, and the vicious multi-armed creature seemed intent on lashing any who came within striking distance.

'We'll have to climb over it!' Leah yelled, but doubted whether the other two heard. 'I'll hold the branches.'

Just as she started forward she heard Sarah shriek, and turned. The girl was pointing into a corner of the porch, a dark recess where something heaved and writhed, an indefinable shape convulsing in agony. *Oh, merciful God, it's that girl who was raped and strangled!*

It wasn't, it was a pile of rustling, shifting leaves, elongated and stretching one moment, bunched tight the next, frightening at first glance in the dim light from the streetlamps.

'It's only leaves,' she shouted in Sarah's ear. She grabbed the child and found a hold on Sam. 'Now, come on.'

A waving branch lashed Leah's face, making her cry out as she grabbed it and fought with it. She straddled the trunk. It was moving, trying to throw her. Sam went first, wriggling low on his stomach until he made it on to the concrete on the other side. Sarah next, her skirt tearing, a ribbon of material fluttering behind her like a bizarre tail.

Then Leah, and the three of them lay in a heap on the pavement. Something smashed close by and threw shards in every direction – a tile bursting like exploding shrapnel. It had become a hostile, macabre world where Man fought for survival.

Leah kept the children close and tried to shield them with her body. An overturned car blocked the pavement, so they had to make a detour into the litter-strewn road. Glass powdered and crunched beneath their feet.

Then, without warning, everywhere was plunged into deep darkness.

Sam and Sarah were whimpering up against her. They clearly could not remain here. She thought about seeking shelter in one of the adjacent houses but decided against it. They would be safe in the underground; the storm could not penetrate there. She followed the pavement, an arm outstretched to warn her of any obstacle in their path. They turned left, went a few hundred metres, then crossed the road, skirted the waste ground, crossed another road, and the tube station entrance was on their left.

Not once did they pass another traveller. It was as though the inhabitants of this besieged suburb had fled, gone elsewhere. That was ridiculous, she told herself. Everybody was sheltering in their frail houses, as they had done during the air raids nearly half a century ago.

Leah cursed her mother, for they could have been safe away from the teeth of this storm; instead, they were fugitives in a hostile city.

The underground station was closed! Leah fought against despair. On her own she might have given up and just lain down to die in the barricaded entrance. A uniformed ticket collector with a paraffin lamp was waving away any who might seek escape or safety below ground. Impassive, merciless, he shouted something, but the gale took his words.

There was a brief respite in a shop doorway. A car passed, braked, then reversed into the side of the road. In its headlights Leah saw a van on its side; the driver might have been dead inside or he might have abandoned his vehicle. She didn't care which, her only concern was her children's safety. Damn you, Mother, she thought. And damn you most of all, Joseph Nason, or whatever your name is!

There was no question of going back to Number Thirteen. They would never make it, but, in any case, rather this hurricane than the evil that dwelled there. She wondered about the police station; she had no idea where it was, but there had to be one. Hugging the shop fronts, they moved on down the main street. There was the pelican crossing without its lights. Don't look in case you see, she told herself. She thought she heard a scream borne on the wind.

A telephone kiosk! Her outstretched hand touched it.

Miraculously the thick glass was unbroken. She would phone for help. Sam and Sarah tugged at the heavy door. Somehow they got it open and squeezed inside. Leah fumbled for a coin, found the slot and tried to work out where the 9 button would be. She found it just as she discovered that there was no dialling tone. In all probability, she realized, there was not a telephone in London that was working.

'Mum, what are we going to do?'

She tried to think up an answer, any meaningless words, in the vague hope that she might allay their terror, because there was nothing they could do. Then, without warning, the streetlighting flickered back on.

Dim and eerie, its feeble glow taunted them with silhouettes of devastation: a roof that had collapsed and avalanched into the road, buried parked vehicles, gaping shopfronts ready for –

And as if the wan lighting had been their cue, the looters came out of the wreckage, sinister flitting shapes, human vultures arriving to prey on the remnants of civilization.

'Keep still!' Leah whispered even though the advancing mob would not have heard had she shouted. Huddling in the cramped glass cubicle, praying that they would not be seen, she cried her terror aloud as a torchbeam found them, dazzled them. *No, please spare my children!*

Faceless creatures of the dark hiding behind their torches, the rabble saw their helpless victims trapped in a glass cell and came for them. Leah tried to hold the door shut, but it was only a token protest. A forest of lusting hands like tentacles reached out of the storm, a fallen tree that had come alive.

They had her, and dragged her out into the open. Sam and Sarah were screaming but she could not see them. She struggled and then gave up, closing her eyes as her clothing was shredded from her body. *No, please spare my children!*

She was aware that they would spare nobody, for the night storm would hide their foul deeds. Her arms were pinioned; she thought they would snap. Her legs were pulled wide until she thought they would dismember her. Only her head was free. She turned it in an attempt to find the children, but there was no sign of them. Bodies crowded, human rats were swarming.

Suddenly it was as if the whole world had exploded. The rumbling and crashing was even louder than the hurricane itself. Missiles flew and found their mark. Leah felt that bone-snapping grip on her relinquish its hold, and was aware that she was coming free of the man who thrust and powered into her. She fell back; it was a soft landing, and she lay there, looking up in vain hope.

Powdered glass like sea spray scintillated in the street-light, which revealed a bizarre, unrecognizable, devastated landscape. Buildings had gone; there was just eternal blackness beyond the restricted radius of the lights; and mountains where previously there had been a tarmac plain. Above Leah, that monster whose comrades had held her for the forced mating tottered uncertainly.

Fearfully her eyes travelled up from his obscene bared thighs. His clothing had gone, his heaving torso was awash with crimson . . . a thick neck, then nothing! *Just a ragged stump that pumped dark fluid, a bizarre fountain in a pool of carnage, like a beheaded chicken held upright by its nerves amongst the slain in the slaughter shed!*

Mind-blasted, numbed, Leah clawed her way out of that landslip of brickwork and corpses. She smelled death, tasted the bitter iron flavour of blood, but ignored it and thanked God that she had been spared to search for her offspring.

Clawing at the debris, trying to dig, snatching her

fingers away from bodies that were not her own kin, she called out for them, sobbing her terror and frustration into the wild night.

She tried to stand up but fell sideways. Something cut her hand but she was scarcely aware of it. Pulling at a thick timber above her, she hauled her body off the ground. And realized as she collapsed a second time that something was dreadfully wrong.

The streetlamps gave one final flicker, fought for a second or two to survive. The cruel moments of dimming artificial lighting were time enough for Leah to witness her own mutilation. She screamed hysterically as her eyes alighted on her bleeding thigh stumps, then travelled on to where her amputated legs still twitched like landed eels in a pool of blood.

The Stygian darkness surged back, and somewhere in its unholy depths she thought she heard Sam and Sarah calling for her.

24

John Strike stood there in the blackness, bewildered. A power failure was a factor he had not taken into consideration until the first flicker of the lights a few minutes ago. He had never had a fear of the dark, even as a boy, but now it was terrifying – a strong disadvantage when he was alone in the house with Joseph Nason.

He tried to listen, but all he heard was the storm outside. Tiles were cascading off the roof and somewhere not very far away he heard a tree come down, probably that big Corsican pine in one of the gardens at the back, he decided. The grinding and tearing were followed by a crash that vibrated the brickwork. But that wasn't his worry.

Nason was here all right, he had no doubt about that. He could sense him in the cloying cold atmosphere and feel the clammy touch of his icy fingers. They were snatched away when he turned round; Nason was playing with him, wearing him down.

John edged his way into the kitchen and groped in the units until he found the box of candles that was kept for a remote emergency such as this. He wondered if the first one would light or whether the wick would be as ill-fated as that fire he had built in the front room. He struck a match, and with some reluctance the tallow caught, its eerie yellow light creating a multitude of shadows. With trembling fingers he lit two more, stuck them in saucers and placed them at strategic points in the kitchen. Then one more for the hallway, its flame flickering in a draught that came in beneath the front door. It would probably blow out before long.

In a way the candlelight made it worse, leading him to imagine all kinds of things. Shapes changed when he looked hard at them; others tried to sneak up behind him, then fled when he turned round, constantly moving; it was another dimension. Like Nason.

The storm had to be at its height now, surely. Upstairs something fell, then rolled. One of those ornaments on the dressing table probably. But the wind could not touch them!

Leah hadn't phoned. The sudden realization came as a shock. She had been gone an awfully long time, two hours at least, he reckoned. Now he found himself listening for the telephone. Eleven o'clock and it still had not rung. Maybe she had had difficulty finding somewhere to book in. It was bloody stupid coming back from Wales at a time like this. That cow Marjorie had done it to spite him, he knew. *You go back home, Leah, and find out what that man's up to.*

The gale was shrieking harder than ever now, rattling an upstairs window frame, threatening to tear it out. More slates were going, sliding and bumping down the roof, splintering on the pavement. He heard a metallic bang; one had hit a car parked outside. He hoped it wasn't the Suzuki.

Leah wasn't going to ring. It was after midnight; she would leave it until morning now. Or perhaps the phone wasn't working, he thought, suddenly relieved because there might be a perfectly ordinary reason why he had not heard from her. He almost ran into the hall; the candle spluttered and nearly went out. He grabbed the receiver – not so much as a dialling tone. Dead, thank God!

That was when the candle flame blew horizontally and

extinguished. There was just the light coming through the kitchen now, an unearthly glow. He'd better get back in there . . .

'*Dad!*'

He froze. The cry seemed to come from somewhere upstairs. Recognition sent an icy chill over him; it was like the whimper of fear Ben used to make when he woke up and was scared of the dark. Any second he would come sleep-running out of his room, dash for the stairs. John had to stop him, he might fall and . . . Except that it was not Ben's voice. *It was Sam's!*

John was at the bottom of the stairs before he checked himself. It could not be Sam because he was with Leah, holed up safely somewhere. It was a trick to lure him upstairs . . . so that vertigo would make him fall, maybe breaking his neck this time.

'You don't fool me, Nason!' John yelled angrily, but the noise of the storm drowned his words. He was sweating heavily and his shirt was sticking to his body. 'Come on out and face me, Nason!'

Only the wind answered him, banging angrily at a window up above.

Was that somebody sobbing? He strained his ears but the sound was gone now. He had thought for one awful moment that it was Leah. He went back through to the kitchen.

He was tired; more than that, exhausted. He had not slept for two nights now. You're not achieving anything by staying here, he told himself. Nason's dead; you can't harm him. And then there's tomorrow night, and the night after that. You'll crack before he does. Be logical, he wants to get rid of you because you're in his house; you want to go, so where's the problem? The problem is he doesn't want the house sold again, just wants it left for him. *And I'm not paying a bloody mortgage for a fucking spook!*

A cry. That was Sarah's voice, no doubt about it, loud and clear in a lull between the gusts. He didn't catch what she said, but there was no doubt that she was in pain and frightened. And she was just at the top of the stairs.

'I'm coming, my darling!'

He rushed into the hall, then stopped. He's fooling you again, he thought. *But I have to be sure*. The candleglow seeped up the stairway wall and patterned the rail on to the emulsion like outsize prison bars; one of the struts seemed to be broken and something was suspended from it. *A body, swinging gently*.

John almost screamed, but when he looked more closely there was no break in the row of uprights. No body. A trick of the candlelight. Another trick of Nason's.

'You're a dirty fucking bastard!' he shouted up the stairs. A loud bang answered him, followed by a crash of splintering glass. The window had finally gone.

It was pointless staying here, he decided. He stood to gain nothing, not even a chance of revenge. Far better to leave now, and hope to sell the house. *Go on, then, there's the door, coward!*

He had half expected that agoraphobic barrier; he'd had a premonition before he encountered it. It was a feeling akin to blundering into an electric stock fence – he had touched one once many years ago. It hurt and gave you a fright, but didn't do any real harm. You just made sure you did not go near it again.

He knew it was there in the same way that grazing cattle know where the electric fence is. He backed off and licked his dry lips. One thing was certain, he wasn't leaving this house tonight; the rear patio door would be barred to him, too. It was a waste of time even checking it. Nason was pulling every trick.

'Look.' He spoke in a voice that quavered. 'Why don't we talk this over? I'm prepared to leave if you'll let me go. And I won't come back.'

No answer. Just the hurricane renewing its efforts to strip the roof, trying to get to him. Nason didn't have to do any deals; he was calling the tune, had been all along.

We should have left at the outset, John realized. If we had, then Ben and Ruth would still be alive. And George. He wasn't sure about the burglar, or that girl who had been strangled in the porch, because he had had no control over them. Now it was too late.

Somebody was walking about upstairs, in the main bedroom directly overhead. The slow, dragging steps paused. Then an object fell; glass broke and tinkled on the floor. The wedding photograph, John guessed. Nason had been intrigued by it again and had maybe broken it deliberately. The footsteps did not come again.

Christ, it was hours until daylight! Nason had got John on his own, sorted him out of the herd like a cowboy singling out a bum steer. Some he had killed, others he had sent away. He was playing with him, slowly driving him mad. I won't let him! Ben's dead, Leah and the other two are safe, and if I hear voices it's only a trick, he told himself.

Somewhere water was running. It must be the bathroom; the taps had been turned on. Well, that's fine, he thought, I'm not going up to turn them off. If the bath overflows and brings the ceiling down, then tough shit! The insurance will pay for the damage, the roof will cost them a fortune, anyway. I couldn't give a . . .

Sudden terror took him by surprise, caught him off guard. As it had at the swimming baths that day. One second everything was fine, the next he was on the verge of blind panic. He could smell chlorine again, felt it stinging the back of his throat. Breathing was difficult. He was gasping for air as if he was . . . *drowning!*

The house was going to flood. Water would come pouring down the stairs and would not be able to escape because he could not open the doors to let it out. When the level rose, he would climb on a chair, then stand on the table, but eventually it would reach right up to the ceiling. He would be drowned like a rat in a cage trap dropped into the river. There was no escape. Stupid, but it was true.

The bath was overflowing. He could hear water splashing on the linoleum floor. He wanted to shout, to plead with his tormentor, but no words came. He scrambled up on to the units; it would not save him, merely prolong his torture.

It was as if the hurricane was concentrating its entire force on Number Thirteen, raging in at the open window upstairs, devastating the bedroom, piling the furniture into a corner and starting to smash it up. It had breached the defences, infiltrated this suburban fortress. *And somewhere amidst the noise John heard Leah screaming that her legs were gone.*

The water was real, the storm was real but everything else was Joseph Nason's trickery. John looked up and saw water starting to seep through the bowing ceiling. Any minute now it would come deluging down. He slid down off the sink unit, went through to the hall and relit the candle by the telephone. Now he could see the stains on the wall left by the blood. It wasn't just shadows. That fellow hadn't made a very good job of washing down the emulsion.

Leah was still screaming somewhere – it might have been inside his head – shouting for the children because she had lost them in the storm. That was ridiculous, because by now they were undoubtedly snug and warm in some dingy hotel bedroom. He wished that he had left with them.

Funny, he couldn't hear the water now. Somebody must have turned off the taps. Nason, probably. John sat down on the chair and waited. There was nothing else to do.

The wind had risen again with renewed force, as if it had paused to gather all its strength for one final assault. There could not be many tiles left on the roof now and it sounded as if another upstairs window would go before long.

Suddenly the lights came back on. No warning; one moment there was eerie candlelight, the next dazzling brightness. They flickered, went off again, then came back on. They were not so bright this time, just a kind of ethereal glow. But even on reduced power they were brighter than the candles.

He checked the telephone but it was still dead. Then he went through to the kitchen. The ceiling was holding. Just. It resembled the underside of a punctured waterbed, with a steady drip-drip from the far corner. But he wasn't going upstairs to check; he wasn't going anywhere.

A scurrying movement made him turn. He saw a grey furry shape dart across the hall and into the front room. Then another; and still more, some large, some small. *Rats and mice!*

A feeling of revulsion engulfed him and he climbed back up on to the units. Doubtless they had come down from the attic, driven from their hiding place by the force of the hurricane. They were deserting the sinking ship, leaving the humans on board to drown when it went down.

He could hear them in the other room, squeaking in terror, running back and forth. Some more crossed the hall to join them. So long as they kept out of the kitchen, that was fine by him.

The lights dimmed still further. The fluorescent strip overhead reminded him of a red-hot soldering iron. There was nothing he could do except wait for the dawn, but he knew even daylight might not be his salvation.

His thoughts turned to Ruth. He felt grief but it was different from his sickening sorrow over Ben. Just another affair, in the end it would have come to nothing. But the responsibility for her death was his, as surely as if he had strangled her himself. Because he was the cause of her coming to this house of evil.

He found himself feeling sorry for Joseph Nason, the poor lonely old man whose phobias had killed him. It wasn't Nason's fault; he was a victim of his fears. A victim of society, really. Denby had tried to help, done his best, but it was too late by then. Others had known, but ignored him because it wasn't their problem. There had been no social workers to check up on a recluse.

And I'm as bad as the rest of them, he thought. All I want is revenge that won't do any good. It won't bring back Ben. Or Ruth.

Another movement, one he sensed rather than heard, and a deepening of the shadows out in the hallway. Tensing, pressing himself back against the wall, he drew up his legs, and not just in case the rats and mice swarmed in here. A shape materialized out of the darkness, a wretched figure in a long frayed coat and worn trilby, and stood in the doorway, watching him.

And there was no doubt in John Strike's mind that Nason had arrived for the final confrontation.

25

Even the shadows were unable to hide that corpse-like face, the emaciation, the wasting flesh, the eyes burning deep in the black sockets, the nose little more than twin holes above the twisted mouth. But gone was the smouldering hatred that John Strike had witnessed in the man who had called himself Matheson; instead of arrogance and defiance there was now a marked wretchedness that was evident in the hunched shoulders, the posture of dejection. Cowering, he was almost . . . pleading.

'So you've shown yourself at last, Nason,' John said evenly. 'Or should I call you Matheson?'

'You have tried to drive me out of my home.' The voice was a cracked, whining whisper. 'The others left but you tried to destroy me, even attempted to burn down this house which is rightfully mine. The house you *stole* from me!'

God, how the hell did you try to explain to somebody that they were dead? 'I bought it, Nason. So did the others. Can't you understand that?'

'It's *my* house!' His petulance was a cry of defeat and despair. 'You don't understand, I live here. And you've let the rats and mice breed again, you've destroyed everything. If you had just gone away then these people would not have died.'

'You killed my son, others as well!' John had to control his anger. Suddenly the entity, the spectre which had terrified them by its very presence for months, was no longer a fearful prospect. Revolting, malevolent, yes; but not frightening. All that was frightening was that which Joseph Nason had created.

'Why don't you just leave?' The skeletal arms attempted to spread in a gesture of resignation but fell weakly back. 'Go now.'

'I can't. I can no more pass through the doors of this house than you can. Your agoraphobia has got me, too.'

'I have not been outside for many years.' Nason seemed to cringe. 'Outside there is death in many forms, as there is now inside. The vermin will spread disease, the water will flood and drown us. Go upstairs, and you will fall down and break your neck. There are knives, too, with which you might cut yourself and bleed to death. And only *I* prevented us from being burned alive.'

The storm was raging, throwing everything at the house as if it was determined to demolish this breeding ground of fears. There was a clatter, then breaking glass – another window had been ripped out. Leaves were rustling at the front door, trying to get in. A snapped branch was banging on the patio door.

A rush of rats and mice in the hallway retreated in panic to the other room. Joseph Nason gave a wheezing scream and seemed to shrink in size as his bony shoulders hunched still further. 'Even now my home is being destroyed. But I will not leave. I cannot, no more than you can, my friend!'

The kitchen ceiling had sunk another foot. Water was oozing through the cracks, dripping steadily. It could not hold up much longer.

'Perhaps we could try and leave together.' John slid off the cupboards, edged away from the pending waterfall.

'*No!* I will die here as I have lived here.'

John thought he detected a faint smell of burning; it might have come from the candles. The one in the hall had been blown out by the icy draught rushing down the stairs, and the extinguished wick was still smouldering. He told himself it had to be that.

A tearing, rushing sound interrupted his thoughts, making him leap for the doorway as the kitchen ceiling capitulated in a rush of water; a deluge, a miniature tidal wave, foamed upwards, sweeping a chair and table with it. He dived for the doorway as the wave hit him, knocked him to his hands and knees and saturated him. The water crashed against the front door, then swirled back. There was debris everywhere and . . . *oh, Jesus Christ, the rats were swimming for their lives, climbing up on to the furniture like shipwrecked sailors on rafts.*

He heard a scream, a shriek of terror that no human lungs could have produced, a sound that surely came from beyond the realms of the living! John knelt there and looked back. The kitchen light had fused as it came down; only the glow from the hall remained. But it was enough for him to see Joseph Nason clinging frantically to the stair rail from the third step, driven up the stairs because there was nowhere else to go. His features reflected the torments of hell, an unearthly body in excruciating pain, his festered mind pushed beyond the brink of endurance.

Rats and mice were everywhere, some floating belly upwards, drowned by the sudden flood. *They huddled at the bottom of the stairway with water lapping at them, but not even the threat of a watery death would drive them upwards. No way would they venture past that corpse-like creature above them.*

John staggered to his feet and leaned back against the wall. The telephone hung by its cord, submerged; the table on which it had stood had floated away somewhere in the semi-darkness. Rats brushed against him and he almost cried out. Filthy icy water all around, to a depth of perhaps eighteen inches, no more, was finding its level, frothing and settling. There was just one flood. Maybe the tank in the attic had come down, he thought, or it was just the flood in the bathroom; there was no sound of water pouring through the kitchen ceiling now, thank goodness. A domestic flood, damage which the insurance would pay for, along with that sustained from the hurricane; no lives lost except those of the rodents. He would not drown, it was no cause for panic.

Only Nason had given way to panic. He was gripping the woodwork, his wasted features a terrible mask of terror as his long-time fear of water became stark reality. Below him the surviving rats were squeaking their fear, forcing him up to where his phobia of heights began. He writhed as vertigo took its hold; he might fall, drown or be ravaged by those filthy scavengers.

Or burn, because now there was smoke drifting down from the landing above.

'The . . . house . . . is . . . on . . . fire!' John was not sure whether Nason shouted or mimed the words. Did he really hear him or was it all in the mind? Right now it did not matter, because he could hear the first crackle of flames, a roaring fanned by the hurricane which had finally breached the defences of 13 Schooner Street.

A grotesque serpent of thick black smoke was oozing its way down from the landing, a beast of suffocating death in search of prey, enveloping the living dead thing which cowered before it like a foetus in a womb.

The storm had started the fire, John decided, a combination of the collapse of the wiring in the attic and the flood. Possibly the electrics had been gnawed by the vermin in some kind of predestined preparation for this terrible night. He could hear the wind shrieking its delight at victory, driving the flames into an inferno.

He glanced back at the door. It was the only remaining escape route, a matter of feet away. All he had to do was to breach that invisible barrier which had held him prisoner throughout the night hours. He began to splash his way towards it and felt dead rats and mice bobbing against him. He heard a shout that had to be Nason, followed by incoherent pleadings not to be left alone – in a place where he had craved reclusion for half a century.

Half a metre from the door, John could go no further; for no logical reason. Something barred his way. He knew it would have been invisible even in full light. All in the mind, as they said, but nevertheless it stopped him going where he wanted to go. As simple as that. He could reach out, touch the door, maybe even open it; but he could not pass through it.

Which was how he had expected it to be; he had steeled himself in readiness. Autosuggestion, in fact. He did not curse or beat his fists on the woodwork. There was no point. He turned round, and coughed as he breathed in acrid smoke. The water level remained constant. It wasn't going anywhere, either.

He could barely see, and thought for a moment that Nason had gone. Then he saw him through the smoky atmosphere. Nason was sitting on the stairs, clutching at the rail with both hands, head bowed on his chest. One old man was responsible for all this, but in the end John couldn't hate him for it. It was *their* fault, not Nason's. *Them*; those people out there in Schooner Street. Folks like the Johnsons; they hadn't changed over fifty years. Their idea was to create an impression, and fuck everybody else. In the end somebody had to pay the penalty. The Strikes were the unlucky ones, the fall guys.

John knew that Leah and Sam and Sarah were dead. A sort of slow realization had been breaking itself gently to him for some time. He didn't know why he knew, just that none of them were going to come out of this alive. Another reason for not attempting to escape.

He dragged his feet slowly through the water, creating a wash that came back at him off the wall. Rodent corpses nudged him as they swept past him. Stooping, he looked for those huddled on the bottom step but they had gone. Maybe they had discovered a way out somewhere.

He sat down alongside Joseph Nason. A sideways glance showed him only a dim smoky outline of the old man's hunched form. He sensed his presence, but when he brushed his elbow against him there was nothing. There probably never had been.

John could feel the heat now. Any minute, he knew, the flames would break through to the landing up above, then rush down the stairs, roaring so loudly that they masked the noise of the hurricane. He heard the rafters collapse, bringing down an avalanche of the remaining tiles.

It was almost impossible to breathe now. The smoke would get him before the flames. His cremation would be no different from George Bourne's because John would be dead by then.

He cast one last sideways look at Joseph Nason, but there was nobody there. In the end they had all deserted him, even the rats and mice. Just as forty years ago an old man had been left to die here whilst life went on outside. Another cycle was about to begin.

GAME FISHING TACTICS

By the same author

THE ART OF LAKE FISHING

PIKE ON THE PLUG

CLEARWATER TROUT-FISHING WITH WORM

THE SPENCER LAKE FERTILITY CHART

SALMON AND SEATROUT IN WILD PLACES

NEWLY FROM THE SEA

WAYS OF FISHING

Frontispiece

I

PORTRAIT OF THE AUTHOR

GAME FISHING TACTICS

By

SIDNEY SPENCER

H. F. & G. WITHERBY LTD.
5 Plantain Place Crosby Row London SE1

First published 1974

ISBN 0 85493 113 9

Printed in Great Britain by
Ebenezer Baylis and Son, Limited
The Trinity Press, Worcester, and London

Under the fern, arching from shore in the islet's quiet lee and far from the surge of open water, a small jewel shone bright among breaking wavelets on a beach of sand golden in sunshine. It hovered and it darted in vibrant quest for the motes of life that are the quarry of very little trout. There was in it, small but clear to see, all that exultant mastery of element that is in a plunging salmon in a thundering surf. There was the confident poise alert in the wall of the roller and the swift foray into the tumble of backwash. There too the gleam of grace in barred and speckled flanks – of power in the sweeping tail.

You forgot the little-finger length of it and the puny scale of its environment and you saw only an accomplished trout following the ways of his kind in a sun-dappled world he had made his own . . .

Foreword

by Hugh Falkus

Whatever his degree of experience, any game fisherman will find this book invaluable. It is not only immensely readable, it is a compendium of game-fishing lore that results from a lifetime's experience. Together with *Salmon and Sea Trout in Wild Places* and *Newly from the Sea*, it makes up a trilogy of modern loch-fishing strategy and tactics that could hardly be bettered.

Having fished with Sidney Spencer I know something of his mettle. He is supremely good at catching fish, and the reason why is not far to seek. It is summed up in this passage from that lovely book *Salmon and Sea Trout in Wild Places*:

> A good angler (and I do not necessarily mean a man who can cast X yards) is almost always a good amateur naturalist. He need not know Latin names for wild creatures, flowers or insects, but he needs to know about otters and elvers and why insect-feeding birds feed here and not there, why some types of vegetation grow in some waters and on some shores and not in other places. He must be able to smell weather, to have an eye for wind and cloud and light and most of all perhaps have the ability, understanding currents in loch as in river, to visualize the life of the fish in relation to its environment.

That paragraph holds the secret of Sidney Spencer's success. A poor naturalist never made a good hunter, and it is the sharpened instinct of the hunter that makes Spencer the fine angler that he is. This affinity with wild life comes out strongly in his writing, and he has the gift of making it all come true on the page.

In his mind's eye the scene is ever vivid, ever fresh. The lonely waters of the west that mean so much to him; a sweep of moorland; distant mountains, blue as turf smoke; a bent blackthorn stark in outline against a fading sky . . .

His prose evokes the honey scent of gorse and bog myrtle, and the sound of lapping water. When I read it I too can see the long light on the lake—and hear the curlews crying.

Cragg Cottage
1974

Contents

Illustrations

Introduction

If you are what I have called in this book a dedicated fisherman you have three main preoccupations, first the fishing itself, second the talking about it, and third the reading of its literature. If, in addition, you have an urge to assist those less experienced but equally keen, you write about it, so quite openly quenching, lest you be accused of too much purity of motive, your own overwhelming nostalgia. The urge is the reason for this book.

Every angler of long experience and reasonable proficiency sooner or later comes imperceptibly to the stage at which he derives as much delight from assisting one of lesser experience to catch trout or salmon or seatrout, as he does from the taking of the fish himself. The faint subconscious competitive element has gone with the years and there is no place for envy. I remember as a boy sitting one darkening autumn evening in a train at Helensburgh station after a long day's fruitless flogging of that attractive Loch Lomond feeder, the Fruin. As the train began to move a man flung himself into the compartment complete with tackle and grasping by the tail a somewhat red salmon of about fifteen pounds, which he deposited under the seat opposite to me. He, like me, had been on the Fruin. I can see that fish now. I hadn't caught many salmon then and I was, I know, utterly emerald with envy. Since then I have noticed many young, and some not so young fishermen looking at *my* salmon and hiding their feelings as I hope I hid mine that day long ago.

In time those lookers-on will be able to go out with confidence in their own ability to do well, not only because of their acquired perfection of technique but from weather-wisdom, from observation and understanding of the fish and not least from the mass of fishing lore that they will, like all of us, gather to themselves. Some will have too few opportunities to garner it in less than a lifetime and to them these writings of mine may be a help in the interval.

For my part I have listened long to the sough of the sweeping wind over mountain, river and lake, to the rush of torrents and the surge of the sea, and I have communed at equal length with the fisherman's profound spirit of the wide open sky, under whose benison my fishing life has been a treasure beyond both price and my capability of description.

So may it be for all whose hearts are in fishing.

AXMINSTER SIDNEY SPENCER
March 1974.

I

Problem River

A spate river of the Hebrides provides a challenge all its own.

THE PONDEROUSLY humped mountains had each its Norse name, the deep green loch in their dark recesses had one and so had the little river I had come to fish.

It was now pouring its flood water, very faintly brown over the white shell sand, into the bay where ocean rollers thundered with the rising tide and the urge of an onshore breeze. Wind and tide I had anticipated – a spate to meet the top of the tide was an unforeseen bonus. It can rain heavily in the heart of the hills, and a few miles away you might suspect it but you wouldn't know, or the situation could be just the reverse: when you travel far to fish a spate river you gamble heavily.

Looking down and seaward from my perch on the last steep drop above the river, I could see some way northwards along a coast armoured with shattered pinnacles, riven cliffs and skerries awash in a creaming surf. Down here from the north had come the raiders whose legacy was the Nordic name to almost every feature of the island land. On such a day, far in the dimness of the rapacious past, the longships might have come. The fancy suited the induced mood and I remembered lines from the saga's 'Song of Harald' in honour of King Harald 'Comely Hair' –

Methinks you know the King
Dwells at Kvinne
Head of the Norsemen
Master of deep keels and scarlet shields
Tarred oars and spray-drenched boards . . .

and having thought of it, couldn't get it out of my head until a salmon leapt glittering in the tide rips on the north shore of the bay – and then another. The fish were coming in with the tide and with the river up would run its two miles very quickly to be lost to fishing, until they were settled in the big loch itself almost unfishable because of inaccessibility. In those two miles there were a few shallow pools and two deep rocky basins whence a resting fish might be snatched: I use the word to express urgency – not method!

This little river to which I was presently hastening is a problem stream for two reasons. First it is too shallow generally to hold fish so that they literally rush through it and are gone in a few hours – the number of hours depending on the duration of spate conditions. I have known it full of ascending fish and as nearly empty as makes no matter two hours later. Second, such places as may hold fish for brief halts during the run are so small that they are extremely difficult to fish. I know plenty of small and high ground rivers that run off quickly, the feature is far from unique. All you have to do is to know your river and get your timing right. But combine a quick run-off with tiny bare pools and the problem of working a salmon fly or in fact any fly in them, and you have something almost baffling. The saving factor in the present case is the huge run of fish – were it not for the multiplication of chances due to the numbers of fish this little watercourse would not be a fishery at all and your efforts would be of necessity confined to the loch above, and to the estuary below.

But, over the years I have found ways of taking both salmon and seatrout – by the use of some exertion and a pretty fair knowledge of the river bed. There is however much in the manner of doing it which is just as applicable to any of the many *small* spate rivers which drain the western seaboard wherever the watershed is close to the coast and for this reason giving you a quick run-off. On a day such as I describe seatrout may enter in a steady stream as long as there is a running water but salmon seem to have the shoaling habit more deeply implanted and will come in fairly compact companies with intervals of varying duration between one lot and the next.

The tide was approaching full when I reached the seapool and one bunch of salmon was constantly in evidence outside the almost covered gravel-bar – approaching with dorsals arrowing the surface, nosing up to the fresh water and darting away again with spurts of foam from flirting tails – momentary communal panic. Some might easily have entered unnoticed however and since this is a fishing of opportunity I got me down with all speed to the turfy rabbit-shorn banks twenty yards above the bar where the true tail of the pool really begins. One thing and one only is simple on this river – the choice of fly size, since the same size, a 7 or 9 according to water height – will raise both salmon and seatrout. And the best patterns for both are Butcher and Black Doctor or in a foul peaty spate which is rare, something bright such as a Silver Doctor. The accepted and successful dressing for peat-stained water is, of course, the Fiery Brown or the old Irish Claret but I confess I have never tried either in the Islands, where the need is not apparent.

The fish were not lingering in the seapool which seemed to

be full of finnoch and small seatrout. I kept a brace of the latter but the finnoch went back kicking like small steel springs and I moved on. Above the pool the river churned through a steeply inclined jumble of broken rock now smothered in white water and quite impossible to fish except for a six-foot wide basin at its upper end. This pool, about five feet deep and as bare as a board must have been floored with seatrout. They went in an unending stream up the gout of water falling into the basin from above – among them an odd salmon. It is an awkward place because banks are high and one is casting down with a short line in a curiously inelegant and unsatisfactory style – the line angle as wrong as can be. The fly worked under the foaming surface by rod action that was little more than sink-and-draw.

Be that as it may, in half an hour I had six beautiful seatrout of rather over two pounds – a lovely even lot – short and thick-shouldered and fighting as only a prime-conditioned seatrout can, and one salmon of about six pounds. This fish gave a wonderful display. He had no room to run, of course, but made innumerable jagging circuits of the pool, jumped four times and finished by going up the incoming torrent to the broken water above in one flashing leap. I had no choice but to apply, dangerously, just enough pressure to induce him to tumble back into the pool. The hook, miraculously, stayed in place and he soon came to the net.

By now, I calculated, there were more fish upstream than down here near the sea and with a thought for the ever-present hooded crows and black-backs, I concealed the fish deep in the heather and scrambled along the gorge side through a maze of ankle-breaking rough rocks and hidden holes. You pass about a hundred yards of very broken and quite unfishable water in so doing and then come to a small narrow pool with a low bank on your side and a high deeply-undercut rock on the other. Here a couple of casts delivered from a kneeling position but in relative comfort, produced another two pound seatrout. The difficulty here is that the 'pool' is so narrow that one must fish upstream or down and this last won't work because the fish see you. And when you fish up the fly only fishes momentarily because of the speed of current. In most rivers of my knowledge this procedure would be useless but these fish are incredibly quick and except in the whitest of water are capable of snatching the fly in spite of its speed of passing.

The next stage upstream presents one of the only two opportunities on this tumultuous little river to throw a longish line and to hang the fly. Here under a steep heathery hillside is a long chuckling shallow over gravel with here and there a bigger stone and its accompanying eddy or quiet patch of water. But the bank is flat and low on the fishing side so that you have to stay far back and use some line. Here I have twice hooked salmon from behind quite small rocks – from little depressions holding eight or nine inches of water and on the face of it too small and shallow to hold a fish. A stranger would certainly pass by.

I knew that today there must be fish resting here and there in this water and I did find one behind a smallish boulder. The Black Doctor washed over the stone and was taken instantly. This fish must have been tired because he hardly moved two yards from the lie and after some dogged pulling washed quietly back over and into the waiting net. A small party of hinds watched the proceedings over the shoulder of an upstream knoll, only cantering off as I moved in their direction. From here upwards the hillside on both banks grows steeper down to the water and it is wise to concentrate on your footing among broken rocks, peat holes and water-filled cavities of unknown depth, rather than try to fish the very few places where it is just possible to place a fly. I have, indeed, fished this stretch without result in very good conditions and now leave it – heading instead for the one big pool in the river.

It's a study in itself, this pool and it took me three seasons of many occasional visits to learn how to fish it. Both banks are rock and vertical except at the head where they recede in grass and heather sufficiently to enable you to scramble down almost to water level. Arrived there you can see that on both sides the rock walls are deeply undercut into deep water and here, surely, you will say to yourself is the lie – on one or both sides. These dark caverns offer perfect cover for salmon. They are washed, moreover, by a briskly flowing current which empties out over a fan of gravel at the tail. If you don't know the pool you approach it upstream via a steep track which traverses the hillside thirty feet or so above the water, across the top turf of the rock wall. In so doing you pass the tail and presently find yourself fishing down the pool from the only possible stance at the head. Your fly fishes beautifully down the centre current and, with a certain amount of leading, into the undercut on both sides and you cannot imagine likelier looking water or a better working fly. But you will be wasting your time and I know why. The fish are there all right, finning gently under the rock but you've disturbed them and they will *not* take.

You see, despite all appearances, the lie in this gorge pool is not where, theoretically, it should be, but on the open gravel at the tail and every fish lying there saw you on the steep path above and shot, alarmed, into cover upstream.

The tail must be fished from the pool's head stance because it cannot be approached inconspicuously from below and will not, in any case, fish well upstream since you cannot hang the fly over the lie. No, you have to make a long detour completely out of sight of the water and approach the pool head stance by slithering on your back down through grass, heather and odd proddings of rock. Crouched on the edge of the ingoing torrent you throw a longish line to the tail where, if fish are in the pool at all, you will get a rise.

You would think that in such a place there would always be fish but I am not so sure despite the ample cover and any number of apparently desirable features. An odd black and dour fish doubtless lingers in the holes under the rock but except in spate conditions when fish are running, this lovely looking pool is generally unproductive – at least in my experience.

On the day I am recalling I had one fish from the tail gravel at the first cast – a biggish fish for this river – about 9 pounds and he – or rather she – so upset the pool with plungings and surgings in and out of cover along the rock walls that I judged it useless to fish further when the net had done its work. But I saw half-a-dozen fish pass upstream through the thin water ahead while I rested the pool very briefly and I had a feeling that the run was going beyond me and far up into the unattainable recesses of the river's bog land leading to the distant big loch. The fact that now I could not raise another fish in the pool tended to confirm the suspicion – it looked as though fresh fish had ceased to enter.

For this reason I went on upstream – making what speed the broken ground would allow: the river was falling while I watched, the cause apparent in the clearance of weather upwind where a jumble of hills flaunted colour in sunshine where an hour ago all had been gloom and writhing cloud. An eagle rose heavily from a high knoll as I came out of the river defile into open ground. The river ran swift and thinly here with one last chance of a fish, or maybe more, from a broad shallow pool formed by the entry of a tributary torrent on the left bank. A broad band of foam on rapidly drying ground in the margin showed how far water had fallen and a hastily inserted heather stem by way of gauge at the limit of lapping water was high and dry in minutes, so fast was the river emptying.

This junction pool, lying as it does on moorland as level as you will ever find in that wild country, is the only one suitable for conventional approach: it helps to kneel because banks are low and you are very prominently in view but you can throw a normal line and fish each cast out. Fish are inclined to rest here briefly after negotiating the long series of shallows and tiny potholes between here and the big pool. However as I have said, the water is shallow and fish do not stay long. If you are really lucky and catch the level right you can take as many salmon from here in a short hour as would be reckoned highly gratifying for a whole day on many a well-known river. But to catch it just right is a rare thing – there is a short stage in water height movement when fish rest: apart from that the characteristic behaviour of fish in the whole river is very marked here – the haste to get on and up. It's as though the fish know how quickly the river falls and how shallow and coverless are the moorland miles leading to the loch away there deep in the high hills.

Today I was late, having dallied too long with my seatrout from the lowest pool above the sea. My first cast down and across finished with the flies deep under the foam in a down-stream embayment and here came a vigorous pull without surface sign. By shifting position I got him out of the tail, where is the taking place – and presently landed one of the five-and-a-half to six-pound fish typical of this little river. What they lack in size these fish make up in vigour and in beauty: they have tiny heads and thick shoulders and are so short that a five pounder looks at a first glance as though he was no more than three-and-a-half pounds. I had another similar fish from the foamy corner downstream but that seemed to end it. I rested myself and the pool for half an hour and then fished it again to find it full of finnoch and, apparently, nothing else. The day was done and I was left with the question – still unresolved these years later – whether it is wiser in exploiting these lightning runs of fish to intercept at one of the few pools or to traverse the water as I had done. Comparison of the results of two rods of equal experience and capability and exploiting one procedure each, might throw up an interesting conclusion.

I collected my five salmon and nine seatrout and presently handed them very gladly at the appointed place and time to the ghillie sent to meet me and the contingency that I might have caught the problem river right and had a big day.

2

Rise Forms

The way that fish come to the fly must dictate the manner of your striking.

SEATROUT RISE FORMS differ widely one from the other, their diversity dictated by weather, wind and wave and by light conditions – mainly I think the latter. Or you can say that the mood of the fish will determine the way of their taking and this is really the enveloping truth: since, however, that same mood is governed by prevailing atmospheric circumstances we are back at square one and the inescapable conclusion that weather is the prime factor. Light first and air temperature second play the larger parts in inducing the firm determined take that we like to think is typical in seatrout. There have been countless times in my experience when weak splashy rises or half-hearted swirls at the fly have given place to real solid takes within minutes of the onset of cloudy conditions or of a marked rise in temperature and unquestionably seatrout do respond very quickly to certain weather changes. So do salmon but their reaction is more to change – almost any change – than to that which is necessarily an improvement by human standards.

Brown trout rise forms owe their variety mainly to the character of the feed on which the majority of the fish are concentrating at any given time. Nymphing fish for an obvious example are unmistakable and can be dealt with in choice of fly and its presentation. There is not the element of moodiness noticeable in seatrout; there is identifiable reason in the behaviour of the rising fish and in the way they come to both the natural and the artificial. The conversion of a rise into a hooked fish where brownies are concerned calls for some nicety of judgment in speed of strike but I have never considered it as critical as can be the case with seatrout in some of their moods.

Some writers on seatrout fishing believe in fast striking at the rise, some in the absolute opposite or in a slow deliberate lift of the rod and I think they both make a mistake in ascribing too much uniformity to seatrout ways of moving at a fly. So very often the fish change from day to day or even in the course of a single day in the way of their taking – moods again. There are days or hours when you will get sly touches at the fly with little or no surface sign and other times when the rise is a fussy splutter and again the faint touch. The 'feel' in both cases is similar to the quiet touch you get from seatrout at night when the taking move in a pool tail is 'sneaky'. At another time there will be a deep boil or no surface indication whatever but simply the pull with which instant reaction from the rod will mean a hooked fish. But to say that in most cases you must strike like lightning or, on the other hand, tighten slowly is unwise. The idea's only virtue is that it is positive but it is not good advice. It is more constructive and wiser in my view to say that your reaction at any time to a seatrout rise should be instinctive and quick. If the day's conditions are such that the fish are behaving in some manner that you cannot analyse but which clearly results in your taking the fly away without hooking, then you must modify the strike timing to suit. I do urge the belief that it is possible to match the mood of the fish and that instinctive recognition of what is required to counter it, is in the armoury of every experienced seatrout fisherman. There is no short way to learn how to hook the 'difficult' seatrout and you will never, whatever your craftiness with these temperamental fish, hook all that rise to you. The fish of one season vary from another and the fish of different runs in the same season may and often do differ in behaviour: above all the way of taking may change, as I have already said, in the course of a single day. With seatrout I take the problems as they arise, modifying presentation and tactics at the bidding of that shadowy knowledge we call experience and not hesitating to re-modify until, as can happen, I come to the limit of inspiration.

The type of rise has no relation to the subsequent play of the fish except that in very general terms I would say that the usual firm take of an eager fresh-run fish will be followed by the usual vigorous play. This is not to say that a stale fish will not provide equally good sport because in fact, very many dark fish play extremely well. But a really big dark fish can be frightfully dull and dour. And if stale seatrout know some vagaries of taking that fresh ones do not or have forgotten and are even harder to hook at times, at least the hook once in will usually stay in place in their harder jaws.

Grilse are in a class by themselves, especially in very quiet river pools or in the lake and in these places I rate them the fastest risers of all – far quicker than either brown trout or seatrout. Some big fish rivers breed big grilse and these may be as heavy as the average adult spring fish of other and smaller rivers. My own experience of big grilse is limited and I write here of the class that runs from say three-and-a-half pounds to six pounds and probably averages four-and-a-half. These are the lightning fast risers, taking the fly in a flash, turning away and almost doubling the body in so doing, so lissom are they. In play their ability to twist and turn – their 'contortability' – can wrench the hook free in a manner and with an ease that you don't meet in any other fish – the result often attributed to softness of mouth. There is not much diversity in grilse rises. If they are 'on' they take well and without subtlety and their normal reactions to weather are those of salmon rather than seatrout.

Adult salmon, of whatever run class, do however display more versatility in the manner of their coming to the fly – some behaviour conditioned by weather and altering very obviously in step with weather changes, and some much less easy to understand. I distinguish five main forms in which interest in the fly may show itself. You come to know them as quite typical in certain circumstances and in some cases as recognisable symptoms of something amiss – something very wrong in the day or in your presentation. Or if you know your water and the ways of its salmon, there will be the happy outcome in the shape of a fish well-hooked. You then know that to some extent anyhow fish are 'on' i.e. taking, and that your speed of fishing and the pattern and size of fly are right.

By far the commonest kind of rise is signified by the boil which is the surface indication of something which has already taken place – the swift turn of a fish at or away from the fly. If you are not so keyed up that you strike at once – and how many anglers do exactly this knowing perfectly well that it is wrong – you will, as you see the line leading into the fading remains of the boil, also feel it drawing taut. Aid the tautness by rod lift and you have your fish. However, a great many rises of this kind are what I call 'soft' and however judicious you are in your attempt to set the hook, you find no line tightening – nothing. Such 'soft' boils are frequent when fish are fresh-run but not settled or only just coming on to take; the fish are attracted by the moving fly but only come part way to the level at which the fly swims, the turn of the body and the sweep of the tail causing a disturbance which comes to the surface. It is a rise only in that it betokens the interest of some fish in the fly but is not a serious attempt to take it. Pattern is probably right for the light and water colour and more than likely is wrong for size. An odd 'soft' boil can occur at any time and has no special meaning but one after another make the clearest signal to go down a size or better two sizes in the same pattern.

Then there is the quick splashy rise which gives no impression of the size of the fish and might almost be caused by a trout. It's often quite impossible to analyse because it happens so very quickly. Usually the fish makes no mistake and has the fly firmly on a line instantly taut. I find it significant that this rise form is seen more often when the fish comes to the dropper – i.e. to the fly which, properly fished, is tripping the surface, as it should be in lake fishing. The ghillie, seeing the rise from a slightly different angle, will sometimes have a better idea of what size of fish is involved. My ghillie often in this way sees something I miss and will say 'That's a bigger fish than you'd think – I saw his tail as he went down'. This is neither imagination nor a desire to please because so very often when the fish shows in play or is boated he is proved to be right.

Linked also with the kind of behaviour you get when fish are interested but not really taking is the third type of 'rise' which is not in cold fact a rise at all. Some places are worse than others in respect of salmon acting this way. I refer to the maddening habit of following the fly without making any attempt to take it. You see, in its more common manifestation, a wave following the fly as it is recovered towards the boat, the fish turning away in leisurely fashion at oar's length. You can speed up or slow down in working the fly, or you can change pattern or size quite without result. If you are wise you will stifle your frustration and reflect that this conduct on the part of the salmon may easily – very easily – mean that they are in process of coming on and will take properly tomorrow or the next day.

Several times but not very often I have seen this following habit take an exaggerated form in which the fish swims on the surface – shoulders and back awash and upper lobe of the tail in air – in close pursuit of the fly. This is an agonising business because you are so helpless. No variation in the way of fishing seems to make any difference and I once spent a whole exasperating day on an Irish lough driven to distraction in this manner. You would have seen two very thoughtful men coming in blank off the lough that evening. But you would also have seen those two men bringing in fourteen fresh salmon during the good take that lasted over the next three days.

The fourth type of rise can be difficult to convert particularly if the fish carries out the move slowly. It is the rise we call 'head and tail' and when fish are hard to come by it's the one we pray for. A clean moderately fast head and tail rise usually means a firmly-hooked fish because a salmon making this move to a fly does it with deliberate intent to seize that fly: he will certainly do so if the fly is left long enough before him. Take it away by an ill-judged rod movement and he will slide down disconcerted by its disappearance and, usually, he will not come again. If, as sometimes happens, the fish porpoises in this move in slow motion, the tension is almost unbearable. You need nerves of steel, and skill to keep the fly moving slowly before the open mouth until his head goes down and the cast and line straighten. These slow fish, like almost all salmon, hook themselves – the difficult thing is to allow them to do so. I know several fishermen who seem petrified by this kind of rise and it's fortunate that it is not very common since they either snatch the fly away or are so fascinated by what is happening that they cease to put life into it.

The deep take is another move not truly a rise. It tends to occur more with stale salmon than with fresh or relatively fresh fish. You generally find that a fish which has been occupying one lie for a few weeks or even months will wake up one day in response to a weather or water height change. You probably know that fish, having seen him plunge occasionally and in time you are convinced he is uncatchable. But one day, fishing without confidence over the lie, the searching fly will stop dead and for a few seconds the tight line will suggest snagging. Then the snag will start to move away and when it surfaces later you know that your dark acquaintance has come to the fly at last. But, of course, you can catch one of these stale fish at any time and anywhere: the chances are that there will be no rise but just that deep stop or pull and then a very dour fight. When you meet the deep unseen taker you can be pretty sure that you have a coloured fish and you just hold on.

In some seasons, not necessarily those with continuity in weather conditions over long periods, you will find all of the class of fish present in the holding areas are behaving in a similar manner and this is particularly likely if those fish belong to the same run. It frequently happens that high water of the right temperature and duration brings a run of fish all of the same class, age group and approximate size. And it also often happens that there is no running water for weeks afterwards so that fish of other classes do not enter and cannot mingle with the earlier runners. A normal stock in most places in say August, will be a mixture of salmon from the very early runs – the big spring fish, probably only a few of them – and the main run of smaller spring fish plus any summer runs that may be. This mixture produces a range of differences in behaviour, some classes show freely and others do not for example, as well as a diversity in their ways of coming to the fly. The season of 1973 produced, where I was fishing in Ireland, a remarkable uniformity in salmon behaviour due entirely, in my appreciation, to the fact that the fish were all of one run and all of the same age class. They held to their shoal habit longer than usual and they were all above average weight for the water. They were not mixed with other fish until the grilse arrived very late in the summer.

The intriguing feature of the fishing was that these fish all came to the fly in the same way with a very quick but unobtrusive little rise and a small splash like that of an eager brown trout taking a drifting fly. They were in no sense difficult and out of twenty-seven fish hooked in four weeks of patchy weather there were no slow deliberate takes, no head and tail rises, no 'follows' and one only taker below the surface. All were between ten and fourteen pounds and very strong, well-made fish of rather better than average activity in play.

If I had been endeavouring to show to a beginner the great variety in the ways of salmon with a fly, I should have indeed been in dire straits. But he would have learnt the rule common to all processes of hooking salmon on the fly – don't tighten till you feel the fish.

3

These Things Need Saying to a Young Fisher

Having the priorities right is important in the beginning years.

WHEN WE FISH today for sport we perpetuate an activity that is incalculably ancient – nearly as old as man himself. The urge of the hunter and his waterside activity which is as it always has been, compounded of skill, experience and instinct, is no longer dictated by the sheer need for survival but it remains strong in some of us. It stays for a man's lifetime if he is one of the company of dedicated anglers and this, I assure you is a very select company. If your interest in fishing proves itself as the seasons go by to be no passing phase so that you grow ever keener and more deeply involved, you are fortunate, on the way to dedication and to unlimited interest and enjoyment.

I am not thinking of your killing vast numbers of fish. A small boy asked me recently 'What is the biggest bag you've ever made?' and I told him that I couldn't remember, which was the truth. My diary would provide the answer he sought, of course, but that's another matter.

A big bag will naturally make a memorable day but the more you fish the more you come to know that the joy of a day lives on in its wholeness, in the use of your basic hunter's urge in a way that we now consider sporting. Your aim should be to catch *some* fish without taking part in senseless destruction. I have been fortunate in my opportunities to fish in very productive waters and you might with justice say that it's all very well for *me* to talk. I can only tell you that I rarely keep more than a brace of trout, two brace of seatrout, and that I have returned alive many salmon – on one occasion seven fish in the day. The simple answer is that I fish for pleasure and not because – as my ancestors of ancient times doubtless did – I am hungry. And, in any case, stocks are under great strain today and should be drawn on lightly as a matter of principle.

There was no intention to make these notes into some kind of homily but I do beg of you to take to heart – and the earlier in your fishing career the better – the great truth that the rewards of our vocation as anglers cannot be measured in terms of dead fish. We look for our pleasure in other things, the skilful use of good rods and tackle of course, but beyond this, in our close association with nature and with the world of the fish we seek to lure. Birds and animals too, the sea and the sky and the sounds of the wild – these surround you and should be a highly-valued part of every fishing day. Get far away, sit on the shore and listen to the waves, watch the blowing of the reeds and be conscious of the voice of the wind from the hills – these sounds and sights are unchanged in measureless time – a humbling thought this, and good for a man every now and then. And dedicated fishers are humble men.

It is a vital part of your overall knowledge that you should understand the life histories of the fish as affecting their movements, feeding habits, and general behaviour and even their reactions to your endeavours to deceive them. There is, besides, the simple fascination of the subject as a study. But do not listen to every half-baked tale from people who think they know. Half the men you meet on the river cannot distinguish between a four-pound seatrout and a grilse of the same size, and have the vaguest of ideas about the age of a trout in the hand – even when they know the river and should know its approximate growth rates. Some ghillies are extremely knowledgeable especially those who couple some reading with years of personal observation, but there are others with fixed ideas which are, to say the least, unreliable. You must know the truth. Read and watch and learn for yourself.

You may think that the study of life histories of fish is far removed from devotion to fishing but I consider it not only adding hugely to your enjoyment but necessary. Without some comprehension of background, how could you anticipate the taking habits of say, big deep-lying spring salmon as opposed to those of summer runners or autumn fish – of fresh as opposed to stale or staling fish – of some strains of trout as compared with others. The starting point is the history of the fish – the rest is the condition of the moment – weather, air and water temperature, water colour and height and overhead light. These latter belong to the other and wider general lore of angling only to be acquired by observation and long hours by the river or on the loch.

One more thing about the life of the fish. Stay interested all the year and don't put the rods away at season's end and forget. I don't think you are likely to do that but you should do more than spend the winter lost in nostalgia and in longing for the opening of a new season. Go, if you can, and watch the fish spawning. There is a very great deal to be learnt this way including a curious attachment to the fish, here ensuring the continuity of their kind as they have done since the last ice left these islands – possibly before.

Where you find your fishing is a matter for you. Today

there is rather more leisure so that one can look farther afield than was possible for the average angler a few years ago. It can happen that you can find some small, and because small, unfrequented river or lake. If you do, rent a right to fish and indeed this is sound practice almost anywhere, granted, of course, that the quality of the fishing is commensurate with the rent you are asked to pay. Having a rod on a reasonably good water which is well-managed and not over-fished is the next best thing to having your own fishing. An exclusive right or outright ownership is often beyond reach but if it is practicable it's a great treasure and an unending joy. I can think of no more worthwhile ambition than to aim to own some fishing and with patience and perseverance it can be done. I know some very happy men who have done it from rather unpromising beginnings. But it must be admitted that it is not becoming easier with today's strong demand for fishing and its consequent high cost.

To tell anyone how to fish you need to be with them day after day on the water and any writing like this can only touch the fringes of a subject which has produced thousands of books, of varying authority and usefulness. Some of the best of them are mentioned in Chapter 16 and these could form the nucleus of a library.

There are, however, many things that you will not find dealt with in the traditional media for imparting angling advice and others that, if they are mentioned, are not adequately emphasised. These omissions, for the most part, concern the finer points of our craft and of course, they affect the entire range of technique and methods including dry and wet fly for trout and seatrout and sunk fly for salmon. I cannot in good faith help you with dry fly; I am not sufficiently knowledgeable having devoted my fishing wholly to sunk fly in its various ways of presentation. I therefore write all the time with wet fly in mind.

But mention of dry fly does bring to mind a curious phenomenon that I keep encountering – the habit of continuous false casting of a team of wet flies. I have seen it employed in casting a single fly for salmon! Why do people do this? The flies do not require drying – indeed they and the cast are better wet; it must be some kind of confusion with dry fly practice. It really has no sound basis except in the very infrequent case where you false-cast a growing weight of airborne line in order to throw an exceptional length. There are occasions where for example a salmon has surfaced head and tail beyond normal casting distance. To cover such a fish while he is 'up', you will, if you react as I do, tear off line from the reel and make a fake cast or two to get most of it aloft before shooting the remainder. You rarely get a chance to make more than one dummy cast – so often the fish is yards away before the flies can alight. Persistently to throw a line so long that it requires false casting is bad practice. Nine out of ten fish, of whatever species, are risen and hooked at medium distance and within comfortable reach. Some river pools may call for long casts, admittedly, but casting to the limit of your own capability and that of your rod is seldom rewarding.

And whilst on the subject of casting whether blind – i.e. fishing the water, or to some specific fish, there is a small but extremely important point which does not appear in print or in verbal instruction as often as, in my opinion, it should. It concerns the point at which the fly or flies cease to have forward impetus. That point, with very many, probably the majority of casters, is the water surface and this is in order if you are trying to stun the fish or see how big a splash you can make. But you will catch more fish if you aim two feet above the water and then allow the flies to drop of their own weight. This is a habit to be cultivated. It is not made into a nonsense by the fact that very, very occasionally the plop of a biggish fly will attract the attention of an alert salmon.

Again about casting, there is a common misbelief that it is necessary to throw a straight line. It is desirable to be able to do so and in most fishing situations you will do it, as I do, without conscious effort and it serves very well. Now in the river the current will contort that straightly-laid cast and its flies' path almost at once, but not so in still waters where cast after cast shows the flies to the fish from the same angle relative to light and wave drive. Here you need the ability to throw a curved line or, more accurately, a curved cast which I call the 'S' cast. It looks untidy but if the degree of check you apply in the final stages of forward drive is correct – and this is a matter of judgment which needs practice to attain – the flies will not fall in a heap but will be so placed that the first few seconds of recovery will lead them on a curved course. This brings rises. I use the trick regularly, alternating with straight casting in the same way as I switch to and from fishing across the wave to working along their hollows.

Accuracy in casting is another matter. In dry fly work it's vital of course and in wet fly on rivers too, in cases where fish are lying in weedy channels, under bushes or bank overhangs and so on. The 'S' cast has no place here, it's essentially for open pools and still water and I would never belittle the virtue of good, clean well-directed casting. But, in practice, in general wet fly fishing *extreme* accuracy of aim is seldom required.

Very many anglers make fishing into work and you can find it wearying just to watch some of them. I've already referred to unnecessary false casting which is one element of the 'work': the other is the simple fact that the angler does what the rod should do and is perfectly capable of doing – he drives the line forward and out instead of providing the initial impulse only. So many people do not use the power of the rod and largely as a result they find that a long day's casting is tiring. There is absolutely no sense in this providing that the rod is suitable for the build and wrist strength of the fisherman. Your rod weight and action if single-handed and your use of its qualities of flex and recovery should be such that you can cast without conscious effort by little more than wrist action and go on doing it all day. The feel of a good rod, properly used, is a delight and no mean part of the joy of a day's fishing. The clean lift off, the pause for line swing behind, the forward drive *in which you do no more than provide the impulse* and the follow through – all these any reasonably balanced outfit will do beautifully and in silence. Show me a man who casts to the accompaniment of whooshing noises and I'll show you a man who either needs a lesson in how to use his rod or who needs a new one.

Reel and line must balance of course. If the reel is too light the action of the rod will not come out in casting – if too heavy it will make tip action too lively. I like the reel, full of line, to be fractionally too heavy for the rod, and its heaviness to be derived from the use of a line *very slightly* too heavy for the rod. Thus, with a normal length of line out there will be a shade more forward weight in the air and this will help the rod to do the work by bringing out its action. Reel and line weights should vary from their theoretical suitability only in a small degree, which unfortunately cannot be defined. I say only that if you have a weight choice within the accepted limits of suitability for your rod – choose the heavier. And you cannot really judge in the shop – you really need to be on the lawn (or better the river!) and then make a series of casts with the outfit assembled in fishing order. I am not, of course, suggesting the use of lines either distinctly too heavy or too bulky in order to bring out the action of a given rod because you pay the price in the shape of greater line visibility for one thing and bulk is quite unnecessary anyhow with modern tapered lines with sinking tips and so on.

You may hear some talk about double fly irons and indeed you may see them in use. Some anglers think they get a better grip than singles and I know a few who regularly use them. These people lose as many fish as the rest of us and I feel that there is much rather ill-founded faith in the double hook. Those who don't like it argue that it tends towards loss of fish because one point exerts some leverage on the other and this seems possible if one hook is firmly embedded and the other free. But if both are well and truly into the tissue of a fish's mouth – how can one exert pressure on the other? My opinion is that a very small double will usually get a very firm grip but a larger one, as in an average salmon fly size will not necessarily do so, and that in sizes above say eight the single hook is far preferable. The tiny triangle of a tube fly is the best hooker and holder of any. This is fact and so beyond any suspicion of doubt.

There is one other consideration – reverting to double hooks – and that is that if your cast and line are well-balanced and if as a result you have a 'fine feel' of the tackle in the action of casting – you will detect a faintly objectionable something when the hooks are double. The weight difference must be infinitesimal but the flies do not cast as cleanly. My advice is to let those who wish use doubles while you stick to sharp well-tempered singles. There are, by the way, some badly-tempered hooks on sale in recent years: the main defect seems to be softness. I have a number six

Torrish by a famous tackle-maker in front of me as I write – the hook all but straightened by one not particularly violently-playing salmon. Other hooks are brittle and break off short at the bend. I don't know how you avoid this kind of mishap since you can't detect the weakness until it shows itself. However, one can avoid hooks exceptionally fine in the wire, attractive as they look in the tackle shop.

The hook manufacturer is, I must say in simple fairness, often blamed for the breaking or turning of hook points and barbs when, in truth, the fault lies with the man unhooking the fish. You will take care but some ghillies or boatmen are prone to carelessness – twisting and wrenching at any hook firmly embedded. The rough handling that a salmon especially gets when netted and hit hard with the priest seems to set the tempo and manner of the unhooking. I don't blame all ghillies but some deserve watching and since I always re-tie the fly to the cast after taking a fish, I use the opportunity carefully to examine the hook point and barb as well as to wash the fly and re-furbish the bedraggled dressing.

And so in the end, as it should be, to the object of all these exercises, the playing and landing of your fish. This is nine-tenths a matter of 'hands' and one-tenth the observation of a few rules which I do not think it necessary to dwell on here. But there are two prime rules – well known since the beginning of rod fishing which, fishing as I do on most fit and suitable days throughout each season for salmon, seatrout or brown trout, I see broken day after day with resultant sad tales of lost fish. Keep the rod up is the inflexible rule of all fishing rules and running it a close second the axiom – never, if you can avoid it, give any slack. Yield line to a strong fish if need be by all means, but not any slack. Always keep a firm but not harsh hold and this is above all else, again a matter of 'hands'. Disregard of these two disciplines is responsible for more lost fish than all the stratagems of the most cunning of hooked fish.

One other thing – when fish are feeding or moving you should be fishing but when they are not, and when opportunity offers, sit long by the shore. You learn, sitting there and watching.

4

A Strange September

Weather and fish behaviour can both be abnormal and baffling.

MID-SEPTEMBER AND the warblers are still here. On the lake the dabchicks are escorting small young — presumably the survivors of second broods. The rowans along the rocky shore droop with the weight of clustered berries and the heather is still bright in bloom. But there is, and this at least marking the progress of the year, the robin's little autumn song, melancholy sweet and in it the essence of summer past.

Another feature of this strange September has been the behaviour of the flying ants. I have noted in years gone by that the ants usually appear in quantity on two successive days – rarely three – and in our part of Ireland usually in August but dependent on weather. Hot quiet days seem to provide the optimum conditions. This year in late August and up to the middle of this month they have appeared on six days and in my observation the trout have ignored them.

Day after day it is bright for an hour or so in early afternoon. Morning and late afternoon are heavy with haze and the wind blows lightly but without intermission from the east. Mountains and distant shores are hidden from view and the lake is uniformly grey. As I write there have been three weeks of these deadly conditions and in the process of catching seatrout and salmon – in which matter I profess to know a little – I have been singularly unsuccessful. Such results as I have had with seatrout have come in brief intervals of fresh wind and temporary lifting of haze – in what in short we call 'open' periods. Salmon exhibit the ultimate degree in dourness and I begin to think them so stale that we shall not get a 'take' on them before the season closes.

On the other hand, I have seen in other seasons days when some sort of madness seemed to possess even the dark be-jibbed cocks that have been lying since April in the gloomy recesses between the bottom's boulders so that they came avidly to the fly. You can apply all the stored lessons of long experience and still be forced back on the triteness of 'you never know'. Indeed hope alone must take the place of knowledge if one is to go on fishing in conditions which to human eyes look decidedly less than hopeful. No-one can have studied the behaviour of salmon and seatrout more earnestly than I have throughout much fishing and this has resulted, of course, in identification of a wide range of factors which normally produce predictable reactions in the fish. But sometimes – quite often in fact – the fish don't obey the rules – and it is at such times that you could be disheartened to realise how very much remains hidden from you.

There were, for example, prior to the deadly dull period which is prompting this writing, several days when my ghillie and I – both of the same lough-studying persuasion – were as certain as you can ever be in fishing of getting salmon to move to the fly. We had broken light, a soft and warm but brisk southerly wind, water temperature not too high and a lovely rolling wave. I looked for a taking fish in the trough of every wave – the flies fished beautifully. Yet we came home several times with one fairish seatrout from the only rise of the day – not having seen anything else, no salmon, no other seatrout and not a single brownie. Normally in this lough the latter are so numerous as to be a nuisance and there is a significance in the fact that the brownies are 'off'. There are, it is true, no fresh salmon at this season but there are plenty of fresh seatrout and the innumerable brownies aforesaid. What is the factor which keeps *all* these fish down? I suspect water height which has been greater than I like, but I am not absolutely sure. There is something here which eludes me in spite of all my fine talk about a lifetime's experience – something quite outside my current thinking. This is at once tantalising and challenging but its serious aspect resides in the intriguing question – if fish will not take in what experience classifies as ideal conditions, when *will* they take? I am almost disheartened.

When you deal with a fish which does not feed but which takes a fly or a lure on the bidding of a whim how can you predict its behaviour? Once again you never know. And the proof of this will be evident one of these days when, everything according to our fisherman's book being wrong, the stale salmon will emerge from their torpor and take well. This madness will not last long, of that I am quite certain; the taking time being not more than half an hour – and perhaps less. The trouble in such a case can be that a dour slogging fighter in a big lake like ours can take fifteen minutes to boat and lead you far from the taking place. You can be back on the ground only to find the fish down again and the lough as dead as ever. One fish in the boat is some consolation but you may have to wait a very long time for another taking time.

* * *

I wrote what you have just read designedly for inclusion in a suitable context in this book and within a few days it had fallen into place by virtue of events. These original notes made in a bad period remain as at first written and those that follow simply record subsequent events. I leave you to find the moral.

* * *

Monday September 17th was in loch fishers' terms a real dirty day. A gale blew from the south-west, sweeping away the haze and the amorphous shroud that the hills had worn for so long, but it was cold – unusually so considering the source of the wind and the sky was icily blue between squalls. It had rained heavily in the night far back in the mountains at the river's sources: as my mark at the boat-landing showed the lake was far too high. Above all that, the day was a 'hard' one: I had little hope but we went out because although there was a nasty big sea, conditions were decidedly better than they had been and maybe – just maybe – the change would have brought fish 'on'.

We had a rough and squall-ridden passage to the fishing ground and in the calmer intervals a bright sun glittered dazzlingly on very broken water. I didn't like the glitter and still less the peat stain that we found off the river mouth when we arrived on our chosen area. But when we left in mid-afternoon, wearied by the unending lurch of the drifting boat, we had four good seatrout and a shapely cock grilse of five pounds. All five were on a rather simply-dressed Dunkeld size eight and theoretically too small for the big rough wave. The traditional peat stain patterns seemed quite ineffective and I had switched to Dunkeld because of the bright sun in the between-shower intervals. It worked.

Weather on Tuesday September 18th duplicated that of

the previous day except that there was slightly less wind and a nicer light. A good feature too was a softer air but there had again been some overnight rain and as a result the lake had kept its high level. Evidently, however, the worst of the sour peat water had been washed out of the moorland bogs by the earlier rainstorms and some of the peat stain had gone when we arrived once more on the fishing ground. However that might be, it was quickly apparent that seatrout were dead 'off' although I had two small finnoch in the first few minutes. We saw several better fish take natural flies and I looked for a taker of better proportions with every cast. Yet I simply could not raise a single fish and I think the two finnoch's taking merely signified the end of the take for the day. In this lough seatrout seldom take – though you will get the odd one – more than once, perhaps only for half an hour, each day.

By one o'clock sun time I might have called it a day but for the fact that, aside from a growing brightness I didn't much care for, the day still looked good. We had a medium-sized broken wave rolling from the right quarter and a soft air – soft that is by contrast with the previous day's hard cold blast. So we continued with drift after drift for another hour largely on the basis that our fish of yesterday had moved round two o'clock.

I was casting mechanically when out of the corner of my eye (and isn't it surprising in fishing how very much you see 'out of the corner of your eye'?) I saw a break in the wave twenty yards downwind and to our left. It was either a very big seatrout or a salmon: it surfaced unhurriedly and was gone. You couldn't say it was a cruiser because it appeared only that once but it certainly looked like a taker, if one could cover it. I calculated that the boat movement necessary to put me in comfortable casting distance would offset any

2

SEA TROUT TAKEN IN SALT WATER
DURING TWO TIDES. See chapter 8

3

GREENLAND
A DRIFTNETTER IN PORT. NOTE THE MILES
OF NETTING IN THE STERN ENCLOSURE

virtue in the opportunity and we continued to drift, with a little inclination leftwards. I had 'marked' that fish down and knew where he was but he surprised me when he rose to the fly – coming at it like a tiger and racing away in a long run as soon as the hook went home. He turned out to be a fairly fresh salmon of eight pounds.

Now the odd thing was that we found this fish in an area we had condemned as fishless because we had failed over several weeks to raise anything there at times when fish were rising freely in surrounding places. It had in former years had a good reputation and I have had many fish from it, but for three or four seasons the fish seemed to have deserted it. Salmon do this kind of thing, of course, and in a river the reason usually is not far to seek. The scour of winter floods moves gravel, destroys old lies and creates new ones, and the fortunes of individual pools fluctuate considerably. But in a lake it's a very different matter and other than at river mouths where deltaic deposits may alter the lake floor during big floods it is difficult to discern any reason in fish forsaking a favoured lie. In the case I mention I have not been able to detect any change in the bottom. Its location is far from any entering river and not especially exposed to storm, shore erosion or any other factor likely to affect the character of the bottom.

Anyhow we had been looking, as I have suggested, with some disfavour at this area but now with one fish from it in the boat we argued that where there was one salmon it was likely there were others. James placed the boat as nearly as possible where we had begun the successful drift and we started again. Conditions were good with a pleasant lively wave and at that moment a broken subdued light overhead. Now it is quite impossible, on a big sheet of water and from a distance, to pinpoint any one spot other than very roughly but I'm prepared to swear that the flies were working within ten feet of where I had hooked the previous fish when I had another hard, firm take and was fast in a second fish. This one I saw as he turned away with the fly – a bigger fish and a stale-coloured one. He made a rather ponderous long run, apparently over-running a rising seatrout as he went. I saw the taut cast cut through the rise.

It was a long and not very exciting fight though by hard pulling he twice had me down to the backing. After that he kept circling the boat and I simply could not get him up using all the strain the eight-pound cast would stand. It was like trying to lift a dead weight and more than once I had to feed a little line to ease the strain on the doubled rod. I couldn't get more than the loop of the cast clear of the water and I couldn't tell whether he had dropper or tail fly. 'There is,' I said to James, 'something very odd about this.' And then the pressure eased momentarily and the dropper came nearer the surface to show me a seatrout of about a pound being dragged thither and yon by whatever I had five feet lower down on the tail fly. It was a long time before we saw the yellow gleam of the bigger fish, about six or seven feet down: I had no straight pull on him – the seatrout seemed to absorb any lift from the rod and I expected the tackle to part. But it did not, the fish came slowly up and at last James had a chance with the net: he wisely took the salmon, the seatrout being dragged headlong over the gunwale as a twelve-and-a-half pound slightly-tinted fish was dumped into the boat.

That stubborn fish had taken us a long way and when we were at length back on our drifting area the lake seemed dead and an hour's fishing proved the take was over. I trailed the flies on the slow way home upwind and so doing had one more smallish seatrout.

The wind blew chill now and tossing seed plumes on the reedbed forests were a mist of purple. Yellowed oak leaves were drifting far out on the lake. You knew it was an autumn day.

5

The Sea Life of Salmon

Our knowledge is far from complete but the gaps are slowly being filled.

LONG PRACTICE WILL enable you to gauge the weight of a salmon, when you have landed it from some water you know well, to within about eight ounces of its tally on the scales. When you want absolute accuracy you use scales and not the spring balance which will yield an approximate reading when it stops dithering. You will also be able to assess how long the fish has been in fresh water – its sex (not always at once apparent with a young absolutely fresh specimen), the class or run to which it belongs – i.e. spring, summer – or grilse and from this its probable age. Or you may be able to distinguish little beyond sex and a rough run or class estimation if the fish is a stranger and clearly belongs to another river system. This last distinction can only be made if you have much experience and have made careful observation of many fish truly belonging to your river.

Salmon do vary in the relationship of weight to length, girth and general build, but the overall features and the whole 'air' of fish belonging to the breeding stock of any individual water are common enough to be seen in the vast majority from that water. There will always be odd fish, in every river system which do not develop quite like their fellows, perhaps due to a poor smolt history or to indifferent sea growth from some reason at which we can only guess. We shall return to this latter presently but in my opinion it is less likely to account for some aberrant feature in individual fish than the influence of very early history. The critical phase seems to coincide with the pre-smolt or smolt stages and to relate to the condition of the young fish at the point of first migration to sea. It is well known in artificial propagation practice that better alevins, fry, parr and eventually smolts are derived from large ova. Such smolts are usually larger and stronger than those derived from small ova of small parents and it would appear, though not proven beyond all doubt, that these fish, better suited to take advantage of sea life in all its richness, have a better survival rate than smaller smolts. Heredity can be demonstrated to play another part too because it is notable and very noticeable in handling smolts trapped on migration that those belonging to wild stock and having made their growth by 'wild' feeding in the river, are stronger (though not necessarily larger) than those coming from hatchery-fed conditions up to the small parr stage. The wide difference in the muscular strength of the two classes can be felt in the hand very easily.

So much – and it's very little on a subject of unlimited ramifications – for variations from the norm in the adult salmon one is trying to appraise. It brings us to the conclusion, inescapable in any event, that to check the aptness of our observations and to make sure we are indeed as prescient as we like to think, we have to read the scales of our fish. The actual process is simple enough but the interpretation, useless unless accurate, takes years of experience plus a wide knowledge of salmonoid migrational behaviour in general terms. A close knowledge of the river concerned is an enormous help because you get growth characteristics showing up on the scales which you come in time to know are typical for that river or are equally clearly recognisable as strange.

I take scales and later read them from any of my fish which exhibit unusual features, good or bad condition factors, an uncommon build or marking, or perhaps the mere fact of coming to hand at abnormal season or place. The result, checked and double-checked, is compared with my earlier visual assessment of the whole fish and this is a fascinating exercise and as a rule rather gratifying. The odd puzzle where evidence conflicts does three things: it keeps one humble, gives plenty of food for thought and adds to one's knowledge.

It ought to be said, before leaving the subject of scale-reading, that salmon scales are relatively, repeat relatively, easy to decipher. Brown trout scales and those of larger seatrout need vastly more study and scrupulous care. So many brown trout scales have bad centres obscuring early growth and growth itself is so often very slow, while those of seatrout with their blurred record of repeated migrations and spawnings will tax patience and imagination. Scales from elderly seatrout are the most difficult of all and I've seen plenty on which no firm conclusion could be made and of which one could only say 'It looks as if . . .' or 'I think'.

What now of a salmon smolt on the way to the boundless ocean and the hunting grounds of his kind? We know something of the hazards he must surmount if he is ever to return to his native river, something of the legion of enemies that await him, from cormorants when he is small and seals when he is larger, and a little – a very little – of the sea areas he will visit in his wanderings.

It is a wry commentary on our increasing knowledge under all headings that it comes to us because of increasing exploitation of the salmon in the sea and because of the growing toll taken of the fish in the ocean-feeding phase of its life. On the one hand we learn more and more of the fish that provides our interest and our sport and on the other we may possibly be seeing, as a price for that knowledge, the last years of a disappearing race. The thought must depress us beyond any words I can find and I am not pursuing it further at this point.

Nor can we do more than speculate about the movements of our smolt for something like most of the first year of sea life, apart perhaps from the first few weeks when he may feed with shoals of his age-group in areas adjacent to the river mouth. Bit by bit however he will cease to feed in the estuary with the shallow-haunting seatrout and he will go out to deeper water. Here begins the mystery because he is unlikely to come into human ken again until, and if he surfaces and approaches shore and his native river, he is a grilse. In the intermediate stage the vast ocean conceals the extent of his travelling, the depth at which he feeds and to some extent the food itself. We know much more about him once he is a full grilse because at this size and state of development he and his class become the main catch in the offshore drift nets round these islands – his weight varying according to the characteristics of his native river, from five to say nine pounds. If he belongs to a river producing small adult salmon he may as a grilse weigh no more than three pounds.

In summer the grilse will pack together far out at sea and feeding as they come, follow routes which will bring them to the general offshore area, where at some unknown stage they cease to feed, of their home rivers. Shoals will contain individuals from many rivers and according to season fish of classes other than grilse, first-return older fish and possibly some second-return fish surviving from earlier spawning runs, though these latter do not figure significantly in the open sea net catches.

The southwest Greenland fishing ground has become famous or infamous by reason of the toll taken from the vast concourse of salmon from both sides of the Atlantic which make the long journey to feed there. In the peak season of this fishing the catch was approximately three-quarters of a million salmon. By what route the British element in this huge annual gathering of salmon travel is not known. Somewhere in the depths of the north Atlantic the fish from our rivers mingle with those from Norway, the Swedish West Coast and Iceland, Canada and the eastern United States, to share with the ocean-going char and small native salmon of Greenland this fabulously rich feeding ground. Their diet is the Capelin (a small fish of the smelt family, not to be confused with the European *Capilanus gadus* the 'poor cod' which the French fishermen call 'capalan'), sandeels and some herring and the larger animal plankton akin to our shrimps. The salmon shoal very close to the surface at night when the plankton rise from the depths and with them the capelin and other surface-feeding fish whose diet is almost exclusively plankton. This surface-feeding habit of the salmon is proven, if proof is needed, by the fact that almost all are taken in the upper meshes – the top two feet – of the drifting nets. This is a late summer and early autumn fishing and the bulk of the fish caught far offshore are of the class which would, if unmolested, form the greater part of the spring and summer runs of the following season's fishing in their home rivers. Even little rivers with scanty native stocks will contribute to the Greenland catch as we know by recovery in that area of tags applied to migrating smolts as they leave our rivers. There is reason to think that in many cases the native stocks, already alas depleted from a variety of causes, are not strong enough to withstand this additional strain.

Unfortunately the walls of drift netting are to be found in other areas as well as off Greenland and our own offshore waters are yielding enormous catches of salmon which would otherwise reach our rivers as they did in the past. In this context an analysis of the total Irish catch of salmon over the last eleven years is both illuminating and saddening when you look at it from the joint standpoints of anglers and conservationists. The annual rod catch is relatively insignificant and tends to decline; the take from the traditional operation of fish boxes, shore and estuary nets whilst fluctuating considerably is not on average markedly greater than eleven years ago, but the offshore driftnets catch has rocketed from 97 tons to the staggering figure of 1,000 tons. This stock-devastating industry is not generally operated on the old local and traditional basis though an element in the manning may be local. Very many of the boats are big and modern, lavishly equipped with the latest electronic gear, and enormously expensive. Netting our noblest fish at sea to fulfil a western world 'status symbol' demand has become big business with its only apparent object, to anyone interested in the survival of the Atlantic salmon, to make a quick killing, in more senses than one, while the species remains to be caught. I personally can imagine no other explanation for the wholesale decimation of breeding stocks on which the future of this netting industry must depend. This fishing seems to depend on interception of the shoals, mainly grilse, coming from distant waters but still far at sea. Again there is the noticeable mixing of fish of many origins and they are still feeding. The season just ended when this was written produced very large catches off the west and north-west coasts of Ireland and this included, to judge from evidence of marking, many salmon from English, Welsh and Scottish (east coast) rivers, mingled with the bulk which were Irish-bred fish. Which route those from far-off rivers followed to join the Irish fish we cannot know. Did they round the north of Scotland from the east, or pass west and north through the Channel and Irish Sea and there join forces, or did they gather together in some distant ocean-feeding ground of which we can only guess? The significant fact, and it *is* a fact, is that they were still feeding far out at sea in the summer as their stomach contents showed and, most unusually, many of them contained mackerel. Or do such fish normally follow the mackerel shoals and feed on them and we simply have not realised that mackerel form a not inconsiderable element in the diet until now? I hope and believe that the question is being studied.

It's a far and a sad cry from the days, which I can remember very clearly, when a salmon caught by a commercial fisherman far out at sea was an event worthy of mention in the angling press. But it's not so long ago in time.

Back to our smolt we must imagine – for peace of mind! – that he has survived the horrors of predators, the hungry saithe, the congers and all the ravenous hunters of the kelp forests and the continental shelves, the porpoises and the seals and those enveloping nets, and returned to the brackish inshore waters. This is the stage at which the homing mechanism has to be precise in action if he is to find the river whence he first emerged as a newly-silvered smolt.

We used to say that returning salmon entered their home rivers on arrival from sea at the bidding of some undefinable homing instinct, that indeed most examples of migratory movement in wild creatures were governed by some mysterious guidance system we call instinct or sense of direction. In the case of the salmon we now know rather more about that part of its make-up which prompts entry into the appropriate flow of fresh water when the fish encounters it in its coastwise movement. Research has shown that when the nasal sacs are flushed with water from the fishes' native river there is a strong reaction in that part of the brain associated with the sense of smell. This reaction can be and is measured electrically, but does not occur when water from other rivers is used. The reaction is strongest when water from the spawning areas of the native river is the stimulant, but water from the river throughout its course will produce the effect to some marked degree. Further research has also shown, and this phenomenon is still under study, that the 'smell imprint' which brings the returning adult salmon into the home river from salt water, is impressed in the closing period of the smolt's river life immediately prior to its departure from fresh water.

He would be a singularly unimaginative man who could, without marvel, look either at the salmon he has captured from an infinity of waters, or at the migrating smolt on its way to ocean adventure far beyond our ken and the limits of our imaginings.

6

Weather Change

On a big lake the unexpected may be a blessing and unpleasant at one and the same time.

IT BEGAN WITH a shift of wind. Before then the day had been just another of light breeze from a not very favourable quarter – the north-west to be precise. That source of wind didn't suit the south-eastern fishing ground because of the three-mile run of waves it provided there once it had what I call salmon-fishing strength. Rough lively waves are one thing but big rollers lurching too steeply for a drifting boat are quite another.

So, with the north-west wind despite its no more than medium weight making the southern area of the lake a doubtful proposition we had gone, James and I, to the north end which we preferred anyhow given a suitable breeze. Salmon were inclined to be dour but a north-west driven ripple would suit the seatrout admirably and I looked for a good day's fishing in fair, if not first-class conditions.

I was wrong. That wind did nothing for us. It was inclined to fluctuate from pleasant steadiness to near squalls but that was hardly enough in itself to account for total non-response in the seatrout. We covered ground where we knew seatrout were present in newly-arrived shoals and we saw a few small brown trout. I thought that the time was wrong – as it so often is with seatrout – and that there would be a rise sometime before one o'clock sun time. The light was fairly good through broken cloud and the air was warm. We idled in the boat watching the sandpipers on the shingle and testing our skill to call the curlew flighting overhead. They are hard to deceive but you can make a bird swing round and down just once – and only once.

Theoretically we should have been fishing intently because it had come to eleven-thirty and we had not so much as a scale in the boat. We had been wasting time and then suddenly without warning it was calm. On our lough and indeed on most that I know, a calm will be followed by a change of wind, beginning with a few puffs from any and every direction and followed by a settling in from one of them. I said as much to James who kept studying the horizon and was concerned mainly lest it should back and blow too freshly from the south – indicating a hard pull home.

But it did not come from the south – it came down due north from the mountain – a real cold fresh breeze and in our situation, blowing directly offshore. Worse still it was gusty, scuttering black patches across the lough, and aloft it was filling in with uniform dark cloud everywhere. I didn't like it one little bit because with us it can blow really hard from the north. And I do not like fishing, as we were now forced to do from shallow into deep – whatever the wind's source.

I have been fishing for seatrout a very long time indeed and they still surprise me. They surprised me now because in that cold gusty wind and very poor light, they began to rise. They didn't take well but they did rise. At one time to the Donegal Blue and a small Silver Doctor, I seemed to be rising fish to every cast that I could fish out between gusts. I think that in half an hour or thereabouts I must have risen thirty fish. A few were obvious finnoch but the majority, fish of one to one-and-a-half pounds; and when they ceased to make swirls at the fly we had ten of them. Neither gust nor chill seemed to put them off while the general move was on them. I have seldom seen less promising looking water. It was broken into little ragged heaps without concerted movement, tortured into miniature maelstroms of gust-blackened waves and above all carrying that abomination of all water-surface conditions, a wave on top of the wave. If I had not seen it I would not have believed that fish would come to the fly. Nor would James, and I have a feeling that lesson will keep coming to mind.

When we pulled in to the shore for lunch the wind had increased markedly and the body of the lough was breaking into white horses everywhere.

Under a rowan bush on the turf bank behind a little sandy beach we were comfortable enough and indeed must have so looked because we were presently joined by another boat – angler and ghillie both of our acquaintance. They had had a long rough pull up the lough and were glad to shelter. The fish in our boat astonished them: they had tested some of the best points along the shore wholly without result. Clearly our take was local. We agreed that there appeared little hope for the remainder of the day. If anything the wind was strengthening and it looked like building into one of those days of the big rolling combers that lift the silt on the shallower fishing grounds and make much water useless until some hours after both wind and silt go down again.

We stayed ashore for some time. Normally we forget lunch until we are sure that the usual midday taking time is over and then take our time over it. But we don't normally waste good fishing time: today was different for, to be truthful, I didn't know where to go. The only water sheltered from the blustering north wind and on the way to our home landing was a weedy bay full of hungry little brownies and little else so that further fishing for anything worthwhile appeared non-existent. A boat could no longer be held in position where we had found our seatrout so that all that was left seemed to be a straight run home.

Even that defeatist course held some problems because if the lough lapping our beach at the head of this wind was rough, what would it be like at our home landing where the wave would have had two miles of open water in which to build up. Even at that distance we could see flickering fountains of white spray bursting on the southern shore rocks and we knew that no boat could live in that sea. Unless you fish big lakes you can have no vision of the kind of roughness that can develop from mountain-derived winds of any strength.

But plan for the return there had to be and it could take one form only. There was, about three-quarters of a mile downwind from us, a long low point jutting athwart the wind and at its landward end a great sandy shallow thickly grown with reeds. If we could attain that place we could safely allow the boat to be driven or to be washed ashore through the sheltering reeds, and thence walk home knowing the boat to be high and dry and beyond harm on the beach behind the aforesaid reeds.

This plan had two defects in the shape of two hazards. At one point on the route the wind, now freshened to something like a full gale, was funnelled between a high rocky timbered island and the shore, and here in the shallow channel there would be a steep boat-swamping wave. Beyond that lay four hundred yards of open water which we must cross to reach the reeds. The wind would be dead astern all the way. I said that our home-going plan could take but one form but we did very briefly consider the one alternative which was to leave the boat where she was and walk from there. This would require the tortuous traverse of over a mile of densely-wooded hillside before we could reach open ground. Fresh and alert and unburdened one can, in fact, negotiate those woods but in a lifetime of scrambling I have never known such a jungle – its floor littered with broken rock, gnarled roots and fallen trees, hanging lichen swamping the lower branches of living timber – true primeval forest. Today with rods and miscellaneous gear to carry, its passage would be both exhausting and temper fraying.

If this is a long recital with precious little fishing to enliven it I can only plead that days like this will occur as a part of fishing and that however well you know your lough and your local weather, you cannot anticipate every wind shift and you must occasionally be 'caught'.

The other boat, talking vaguely of waiting for wind drop, wished us luck as we pushed off and even went so far as to say 'Ye'll get yer salmon on the way home!' We thanked them, of course and we parted with no shadow of hope. But I did take off the seatrout cast and replace it with one of 8-pound nylon carrying two sixes – one a Dunkeld and the other a Sweep: as we left the shore I put out about fifteen or twenty yards of line and allowed it to trail astern. In a rough wave salmon will often take a trailed fly when they won't look at one cast to them and worked. We would pass a very small area of good salmon ground on our way.

Conditions in the channel between island and shore when we reached it, were on the borderline between what is passable and what is so bad that only a fool would try it. So great was the pressure of wind and wave however that we had no choice: we were committed and could not turn inshore since any single wave on quarter or beam would have

4

Photo: John Marchington

FEEDING TROUT—AN UNUSUAL RISE FORM
THE CAMERA SEES MORE THAN THE HUMAN EYE

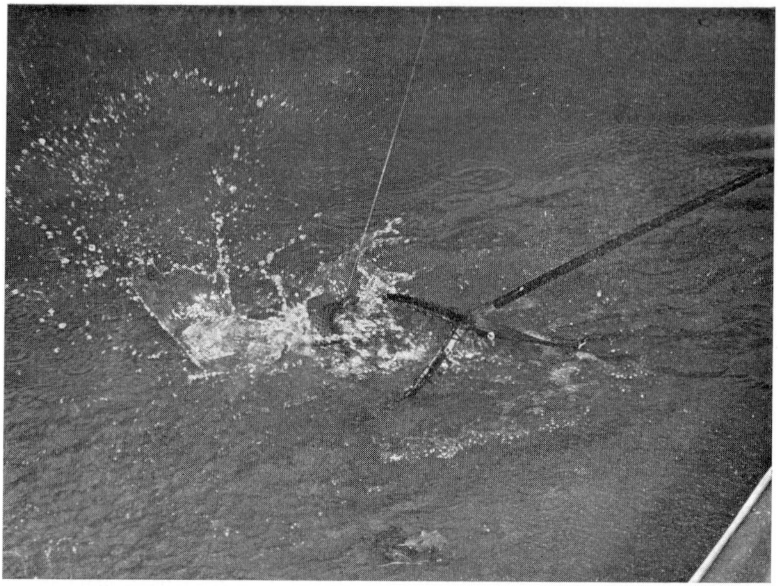

5 *Photo: John Marchington*

IT WOULD HAVE BEEN WISER TO WAIT
FOR THIS TROUT TO QUIETEN DOWN

6 *Photo: John Marchington*

QUIET AND SAFELY NETTED

swamped us. James dug his oars in and held on and we swooped and soared onwards like any speedboat. The wind was curling the wave tops and whipping them off. I sat on the floor and baled the water swilling over the boards, but we caught less wind this way and we took only spray and no solid water.

When we were rather more than halfway through, I hooked a fish. As a fact I had nothing to do with it. I had secured the butt of the rod at a slight diagonal, reel handles uppermost and had all but forgotten it when the reel screamed and went on screaming. Backing was partly gone when I got the rod up to a sensible angle and clamped a finger on the line. And there I sat in an inch or two of dirty water holding the rod butt nearly vertically and literally dragging that fish with us. James was helpless and could only cling to his oars and try to slow us down while I waited for the break. I thought it had come when for a second or two the pressure eased completely. But it came on again with a sudden snatch as we sailed on. Generally speaking, that fish came quietly – surging along behind us and now and then showing in the wall of a following wave.

Now there was a place where the channel splayed into completely open water, on our left and on our right, into an indentation hardly deep enough to be called a bay on the main shore and here the rough water eased down a little to become a heavy surge – uncomfortable but relatively quiet. A touch on one oar and we shot into the 'shelter' of this semblance of a bay. Twenty yards more and we were close inshore where tall mixed timber stood as a partial wind break at the water's edge on a steep beach of broken rock. In terms of being pulled by the head that fish had had a rough time, but in terms of resistance he had come like a lamb for something like a hundred and fifty yards – and now he woke up. If, a few moments earlier, he had used all the tricks he now employed, we should never have got him so far. He went straight down, smacking the cast hard. Water was very deep here and looked safe enough until you looked closely, when you saw the maze of fallen larch timber with laddered branches that cluttered the bouldery bottom sliding steeply into the gloom of great depths. It was a horrible place in which to play a fish and James and I looked at each other in something like amazement when, at last, we had a very fresh-looking ten pounder in the boat.

There were two separate and distinct hook tears in the mouth so that I had come very near to losing him before that snatch had signalled a fresh grip of the hook. For what it was worth he had taken the Sweep but I thought then, and still think that the impulse to take came from the speed of the fly, the lure of a darting shape passing at high speed and not from its pattern.

We sat in the rocking boat close under the trees for a while, studying the look of our final hazard, the open gale-torn stretch between us and our designated haven behind the reeds. This stage was twice as long as the passage through the island channel which we had weathered very well, but in the open the waves were longer crest to crest and less broken. I cannot say that we made the crossing, when we did finally leave shelter, with any comfort, either mental or physical: I am quite sure that boat had never travelled so fast in her history but I was very wet from sitting in sloshing water when her nose drove into the reeds. Successive surges damped down by the forest of stems but still full of drive, carried us shorewards until we grounded in a few inches of water over firm sand.

We emptied the boat of all her movable gear, rods, sodden fishing bag, lunch bag and the fish and hauled her high above flood marks, there to lash her to a tree with the long nylon painter I carry for this purpose. A short painter is always an abomination, but a long one can be a great blessing in any boat when water is low or she has to be left as on this occasion away from the usual mooring.

Oars and rowlocks concealed in the bracken, we turned our backs to the wind, glad enough to have something solid under foot and content to carry between us about twenty-five pounds in ten seatrout and a salmon got most unexpectedly on a very 'bad' day. You never know do you?

7

Boats for Fishing

Suitability for purpose is vital in a fishing boat because its character can mean the difference between happy fishing and endless irritations.

INCREASINGLY I AM asked about boats for fishing and the conclusion can only be that there is growing interest in lake and sea fishing. Indeed there is other ample evidence of this. To me it indicates first the growing scarcity of available river fishing, second, the current development of still-water facilities – reservoirs, artificial lakes, ex-gravel diggings and third the ever-widening use of the car to get to distant lakes and to the sea.

Once upon a time you went to Scotland or to Ireland or otherwise far afield and you there hired a boat and a ghillie for the duration of your stay or day by day. This, of course, is standard procedure in most well-known fishing places but today many anglers have their own boat which they either keep on their own fishing or by arrangement on some favourite lake to which they have access. Others carry the boat on the car roof – less often on a trailer, launching it on arrival. I am sorry to say that some owners in the 'carry your boat with you' class are doing fishermen and fishing in general a disservice by reason of their failure – and this is becoming quite common – to obtain leave before they put their boats on any promising-looking water they may come across in their touring. The touring angler is welcomed everywhere because he is, as a type, inoffensive and law-abiding and he helps the local economy. But I do know from personal observation and experience that the welcome is becoming distinctly cooler in some inland areas where private rights are ignored and the visitor simply helps himself. There have always been people who would fish without leave, of course, and this practice has not done the rest of us any real damage largely because such 'poaching' has been done from the shore with consequent limited harm to the fishing. Boat fishing, especially while using an engine, is a very different matter. It has occurred several times on my own fishing when the lake, kept quiet as a matter of fishing policy, has echoed from shore to shore with the chatter of an outboard on a boat launched without permission from the lakeside road. I do feel strongly about this sort of behaviour but the issue is not a personal one – I know many other sufferers and the practice seems to be growing with the introduction of small light boats capable of being carried on a car.

It has been necessary to write this to make clear that in notes about boats, boat owning and the carrying and use of boats for fishing, my purpose is to assist in the use of boats in ordinary fishing by the ordinary decent angler. This said I hope you will forgive my fulminations about the few whom we must disown and discourage.

In practice the numbers of trout, seatrout or salmon lakes where you may use a private boat are limited but there are plenty of small, unfrequented trout lochs and lochans in Scotland and Ireland where leave to put a boat for a few hours is readily given and sometimes by this means it is possible to take fish uncatchable from the shore. There are places too where the shores are near liquid bog or widely fringed with lily-beds or reeds so that shore fishing is impossible. The little hill loughs rather often harbour in their acid waters hordes of ravenous little black trout but occasionally you will find one, situated on or drawing its water from a limestone outcrop, where you may find good trout.

There is, of course, sea fishing in open water to justify owning and carrying a boat and in some coastal areas there is little other fishing use for the boat. This is not true however of much of the western and north-western coasts on both sides of the Irish Sea where the sea lochs offer a variety of fishing – including some good seatrout water – in safe and attractive conditions. I am all for carrying a light rigid boat over the border or across the sea specifically to exploit such possibilities. For this kind of use, the thin-skinned inflatable boat is not advisable: there are lakes and sea lochs which bristle with hidden rocks forming a high hazard for this type of craft in the hands of a stranger. Apart altogether from the question of safety the inflatable boats though commendably low in profile, are not ideal fishing platforms. You have little command of the water and the boat which is really a keelless raft has too little grip and skates about too readily at the bidding of any appreciable wind. That said, I will admit to having had some very good trout fishing, and some excitement, by packing a very small inflatable life-raft up the weary miles to certain very high mountain lochans in Scotland – the sort of places of which it is said that 'there are good fish there but they only seem to rise far out in the middle beyond reach'.

Clearly, however, the transportable boat should be rigid and there can be no doubt that fibre glass is the material giving maximum strength and lightness. Size must be related to method of carrying and generally to car size. Usually this means a very small boat of somewhat prescribed build and equipment. The one important point on which it can conform to good fishing practice is in its colour. Almost all those that I see are white. They should be dark grey if they are to be used for trout or seatrout fishing.

Conventional style fishing boats, for location in one place offer far more scope for approach to complete fitness for purpose. Size, within limits, is governed by the type of water and a little nine or ten footer will serve perfectly for the small lowland lakes and ponds, but would be quite inadequate for the bigger waters where something more substantial is needed for rough conditions and required to carry, if necessary, two rods and a third man at the oars. Much of seatrout fishing in lochs and all of salmon fishing there really requires that the rod should concentrate on fishing. You *can* fish salmon, play them and boat them single-handed: I have done it several times but it is not really 'on' and you need a man to handle the boat. Seatrout are no great problem to the solo angler in one way but lack of boat control results in wasted water and the putting down of fish that would rise to a rod fishing from a boat well-held on its drift.

Fourteen or fifteen feet is a good average length for a boat to take two rods and a gillie and indeed a foot or two more will do no harm provided the boat has a good entry and is an easy puller. You have to remember in the size context that the boat has to be light enough to beach on occasion — over and over again if you have no dock or landing stage. Also, it is a fact that the bigger she is – i.e., the longer, the more free board she will have and the more wind she will catch on a drift. This effect will be very obvious too when there is one rod only aboard and he occupies, as is usual and natural, the stern seat. Then the bow, slightly cocked up because of unequal trim, will catch the wind and swing, the ghillie will swear and he will get no rest if his charge is to drift straight. So excess length is to be avoided.

I fish alone on most days and even my fifteen-foot boat is not free from the bow-swinging fault when I occupy the stern but a biggish stone in the bow cures this and serves, incidentally, to steady the bow when we have to pull home against wind and wave on a rough day.

Choice of material in a boat is critical. Wood, larch for example, is excellent and traditional and is handled skilfully by small boat builders who usually know what is required by way of 'lines' in a boat for fishing in their localities. But wooden boats of whatever construction incorporate a great deal of hand labour and are costly today. They are also, unless well-maintained, relatively short-lived. I like a timber boat, but far better for our purpose in my view is the modern fibre-glass job but there are snags, so very much in a good boat for fishing depending on hull contour.

I had a sharp lesson in this regard a few years ago. A boat was moulded for me in fibre glass and conformed precisely to the specification I had indicated in all respects and admirably, except in hull contour. She was of 'hard chine' shape or profile and I can best describe the result by saying that if she had been wooden she would have one smooth broad plank from gunwale to bilge keel and another sweeping in sharply from that line to the true keel. If you looked at her bow-on she had no curve from gunwale to keel but simply two flat planes. She looked good. Broad in the beam and more stable than any boat I have ever known, she refused to list far enough to ship water when two heavy men sat on the gunwale. Buoyancy tanks were fitted under thwarts and she was unsinkable. She was for use on a very big Scottish loch where we often had to travel miles to the fishing ground of the day and so used an outboard motor. Top speed in big waves left her bone dry and she went under power like the proverbial bomb. But, and this was wholly my fault for not giving enough thought to the hard-chine principle and its possible effect – she would not drift at anything remotely resembling fishing speed. She slithered sideways, spun round and reduced half-a-dozen hard-bitten ghillies to near tears.

Since then I have seen and fished from glass boats completely free of faults and these boats have been moulded from clinker-built timber craft, so that one had to look closely to detect the construction material. The master from which the mould was made was clearly a good boat and the copies, faithfully reproducing the lapped planking and relatively deep keel, are very good indeed on the drift. Were I buying a boat today I should certainly choose this type, specifying among other things the unsinkable quality derived from sufficient plastic foam buoyancy bags, a general low profile and adequate beam. This question of beam in relation to stability is important especially in salmon fishing where, if you have my habit, you like to stand in the boat in the closing stages of play when the fish is coming to the net. This way you can see the fish and so anticipate any last moment moves such as a dive under the boat. It's a great thing then to be able to stand firmly in a boat which is stable and not in any degree 'cockly'.

Badly arranged seating is a common boat fault. To begin with the stern seat should be deep and run right back to the transom and the thwarts and their related rowlock sockets should be so placed that if there is need due to bad weather for example, for two men to take an oar each, the man in the main and usual rowing position will not on his forward movement bump the back of the man on the sternmost thwart. This kind of thing more than offsets anything gained by having the strength of two men to the pair of oars.

External colour in a boat means, in my belief, the difference between good and poor results in some lights and conditions – as for example when you are drifting into the sun. Since the fish if trout or seatrout, are feeding head to wind and wave, it follows that they face the oncoming sunlit boat and if that boat is white or very light coloured it will show up in a most unnatural and glaring manner. This will certainly put seatrout down. After much experiment I like dark grey best of all for the outside of any fishing boat: not pretty, it's extremely practical.

Some boats beach, or better can be beached, more easily than others but this rather depends on the nature of the beach. Some sandy beaches might be coated with glue, so firmly do they stick to a boat and I think small pebbles provide less trouble on the whole, so that if there is any choice you should avoid the sand. Of course the point has no significance for temporary landings at lunch time, or for leg-stretching. But if you lack a landing stage and your lake is subject to considerable fluctuation in level you are obliged, as I am, to take the boat well up, in inches of water, or on a dry shore. Then weight and beachability are factors to be taken into account. Straining and pulling to excess are bad for both rod and ghillie at start or close of a day. On water-level fluctuation and its influence on safe boat bestowal I suggest a stout and very long nylon painter. I carry a hundred feet of light nylon line which is a great convenience when in low water the boat grounds in shallow water far from shore. If the lake rises as a result of heavy rain in the night, I know that at least she is tied securely and cannot drift off.

The possession of, or the right of access to a really sheltered boat landing is a great asset and comfort: to wake in the night, listen to the howl of a gale and wonder what is happening to the boat is a wretched thing. Lacking shelter in such weather you will assuredly find the boat in need of attention on the morning of a day which promises to be the best for a very long time were you able to get afloat!

My boat landing is a safe place. It is also in its calm seclusion a little world of its own. From its calm in the morning you set out on the wildness of open water with the momentary tinge of apprehension born of contrast, and you return gladly in the evening to its welcoming peace and shelter. There are many birds in the sheltering hazels and the high timber behind them. Here I often see over heather and bracken, the swift blue-grey flash of a hunting merlin – the elegant little falcon. To my joy, a pair of badgers have lately opened up a new sett under a shelf of limestone near the boat, daily evidence of their industry, a huge and mounting pile of shaley earth. The sett is unusually near the water – six feet away – and I wonder if in their crepuscular activities the tenants encounter the big dog otter who holes up nearby and on occasion pursues the big seatrout that haunt the area in spite of him.

8

Distant Dinner Party

Salt water fishing for the seatrout of Problem River and all that was involved in a twenty-four hour exercise.

PROBLEM RIVER, WHICH has and richly merits a chapter of its own must be for its size one of the very finest seatrout fisheries in these islands. The head of seatrout is phenomenal but you have to remember that although it is a small waterway, it leads to an area spread with mountain lochans and two big lochs with their feeders – the whole an anonymity of distance into which in running time hordes of seatrout (and almost as many salmon for that matter) ascend and vanish.

It follows that despite the smallness of the river itself and however in consequence its fishing may be difficult, the adjoining sea area must carry a heavy stock of seatrout and, as a fact, the fish in due season are present in shoals innumerable in the long narrow sea loch into which at its head, the river empties. At the point of entry the loch is relatively shallow over clean, smooth sand broken only by a few rather deeper channels and several turfy islets. The shore is fringed by a singularly awkward kind of beach, steeply sloping and composed of a mass of stones of all shapes and sizes, the weedy ones at tide level and below exceedingly slippery and all of them potential ankle twisters or worse. The fringing weed hangs limp at low tide and conceals the pitfalls and at high water floats as a shelf of tangle, its seaward edge the feeding ground of seatrout.

Behind the beach, the hillsides rise sharply, heather and rock and peat bogs – domain of the deer and the eagles, the grouse and golden plover and the flitting wheatear. The sharpness of the ground's rise behind the narrow beach has some fishing significance because unless you use some kind of modified steeple cast, are extremely lucky, or find a place where the weed fringe is narrow and you can use a short line, you will assuredly blunt or break many hooks in the back cast.

So much for the character of the estuary – the river itself is described in Chapter I.

I like the river but when water is low and the fish cannot go higher than the sea pool even at top of the tide there is the estuary and its multitude of restlessly-cruising seatrout. Thus Problem River and its outlet to sea, treated as one fishing, is capable of providing sport once fish have come in from the open ocean, at almost any part of the season and any time of the day. I say 'almost' because of course, there can be enormous floods in the river to make fishing impossible and there can be very low tides that take fish far away down the sea loch. And the weather is always beyond control. But generally, if the river is low and its rocky pools empty of fish, you can confidently fish the salt water and if the river is high or even reasonably high, you can ignore the estuary and fish your way upstream. A remarkable place – its matchless potential due, of course, to the tremendous stock and to its privacy and remoteness.

Knowing it, and if you know it you are drawn as if by magnet, the feature that you must come to terms with is this very remoteness. And thereby hangs a tale which contains at once some elements to be noted for other times and similar places, and some which I cherish for their own sakes.

For some years in late June and early July I had been able, by grace of a good friend and very kind host, to make repeated short visits to this fascinating place and I came to know it rather well. I always felt, however, that I left it unexploited because of its situation on the Atlantic fringe across very rough wet moorland and eight miles from fishing headquarters. The fishing day became rather short, even in the clear northern June, when you had to allow for a really punishing walk of sixteen miles in the day in addition to your ramblings up and down the river or along the shore. And since, if the weather had been dry and the river was low your fishing had to be in the estuary, you had a further limiting factor in the state of the tide. Ideally you would fish half-flow and half-ebb.

The answer broke through my frustration like a shaft of sunlight through cloud one day in early July. Why not contrive a major operation to last twenty-four hours and so strike the range of tide conditions? The weather was settled and even if it broke as can happen in that place without any real warning, we had for shelter a keeper's cottage out of use for some time, but sound enough and furnished after a fashion – just the place for a meal and an hour or two's rest at full or slack tide or through the small hours. You shall learn how it worked out.

Sharing my solitude in the islands at this time was a friend of many years and so, with the ghillie John, we were a party of three. My host's admirable house staff used miracles of ingenuity to provide twenty-four hour provender for three hungry men and in so doing put together what felt like about half a hundredweight of the best tableware. And since the unfortunate John had to carry this load plus food and any oddments of his own over all those miles, I had to intervene to make drastic changes and many cuts. This by the way. As it was John had a heavy load. He is small, wiry and astonishingly strong and has several times carried big loads of salmon for me from distant rivers and lochs – burdens that would have floored lesser men. He loves fishing and if a little impetuous with a landing net, is a good ghillie and a helpful personal attendant in an age when that kind of support is rare. He carries his load, whatever it may be, on his back with the supporting strap across his chest and upper arms and so laden goes tirelessly for hours. Any attempt to take part is repulsed with dignity.

You would have seen us that morning, tramping not fast but steadily, in single file across the moor; John in the lead, Hector and I following at his speed. Peat hags and deep water-courses, quaking bog and rocky crests were taken in turn until in about three hours we stood on the hill overlooking the river and the little grey cottage that might have been at first glance and, but for the blue of the slate roof, one of the giant boulders surrounding it. A party of hinds on the green by the river gave us a hard searching look before trotting off.

Our tide calculations had been made by guesswork based on the tide table for the nearest quoted port and turned out to be accurate enough for our purpose: from the top of the hill we could see only a narrow fringe of weed along the shore and we had clearly arrived within an hour of high water. We could see arriving shoals of seatrout and occasional leaping salmon, all heading towards the stony bar where the shrunken river trickled seaward through the gravel to meet the upward creeping tide. At another time and place we should have been lunching first but now that function was an irrelevancy; we had a thirst-quenching drink from the icy spring beside the cottage and were away to the shore leaving John to open doors and windows and get a fire going in the ancient stove. He had announced that in virtue of his once having served as cook in a trawler, he was dealing with the evening's dinner and would in fact serve it – all in due course.

In five minutes we were on the shore at points a hundred yards apart. I had a ten-foot trout rod with an old reel and an equally elderly but sound line, a six-pound cast and a tandem-hooked lure of blue and silver. There are times when these seatrout will take a spun Devon better than any feathered lure whatever its type, and I had as reserve a short spinning rod with a South Bend multiplier, terylene line, eight-pound trace of nylon and an inch-long Silver Devon. All the gear was 'second best' – concession to my dislike of using top grade equipment in corroding salt water – but it *was* sound.

Weed tips were showing in a belt ten feet wide, and beyond the weed crystal-clear water four or five feet deep over clean sand. The seatrout, in companies of anything from ten to fifty fish, were just visible once you spotted the slight surface ripple that indicated their approach. You might get the odd fish by casting blind between shoals, but I always prefer to fish to an oncoming shoal because the hooking and playing technique is exacting and it pays to stay fresh and unflurried and to rest the rod arm.

I had been waiting with plenty of loose line ready to shoot for a few minutes before the chance came. I put the lure a yard in front of an oncoming shoal and brought it across the leading fish (or where I judged the leader to be) rather smartly. The shoal turned in pursuit like one fish to scatter and go on as the lure was grabbed by one of their number. I never cease to marvel at the strength of these salt-water

Photo : John Marchington

7

THE LURE CAST UP AND ACROSS
SWINGS ATTRACTIVELY IN THE CURRENT

8 *Photo: John Marchington*

HELD HARD—A FIGHTING SALMON IN A MOORLAND RIVER

9 *Photo: John Marchington*

A PLEASANT BASKET OF TROUT

seatrout and this one knew all the tricks as well, leaping and boring and finding new reserves of pulling power each time I had his head up to slide him across the weed to the net. But he came at last, about two pounds and bright and covered with lice. It was a beginning.

He was quickly unhooked and laid in a weedy hollow up the beach and I took another from the next shoal and a third from one far out – slightly smaller fish these. Then I hooked a much bigger fish which gave me a spectacular fight in clear water before diving quite irresistibly into the weed. He was under the rod tip and not far out of reach but the beach shelved too steeply for me to go in. I slackened line and hoped he would go out again of his own accord which indeed he may have done. But the lure – with fish or without it – was firmly anchored and in the end I had to break. I was being tantalised, as the minutes passed in re-tackling, by the unending procession of dark ruffled patches moving up with the still creeping tide and I knew there would shortly be an 'off' period at full tide followed by another take on the ebb.

My next fish was a three-and-a-half pounder which I netted after plenty of trouble – a lovely shapely fish and all that a richly-fed fast-growing type of seatrout should be.

Then I began to lose fish in the weed, or in some cases, by the fish simply coming off for no apparent reason. I discovered a possible explanation of the latter trouble, in one pointless hook – the tail one: whether broken in a fish or in the backcast I could not know. While I was replacing this tackle I saw a biggish company of salmon coming along the weed-edge towards me and I did a foolish thing – I switched to the spinning rod. I took no heed of a little voice telling me something I knew very well indeed from long and bitter experience – that salmon will not take in shallow water and so far up inside the loch. I could have predicted what would happen with absolute accuracy because I've seen it so often. I could see these salmon in the clear water – fish of five to ten pounds and I put the Devon across the spearhead of the shoal at a medium steady speed. The leaders turned to follow and like so many sheep the entire company after them. They followed the bait up to the edge of the weed and I could see them quite clearly. The leading fish never came nearer than three feet from the bait and as they turned away I would have sworn that every fish had a mouth tight shut! This behaviour is typical in shallow water: further down the loch where the fish shoal at the surface of relatively deep water you will find fish coming open-mouthed at the bait and though you will not get all those that take, for they are terribly soft-mouthed and violent in play, you will get some of them.

That particular shoal circled round and came past me again but I could not induce a take, nor any from the next lot. I put the spinning rod away having wasted some good seatrout time. I saw John come down from the cottage and talk to Hector and I saw them obviously examining his catch – his net had been in use several times when I had looked along the beach. Waiting for John, I found I had eight fish and also that breakfast had happened in the now rather-distant past and some nourishment was urgently needed.

John had turned out to do some ghillying and to discover when we proposed to dine, but I decided that whilst an evening meal could wait until well on into the ebb, tea was an urgent current need. So tea it would be and one would fish again before dinner. John hastened off to his tea-making – we followed bringing fourteen beautiful seatrout to be put in a cool place and free of the rats that swarm on this and many other island beaches. It began to look like a real bag and we still had the ebb and tomorrow's flood to fish.

The light had been very good, filtering softly through filmy cloud of the kind Donegal men call 'goats hair'. Any movement of air had come from the north-west, crinkling the water without producing anything like a real ripple. Now, as we sat on the rabbit-cropped turf by the cottage door, waited on by John with relays of buttered toast and tea to trawlermen's standard, that zephyr died away as is the way towards evening of any wind with an appreciable element of north in its make-up.

From the water's edge an oystercatcher whistled and there appeared a curl of flow at the seaward ends of the little turf islets – the tide had turned and presently the fish would go out with it. At about half-ebb they would take again if – and I gave nothing for the chances – we had a ripple. The western ocean water along unsullied beaches is crystal clear and in flat calm you won't move a tenth of the fish that will come racing after the fly when it fishes under a broken surface.

However, we had to have a plan, not least because of John's domestic endeavours. He had been busy – fire going and the room like an oven, provender unpacked, floor swept with a bunch of heather and two broken-down easy chairs and a settee in a similar state of decrepitude, carefully arranged for a social evening. A bottle and three glasses were prominent. From the doorway we could still see an occasional seatrout splashing but there was now nothing like the earlier showing of fish. The dimplings and minor curls on the placid loch surface could be shoals of cuddies or almost anything. The sinking sun was off the floor of the glen but still high and bright beyond the hills' rim when, later, we went down again to fish the ebb.

A pair of eagles wheeled without apparent effort above the slope of the north hill, a black-throated diver appeared on the loch and the evening air into the far distance was filled with the plaintive pipings of the golden plover. It was very peaceful – the blue reek from John's turf fire columned straight aloft and there wasn't the faintest shift of air. The fish were moving out with the tide but they were further offshore in this movement and I counted myself lucky to get two one-pounders. They ignored the fly for the most part and when we compared notes I found Hector having an equally frustrating time. At this stage, beginning to be conscious of the length and extent of the day's exertions and becoming the targets for legions of midges, we became aware of the approach of a strange figure.

You should know that John is a rather wild-looking small figure when he is about his ghillying, clothes and old boots liberally plastered with black half-fluid peat so that on the moor you could find him difficult to separate from his surroundings – a thing that made him the good stalker he is – but now I could only stare. His weather-beaten face was shining, his coat had been brushed and his boots washed. He bore a serviette draped tastefully over one forearm and he carried – very carefully as he stepped among the boulders – a bottle of the wine of the country and a bottle of water.

Arrived beside us he produced, from pockets, two glasses. With these and the bottle secure on a flat rock, he said very solemnly 'Dinner will be served in half an hour.' and as a kind of afterthought 'I've washed my hands!' 'Did you also,' I asked, 'bring another glass?' The shining face creased fleetingly and out of an inner pocket came the third glass.

The air outside had that luminous night quality that belongs to the Isles and to the Scandinavian north, when we sat down to dinner. John plus serviette, waited on a table complete with white cloth and correctly laid. In a kind of daze, I watched him produce in succession soup, Parma ham and melon – biscuits and cheese and coffee and none of which we could have faulted had I wished to do so. It's true that the melon was piled on the ham but we meant our thanks and our compliments. 'Ach' said John, 'it's no me you should be thankin' – it's the girls in the kitchen.'

However that might be, we gave him in gratitude first choice of a place to sleep. He chose a chair and so did Hector and I had the settee. Within five minutes of lying down I would gladly have changed that settee for either of the chairs. The stuffing had long since fallen out or been stolen by mice or rats for their nest making and springs protruded in all directions – all painful. The fire in the old stove died down and the room was filled with rustlings and scrapings – muttered imprecations from the would-be sleepers and groans of discomfort. I do not really know how we got through that short night. John can sleep in a heathery gully on the hill in bad weather but even he was beaten by that furniture. When the new day had lost its early chill we were all hard asleep on the grass outside – heads on fishing bags and for cover our oilskins.

Later, Hector wanted to photograph some hinds and we used most of the morning and early afternoon in fruitless minor stalks. At three-quarter tide we were on the beach again but this day was different altogether. The fish may have been there but they hardly showed and only a very big shoal and (I suppose) its greater competitive characteristic would produce a take. By top of the tide we had six seatrout between us having returned any number of finnoch on whom the calm clear water seemed to impose no restraint. But, and this is significant, we lost ten good seatrout in play as distinct from the odd one lost in this way on the preceding day. The fish simply did not take 'properly' in the prevailing conditions and the fly pulled away time after time. I won't say pulled 'out' because I don't believe that in these cases it was ever 'in'. The lack of ripple had beaten us.

And so, in the late afternoon, homeward over those gruelling eight miles.

You may feel that there is a great deal in this account of a twenty-four hour exercise which is not fishing. It is quite simply a factual record of all that was involved in an attempt to catch seatrout from the sea in a very remote place. Perhaps the best commentary resides in a summary of its results which were: landed 22 seatrout weighing 37 pounds – plus eleven fish lost in weed or from breakage, plus ten which came off in play and finally, hooked, landed and returned about 30 finnoch.

9

Seen While Fishing

The success of the day is not measured in terms of dead fish. Other things contribute importantly to the joy of fishing.

IF YOU ARE A fisherman and as observant as you should be to make the most of your rod handling or even to succeed to any degree at all, you can hardly avoid being something of a watcher and student of living things. In that capacity you are what used to be called a naturalist, but it seems to me that we hear the word less nowadays: perhaps it has become old-fashioned. There are far more students of nature than there used to be but they specialise in birds or mammals, insects or plants, reptiles or soil organisms or fish. Their interests generally are narrower than yours though you too are a specialist with the difference that your principal subject cannot be studied without awareness and some extensive knowledge of the wild world of which the fish are part. On the reverse side of the picture, I know at least one man highly and properly esteemed for his specialised knowledge of the salmon kind, who has never held a rod.

In my own case a lifelong dedication to fishing and a deep-rooted interest in wildlife of all descriptions seem always to have been quite inseparable and wholly complementary. Looking back it appears to me that no day outside has ever been lost: often there have been highlights – great fishing days or times when events in the simpler background of fishing have provided reason for instant pleasure or for recurrent memory. But mostly the features marking the days have concerned minor occurrences – small things easy for the unobservant and unquiet to miss – bird voices and the behaviour of their owners and of animals, the finding of a rare plant or the teeming life of insects on or about river and lake. And above all and always vital, the doings of the fish as a part of their life pattern and as affecting their catchability.

Consider then, as a change from purely fishing talk, some small pleasant matters which have illuminated fishing days and given me something to ponder as well as delight in recollection.

One golden September day I was sitting by a pool on a beat which I then had on a North Devon river. If you ask me why I was sitting instead of fishing, I will tell you that it was mid-afternoon and generally a rather dead time as far as any movement of salmon is concerned, that I had taken one fish from the pool in the morning and was content and finally, that it was hot and bright and very conducive to just sitting.

It is an interesting place in which to sit quietly. The bank is luxuriantly grown with grasses and all manner of wild flowers in their seasons, backed by a fringe of sprouting alder stumps and edged below with the shingle beach which is the fishing stance. Opposite, across the pool, is a near vertical rock face with twenty feet up, an overhanging matt of turf, tree roots and wortleberry. Under this there is, every season, a dipper's nest – worth watching in itself. The pool is slow, twisting of current and deep and ever and anon you will see the back or tail of some restless salmon cruising along the base of the rock. When this happens you can reach for the rod, pull off some line and pitch a fly against the rock in the path of the fish – if by that time he hasn't gone down. Or you can just sit.

I was doing that when I became aware of a curious thing. About five feet from me there grew the tall, now rather withered stem of a foxglove. It was a strange plant because in place of the typical single tapering spear of a flowerhead, this one had branched so that each side of the main stem grew minor stems each with its flowerhead and each bending gracefully down with, presumably, the weight of seed in the withered flowers. What had taken my eye was the fact that the whole plant was quivering gently but ceaselessly. There was no wind and anyhow it wasn't that kind of shiver: there was something at work at the base of the plant and hidden from my view by the grass. I kept quite still and watched, to be rewarded presently by the emergence from the grass jungle of a vole – one of the short-tailed variety, plump of body, beady-eyed and blunt of nose and very intent on some business of his own. He, or it may have been she, proceeded at once to scale the foxglove stem to the fork where the first side stem parted from the main and then to move out towards the drooping seed head. I was tempted to call a warning. The weak side stem couldn't possibly carry the weight and before the venturesome one reached the seed-head his support drooped suddenly and he quite simply fell off. He landed on the tangled herbage kicking frantically, regained his feet and dived out of sight. The foxglove began to shake again and up the stem came the fat little brown climber only to fall again in precisely similar manner. And he did it all once more – three abortive attempts to reach those seeds.

There was a pause. The foxglove didn't quiver any more and I pictured the perplexed little animal somewhere in his tunnel among the grass roots. When he reappeared he was eight inches from the main stem and directly under the drooping seed-head and while I watched in admiration, he stood erect on a pair of ridiculous little hind legs and reaching up with stretching fore-legs pulled the seed-head down so that he could extract and eat the seeds. I kept still until he had finished – I thought he deserved the consideration and all the seeds he could reach. That beady-eyed little clown contributed as much to my day as did my ten-pound fish of the morning!

* * *

I have never really liked eels in spite of the extraordinary interest of their life history. How much ova of trout, salmon and seatrout they consume is incalculable but certainly a very great volume and this quite apart from their predation on fry and bigger fish. A feeding eel will tackle anything that it can swallow and some that it cannot. The really big ones are almost always females and in my time I've seen some whacking great brutes. Just how big a victim they will menace was brought home to me many years ago.

I was in that delightful area where Lancashire and Yorkshire meet in the north of both counties and I was fishing seatrout in a pleasant Lune tributary. I think it was August: we had traditional August weather anyhow and the days were hot, bright and useless for fishing in a low river. Some of my days were spent in marking down the shoals of seatrout and all of my late evenings in crouching about dusk-shrouded pools and in taking a few fish from the aforesaid shoals on Bustard, Corncrake sedge and the like.

When you are idling about a river, bridges have a special attraction and one day I looked over the parapet of an old grey bridge of several arches. Below, the water was eighteen inches or so deep and gently flowing and there, all but motionless, was a seatrout of four pounds or more. I was admiring the short thick body and trying to decide whether he was four pounds or five when an enormous eel appeared. It seemed to be five feet long and as thick as my forearm above the wrist. It came from the left diagonally downstream and headed straight for the big seatrout with aggressive purpose in every undulating line. I expected to see the seatrout edge away to one side or the other as the eel approached but he did not. He turned and shot away downstream as though the devil was on his tail. The eel went back whence he had come.

Now, did that seatrout bolt because he knew the eel was a menace even to a fish of his bulk, or was he impelled by some 'memory' of earlier days as smolt or whitling?

* * *

Seatrout fishing again, down in South Devon this time, I paused in the half-darkness to change a fly, holding the cast up against the fading glow from the west. A barn owl – an individual of several pairs haunting that valley, was quartering the field on the other bank – drifting to and fro like a gigantic white moth. The valley was very quiet. Suddenly I became aware of a curious sound – a high-pitched squeak clearly originating with some sort of rodent. The odd thing was that it came from the air and not from the herbage about the bank. I looked up again in time to see a barn owl pass ten feet above my head carrying in its talons a struggling rat. The bird seemed to have it firmly by the middle of the body and the rat was shrieking from the grip. Victor and victim were quickly out of sight but I could hear the squeaks for some time. An odd little happening that sticks in mind.

* * *

There is a house in the outer Hebrides where for many years I enjoyed unlimited hospitality at the hands of the owner, an old friend. And, out of doors, some superb salmon and seatrout fishing. The lodge stands among its lawns on the edge of the loch and here are always many snipe and rabbits innumerable. In that stark landscape and harsh climate, opportunities to make a garden are limited and flowers are rare – for all practical purposes one saw only the stunted rhododendrons clustered in sheltered corners.

At one time, however, one of the ghillies in a praiseworthy effort to introduce some colour, created a small flower-bed along the lawn's edge. It was perhaps three feet wide and twice that length and here the budding gardener scattered broadcast one of those packets of mixed annual flower seeds. Then with thought for the ubiquitous rabbit he enclosed the little plot in a three-foot fence of small mesh wire-netting. The seeds germinated, to everyone's mild surprise, and we presently had a pleasant little block of colour.

Walking by one late June day I flushed a snipe from among the flowers and when this was repeated a day or so later, I took a closer look and found a nest and the usual snipe clutch of four eggs. Thereafter we avoided disturbing the bird and she duly hatched all four eggs. It then became extremely interesting. The brood were as active as wader young can be but, of course, they couldn't get out. They had to be fed however, and the parent birds developed a technique for this. They would collect the food by the boggy edge of the loch and then fly in fairly high to drop like stones into the little wire enclosure. I watched them for hours when I wasn't fishing and there came a stage in the chicks' growth when the parents seemed to realise that their repeated exercises in aerial navigation were unnecessary because they began to land outside the wire, to call the four hungry youngsters and to feed them through the wire. It was fascinating to see the four lined up inside the wire and the small bills thrust through the mesh in expectation. I didn't see them fly but they were gone very suddenly after about two weeks and I later saw them by the loch's edge.

In my judgment snipe, like all small waders, have a special charm of their own.

* * *

In Somerset, one warm evening in mid-May, on a small artificial lake, I was stalking a trout – a most exasperating cruiser. I had known this fish for weeks and perhaps he knew me. I was prominent enough because his cruise path lay along the base of a high stone embankment and within a very narrow lane between the stones and a dense bank of weed: I could throw a line only from the narrow grass strip at the embankment crest where, unless lying flat in a cast-inhibiting posture, I must have been silhouetted against the sky.

This evening I was moving in a crouch and as low down as I could get along the lower edge of the grass when I saw my two pounder coming towards me and feeding busily. I sank to my knees and began to pull off line. As I did so something moved under my knees and in an instant of revulsion I stood erect and saw at my feet a very big dark adder. You see plenty in that part of Somerset but this really was an exceptional specimen, over two feet long. I expected it to slide away but instead it struck repeatedly at my rubber boots. In spite of the thickness of rubber in the lower leg I could feel the sharp blows in the way that I would have felt smart raps with the shaft of my landing net. It abandoned the attack after six or eight strikes and disappeared.

I caught that trout – two-and-a-half pounds – two evenings

later right off his usual beat and on a ridiculously unsuitable fly.

* * *

There are two of our native wild animals with a very special place in my affections – otters and badgers. Both have an extraordinary charm of their own; both are very ancient Britons. I see them or traces of them with equal frequency – badgers in and about my West of England cottage garden and otters almost wherever I fish. I intended only to mention the otter when I started this small story but the badger came in through a gap in my thinking just as he comes into my garden via a hole in the hedge – and he must go out.

My boat landing, on a rather wild Irish lough, is protected by two promontories of rock, one high and tree-clad and the other low and made up of rocks of all shapes and sizes. The final rock to seaward so to speak, on the low side, is a great flat slab eight or ten feet square. The surface is bare, but in its centre is a vivid green patch of moss and algae subsisting on traces of moisture and made startlingly bright in colour by the fertilising effect of fish remains left by the otter. For this flat rock, like so many others, is the otters' hauling-out place – the dining table. Because I like to know what my sleek friend has been up to in the night, I make a point of looking carefully at the rock when we take to the boat each fishing morning. And unless I have been anticipated by the crows or the gulls, I often enough find the remains of the otters' meal.

One morning last summer I was approaching for my customary inspection when I was halted by the sight of some minor movements of something reddish brown on the rock. I was too far away to see clearly but binoculars fetched from the boat brought the rock to within a few feet. There were three very small young stoats and one medium-sized dead rat. The stoats were ranged on one side of the carcase as if feeding on it but I quickly discovered that they were, in fact, moving it by communal effort – tugging, heaving and dragging their burden towards a little thicket of bog myrtle. This was no haphazard enterprise – there was a remarkable unison in their efforts. Progress was slow but very sure and there was no let-up in the tugging, the small lithe bodies straining under the load. You had to be impressed by the sheer disciplined determination of it all.

The things you see when you're fishing!

10

Lure of the Big Lough

Just as the big water poses its own problems so it has a special attraction and a greater opportunity to study and to learn.

THE BIG WATER, whether lake or loch or lough, according to country, ideally is enfolded by mountains. They should be close here and distant there and, guarding your playground, familiar to you. Islands should be there too with windy straits between and favoured drifts among them and the whole a delight to eye and mind on days of sun and storm alike: in total, a magnificent challenge to your fisherman's instinct.

There is a special quality, coming near to a magic of its own belonging alone to the fishing of a really big sheet of water. The fine mechanics of presenting a fly in such a place are no different from those employed on your smaller loch, but the whole business of taking a fish from a veritable waste of water contains a vastly greater satisfaction and a special joy if you've a mind to act on a compound of knowledge and instinct.

Every sheet of water large or small offers a challenge but it will always be less daunting if you look at it *as an area of ground covered by water*, and you will not really succeed until you know that ground. True, you cannot walk it but you can study it by scrutiny of surrounding contours, by map or chart study, by sounding line and in some cases, by just looking over the side of your boat. And it takes a long time, using all or any of these ways of learning, to know a big lough. When you do you can use reasoned fishing tactics based on knowledge and, possibly most important of all, on instinct for times and places, weather and the probable moods of fish in those places and at those times. This is the precious freedom of the lough: no-one can confer it on you – you have to earn it the patient and the thoughtful way.

It gives you the *probable* answer to that problem which is so much greater than on a small water – where in all that wide expanse, in all those miles – a fish or better several fish, may be found, raised to the fly and boated. And this mark you, in an infinite range of conditions.

I have wondered whether the appeal of the big lough resides for me in the beckoning of distant places – the far-off drifts looking fishiest so to speak and I admit there may be a tiny grain of substance in this. But the width of choice is surely the prime attraction however the motives may merge one into the other. The great elements are wind and weather which can narrow or widen the choice of fishing ground according to the lie of your lough and the character of its shores, its bays and headlands. It is certain however that so long as boat movement place to place is not totally weather-inhibited, there will be some scope for the following of instinct, some ability to proceed afloat at the bidding of the inspiration of the day. It is then that basic knowledge comes into play so that wind and weather can be made to serve your purpose rather than to result in a wasted day or a journey to an untenable fishing ground. True, big lakes breed their own often very changeable weather and there can be mischances – totally unpredictable changes of wind, for example, which can reduce the best-laid plans to the status of a nonsense. On the credit side however the big water affords scope for contingency planning to cover some such events.

If, by way of illustration I take an imaginary day on the big lough on which I spend some months of each year, you may be sure that it is a reflection of fact showing the kind of appraisal of chances both of weather and of fishing success, that must be made before one takes boat. And I should say now that we don't always do that – there are days when close inspection of the lough does away with any hope of fishing. Foolhardiness has no place in fishing any big open water and when a gale makes boat launching difficult, you retreat and return later or another day. It happens to me rather rarely because from my quarters I can see clearly with good binoculars a certain rock in a bay half-a-mile distant. When the wave breaks white on the rock I know that all but very limited and generally unproductive fishing grounds are inaccessible until the wind falls or shifts direction because in existing conditions we should be operating along a lee shore where the wind would blast down to us after an over-water reach of several miles.

In all other conditions there is a conference on the beach before we start. The first query – where are most of the fish lying? we answer easily from recent experience, the second is almost as simple. What parts of the holding areas will fish best with the wind where it is and at its observed strength? This also we can answer from intimate knowledge and the mental picture it gives us of just how that area will look today. But the feeders are running hard and the lough is up two feet since yesterday – will the fish have moved? It's early in the season and while inflowing fresh water will assuredly draw some fish, there will not be the general shifting of ground that you would find in September. So Murphy's Bay and Sandy Bay should be our objectives and the time now is eleven by the sun. We have a pull of about two miles and the best fishing time is from twelve till two so that we can do it. So far so good but there is a last and important consideration – will the weather hold? At existing weight of wind there is no problem. We shall have a following breeze on the way out, good wind and wave on our fishing ground and no real trouble to get back in the evening – *if it doesn't blow up*. What if it does blow up – how do we cover that contingency? – beach the boat, walk three hundred yards to the road and get Pat Murphy and his car to bring us home. Right, then that's it and we'll go. You will observe that the great thing in all this is to be able to visualise conditions as they will be some miles away – that comes from knowing your lough.

On another day with another wind and let us say, much less wind and wave, we shall be calculating which of the promontories are holding fish where they shelve into the deep and of those which will catch that whisper of breeze. Maybe if it turns out that we have too small a wave for salmon, it will be enough for seatrout so we need a long gravelly point that is also a seatrout lie. This is no problem since we know them all, have fished them recently, and can make a reasonable estimate of the density of fish.

It's important in this latter context to know the travelling routes of fish in the days immediately following a run and it's nowhere as vital as in the big lough. Both seatrout and salmon travel in companies which persist for a few days after entry and they will have staging places where they're inclined to rest while travelling. True, odd fish take up permanent lies almost anywhere but the bulk of them will pass long stretches of likely-looking shore without pause and will frequently settle for a short time in places of which the attraction is a mystery. But it's our business to know first the travelling route – usually fairly close inshore – and second the resting places. These may be and usually are, quite different from the permanent lies which numbers of fish together will occupy until they move upstream into a feeder in the late autumn. In a big lough therefore you must be able to anticipate salmon and seatrout behaviour as conditioned by the physical features of the bottom and the shores. Without a guide you could waste days and weeks fishing non-holding areas. In a small lake even without local knowledge, persistent fishing will bring some results – not so in the bigger waters.

You are always pitting your skill against nature in the actual process of fishing, but it is an infinitely more rewarding exercise in every way when that skill is used successfully at a place and time and in conditions of your own choice – a choice made in the light of experience and with an instinctive recognition of the best chance each day has to offer.

I know of no greater joy in fishing than the curious attraction of a long passage to some distant drifts to catch estimated conditions just right and to get one's salmon. You study the lough as you go. You were right to avoid the easterly grounds because there you can see, flashing white in the far distance, the broken white water and high-flung spray, while in the extreme lee of the shore you now follow, the deep bays show still and spruce dark under the wooded mountain. A skiff of rain slats against your oilskins and across the mouth of the big bay the wind has a long sweep and here there's a nice rolling wave – but this is not salmon ground and you go on. You hear, high above, the hoarse voice of the morning raven on some dark errand of his own. That mallard on the outer island has hatched her brood and there they are, a line of frantic, paddling morsels bobbing like corks behind the duck. The otter that uses that turf-capped white boulder for dinner table had a fish last night and two hoodie crows are pulling at what the otter left. A disturbed fish plunges behind the boat as you cross a patch of shallow water and your once-distant fishing ground is in sight now and beckoning you on.

11

A Bad Day

A rank bad day means more than a blank in the diary. It can be more instructive than the day when you cannot go wrong.

THE DAY BEGAN normally. The lough was falling after some days of high water and I knew by my water level mark by the boat landing that we had a good fishing height at last. There is always a water height at which any lough will fish best with a tolerance of perhaps six to nine inches, and you have good reason for a certain basic confidence when this condition occurs. Couple this with a moderate wave-rousing breeze and a broken sky and you can go afloat quite happily, as I did on that nice-looking morning. The objective was a series of salmon drifts, favourites of mine, about three miles away.

Because of the long pull to the fishing ground I had taken the spinning rod as well as the fly rod, with the idea that I would troll a small bait across the deep water en route and once we were clear of the rocky shallows outside the boat landing bay I pulled off a few yards of line, made up a trace and attached a Blue and Silver Devon. Then as we passed the high rock-face where for some reason grows the deepest-coloured heather in a vast extent of heathery shores, I started to let out line. Along this very deep shore are great slabs of rocks in broken layers both above and below water and down below forming shadowy caverns where, in my belief, lurk some of the lake's very big trout. One day I contend, the passing bait will be snatched and in due course a trout of up to ten pounds will grace (or disgrace!) the boat. James knows my conviction about this place and works the boat cunningly along the sunken contours as we pass.

However even with this perfectly legitimate object in view, I don't troll very wholeheartedly and I was rather idly feeding line off the multiplier when the line went slack and I found myself looking at an apparently frayed end: bait and trace and some yards of fairly-new plaited terylene line had gone.

The frayed end was interesting, the tough fibres teased out for quarter of an inch from the break. The line remaining on the reel contained two further abrasions in the centre of the spool and one damaged turn of line overlaid the other. I had never seen anything similar in forty years of using multipliers but I looked first for a sharp-edged rod ring: the hardened steel rod rings were perfect. Had a few coils of line climbed the spool shoulder and been nipped by the spool's edge? – no. Had the line been trodden on by a nailed boot? – both James and I wear soft rubbers.

I pulled line off until all trace of the trouble had gone, mounted a new trace and bait and we went on our way, debating as we went. How *had* that line been chewed like that? Chewed – that was the word and the key, and from it we had the probable answer. Nature has provided me with a rod-rack outside my window at my fishing quarters – a ten-foot spruce tree. My rods stand in the heather – leaning at forty-five degrees on the ladder-like branches of the tree and quite secure among the soft new growth even through a night's gale. And sitting there in the boat I remembered seeing a field mouse scamper away as I went to pick up the rods that morning. He hadn't touched the plastic-coated fly line, presumably because that reel and rod-butt were enclosed in a thick polythene bag put there to keep the reel dry. But why a mouse would try his teeth on an undressed line without scent or other apparent attraction I couldn't think – and I still don't know.

'That's a queer one,' I said to James, 'I hope we don't have any more unexpected nonsenses today.' His opinion was that he'd rather have a bad start and a good day afterwards than a good start to raise one's expectations and a rank bad day to follow. This has always been my own view and if you look back over your fishing experiences you will find beyond doubt that there are few days consistently good from the outset. But there are many that are very bad throughout and a poor start can be just part of a poor day.

Anyhow it looked a good day to both of us: the mouse-nibbled line was forgotten and we went cheerfully through the island straits and past the isle of the single pine where a two-pound seatrout grabbed the all but forgotten Devon and was duly netted. A few minutes later we passed over a gravelly area obviously holding just then a shoal of finnoch. When we'd had three of them I reeled up the minnow, I don't like hooking finnoch even on a fly: the less future stocks of takeable seatrout are interfered with on their first return from sea the better and the tail triangle of a bait doesn't do the mouth of a little seatrout any good at all.

Half an hour later we were on our fishing ground, a big sandy bay renowned for the stocks of salmon drawn to it by the river which comes down to the lough at this point. Most of our season's total of fish in an average year come from this area. Apart altogether from that, it is a superbly pleasant place to fish. Here the lough is cradled in mountains close at hand and since the water is relatively narrow at this point, there is always easily-gained shelter under one steep shore or the other and overhead cover in rhododendron or gorse thickets for lunching or resting on the not-infrequent wild wet days. We know it intimately, James and I, and in particular every feature of the underwater contours, the two weed beds, the steep edges of the delta sand and the snags in the river's channel.

We started the first drift about a hundred yards offshore in a moderate breeze and a gently-ruffled rolling wave. The eleven-foot rod, sinking tip line and three-yard eight-pound cast suited the conditions: the small Dusty Miller on the dropper and the Golden Olive on the tail were right by my instinct and I fished very contentedly looking for a rise in every wave. It came almost at once, a lovely rise resolving itself into the solid pull of a well-hooked fish. After the usual preliminary waverings we had a series of short runs out in deep water and five or six minutes delightfully vigorous play from a strong, obviously fresh fish, hooked as we saw when he finally came towards the boat, on the dropper. He looked like the usual summer fish of about nine pounds and, head up, came quietly enough to the waiting net: by any normal standard he was ours.

But, with net and fish a bare two feet apart and with comparatively little strain on the tackle, the cast parted at the dropper knot and the fish turned down and was gone. The shortened cast whipped away in the wind and for a moment there was a stunned silence in that boat. The inquest revealed the curly end of the cast typical of a pulled knot.

No-one secures every fish that is hooked – accidents do happen. Fish do strange things in play, hook angles alter, fish throw hooks and hooks simply drop out and sometimes, not often, a cast will snap due to nylon degradation or because of poor rod and line management or because a cunning fish has evolved some special trick.

Now, although in my time I suppose I have lost fish for all these reasons, I do not in sober truth lose many fish. This particular loss irked me because the fault could only be mine and mine alone. I consider that after all the years of practice in making up casts that I have had – gut and latterly nylon, I can tie sound knots. I had tied the knot which had failed us on the previous evening with customary care, but obviously without enough care since I had clearly snipped one end of the blood knot a little too short. Test after making up had not shown up the fault nor had a second pull test before we went afloat that morning.

The lesson was and remained all too clear and I am quite sure that like me, you know it, but in this case it has a background which may be worth the record and it's this. I don't really like nylon and I use it only because gut is no longer to be had. I admit the many virtues of nylon but to me it has always had at least one grave defect – its lack of backbone as evidenced by the sloppy 'feel' of it in the backcast. I like to feel or think I can feel the line and the cast straighten in the air and I had been discussing this with a nylon distributor who – to my surprise I must say – agreed with me and produced a specially-stiffened brand of American make. This stuff is as springy as wire, stiffer than gut and completely meets my point about behaviour in the back cast. But what you gain in one respect you lose in another because the stiffness makes it extremely difficult to tie in blood knot style. It was a cast of this description in which I had failed to tie a sound knot. The fact did not lessen or justify my ineptitude. I could however have done with the lesson driven home less forcibly. As a final comment, before I return to the fishing of that day, I will add only that I have since returned to standard nylon of a reliable marque counting any floppiness in the backcast the lesser evil.

The wind was still steady and the day still held some promise and with a new cast – examined and tested with the meticulous care that you use after any tackle failure, we started a new drift. A big fish plunged some way downwind and a few minutes later another. This one was within reach and with an extra few yards of line hastily pulled off, I was able to cover it. Like most plungers he wasn't interested and I recovered line to normal fishing length and we drifted on. I always like to see signs of life and if plunging fish don't usually take, at least the sight of them indicates that fish are up and moving about and not motionless on the bottom.

We were in the middle of the bay and on our line of drift heading for a gravelly point which always looks promising but is in fact useless because of its extreme shallowness. It's the haunt of innumerable small and hungry brownies and when we were within forty yards of its beach James pulled away to our left. Here is a small bay within the bay and here in four feet of water over a clean sand bottom there are always salmon. We had covered most of it before I had the rise I was waiting for. It was an odd sort of rise such as you may sometimes see in very confused rough water – a clumsy floundering rise. But the line came taut and the hook went home and we had what felt at once like a biggish fish.

James turned the boat and headed quietly for deeper water and the fish came with us pulling hard but nevertheless allowing himself to be led fairly easily. When we stopped, however, he did not and he went on going out into the lough. There was no dash about him, he simply pulled steadily but there was a feeling of tremendous power and weight in his behaviour and since line was going all the time we had to go after him. We had had the merest glimpse of him when he rose but his relentless heavy pulling now convinced us that he was foul-hooked in some way that gave him the full power of his tail and the ability to swim straight ahead. I ceased to speculate because he really needed all my concentration. James had managed to keep up with the rate of line loss but I couldn't regain any line. The rod in my left hand was vertical and the strain all the tackle could take.

After half an hour the position was unchanged and my arm was aching.

We kept altering the boat's position in an attempt to turn him and one of these manoeuvres brought the fish to the surface, where he lashed once or twice and then went down again without giving us a clear sight of him. Then he changed tactics, starting to take line again and much faster this time so that we were well into the backing with perhaps eighty or ninety yards out. He made a long curving run into the river mouth and what was infinitely worse into one of the only two patches of weed in the bay – and by some miracle we were too distant to see, came safely out again. I managed to recover a little line but he was still on the backing when another boat drifted into the bay a hundred yards on our left – the occupants ceasing to fish when they saw us playing a fish that was clearly giving some sort of trouble.

The fish was somewhere between the boats with perhaps sixty yards of line out when without warning he started the kind of high speed run you see a fresh fish in the early stages of play. The reel screamed but with so much sunk line I had no real idea of where the fish was until there was a shout from the other boat and a quick turn of heads in the direction of a splash beyond their boat. With a few yards of backing left on the reel I held on while their boatman came to his senses and pulled away: the fish had run directly under his boat and surfaced beyond it.

I was still holding the rod high and in addition to the acute ache in my rod arm I now had cramp in my hand. The steady strain was telling however and the fish came nearer very very slowly. James pulled towards him as I recovered line and presently we had him on the surface, wallowing weakly but still not coming easily, hanging as a dead weight on the pull of the straining rod. And there, as we came nearer and plain to see, was the cause of a struggle that now had lasted a full hour – the tail fly lodged in the dorsal fin of a rather coloured fish of fifteen or sixteen pounds. I began very gently to recover line.

He lay like a log as we approached and I dared not ease the pressure. If I did he would simply sink down again and perhaps be off in another surge of strength. Then as we watched and James made ready to extend the net, the fly split the fin and came free; the fish sank slowly and was gone before the outstretched net could reach him.

He deserved his freedom and we, for our part, deserved to have him in the boat. I was left with an arm that refused to straighten for some time and which ached desperately for the rest of a day that we now knew was, as James said 'Wan o' *thim* days'. You get them, now and again in fishing, but often enough, as in this case, the following day may compensate – for we then had three fish without suspicion of mishap.

12

Trolling

An assessment of a rather dull pursuit – its usefulness in its proper place.

TROLLING IS AN easy and a lazy way of fishing. It has its own techniques and requires a degree of skill or cunning which cannot, even if you bend over backwards in an endeavour to be fair, compare with those necessary in wet or dry fly, clear water worm, dapping or spinning. If indeed we exclude the proficiency needed to play a hooked fish which is common to all methods, the skill in trolling is not that of the rod, but of the man managing the boat. The direction of travel, the speed of the boat and the shape of her course are the telling elements in the game.

There are places where, especially in early spring, your only chance of a salmon is to troll. This can also apply to the pursuit at any season of the very big loch trout that used to be called 'ferox' – a deadly dull business this. The very deep Scottish lochs are good examples of trolling grounds and it would be foolish, or snobbish or unkind – perhaps all three, to belittle the patience and keenness of the hardy souls whose boats spend wintry hours searching the shelving deeps in all kinds of weather. This represents, in fact, trolling in its proper place. It does no harm nor does deep water trolling at any season anywhere. It has the merit that a beginner or a fisherman of limited accomplishment or of limited opportunity can by this means and if he is reasonably lucky catch a fish or two.

I have a personal impatience with trolling and as must be evident from much of my scribblings, I also have an objection to some of it. The objection is that the method is so very readily misused, to the detriment of fishing by more skill-demanding and more rewarding techniques. The complaint is not that it takes too many fish because, in fact, trolling is not so very deadly – but that unless carefully regulated it disturbs fly water. Your confirmed troller will tell you that you (he) can catch more salmon on the troll than you (he) can on the fly. This, except in those deep waters suitable only for trolling, is simply not true. Over a period, a qualified fly fisher on fly water will take more fish than the troller on trolling ground.

I do not begrudge the trollers the fish they catch on ground which can only be fished by this method but I do strongly object to the trolling and consequent disturbance of fly water. This does not arise, I hasten to add, from blind prejudice: over and over again there has been ample demonstration in my experience of the effect of trolling in putting fish down. Areas which have been yielding good sport on the fly day after day will go absolutely dead and unresponsive after a few passes by a trolling boat. You find this particularly galling when there is plenty of perfectly good trolling water available without intrusion into shallow water where fish can see and will rise to the fly. On some lakes trollers are extremely well-disciplined and thoughtful in this regard but I know others where trolling boats will without compunction cut across a few yards ahead of drifting boats fishing fly.

Make no mistake however – I troll. If I have to travel some distance on a big lake on my way to my chosen fishing area, I will take to the edge of the deeps and troll a bait on the spinning gear I carry for this purpose. So doing I get the odd salmon and very rarely the odd big trout which years ago ceased to haunt the shallows and come to the fly.

One very productive Irish lough which I first fished about forty years ago and have been closely associated with ever since, is as good today as it ever was in spite of much trolling in the deeper areas in recent years. At one time all the salmon were killed on the fly and the vast bulk still are. Trolling, and spinning too, are confined, by agreement, to certain marked areas and the trollers neither catch enough to affect the stock, nor interfere in any way with the boats fishing fly. The truth of the matter is, of course, that as I have already suggested, trolling is not a deadly method. At times salmon seem to favour a bait rather than a fly and the trolling rod may do well for a short spell, but by and large the fly rod will do better and over longer periods. This will not hold good however in lochs deficient in water shallow enough for salmon to see and rise to the fly.

There is no great depth of skill in the actual practice of trolling, hence little can be said of the part played by the man with the rod or rods. Choice of bait is at his option and important because a type of bait which will bring strikes in one loch may be useless in another. Size and colour of bait are often governed by season and freshness or staleness of the fish. A blue and silver Devon, say two or two-and-a-half inches long, or a big silver and gold Toby will attract fresh fish in most places though all gold or gold and brown seem to suit some water colours or the nature of the bottom. The salmon, like the ghillies, have local preferences which, if known, it is well to heed. In the early part of the year the Toby can be the size/weight designated 18 gram, dropping to the 12 gram size as the season progresses. Neither rod nor reel are important as to specification so long as the first is just stiff enough to hook a striking fish and the second holds not less than about a hundred-and-fifty yards of line. I use a braided terylene line of twenty pound breaking strain with a one-yard trace of fifteen pound nylon so that a break, due to snagging for example, will occur in the trace only. Lead if used – and some baits go deep without it – can be of the Hillman type and hooked into the eye of the swivel-joining line and trace.

Bait depth is to some extent governed by length of line and so the amount of lead used should take this into account along with proper regard for the average depths of water on the areas being trolled. Line length, that is to say the amount of line out during fishing should be not less in any event than forty to fifty yards. This leaves a reserve on the reel that should be ample to allow a fish to run after hooking. If he takes more than fifty or sixty yards while the original fishing length is still out, he's getting too far away from the boat and must be worked back or the boat promptly moved in pursuit. Fishing with insufficient line out so that the bait is too close astern of the boat is a common fault, in my view.

Line length, lead, bait weight and boat speed decide the bait's swimming level whatever the depth under it. Correct balance of these variables will hold the bait about two feet below surface, but it should travel very much deeper to attract 'ferox' or deep-lying salmon and be altered to suit bottom contour.

The movement of the boat, transmitted to the bait, catches the fish. Salmon lies and the places where they are likeliest to be encountered follow the pattern that characterises all salmon haunts in all lakes and the location of these must govern the boat's course. The edge of the deeps, the mouths of small bays, the fringes of islands (unless shallow), off stony or rocky points and off stream mouths, should be worked by an erratically swinging boat controlled by the oars in such a way that the bait or baits – two rods are often fished after all – follow a curving course. This is sound in principle and a necessity where from local knowledge you follow for example, the edge of a deeply-submerged bank. If two rods are in use there must of course, be a disparity in line length and bait weight or type if the most appalling tangles are to be avoided. The usual practice is to fish a shorter line and a lighter bait on the inshore rod.

If, as I am personally convinced beyond any shadow of doubt, trolling by a boat under oars will spoil fly water, then trolling with the aid of an outboard engine – which is seen in some places – spells absolute ruin to the fly fisher's chances and it should never be done, or be permitted to be done, in any circumstances. Motors are completely out of place on nine out of ten game-fishing waters and their use is justifiable only on the very big sheets of water where you may have to travel miles to the fishing ground. As aids to movement in such places there is clearly a case for them; their use is out of order on fishing grounds and they should be shut off on approach to good water, their intolerable noise stilled, and the peace of the broad waters allowed to work its magic.

To troll is sometimes to get a fish when salmon are difficult to get and it is the only way I know of to catch the very big predatory trout that never come to the fly and rarely leave the deep water or its steep shelving margins. There are periods lasting weeks, particularly when water temperature is high, in which salmon will not look at a bait and at such times the days must be incredibly dull for the rod. But there are other times when fish are off the fly and if you have a guest who is about to return home fishless for that reason you must send him out alone with the ghillie, who has been instructed to get him a fish on the troll. He usually will.

A possible but not infallible way to offset the caprice of salmon when they disregard a troll put past them in the standard manner is to use what I call the 'worked' troll. Its theory is founded on the undoubted truth that the most successful troll is the one which embodies the utmost change and variety in its movements – working now fast and then slowly, going straightly and then swerving, rising surface-wards and then sinking and in the doing of all this simulating a small fish in distress. The 'worked' troll is made to do it by movements of the rod which impart a continuous sink and draw action. Constant line length is maintained but every few seconds the extended rod – at right angles to the boat's length, is drawn forward about three feet and allowed to drop back again. It's a simple procedure which dictates that the rod must be held in the hand and to this extent it has the small merit of giving the angler *something* to do. I know several lochs where it succeeds when the evenly-travelling bait fails to attract. The take usually comes, significantly, when the bait flutters down free of forward pull.

Trolling is for those who like it and perfectly justifiable on suitable fishing grounds and when confined to them. And to end this discussion I add only the advice that if you troll you should carry a big landing net – sometimes all the hooks are not inside the mouth of the fish and the man with the net needs all the margin possible if hooks are not to mesh with meshes.

13

James' Trout

In a place where good trout are hard to come by, a big one marked down is a magnet and the source of much frustration.

IN MY PART OF Donegal there is never any doubt in conversation about the identity of a fish of the trout family. A little farther north and south they speak of trout and of white trout thus distinguishing between brown trout and seatrout, but ghillies and anglers in my fraternity call a brown trout simply 'a trout' and a seatrout by its own proper name. This is good because in other places again both are referred to as 'trout' which is technically quite accurate but in practice confusing.

You will therefore understand that when James said 'I saw a big trout leppin' under thim branches', I knew he meant a big brown trout and not one of the seatrout for which I was then fishing. This was, so to speak, the first sighting. It was in early September of a notably dry season with a preponderance of heavy all-but-windless days and a very low lake. Seatrout were almost uncatchable and going stale at an alarming rate. I like the lough low because it normally fishes well when certain offshore reefs carry least depth of water, but entirely happy circumstances are rarely in combination. The drought producing a far-fallen lake usually has its root cause in too much sun and with it there comes too high a water temperature.

It was the sun and the torpidity of the seatrout in the open water which had taken us to the place where James saw the big trout, for there, surrounding an enchanting bay in the wooded lake shores, was deep water close inshore and vast outreaching and ancient oaks – under them deep shade. If it has its attractions, it also has its inbuilt handicaps for a fisherman, this bay, for the reason that its location generally deprives it of whatever wind there may be – hence, of course, the brooding woodlands of heavy oak, hanging lichens and luxuriant fern. Here, deep under the trees a boat can find refuge from a gale from almost any quarter and it is indeed a much frequented retreat of ours. Half-way between a favourite fishing ground and the normal boat landing it's exceedingly useful and I have many times hauled the boat up under the trees and walked home when the lake has been seething with white horses and the reed beds flat from sheer weight of wind. You can get caught out, you know, on a big lough however well you know its moods. Chapter 6 records one such mischance.

I must add, if you are to visualise the place – that this haunt of trout and seatrout – and the odd salmon though it is not truly salmon ground – and of woodcock and badger and fox ashore – runs deep into the hillside through a narrowish neck which all but cuts it off from the open lake. Inside, apart from the dense forest growth fringing the shores there are great lily beds, the home of that rarity the water rail and patches of tall reeds beloved of reed buntings.

The trout are very numerous and mostly small as indeed they are in the lake as a whole. Every spring the salmon trollers out in open water will get the occasional six or seven-pound brownie – very dark and ugly-headed but generally we call a trout of over a pound a good fish. You get them while seatrout fishing but the really big ones don't rise and years go by without capture on the fly of a fish over two pounds. Not only are they absent from catches but the big trout are seldom or never seen and might not exist, hence our real interest when we see one show, whatever the reason for its appearance on the surface.

In actual fact if you could see the place where James' fish showed you would say 'just the place for a big trout'. The shore is steepish under the trees and in the clear amber water you can see a labyrinth of shattered rocks sliding away into the shadows of unseen depths. Here a big fish can lurk unseen while the small fry shuttle to and fro in the rim of the sunlight filtered through overhead leaves. Truly a wonderful lie for a big trout. I have always thought that good trout must be here because in addition to the normal wind-blown and water-hatched fly life, there is a constant rain of caterpillars and all manner of small insect trout provender from overhead. But the average trout caught here have always belied the fancy and I believe the thought and the hope are by and large ill-founded.

There you have the background and against it I tell a little story with its own lesson in the never-ending series that make up fishing.

Seatrout fishing being as unproductive as I have suggested and the weather too quiet to give us a breeze that would induce stale salmon to move to a fly, I decided to use evening hours to study the area where James' trout had shown and if conditions suited to see whether I could bring him up to a fly. We went out two days later in a pleasantly idle frame of mind making a leisurely passage to the bay across water carrying but the merest crinkle of wave and marked only by the rises of small trout and, in their regular haunts the dimples of the shoaling char. James shipped his oars thirty yards from our previously agreed observation post and the boat carried her way until we were close inshore and under the trees. A tiny deep inlet probed the woods here and on its distant side a huge oak all but dipped its lowest branch in the water. Here was the 'lie'. The sun had only just dipped but under here it was darkish and warm and the midges were extremely active.

We soon found that in that quiet place a too vigorous slap at the creeping myriads would rock the boat and produce unwanted surges on the dark water. I would like to tell you that we saw a great boil made by our fish or, even more pleasant, that I moved him to a skilfully presented wet fly – but in fact we saw no sign of him and presently, in gathering dusk and midge-maddened, gave up and went homeward. What we did see, as we turned in towards the boat landing was a herd – I use the word deliberately – of big seatrout being shepherded by a very big otter. The fish milled round in unhurried fashion, back fins and tails showing – a very good class of fish which were big enough to be grilse. It looked like a game with neither hunter nor hunted in any hurry and I'm afraid our approach spoilt it.

I kept anticipating a weather change and a week later we did have a small wind from a quarter that would give us a breeze in the bay. We therefore devoted a morning (lest the north wind should act normally and die completely at sunset) to fishing round and about and over our chosen area. We brought back seven fat nine or ten-ounce trout and saw a very dark seatrout of about five pounds leaping vertically. But James said no – his fish was a trout. I comforted him and myself with the suggestion that after all one could watch for a single fish for a month of Sundays and never see him – especially in a lake where his lie might be anywhere inside half an acre of water. Still, it was a nice morning and I had been fishing hopefully with Watson's Fancy, Connemara Black and Butcher in 10's on three-pound nylon. But because the waves ran very nicely in under the trees to chuckle among the broken rocks and the wind stirred the overhead cover so briskly, I drifted a furnace-hackled Loch Ordie in on a long line and worked it by twitch and slow draw by turns. It looked, as I intended it should, like a big caterpillar and made a good mouthful for a good fish. All very fine in theory – in practice useless although it was really an ideal place for the Loch Ordie.

Now I know James very well indeed and I knew that he had in fact seen what he said he saw but I was beginning to lose the edge from my enthusiasm. After all, that fish could be anywhere round about the area though it's true big fish normally have a lie and a settled feeding beat. Again and anyhow, he might be and probably was a bottom-feeder and all James had seen was his annual plunge!

The wind, a one-day's wonder, died away again and we had a succession of hot calm days – the lake falling still further but the seatrout as dour as ever. Any fish we did catch were warm to the touch and the water temperature was far too high for fish except greedy little trout to feed at all. But we picked another evening in which, this time, to fish well into the dark and all the way along the wooded bay shore. I tried a small Queen of the Water on the bob and soft-hackled Black Pennells on both dropper and tail and fished them in the calm with very slow fingering and as deep as I could get them. And in two hours, apart from the crash of some crazy salmon plunging out beyond the gloom of the trees, we neither heard, felt, nor saw a fin.

On the way back I told James we'd give it a miss now until we got some real rain or colder winds and a falling water temperature and we did exactly that. To be honest I was beaten in the sense that I simply did not know how to overcome the extremely adverse conditions: as the days went by I almost forgot that trout because salmon fishing began to pick up a little, heaven knows why, and we concentrated on the open water drifts in preference to the fickle and fluky wind draughts of the bay.

And so the last month of the season drifted by until with two days left to fish there came the kind of wind and weather we had lacked since early July. Soft but steady and reasonably strong winds and broken cloud combined in a way that sent us out early in the day along the lee shore of the lough. Here we fished the known salmon lies in a beautifully broken wave that surged up into the waterside ferns. Water temperature was down but not markedly so. There is, by the way, a belief in some quarters that spring-run fish – after months of increasing staleness and refusal to look at a fly – will come on in September. Occasionally they do but in my experience not often enough to justify any great expectation. It was like that, this last fishing day of the season: places which certainly held fish – the pebbly point where the char spawn in the backend and some channels between the rocky islets and lastly a long belt of reeds on a clean sandy bottom were utter blanks. This belt of reeds lay off the mouth of a smallish river which entered the bay of the trout near where it opened out into the lough and drifting baywards from here in a roughish wave I did have a sullen swirl to the dropper. I went down one size in the fly and we covered the fish again without result.

Light was very good and I have seldom seen better conditions for salmon fishing in that lough. We drifted on into the bay because odd salmon do lie there. Down here at the bottom of the wind the wave was bigger than ever and I went back to the number seven Dusty Miller on the dropper. That change produced a fierce deep take from something very hard pulling and dour. I was fishing 8 pound nylon to suit the fly size and I bent the rod hard to produce at the net in a few minutes, a beautiful brown trout of four pounds which had taken the tail Yellow Torrish. That was a big trout for that place.

It really was an exceptionally handsome fish, well-shaped and coloured, deep and small in the head and it came to the fly about twenty yards outside the big oak. If indeed it was the fish we had been vainly pursuing for so long it had refused every conventional trout fly – sunk or surface and every feathered lure I could think of, to take in the end a biggish salmon fly on a relatively clumsy iron. There must be a moral here but I'm afraid it's a little complicated.

Ashore, later, I gave James the trout. He said, as I knew he would, that he was thankful for it but it wasn't the fish he saw leppin'.

14

Bright Sun

A study of the most adverse conditions in lake fishing and the cause of its effect.

As a devoted fisherman you find yourself, willy-nilly, living close to nature in the sense that you are constantly sensible of every change in conditions out of doors. And obviously the greater your intimacy and the more you fish the more important the weather is to you. Awareness of weather change – actual or impending – is not a matter of organised or even conscious observation, but becomes a habit and a way of daily life. Even in winter when I am not fishing regularly I find that each day brings its morning appraisal of the day's weather prospect as a matter of course and of ingrained habit.

Combinations of the elements of fisherman's weather such as wind speed and direction, light, air and water temperatures are endless in range and sometimes the known bad or indifferent factors will be offset by favourable ones, or the reverse may be the case – you may get a good breeze from the best possible quarter which is more than nullified by unduly high water temperature due to a preceding long hot spell, and so on. Try to set up a rule for your own private guidance and you find yourself arguing pros and cons ad infinitum and hedging round your judgment with ifs and buts, until if you are honest you have to admit you just don't know! In the end, at such times, you go fishing on the ever safe and comforting basis that in our faculty of angling 'you never know'.

In my sixty-odd years of fishing I have detected one weather circumstance which I regard as the most intractable of all those we have to circumvent and this is the hard bright day. Some fish, trout and seatrout and salmon, have come to hand on such days, of course, but they are few and the exception: I do not know, after all this time of trying, how to do as well as on almost any other kind of day and what is worse I do not really know why.

A hard bright day by my definition is one in which there is bright sunlight from cloudless or near cloudless skies along with a brisk unvarying breeze from any quarter. On such a day the lake is blue, the lively wave sparkles with small snow-white crests and *looks* as hard as the steady wind feels. It's a hard day in every possible way. The lake *looks* beautiful under sunlit mountains and visibility may extend to forty miles or more. Non-anglers call it a lovely day and if you're of my persuasion and notwithstanding your keenness to fish, you'll go to the beach with the rest of the party.

Of course, sunshine, so long as not continuous and not on a hard day, can be a good thing and you will often find that fish – salmon particularly – will come on when you get a cloud break on a dark day; blinks of sun as part of a broken and changing light can be very effective. Intermittent sunshine, in a word is to be welcomed so long as the day does not settle into a sparkling bright one without sufficient relief from harsh light for either fish or man.

If we really knew why this condition is so very bad – i.e. why fish won't take, we could perhaps devise a means to counter it and there are three possibilities. One is the rather simple and obvious proposition that terminal tackle, however fine, is too clearly seen by the fish. This argues some sophistication in these same fish – an idea that the facts don't altogether support because the effect is seen in water virtually unfished. But it is certainly true that in the conditions I have in mind the finest nylon looks (to the human eye anyhow) like a ship's cable.

The second possibility is simple in conception too and proposes merely that the fish go down by reason of the brightness of the upper water, sinking down to avoid the glare. You would expect salmon, coming from the shadowed ocean deeps, to find the staring sunlight unendurable, but seatrout and trout are relatively shallow-haunting fish with a built-in tolerance of highly-lit water. It is a fact worth noting perhaps, in this general context, and often overlooked that fish have no eyelids and are thus unable to shut out an intolerably bright light as are other animals. Some sharks have nictitating membranes capable of covering the eyes but no other fish has this ability. Observation of river pools clearly shows that game fish exhibit strong dislike of excessively bright sun but whether this is the principal operative factor in the conditions we are looking at, I am by no means sure.

The third hypothesis is one which I have been pondering for a long time and is much less obvious. It concerns the movement of the plankton which are in part the food of trout and seatrout and the food of other elements in the diet of both fish. The non-feeding salmon cannot be directly affected but a connection is possible and, I am inclined to think probable, having regard to the salmon's known carry-over of some aspects of sea habit into fresh water.

Here I propose to leave our game fish for the time and look at our largest British fish, the basking shark, which has been and still is I think to some extent, the subject of a commercial fishing in western Scottish and Irish seas. These fish are taken by harpoon whilst they are feeding on the surface – in the process taking in vast quantities of the plankton which are their only food. For long the appearance of the sharks on the surface was unpredictable and the fishing as a result a somewhat chancy business, but latterly it was noted that the sharks only appeared in dull weather – or at least in non-bright conditions and that the same was true of the herring, also plankton feeders. Then the upper layers of water could be seen to be thick with plankton whereas on bright days there were none. Herring and sharks, both dependent on plankton are up when their food is up and the upward movement is governed by light intensity.

Now we can look at salmon during their feeding life in the sea about which we have learnt a great deal in recent years as noted in Chapter 5. The area providing most data, because of intensive fishing and observation, is again in the Greenland seas where the salmon are always taken in the uppermost meshes of the drift nets, in the top two feet in fact. The fish are feeding on or at the surface on sandeels and capelan which in turn are feeding on plankton which comes to the surface as the light fades. The nets do not do well on bright days because the plankton are down and with them the sandeels and the capelan.

Vertical migration of plankton in the dark hours is a well-known phenomenon in the world's oceans as is the upward movement of the larger organisms which prey on the teeming small life migrating from the depths. It is not peculiar to Greenland waters nor to the western Irish seas or the Sea of the Hebrides, but its effect is similar and we are justified in my view in building a theory if not a firm conviction on it. There is, it is true, one factor of which we know little or nothing and that concerns the likeness in behaviour between the salt and fresh water organisms which comprise the plankton in the two media. My own intuition for what that is worth is that both react in the same general manner to variations in light intensity. May vertical migration of plankton not be behind the surface feeding of trout and seatrout in still water after sunset? You may say they don't all feed this way – very many are active grubbers on the bottom in the dark hours and the fish that take flies in the fast flowing streams and tails of river pools have no link, however remote, with plankton. I am not sure and I admit to it, but there has been lately some evidence that plankton, fairly plentiful in some river water, becomes increasingly evident – i.e. capable of being sampled – with a drop in water temperature such as would occur in the night.

So, what to make of all this. I am coming to believe that there is a link between the fisherman's problem on a hard bright day and the movements of the smallest element in the food chain with variations in light intensity. The salmon, unaffected in fresh water by abundance or lack of food organisms and hence by their movements, may nevertheless take back with them into their natal element the sea habit which keeps them well below the upper layers of water when light is blindingly bright. A reflex of this kind is perfectly feasible if you consider that about two summers and two winters in the sea immediately precede the arrival in our fishing waters of the average first return salmon – other than grilse.

How, out on the lake and rod in hand you overcome the challenge of the hard bright day I do not know and this writing is constructive only in that it may provoke some thought, study and observation. On the basis of slight and occasional success on such a day I suggest only adherence to the 'bright day bright fly' rule and I like particularly Dunkeld and Dusty Miller in small sizes for salmon and seatrout and tiny Dunkelds or wingless Wickhams for trout.

15

Fishermen's Wives and other Phenomena

WE WERE SITTING, my fishing friend and I, having returned from a day on the lake, looking down from his verandah, on woods, mountains and lake softly lit by the setting sun. Present also were his wife and mine, estimable and amiable ladies both, if slightly bored with fishing talk. It had proceeded, this talk, in the somewhat halting tempo which inevitably results from the introduction of extraneous matter, such as the merits of this and that knitting pattern and the outrageous price of drink when paid for ex the housekeeping allowance. At this stage I drew urgent attention to the glorious colour on the mountain while my friend absent-mindedly refilled the glasses.

The trouble I am in as I write this chapter began when my friend asked me a question about something I had written in 'Newly From the Sea' because, that question answered, his wife said 'Why don't you write something about fishermen's wives?' I think now that the query was artless but at the time I was momentarily conscious only of flashing red lights and a loud clanging of alarm bells. The drink that went down the wrong way didn't help either.

When calm was restored I said that I could already think of one or two things that I would like to write about some fishermen's handicaps. I was promptly admonished on the grounds that the speaker knew what was in my mind, that any written expression would be ungallant, unkind and dangerous in divers ways. Further, it was getting late and we were interfering with our friends' dinner arrangements so hurry up and finish that drink.

You can only fight this kind of thing up to a point. Anyhow I knew that any comment I might make on certain wives of my acquaintance would identify them and if nothing else recoil on the heads of the nice fellows, innocent well-meaning fishermen all, who partnered them. Discretion I suppose it is, but I am the only one to know what a coward I am and with what reluctance I have had to abandon certain telling phrases in character delineation.

A true (fisherman's) wife is made I am convinced in the early stages of the marriage when she learns (unless she is country bred and knows about fishing already) what manner of man she has hooked. In all fairness some preliminary warnings should have been voiced in advance but it is impossible for any angler, even with the most noble of motives to cover all the subtleties of behaviour, of co-operation, of forgiveness and yes, of self-sacrifice that may be called for in the course of one fishing season let alone a lifetime of them. No, that happy young woman must drift, learning all the time, into the happier state of being the wife of a man whose prime interest, after her wellbeing, of course, is fishing. After all, it is a career for her.

In the avocation of being a fisherman's spouse some women do awfully well and some of those who are devoted companions themselves take to fishing. This, it must be said, doesn't always work and I have before now detected an atmosphere to which I shall not append a label in a few cases where the wife throws an exceptionally good line and unless she is very discreet, is the more successful of the pair. A great pity this, especially as fisherwomen nowadays already wear trousers. But the ladies who learn about fishing and what it means in their lives and so come to terms with it – and those who fish themselves, are together the great majority.

The wives who do come to terms with what fishing means to their menfolk but who don't fish occupy the lounges or drawing rooms of Highland and Connemara and Kerry hotels, forming associations with kindred spirits, joining their men for lunch by the river, perhaps occasionally on fine days joining them in the boat, or taking the car on sight-seeing expeditions and – though few will admit to it – having a fairly good time. These are the patient and the wise ones and they at least know where their husbands are and what they are doing – which in some circles today is quite a thing.

Once, to my great delight I heard this pointed out to my Aunt Clara. It needed pointing out to her because she had never accepted that her husband, my Uncle Walter, was a dedicated fisherman. He was a little man and meek with it, but he loved to fish. He taught me to fish in the Clyde style for trout with teams of very sparingly-tied spiders on the finest of tackle. We roamed the moors, following the burns to their risings, and laughed a great deal. He did what was a rare thing in those days – he treated a boy as an adult. But always he grew quiet when we neared home in the evening and even I always wondered what my Aunt Clara would say to him – a small St. George with his own private dragon. I can see him now, returning from some adult foray which excluded me and I can hear again the penetrating accusatory voice that greeted him as he began to lay out his trout 'Walter – you've been drinking!' He hadn't, he'd just been having a happy undominated day.

My Aunt Clara's bullying was flagrant and unconcealed and uncommon, but her failing to understand the urge to be on the river that possessed her husband is by no means rare today among fishermen's wives of a certain type. I know men who own or rent costly and extremely productive water which they don't fish as they should because advice from keeper or bailiff to 'come at once river right and fish running' so very often coincides with a social engagement arranged by their wives which takes up the critical day or days. 'You can't go tomorrow, dear because as you know Alice and George are coming for the weekend.' After the weekend, of course, the river will have run down and the big chance has gone. These socially-minded women never seem to understand this and I know at least one case where the husband risks a major upheaval if, for fishing, he misses a cocktail party or some local event of equally trifling importance. Both parties have their priorities wrong, of course, and the whole thing is just nonsense. But it happens more often than we think. An absorbing interest like fishing can lead to selfishness and this must be admitted; happy are the parties who can compromise and fortunate the man who can accumulate good marks by good behaviour while the river is out of order, or whose wife will cheerfully sit in the fishing hut or the car at any time.

A difficult circumstance arises when the wife actively dislikes the kind of life concomitant with a fishing holiday and will neither go nor be content to be left at home. As a result her husband takes short holidays which give him seven or eight days of fishing. Now you can go anywhere in these islands and meet with a week or two weeks' very bad fishing conditions – lack of water, blazing hot weather, river high or dirty and so on and a time-table stipulating departure in a week is quite useless. Take three weeks however and there is at least a reasonable chance of sport. I have before now pleaded for the change in certain cases, and failed in spite of the victims' acknowledgment that I'm right. There is nothing an outsider can do. And the over-all story, since its theme is human nature, has no end.

As a group, nay, as a select company, we fishermen are doubly fortunate, for most of us have charming and generous partners who not only appear to take an interest in fishing but allow us to go forth with encouraging frequency on our piscatorial occasions. They also deal, in most cases with gratifying outcome, with the fruits of our waterside labours and this sometimes under the strain imposed by a plentitude of fish and the problem of disposal. In my household we cook and eat less than one salmon per season and of this we enjoy best of all, the tail portion, when cold and dressed with lemon and cucumber, of the first spring fish of the season. Those fish not distributed to friends who really like salmon are smoked, deep frozen and consumed in the winter.

Seatrout are another thing altogether. You don't tire of them as you do of salmon and your (fisherman's) wife will find or devise any number of ways of cooking them. If she hasn't tried them baked in butter and then lightly browned under the grill with a dressing of sliced almonds in black butter sauce, do urge the experiment on her. Promise her a theatre or a new car – it will be worth it and you can't lose. As they say in Donegal, 'Sure, you'll be sittin' on a pig's back'. Of course, if the bribe turns out to be unnecessary you can always use the money for a new seatrout rod.

Whilst I'm on the subject of cooking – and of Donegal – my friend Scott Swan of that place and formerly of Ballyshannon, has told me of something which should not go unrecorded. In the days of the famous Erne salmon fishing before it was submerged by the hydro-electric scheme, there was also an eel fishing operated by men who had their own unique way of preparing the fish. The pre-requisite was a good hot fire of turf and round it were arranged a number of turves with their flat sides towards the heat. The eels were cut into three or four-inch pieces and fried in a dry pan over the raked fire – cooked in their own fat in fact, and left sizzling there while the fat foamed white round the fish. Each man then had his pieces of eel 'served' on one of the clean hot turves from round the fire. The dry, hot turf, probably just as sterile as the average 'clean' plate, at once absorbed the excess fat from the fish. Hardly a recipe for the modern clinical kitchen but soundly based on good common sense: countrymen everywhere living close to nature, know a thing or two. Incidentally these eel fishers had a name for elvers which I have never heard before – 'liphogs' – which I suspect is local and from the old Irish tongue. Its true spelling I do not know but I have a note among my papers which records the word 'luogs' as being used down south on the Blackwater as a name for elvers.

Coming to mind towards the end of these ponderings on the subject of fishermen's wives is a small piece of advice which I overlooked in writing Chapter 3. I touched there on the desirability of acquiring either one's own fishing or at all events some sort of exclusive right and I neglected to mention a formula devised by two friends of mine. They both married some of the best fishing in the country – one a good beat on a famous Welsh river and the other one in the West Country. In the first example, unfortunately, the compatibility was not as satisfactory as the fishing and my friend eventually lost the case and the beat. The second man is still fishing. The number of prospects – i.e. beats available by this means – must be limited but I command a policy of earnest exploration to ambitious young anglers.

Finally, and since ghillies have wives as do their employers and to that extent rate for inclusion here, I must tell you a small story which originates, as do so many of its kind, from my one-time ghillie Michael. Knowing him, I have no doubt that the tale has been embellished: I can only certify that the characters in their real identities do exist.

There is one Barney Mulligan, a small farmer, in Scotland you'd call him a crofter, eking out a living by ghillying on the lake – a decent little man except when he has drink taken. At such times he can be an entire civil disturbance all by himself, fearing no-one – not even his wife, a big battleaxe of a woman. It is alleged indeed that she is the sorrow which Barney every so often makes such earnest efforts to drown. She is that awful thing – a nagger, and not unlike my Aunt Clara, but worse. The trouble in the Mulligan domicile fed on itself for the more she bludgeoned Barney about his drinking, the more he drank until in the end she decided that what Barney needed was a severe fright. Thus it came about that one night she got herself up in her old black cloak and hood and laid in wait for the bad Barney to come home from the town. Thence he presently came, weaving along the dark narrow road, bottle in hand and crooning drunkenly to himself to be confronted where his own boreen left the road by the menacing dark figure. That brought him to a wobbly halt. 'Who,' he enquired all tremulous and hoarse, 'are ye?' and was too far gone to identify the muffled voice that said, 'I'm the Devil himself'. 'Then siddown on the bank' said Barney, 'and take a slug outa me bottle. Sure, didn't I marry your sister.'

16

Books to Read

ENTHUSIASTIC BEGINNERS in fishing usually read avidly almost any book on the general subject that comes to hand. The possibility is that they have not yet settled into the way of fishing in which, later, they will wholly or to some appreciable extent specialise: the start is probably made on brown trout, but whether in river or reservoir or lake and whether with dry or wet fly is substantially governed by the area and its facilities. A novice in the dales is likely to develop his skill with wetfly or creeper on the becks, another, in Hampshire, may hear only of and probably practice dry fly.

Consider for a moment the immense volume of knowledge required to fish with even fairly consistent success by the many methods and modifications of methods, in use for the three game fish the subject of this book. Almost certainly every developing angler will, for some reason strongly applicable in his case, whether it's opportunity or aptitude or just plain liking, choose to concentrate on one of the three species and to this extent specialise. You will eventually meet in that man a skilled fisher accomplished in most ways of catching say, seatrout. He will also fish salmon when the chance matures and trout too but seatrout will be his love and special study and from the way he first began to catch them, he will extend his capability to cover several of the accepted methods. He may indeed develop some of his own – most of us do. The emphasis is now, not on acquiring basic information and skill, but on its development and the random reading of anything so long as it was fishing, has given place to selective and critical scrutiny of books on the chosen subject.

These books must be authoritative and well-written if they are to make their contribution to the reader's knowledge and in the search for them a very substantial library can be accumulated. My own surrounds me as I write and it is for a private collection, fairly extensive. Yet, greatly as I cherish it I have to admit that its heart is in about a score of volumes which contain the distilled wisdom of men who knew or know about salmon and trout and seatrout and how to catch them.

The fish come first: first because understanding the fish and their ways of living is the first and vital element and no-one can do well in the business of fishing without that foundation of wisdom. This truth prompts my arrangement of a list of fifteen books which alone would comprise an admirable small library.

To cover the life history of the salmon I suggest two books out of the many that have been written over the years. The difficulty here is that our understanding of the subject is never static and some excellent works by competent authorities are out of date and not reflecting current thinking. 'The Salmon' by J. W. Jones, a monograph in the New Naturalist series contains the clearest and most exhaustive study of the fish in fresh water. Dr. Jones is exceptionally well-placed to uncover the private life of the salmon by means of his observation tank on the River Dee near Corwen where the fish spawn a few feet only away from the onlooker behind the glass window and so reveal much that cannot be seen by normal watching at cutting time. This book in its comprehensive review of the infancy, migrations and adulthood of the fish would be sufficient in itself in the library but in view of today's somewhat uncertain status of the salmon we fish for, I suggest also 'The Atlantic Salmon – a vanishing species?' by Anthony Netboy. This is a study, made on both sides of the Atlantic, of the effect on the species of commercial exploitation, pollution and the general harrying of the world's most valuable freshwater fish. It traces the history of salmon fisheries in Europe and America and appraises their present standing. It is not, by and large, very cheering reading but there is a tremendous volume of information here and not all of it is depressing. Extraneously, and since the book appeared we have, of course, learnt that the Greenland off-shore netting will cease in 1975 and the inshore netting will be reduced very materially.

Now to seatrout. Here there is one book, the standard work on this fish, G. H. Nall's magnificent 'Life of the Seatrout'. Patient study and re-study of this work will teach any man, however close an observer and however knowledgeable about seatrout, more than any I know. It is a big book dealing with Scottish, Irish, Welsh, English, Norwegian and other seatrout and with local 'races' (so called) in these areas – their sea and river lives, migrations and characteristic growth rates. If you have an interest in scale-reading there is even more reason why this book should be always at hand. If I were limited to one seatrout book this would be the one.

The best book wholly devoted to brown trout is in my judgment 'The Trout' by W. E. Frost and M. E. Brown, another monograph in the New Naturalist series. Again this is a comprehensive survey of the fish from anatomy to feeding habits, reaction to light and many aspects of trout development in differing types of habitat. There are distribution maps, charts of growth rates and indeed a mass of data in very readable form.

These four books provide sound first-class background, all of it constructive. They also fulfil the equally valuable function of destroying some widely held and erroneous ideas about the fish – some of the old-fashioned misconceptions found among elderly boatmen for instance and from that source current in some fishing circles.

But we should turn now to fishing how, where and when, and following the order already used, take salmon first. There is some overlap in this category between salmon and seatrout and this is natural enough since the fish are so often found together and it is hardly possible to fish for one without at some time encountering the other. Again, some styles of fishing suit both – greased line for example. Anthony Crossley's 'The Floating Line for Salmon and Seatrout' would be my choice on this theme, its title indicating its scope. Second comes 'Salmon Fishing' by Richard Waddington, more thought-provoking than most. It expresses some theories of the author's which I for one, do not wholly accept, but this in no way detracts from the book's excellence. 'Catching Salmon and Seatrout' by G. P. R. Balfour-Kinnear is straight-forward practical advice by a highly qualified writer of great experience and I end this salmon book list with the curiously titled 'Fishing with a Purpose' by Stephen Johnson. Concerned primarily with fishing in Skye and the Tweed, this book is full of good sense observation with some extremely useful material on salt water fishing for seatrout.

Most seatrout fishers will already have, or have at some time read Hamish Stuart's famous 'Book of the Seatrout' which, while concerned primarily with Hebridean conditions, contains an infinity of wisdom about the fish and their response to fishing – mainly wet fly in lochs. Some of its dicta can be, and are nowadays questioned, but Hamish Stuart was a keen observer and the book is a classic which really must have a place in the library; it must top the list in the seatrout fishing section. River fishing is, I think, best covered by Hugh Falkus in his 'Sea-Trout Fishing' which I consider quite exceptional in both clarity and scope. No other book in my knowledge deals with night fishing so extensively and so very knowingly. To be consistently successful at this game one has to be knowing and intuitive in all the ways of this book. Seatrout, salmon and trout swim through the pages of 'A Man may Fish' by T. C. Kingsmill Moore which, however, affords most space to seatrout and to fishing for them in Ireland. Knowing many of the fisheries referred to in the text I can judge the author's quality of perception from personal experience and he has the trick of taking his readers fishing with him. I never quite know which to praise most in this book, the delightful writing or its sheer usefulness.

Of the legion of books on trout fishing I have selected three which broadly deal respectively with the three main aspects of the subject, reservoirs, lake or loch and river fishing. 'Still Water Fly Fishing' by T. C. Ivens is concerned mainly with reservoir work and is the best book I know on this somewhat specialised but nowadays extremely important branch which has some techniques of its own. 'Lake and Loch Fishing' by Col. Joscelyn Lane is a sober, sensible work containing among other things much information about the diet of trout in lakes, lochs or loughs, the natural flies and their seasons and the corresponding artificials. But for the river man, especially if his fishing is in the smaller class of streams, there can be nothing better than F. E. Tudor's 'Trout in Troubled

Waters'. This is not a big book but it imparts a vast amount of information set out by a writer who knows the fast river and its special problems. There is a useful section on grayling.

My fifteenth book is of a quite different character. It is so packed with data useful to a fisherman – there are sections on salmon, seatrout, trout and incidentally pike – that it can readily be in almost daily use. I know this book intimately but never fail to find in it something interesting – something I know but have forgotten – confirmation of some point that eludes me. There are here, presented in brief, all manner of facts on the life of the fish, weather, tackle, methods and so on. It represents a lifetime's collation of information from the diary of its author G. W. Maunsell, its title 'The Fisherman's Vade Mecum'. Apart from its usefulness as a library item, it is worth knowing at any time when a choice has to be made of a book for a keen beginner. No other book that I know contains so much condensed information.

Any library list making pretensions to be full would include the older writers of works which have become classics. The 'Treatysse', Walton, Franck, Stoddart, Webster, 'Ephemera' and many others – one can go on and on. And there are hundreds of others in the middle distance of the past and more recently who have made valuable contributions to our knowledge of the art that is indeed gentle. A very simple account of them would fill a whole book and many are long out of print. Yet they are, if you have them, 'books to read'.

There are two quite deliberate omissions from my short list of fifteen. They are books exclusively on dry fly and 'general' books. I am not a dry fly fisher and I do not write about this fishing, nor comment on the works of those who do because I am not qualified to do so: that I catch a few fish this way is almost fortuitous. The second omission is that of 'general', all-game-fish-by-all-methods volumes. I do not know of one which deals comprehensively and *adequately* with the entire subject of salmon, seatrout and trout fishing and if there is a superlative fisherman somewhere capable of writing such a book, I have never heard of him and certainly have never met him. Some of us spend a lifetime in mastering a few methods – perhaps only one. After sixty-six years in chase of our game fish and many others I have some knowledge of them and of techniques to catch them and I also know how many gaps there are in my knowing. Ninety-nine out of every hundred good fishers will agree. The hundredth might write a 'general book' – but it's not for your library.

I cannot, with any shred of modesty, urge the inclusion in your library of my own writings and I do not do so. I can however say, hand on heart, that there is in 'Salmon and Seatrout in Wild Places', 'Newly from the Sea' and 'Ways of Fishing', a sincere endeavour to pass on some niceties of fishing lore that rarely find expression.

17

Here and There

Greased line wet fly for trout – the mindless spoilers of good water – the value of off-the-track search for new fishing.

AN APPENDIX TO the 1972 Report of The Salmon Research Trust of Ireland records results of a preliminary survey of the animal plankton of a lough – Feeagh. Measurements by volume were taken in one of the outflows from the lough and reflect the abundance of the various water-carried organisms by seasons, water height and temperature etc.

In reading the annual report, always a remarkable and fascinating publication, I was attracted by this plankton study's sampling of the current borne 'drift' – not I must admit wholly by the subject itself but because it focused my attention on the general topic of current-carried trout food. How much of their sustenance trout secure by active hunting and bottom grubbing, as opposed to that which comes down to them on the stream to be secured with relatively little effort is literally an unknown quantity. It is, however, fairly certain that it represents a very considerable component in their diet; if it were not trout would not spend as much time as they demonstrably do in feeding near the surface of fast water. They take some fully-fledged fly from the surface, of course, but the bulk of their fast current feeding is sub-surface and based on nymph forms, free moving and swept away, and on creeping and clinging larvae dislodged by the current and so carried down – the normal assortment of small animal life in the 'drift'.

Started on this line of thought, I turned back to some notes in the diary, made very many years ago when, before most of my fishing time was devoted to salmon and seatrout, I fished assiduously for trout in Ireland and Scotland. They reminded me, these notes, of something I had wholly forgotten, that I had evolved a greased-line method of presenting nymphs to the trout of one Donegal river. This happened long before the greased-line technique for salmon was talked about – I certainly had never heard of it. It came quite naturally from the observed need to present nymphs at current speed and no faster. There was one long rippling stickle full of decent trout and I used to take a few fish from it by conventional wet fly methods. For several reasons it was necessary to fish almost straight downstream and of course, I had drag trouble which I could only partially overcome by feeding free line. Even then I had too much submerged line and too little control. A greased line was used on the nearby lake sometimes to facilitate pick-up and I switched to its use for the river in general and this long stretch of broken water in particular. Sparsely-dressed North of England patterns, little more than shreds of hackle wound on bare irons, were the flies though I later changed to true nymph dressings – mostly olives – things with bulbous heads, thin bodies and little wisps for tails. Pattern didn't seem vital but I used Reed Smut and green or brown Olive types. What was vital was the speed at which they were fished; they had to travel at the speed of the current-borne feed and you would have seen me doing instinctively what years afterwards I did in formalised fashion for salmon – mending and leading. Fishing more or less straight downstream with a long floating line I could work the whole width of the current by leading and mending while the team of three nymphs on 4X gut drifted downstream. In spite of the fact that the fish were usually directly below when they took (I won't say 'rose' because I seldom saw them) they were almost always well-hooked. The number of good trout so taken surprised the locals and pleased me because the better class of trout on that river, the Lennan, were not altogether easy game.

So, a chance recollection of an early application of greased-line fishing for trout with the drifting nymph.

* * *

Now to a less pleasant matter – the offence perpetrated by anglers who, through lack of knowledge, carelessness or just plain indifference, spoil good water. They can ruin the chances of anyone following them on a river by over-wading, blundering about and showing themselves, by prawning or otherwise disturbing the pools and here the results of such behaviour are so obvious that you would wonder that anyone could be unaware of the damage done to their own prospects and those of others.

Behaviour of a similarly low standard on a lake is much less obvious in effect but just as serious if not more so. If you stir up a muddy ford on a river the dirty water will go downstream and in a short time settle or disperse – so also the flow of the river will tend to minimise the period over which any disturbance affects the fish. The river is a moving ever-changing medium – the lake is not. It's by no means as static as one might think but it *is* more stable than the river and the result of any serious disturbance is felt over a period which on occasion can be measured in days. One example has already been quoted in the chapter on trolling. That which I have in mind now is even more flagrant since it is simply contrary to all commonsense whatever the state of the offender's familiarity with fish reaction. I am talking about persistent fishing of fly water *by any method* in conditions of bright light and dead calm. If you own a fishing you can treat or ill-treat it as you wish and if it is very large, you can abuse some part of it with damage to that part only. But if it's an hotel water, or for some other reason its fishing amenities are shared with others, you have a duty to deal with it quietly and properly and no shadow of right to abuse it. And because most fly water is shallow or relatively so, repeated fishing in strong light and absence of wind will wreck any chance of sport for some time after the conditions have changed for the better for the simple reason, particularly applicable to the shy seatrout, that the fish have been driven off the shallow in which they normally rise freely.

This is not imagination on my part: I have seen it happen over and over again on lochs in Scotland and loughs in Ireland. One man who is a persistent offender and whom unhappily I have often to endure, has been many years an angler – in all charity I cannot call him a fisherman – never learns. On a bright hot August day with the lough a gleaming mirror and unfishable he will be on the best beat where seatrout and salmon gather thickly – flogging for hours – the boat back and forth over superb fly water. Evening brings him ashore fishless, unconscious of the damage he has done, unable to discern cause and effect and in a not very sweet temper. The next day may bring us a breeze, a nice wave and a good broken light but that hammered water, instead of giving us a reasonable day's sport, will be dead apart from newly arrived and precocious finnoch. So I dread the calm bright days, not because they prevent me from going afloat but because I know what will be happening on that beautiful fly beat. The sleeping lake, the vision of the swans flying snow-white against the sloe bloom of the mountain – heart-moving things to me – are marred by the inclusion in the picture of one restless boat unmindful of the fact that fish, like men, have a need of peace.

*   *   *

As the number of anglers grows, the available fishing comes under increasing pressure and the search for 'new' water intensifies. There is movement, change of ownership, of management and of development in fisheries as in all other property but the overall picture alters very little and it's doubtful whether the opening up of new facilities in recent times has kept pace with demand. The exception may be in trout fishing where new reservoirs, gravel pits etc. and hitherto neglected south country lakes have been developed. Meanwhile the value and the cost of salmon and seatrout fishing have soared and the situation hasn't been eased by the influx of Common Market buyers and lessees and of foreign investment in our traditional sports. In some places I know in high summer, the angler you meet is almost as likely to be French or German or Dutch, as British. Politics have no place in fishing talk and I shall pursue this angle no further than to say, non-politically, that I could wish there were more fly-fishers among these visitors and fewer with a skill limited to the use of thread-line reels and spinners.

However, this is a preamble only to the suggestion that more fishing may be found if the searcher shows enterprise especially in the less-frequented parts of Wales, Ireland and Scotland, reached only by the secondary roads and byways. It's a fair assumption that any fishing within easy access of the principal main roads is well-known, taken up by renting rods, strictly preserved or over-fished. True, you may find a hotel with a well-managed stretch and I have a feeling that there are fewer over-fished hotel waters in spite of the demand, than there used to be – presumably due to growing appreciation of the value of the asset. But it's the small unconsidered waters, fished probably by a few locals who wisely talk little and which come into the stranger's ken only as a result of exploration, that have most promise. You have to take to the lanes and the little roads after some map study, to find them – and there will be many disappointments and abortive forays. There can be takeable trout in the village brook and the roadside cascade on the moor can lead you to the little lake where it begins. Once, in Wales, I was shown a dark little hole in a tiny stream overgrown with brambles and hazel and told that Evans the milk once found a twelve-pound salmon there. The 'how did it get there' question led me a long way downstream and to some interesting if not first-class seatrout fishing. Perhaps this — seatrout fishing – is the most promising prospect for the exploring visitor to certain areas. Even the best anglers' guides omit the burns and the tiny rivers that drain the roughest of our coasts – and some of the tamer coasts too. These are not recognised seatrout fishings because the fish are too few, but there are very many into which a July or August flood will bring some fish. You won't find them entering in great shoals and thronging the pools, but your burn is probably only four feet wide and short in fishable length so that fifty fish can provide you with some fun. Local enquiry will produce some sort of clue and the publican is usually impartial. Once you find your little river and have some evidence however slight, that it holds seatrout during and after a flood, you lack (a) leave to fish, not usually hard to obtain (b) a flood and (c) sufficient holiday time to allow you to wait for it. This last may well be the rub. The salt water at the stream mouth *might* be worth fishing at half to full tide in July or August, spate or no spate, but you really are dependent on weather for these miniature rivers. Migrating fish are full of surprises and flowing water, if the right quality, will lead them into very small channels: they have no lack of enterprise. Prospecting fishermen should copy, following the by-ways, and developing in time a nose for this kind of fish finding.

*   *   *

An insatiable curiosity about the day-to-day lives of fish and the way they react to the ever-changing media of underwater and above water worlds must, over the years, have played a large part in furnishing records of successful fishing for my diary. The enquiries, the questions, the puzzles that come to mind are often, in themselves and at first sight, so trifling and unimportant as to be hardly worth further thought and still less investigation. But if your interest is as keen as mine, they refuse obstinately to be discarded and they keep recurring until an answer capable of withstanding closer examination emerges. It is however their interpretation that counts. The practical use of the accumulated knowledge comes when the answers drop into place as you recognise how one factor interlocks with another – which is a cause and which are its direct and side-effects.

My regular ghillie, James, is familiar with this questioning habit of mine and it seems to have invested his own habit of keen observation with a purpose, which is good and my gain because two pairs of eyes and two 'fishy' instincts are better than one. So we never cease to learn and we consciously test and apply our conclusions in day-by-day fishing. I commend this practice to you whether you fish with an interested ghillie or alone. Useful always in a general application to all fishing, it is specially valuable in relation to localised conditions when most of your fishing is in one place. James and I never cease to ponder over the fish in our lough and their ways and though there are many discussions in the boat as a day progresses the habit – now a routine – comes out at day's end. The interval that follows the putting away of rods, weighing of fish and shedding of heavy gear is the time for James' dram (and mine) and for the inquest on the day. Weather, behaviour of fish, patterns of flies used, time of the take and of its ending and so on, these are the subjects of our talk. Whence came that curious abrasion in the ventral region of that fresh fish? What made the second fish run round the boat wriggling like a kelt? Why was there no rise whatever of seatrout? Was it because of any thunder in that dirt gathered down in the south-east? are the kind of questions a listener would hear. There will be speculation, some conclusions and some resolve – 'if we get a southerly breeze tomorrow we'll fish the river mouth – did you see those fish plunge there while we were fishing the shore at about three o'clock?'

After years of this kind of thing, I am still lacking many answers, which is one reason why I still hold these enlightening end-of-fishing-day enquiries.

18

Margins of the Dark

The quiet pursuit of night fishing has undertones for the sensitive in some places.

I DON'T FISH at night any more. For one thing night vision is not as good as it used to be and for another, if I am really honest, I don't think, in spite of years doing it, that I really like fishing in darkness – real darkness that is – nor in some places if it comes to that.

In Norway, north of the Circle there have been wonderful never-to-be-forgotten nights with salmon and seatrout in great rivers that filled the valley with the roar of their rapids, the midnight sun making night but the name for a part of the twenty-four hours. That was not night fishing any more than is the fishing you get in June in the northern isles when you need not flinch from a night-long traverse of the peat bogs, a scramble along a rock-littered hillside, or a tide awaiting vigil with the otters for company, by some seatrout-haunted tidal channel. In these places in season there is no darkness, in its place the transparent semi-dusk that has in its quality some element of benificent magic to lift the spirit while the summer gods smile on carefree fishers.

You can, if you have a mind, fish peal in Devon rivers on September's dark nights – not very comfortably but more profitably than on the pleasant moonlit nights when fish as a rule remain what Hamish Stuart called recusant. The mewing buzzards are gone, their place taken by the hunting owls whose calls make echoing caverns of the tree-shrouded pools in the wood. A dark night on a deep-timbered West Country valley holds too many secrets for me – secrets that I cannot resolve although I probably know every fence, every pool and the way down to them. The dimension has changed and distance lost its meaning. When you cast into fathomless gloom from the fringe of some deep swirling hole there can be a small stirring of disquiet. This night is not happening – it has vanished in timelessness and this darkness is the dark of this place down the ages; the fierce pull from the blackness of water sliding silent out there is part of it, this is not fishing but a venture across the margins of the dark. How long you linger may depend, for all you know, on the element in your blood that was Celt. There does exist, with roots fearfully far in the past, a thing called folk-memory. I wonder.

There are many lakes in Wales where fearsome legend has subsisted on the basis of folk-memory, for example Ogwen, and the weird Pryved in Merioneth of which my friend Frank Ward, who in his time knew more about Welsh lakes than anyone else, used to tell me some sinister tales. Oddly enough, our talks about the lakes with their histories in Arthurian legend and beyond often occurred when we fished what was then a new Welsh lake – Trawsfynnyd. Formed when the little River Prysor in Merioneth was dammed, this lake swamped a farming area and the dense woodlands on its valley slopes. For many years the dead and dying trees lined some shores, marching in groves out into deep water where only the tips of the topmost branches were showing above the waves. Inside the margin of the partly submerged forest was generous feed for trout and on occasion, good fishing in conditions which could be a fisherman's nightmare.

Nightmare is an appropriate word because the best of the

fishing came after dark when the bigger trout were either minnowing where the clustered trunks stood in the shallows, or chasing sedges of all sorts farther out among the trees. In high summer this area had a tremendous hatch of the Great Red Sedge after sundown on suitable evenings. It rarely lasted more than a week or so but while it did last there was a chance to catch the bigger trout which otherwise were reluctant risers. As long as there was a gleam of light from the afterglow, the big sedges could be seen scuttering erratically across the surface in the tree aisles, fair game for the cruising trout. It was odd sort of fishing. The artificial had to be presented on the surface yet it had to be moving without making too much wake. That meant that the fly had to have good 'entry' but not be inclined to sink before it could be drawn a yard or two. The pattern we used is no longer in any of my fly boxes and I cannot recall the detail of the dressing except that the wings were tied penthouse fashion, long and low, dark red blotched cinnamon in colour and about three-quarters of an inch long on fine low-water hooks.

While a gleam of light remained in the sky you cast into the path of a feeding trout; when the light had gone you fished blind, false casting to dry the fly because it was impossible to judge when it had sunk and how long you'd been fishing it wet. The trout more often than not ignored the sunk fly but when they did take – whether on the surface or below – you knew about it. The average weight for the water was about a pound but the Great Red Sedge brought up the two-pounders and the game could be exciting among the sunken trees and with 2X gut. The nightmare part of it came with utter darkness and the boat bumping peat-stained tree trunks, unexpected solids in a gloom with all the shapelessness of black cottonwool. On a quiet very dark night you could be fishing among the columns of a darkened cathedral – the illusion shattered only by the chaos which resulted from a careless or unlucky backcast. Even when the fish was hooked, there was always the mind's eye vision of rotting branches spread below the boat and your two pounder diving and twisting among them. In spite of natural hazards magnified in effect by developing darkness, this was a fascinating fishing – the behaviour of the big rusty flies and the difficulty of simulating their scuttering movements well enough to deceive the trout, quite different from anything normally encountered. In some seasons the hatch was poor but it had its own blessing in the form of a better or longer take than in seasons when the flies were plentiful enough for the fish to go off them rather quickly. But I do remember the Great Red Sedges of Trawsfynnyd with something approaching affection in spite of many faintly spine-chilling nights in the graveyard of standing trees. If you love trees a dead one, stark and bleached of limb, has a message of its own – a forest of them holds something akin to a threat.

I was once unfortunate enough, with a friend, to rent, on a Welsh river a beat in which for the period of our tenancy, there were few or no salmon. The beat was low down and big water had taken the fish through to upper beats. It was no-one's fault; in some seasons and on lower water this can happen all too easily. Anyhow, it left us having to be content with trout fishing on our water and in the immediate vicinity and, looking for something better than smallish river trout, we sought advice from sundry old-timers of the variety usually occupying the corner seat by the fire in the local hostelry. One such character, locally renowned for his consumption of cider boasted, I recall, that in his lifetime he had drunk thirty thousand gallons of the stuff. His more interesting, if less impressive, observation was that we should proceed to a certain ancient water-filled quarry in a near-hidden cwm in the mountains, where there were some big trout.

Our guide would be the gamekeeper who lived somewhere on the mountain and might be seen in the nearby town next day which was market day. We duly met him. He led us that evening to his cottage where his wife cheerfully agreed to feed us. There was a spare room which we could have if we didn't mind sleeping on the floor – there were no beds and it was too far from the town for us to return at night after fishing, especially as we wanted to fish the late evening rise. The lake was three miles farther into the hills and too far to reach that night: the keeper was curiously unenthusiastic about our night fishing intentions though he confirmed the existence of the big trout. We had a huge and very good supper and in the morning a breakfast to match: the bone-bruising hours between I still try to forget.

There was great virtue in that lake – we couldn't miss it. The old quarry track led us to it up three winding miles of very narrow valley occupied alongside the one-time road by a plunging stream. There were more ring ousels flitting among the rocks here than I have ever seen before or since and adding some interest to a venture which somehow bore all the marks of one going wrong. The valley opened out quite suddenly and the lake was, literally, at our feet. The track had collapsed here, and there remained perhaps one hundred feet of wreckage – shattered rocks, boulders and shaley rubbish falling very steeply indeed into a huge pit of greenish water. I call it a pit because of the angle of the sides. We looked down and across its hundred yards or so of length and we were appalled. There was one place and one only where the water could be approached, the break in the quarry walls through which the stone had been carried away. The result was a low shoreline thirty paces long – no more, whence you could throw a line. To reach it we had to make our way along one side and round the end of the elliptical chasm. The nearer way from whence we stood at the narrow end was all but impassable without a very long detour.

A faint path could be seen along the rim to the opposite end and we followed it. I have done some foolish things in my time but none worse than this. That ledge was a horror. One Man's Pass on Slieve League in Donegal is a paved garden path by comparison. The surface was loose shale in small pieces – sloping slightly towards the abyss and if we looked down to our left we saw what was in effect a huge unstable scree with just enough angle to stop all the shale from sliding a full hundred feet into an unknown depth of water. Even so, we progressed slowly to the accompanying rattle and splash of slithering debris and in time attained to that small area of low shore at once thankful, elated and slightly ashamed.

We saw a few trout almost at once. What they were taking wasn't obvious and indeed the only fly we saw were dark Silverhorns apparently hatching from the wreckage of a timber derrick which appeared above the water. Trout are not keen on Silverhorns as a rule and we saw none taken. The wind was north-westerly on open ground but down here it swirled gustily from all directions and there was a bright sun. My three-fly cast included a dark Mallard and Black on the tail and with this fly in intermittent fishing whenever we had a surface ruffle on our limited beat, I had a brace of trout of just under two pounds each. My friend also had a brace of similar fish. They were beautiful fat trout, plentifully and brightly spotted and golden of belly. But they were not very discriminating as to fly because my friend's fish in contrast to mine came to the light-coloured Raffia Sedge. In the course of the day we saw, close under that frightening scree opposite our stand and so unreachable, three cruisers that might have been over three pounds, but I don't think the stock was large and we had only those four rises.

My diary says that it was seven in the evening when we left. The sun was still bright on the mountains about but the deep sunk cwm was full of shadows. There would be an early dusk here and a Stygian darkness to follow. We had visions of big trout close inshore and in easy reach but not all the great oxen of Hu the Mighty could have held us there after dark and we went. The hair-raising passage of the scree path was made again and we paused at the track's beginning to look back and down at the water – dark and unruffled now that the breeze had gone.

The place held an air of brooding malignity coming not, as may be discernable in some places, from some traditional legendary menace vaguely rooted in antiquity but from quite another source of evil – the threat that accompanied every step taken on its margins. I have fished in some queer places and in many that were dangerous but this one — !